The
Lost
Vintage

ALSO BY ANN MAH

*Mastering the Art of French Eating: From Paris Bistros
to Farmhouse Kitchens, Lessons in Food and Love*

*Kitchen Chinese: A Novel About Food,
Family, and Finding Yourself*

The Lost Vintage

A Novel

Ann Mah

An Imprint of HarperCollins*Publishers*

HarperCollins books may be purchased for educational, business, or sales promotional use. For information please e-mail the Special Markets Department at SPsales@harpercollins.com.

FIRST HARPERLUXE EDITION

ISBN: 978-0-06-284578-8

HarperLuxe™ is a trademark of HarperCollins Publishers.

Library of Congress Cataloging-in-Publication Data is available upon request.

18 19 20 21 22 ID/LSC 10 9 8 7 6 5 4 3 2 1

For Lutetia

Et par le pouvoir d'un mot
Je recommence ma vie
Je suis né pour te connaître
Pour te nommer
Liberté

And by the power of one word
I begin again my life
I was born to know you
And to name you
Liberty

—from "Liberté," Paul Éluard, 1942

PART I

Chapter 1

Meursault, Burgundy
September 2015

I wouldn't have admitted it to anyone, but the truth was this: I had vowed never to return to this place. Oh yes, I had dreamed of it a thousand times, the sweep of vines marching across rolling slopes, the sun a slash of white heat against the sky, the shimmering light and dappled shadows. But always my dreams twisted dark, the skies dimming with heavy clouds, rough winds stirring the leaves into a hiss of whispered secrets. Always, I woke with a start, my heart thundering a strange beat, and a lump in my throat that sips of cool water could not dissolve.

And yet, here I was, my first morning in Burgundy. From the windows of my room, the vineyards appeared exactly as I had imagined them, lush and verdant with late summer abundance. In two weeks, or maybe three, we would begin *les vendanges*, the annual wine harvest, and I would join the teams of pickers, gathering the crop by hand in time-honored Burgundian tradition. Until then, we watched as the fruit grew ever sweeter, the chardonnay grapes warming to chartreuse, the pinot noir deepening to dusky black—and we waited.

A knock at the door made me jump. "Kate?" called Heather. "You awake?"

"Morning!" I said, and she stepped into the room. Her smile was exactly as I remembered it from college, a merry flash of crinkled eyes and small, even teeth.

"I brought you some coffee." She handed me a mug, and pushed back her dark curls. "Did you sleep okay?"

"Like the dead." After traveling for almost twenty-four hours from San Francisco, I had fallen asleep as soon as my head hit the pillow.

"You sure you're okay up here? I'm afraid it's a little Spartan." She glanced around the room, empty except for the narrow bed made up in crisp sheets, a bentwood coatrack filling in for a closet, and a battered desk by the window.

"I'm fine," I assured her, even though she was right: Despite the bouquet of flame-colored dahlias on the mantel, the polished floorboards gleaming like honey, these empty attic rooms couldn't shake their forlorn air, the walls peeling faded paper, the windows gaping naked. "I don't think these rooms have changed since I was a kid."

"Oh yeah, you came here with your mom, right? I forgot this was where you used to stay. It's been empty for about twenty years. Ever since your grandfather died. But don't worry—like I always tell the kids, there's no such thing as ghosts." She winked and I laughed. "Anyway, I'm sure we'll find some more furniture in the cellar. I saw a bedside table down there the other day."

"You guys have been so kind," I said impulsively. "I can't thank you enough for inviting me to stay." Heather and I hadn't seen each other for years, but when I emailed her three weeks ago to ask if I could volunteer at their wine harvest, her response had been swift: "Come as soon as you like," she had written. "*Les vendanges* will be sometime in mid-September—but in the meantime, you could help us with another project."

Now she brushed away my thanks. "Don't be silly— you're family! You know you're always welcome here. And like I said, we've been wanting to clear out the cellar for ages. The"—she hesitated, throwing a sudden glance toward the window—"the timing is perfect."

"This is my first vacation in years," I admitted. Back in San Francisco, my job as a sommelier meant long hours on the restaurant floor. Any free time was devoted to studying wine, and any travel reserved for wine research. I always scheduled red-eye flights so I could race from the airport to the lunch service.

"I dreamed of eating at Courgette," Heather said wistfully. "I still can't believe it closed."

"It was a huge shock to everyone. Especially after we got that third Michelin star—"

But before I could continue, the roar of an engine thundered outside and, glancing through the window, I saw an orange tractor rumble into the courtyard. My cousin, Nico, was behind the wheel. Beside him sat another figure, tall and lean, his face hidden by shadows.

Heather moved beside me. "There're Nico and Jean-Luc. They took the tractor to the shop this morning."

I set my mug on the windowsill so that the coffee wouldn't spill. "You guys see Jean-Luc a lot?"

"Oh yeah. He and Nico are still supertight—and supercompetitive, of course." She laughed. "Although Jean-Luc has the edge, much to Nico's chagrin. No wife, no kids—he's got complete liberty to be a total workaholic."

I crossed my arms and forced a smile. Though I couldn't hear the men's conversation, the timbre of Jean-Luc's voice reached me through the glass. I hadn't heard it in over ten years, but I knew it.

As if he sensed me, Jean-Luc turned and glanced up. I froze, hoping that the shutters shielded me from his gaze. And then Nico moved toward the house and Jean-Luc turned away, bending his head to examine a clipboard. Slowly, I let out my breath.

"Bruyère!" Nico's voice floated up the stairs. "Have you seen my rubber boots?"

"Be there in a second!" Heather called.

"He still calls you Bruyère?"

"Yeah, after all these years, your dear, darling cousin still insists the name 'Heather' is impossible for French people to pronounce." She rolled her eyes but still I caught a hint of indulgence.

I remembered that from college, too. "Eh-zaire? Eh-zaire?" Nico used to say, growing increasingly frustrated until, one day, he finally abandoned her real name altogether in favor of "*bruyère,*" the French word for the flowering shrub heather. "It's kind of cute that he has a special nickname for you."

"Kate, please." She paused with one hand on the doorframe. "The entire village calls me Bruyère." A rueful expression crossed her face, and then she slid from the room, calling over one shoulder, "I'll be downstairs if you need anything, okay?"

I listened to her feet flying down the steps, followed by the sound of Nico speaking rapid French, the clamor of small voices, and the clatter of a million plastic toys scattering on hardwood floors. "Oh, Thibault!" Heather scolded her son, but there was laughter softening her exasperation.

I stole another glance out the window. Jean-Luc was leaning against the tractor, one arm raised to his eyes to block the sun. From the back, he looked remarkably unchanged, his frame still tall and narrow, his brown hair glinting gold in the morning light.

I hoped he hadn't seen me.

The house had quieted by the time I had unpacked and braved a lukewarm shower in the salmon-pink bathroom. I carried my mug downstairs to the kitchen in search of more coffee. On the counter, I found a note from Heather: *Dropping kids at day camp. Help yourself to coffee and toast.* Scribbled arrows pointed at the French press and a loaf of bread.

I fitted a slice of bread into the toaster and leaned

against the counter, waiting for it to pop up. Sunshine was flooding the rooms, filtering through crisp linen curtains onto bookshelves and wide floorboards. Still, the morning light revealed signs of age I hadn't noticed the night before: faded wallpaper and cracked ceilings, paint flaking from some ancient water damage. I glanced at the mantel of the kitchen fireplace, where Heather had displayed a few family photographs in silver frames. She and Nico looked so young in their wedding portrait, their cheeks smooth and baby round. The stiff bodice of her strapless gown kept her secret: the bean of their daughter, Anna, nestled deep within. I'd helped her pick out that dress at a bridal shop in San Francisco, though I hadn't seen it again until today. Could it really have been a decade? I still felt guilty about missing the wedding.

Heather and I had met at UC Berkeley—we were friends and fellow French majors who decided to sign up for the same study abroad program. When we first arrived in Paris, she could scarcely order a croissant at the *boulangerie*, and was so homesick she talked about leaving early. But then I introduced her to my French cousin, Nico, and—seven months and one surprise pregnancy later—their whirlwind romance had turned into something permanent. I would have been skeptical, except I'd seen the way they looked at each other when they thought no one was watching. Now they had two kids and lived at the family winery where Nico worked with his father, my uncle, Philippe.

With the pop of a spring, my toast leapt into the air. I found a knife and sat at the table, spreading butter and jam that sparkled like stained glass. *Confiture de cerises* was my mother's favorite, made from a cherry tree in the domaine's garden. Its bittersweet tang reminded me of my visits here as a child, when she would stir a spoonful into my yogurt and watch until I had finished every bite, anxious that I'd waste food and raise her father's ire. I think we were both a little relieved when Grandpère Benoît died and those visits ended; shortly after that, she and my father divorced, and her job transferred her to Singapore. "I've lost patience with Europe—it's so provincial. Asia is the future," she always said. I couldn't remember the last time my mother had set foot in France. As for me, aside from the year I'd studied here in college, I hadn't been back, either.

I crunched through the toast, and then carried the crumb-strewn plate to the sink. A glance through the window showed Nico and Jean-Luc walking up into the vineyards, about to disappear over the crest of a slope. With a sigh of relief, I began moving around the kitchen, wiping counters, rinsing dishes. As I scrubbed at a particularly sticky patch of jam, my thoughts drifted to the real reason I had come here. The Test.

It had been eighteen months since I'd last sat for The Test—I couldn't help but think of it capitalized— but I still remembered the four-day exam in vivid detail. The shape of the plain glass carafes that held the wines for the blind tastings. The sound my pen made as it scratched across the paper, composing short descriptions of each wine, where it came from, and how it was produced. The taste of toasted almonds, elderflower, and flint that made up the white Burgundy that stumped me. The squirmy feeling of humiliation that engulfed me when I realized I'd misidentified one of the world's most revered wines—the same wine my French family had been making for generations. The wine they believed ran through our blood.

Of course, I knew that passing The Test didn't guarantee success. I personally knew scores of respected wine professionals who scoffed at the title of Master of Wine, viewing it as a silly and expensive affectation. But another part of me—the part that scoured *Wine Spectator* with a steel brush of envy, the part that stayed up until dawn making flash cards—that part felt like a failure without it. The qualification "MW" was like a Ph.D., or M.D.—but even more prestigious, considering there were fewer than three hundred Masters of

Wine in the world. I'd spent five years preparing for The Test, investing hundreds of hours and thousands of dollars swirling, sipping, spitting.

I'd taken it three times. The first had been a disaster, an embarrassing blur of questions that only made me realize how much I still had to learn. A year later, I passed the theoretical portion—a series of essay questions on viticulture and winemaking, on selling wine and storing it, and the best ways to drink it. But I still needed to pass the other half, the practical, a nightmarish examination of blind tasting, a forest of stemware filled with dozens of different wines that I needed to identify from only a couple of sips. The Master of Wine program proudly proclaimed itself "the hardest test of knowledge and ability in the wine world"—and it also proudly failed the majority of candidates every year. I only had one more chance to pass The Test before the starchy British Institute of Masters of Wine cut me off from ever taking it again.

"Your Achilles' heel is always France. And not even all French wine. Just the white," Jennifer observed a few months ago, as we went over one of my practice exams. "It's funny because The Test covers so much more than when I took it. Not just South Africa, but Lebanon, Australia, Oregon, California . . ."

"New World wine did exist all the way back in the

olden days," I teased her. "Even in other places besides South Africa." Jennifer was born in Cape Town and was a tireless champion of pinotage.

"But you're brilliant on the New World. You always have been. Even when you were just starting out. No, it's the Old World whites you need to study. You're my exact opposite." Jennifer looked at me over the top of her glasses. "Have you considered going to France?"

"France?"

"Don't look so dismayed. Yes, France. You know, that country that produces, oh, just a little bit of wine? Look, Kate, as your professional mentor, it's my job to offer unsolicited advice, so here it is: If you want to pass the bloody exam, you need to know French wine. And the bottom line is, you don't. It's strange. It's almost like you have something *against* it." She drilled me with a look that combined maternal concern with professional authority. Jennifer and I had met at a Spanish restaurant in Berkeley when she was the restaurant's head sommelier and I was a college student waitressing for extra cash. She had taken me under her wing, encouraged me to further my wine education, mentored me through the Master of Wine program. Without her support, I would never have made it this far.

I flushed under her gaze. "I think I've made a lot of progress with the Bordeaux labels."

"Oh, you know enough to get by." She flapped a hand. "But I mean *really* know it. Not just the differences between regions, but the difference in appellations. You need to understand the terroir, to be able to taste the distinction that three miles can make. Visit vineyards. Meet producers. Drink wine. Most people would kill for your problems." She shifted in her chair. "You still speak French, don't you?"

I stared at the row of half-filled glasses. "I could get it back if I tried."

"Think about it. A long vacation. Three or four months at least. You'll need to travel and you should be there for the harvest. Witness the process firsthand."

"Three or four *months*?" I only had ten vacation days a year. "I can't get that kind of time off."

"Why not? You did that stint in Australia."

"That was right after college," I protested. "I have responsibilities now. Car payments. Rent." *It's France,* I screamed silently in my head. *I can't go back.* Instead, I said: "It's too complicated."

"Just give it some thought."

"I will," I said, prepared to forget all about it.

But then a few things happened.

First, I got a phone call from a headhunter. I loved my job as wine director at Courgette and usually cut headhunters off before they could begin their spiels.

But this time before I could interrupt she uttered a word that made my heart leap: "Sotheby's."

They were putting together a list of candidates to open a wine department in the Napa Valley, she said. Master of Wine qualification was highly desired. A long process, but interviews of the short list would take place after The Test. I came highly recommended by Jennifer Russell. Was I interested?

At first I equivocated. Courgette was critically acclaimed, triple-starred, and wildly popular. On the other hand, I knew I couldn't remain on the floor forever. I wanted to sleep when the sun went down, not the opposite. I wanted a relationship with someone who went out for dinner on Saturday night, not worked it. And lifting heavy boxes and standing on my feet for fourteen hours a day wouldn't see me into old age. I used to joke that I was one hernia away from unemployment—until I actually got promoted when Courgette's former wine director had to quit because of a hernia. The allure of a career change beckoned, especially one at a prestigious auction house like Sotheby's: working with vintage wine collectors, organizing sales, a steady, well-paid, coveted job with full benefits. Yes, I told her, I am interested. No, I assured her, The Test won't be a problem, and I crossed my fingers.

The second thing that happened shocked us all.

One grizzly July afternoon, the type of chilly, grey day you find in high-summer San Francisco, Bernard "Stokie" Greystokes—*bon vivant*, oenophile, owner of Courgette—was arrested on charges of embezzlement. The feds took him away in handcuffs between the lunch and dinner services. A few days later, we came to work and learned the grim truth. Stokie was broke, the restaurant was bankrupt, and we were all out of jobs. After fifteen years, Courgette was shutting its blue-and-white-striped doors, forever.

We convened at the dive bar three blocks away. Margaritas gave way to shots of tequila, and then even more tequila, drunk straight from the bottle. We clung to each other, shocked about Stokie, grieving for Courgette, panicked about our bank accounts. But later, when my throbbing head woke me in the small hours of the night, I forced myself to be practical. I had some savings, enough to cover a few months. But The Test was still almost a year away. I needed to find a new job.

"Why not take this time to completely immerse yourself in exam preparations?" Jennifer said, when she called me the next morning. "From where I'm sitting, this looks like a perfect opportunity to do some extended wine travel."

"Except for the pesky problem of money."

"Airbnb your apartment. Use your savings to buy

a plane ticket to France. Don't you have family with a vineyard in Meursault?"

"Ye-es," I admitted.

"Ask them if you can stay for a couple of months. Tell them you want to help out in the vineyard in exchange for room and board. Trust me, I've never known a vigneron to turn down free labor. And," she said, warming to the idea, "if you start planning soon enough, you could even be there for *les vendanges!*"

Jennifer could be opinionated and meddlesome, but in all the years that I'd known her, she'd never given me bad advice. I swallowed my pride, wrote to Heather and Nico, and, a couple of weeks later, found myself in the last place I ever thought I'd be: on a direct flight bound for Paris.

Chapter 2

"Here we go." Heather twisted the knob and the door opened with a creak, revealing a flight of stairs descending to a pool of darkness. "Brace yourself," she added.

I followed her down to the cellar, breathing in the cool air, damp with the suggestion of mold. A naked bulb swung from the ceiling, casting a weak light on the mounds of junk filling the room. Old clothes spilled from gaping boxes, magazines and newspapers slid into heaps, stacks of broken furniture threatened to topple and crush us. I saw televisions that predated remote controls, a radio that predated television, a cracked globe that predated the Soviet Union, and several fans that might have predated modern electricity. And that was only the area in front of us.

Heather tipped her head up. "Good gravy," she whispered. "Does it breed and multiply while we sleep?"

"This is like an episode of *Hoarders*."

"Huh?" She tore her eyes away to glance at me.

"You know—that reality show where they put on hazmat suits and clean out people's houses."

"There's an entire *TV show* about this? God, sometimes I feel so out of touch with the States."

"People die from hoarding. All the stuff collapses on them and they suffocate."

"Are we the dudes in hazmat suits, or the people getting buried alive?"

"We could be both."

"I would laugh," she said darkly. "But it might turn out to be true." She unfurled a roll of garbage bags. "Come on. You start on that side, I'll tackle this side, and we'll meet in the middle, probably some time next February. Sound good?"

"Sure." I nodded, and she ripped off a wedge of black plastic sacks and handed it to me.

After lunch, Heather had wanted to take me to Beaune, to stroll the crooked streets of the old town and sip lemonade on the place Carnot. "It's your first day," she had said. "We have plenty of time to clean out *la cave* before the *vendanges* begin."

And yet she had seemed almost relieved when I suggested we start working right away. "I want to help you as much as I can," I had said, which was partially true. I didn't add that I wasn't ready for an afternoon of reminiscences or the confidences exchanged by two friends who hadn't seen each other for a decade.

Now we worked in companionable silence, the only sounds the rip of cardboard, the rustle of plastic bags. Occasionally I'd call out the contents of a box. "Stained onesies. Cracked pacifiers. Ratty stuffed animals."

"Chuck!"

"About a million cloth diapers."

"Chuck!"

"Some sort of medieval torture device?" I held up a plastic object flailing with rubber tubes.

"Oh Jesus, my breast pump. Chuck!"

It was strange, I mused, rummaging through these mementos, trying to assess them without knowing their sentimental value. Like this pile of polyester shirts crackling with primary colors and static cling. I held one up, blinking at the bold yellow and blue stripes; the name "CHARPIN" was printed on the back with a huge number "13" below it. "Soccer uniforms . . . maybe Nico's?" I called out.

"Chuck!" And then, more quietly: "But don't tell him."

I placed one of Nico's soccer jerseys in the keep pile

and slipped the rest into a garbage sack. When I opened the next box my fingers brushed soft leather, and I pulled out a pair of tiny booties laced with faded pink ribbons. Turning them over, I saw a name—Céline—embroidered on the soles, and I knew the shoes had belonged to my mother, who had grown up in this house. Try as I might, I found it difficult to picture her as a baby wearing something so sweet. In my mind's eye she appeared always the business professional, crisp and polished, her blond bob impeccable.

I hesitated. Should I save the shoes for her? She had never been sentimental about her heritage. In fact, by the time I was born, she had abandoned her mother tongue—shedding even her accent—and relinquished her French citizenship "for tax purposes," passing neither to me. Still, these tiny shoes were one of the few things left from her childhood. I placed them in the keep pile for now.

At the bottom of the box, I found a miniature sailor suit in yellowed fabric, with a square collar and brass buttons. "Oh, look!" I exclaimed. "This must've belonged to Uncle Philippe." I reached for an empty carton. "I'll start a box for him and Aunt Jeanne."

Heather came over and took the outfit from my hands. She hesitated. "Nico's parents are on vacation in Sicily."

"Right, but they can sort through everything when they get back."

Again she hesitated, and even in the gloomy light, I saw a flush rising to her cheeks. "I suppose you're right," she finally said, and moved back to her side before I could ask any questions.

By late afternoon, we were wading through a sea of brimming garbage bags. And yet, the cellar appeared strangely untouched, still overflowing with mountains of junk. "I swear it mushrooms every time we turn around," Heather groaned as we carried boxes and plastic sacks up and out, heaving them into the bed of Nico's pickup truck. But after a cup of tea and several shortbread cookies, we both started to cheer up. Back in the basement, we reshuffled a few boxes and managed to expose about three square feet of cellar floor. Heather dragged a suitcase into the space, a boxy rectangular relic of another era with hard sides, scratched leather trim, and a brass clasp. A thick leather handle dangled from the top.

"Can you imagine lugging this thing around? With no wheels?" She knelt to unlock the clasp. "Humph."

"What is it?" I looked up from a box of books.

"It's stuck."

"Here." I squeezed past a metal shelving unit. "Let me see." Kneeling beside the suitcase, I saw a nameplate next to the thick handle, a worn leather tag bearing the initials H.M.C. I squeezed the clasp. "It's locked. Is there a key? Look on the floor."

She switched on her cell phone's flashlight and trained its beam on the ground. "I don't see anything." She tried the clasp again. "Maybe we could force the lock? Is there a toolbox down here?"

"We could try"—I felt around in the pocket of my jeans—"this?" I held out my wine key.

She laughed. "Do you always carry that thing around with you?"

"In case of emergencies." I handed it to her.

She inserted the tip of the corkscrew into the lock and pounded the end with the spine of a French-English dictionary. "I don't know if this'll work." She winced as the heavy book hit her thumb.

"Let me try." I grabbed the dictionary and took careful aim, hitting once, twice. I felt a sharp, sudden pop, and the clasp sprang open.

"I will never make fun of your wine key again," Heather vowed, lifting the suitcase lid. "Ugh. More old clothes. Can you believe it?"

I knelt and pulled out a faded dress in a flowered cotton print. It looked like it was from the 1940s: a modest square neck, short puffed sleeves. It also looked well-worn: dingy stains under the arms and, scattered on the skirt, a constellation of tiny holes radiating around a large one, as if the material had been scorched. Underneath it lay a second cotton dress, the style the same, but made up in red-and-white polka dots, with more nibbled holes on the skirt. A sensible pair of culottes in thick brown tweed. A pair of T-strap sandals, the grey suede worn shiny. A smashed, fawn-colored hat with a moth-eaten brim. Several pairs of crocheted ladies' gloves, and one loner in nubby black silk piqué.

"Whose clothes are these?" I held up the polka-dot dress. It fell just below my knee, cut for someone who matched my height. "This stuff can't have belonged to my grandmother. She was tiny."

"Look." Heather was still digging through the case. "There's some other stuff. A map." She unfolded it. "*Paris et ses banlieues.* Paris and its suburbs?" She dug to the bottom. "And . . . an envelope!" She lifted the flap and revealed a stack of black-and-white photographs that proved too difficult to examine in the dim light. "Should we head upstairs? I need to start dinner, anyway."

In the brightly lit kitchen, we washed our grimy hands before inspecting the photos. "I'm almost positive this is one of our parcels of land." Heather held up a snapshot of vineyards punctuated by a small stone hut with a pointed tile roof. "I recognize the *cabotte.*

It's oval, which is kind of rare—they're usually round."
Next, a picture of two young boys beside a yellow
Labrador retriever. The last was a posed group shot in
front of the house. In the center stood a stocky man
with a dark moustache, the hint of a smile on his lips,
a peaked cap shading his eyes. A slender woman stood
beside him wearing a checkered cotton dress and a stiff
smile on her porcelain features. In front crouched the
same two boys from the photograph with the dog. The
smaller one scowled at the camera, while the other,
slightly older with rumpled hair, gazed into the lens
with dark eyes set in a pale, thin face. Towering beside
the kids stood a teenage girl, wavy brown hair falling
to her shoulders, clad in a flower-print dress, with a
pair of round, tortoiseshell spectacles on her face.

"The girl's dress," I said. "It's the same one from
the suitcase."

"Who is she? Do you recognize anyone?" Heather
asked.

I shook my head. "My mom's never been big on
family history. But this kid"—I pointed at the scowling
boy—"looks exactly like Thibault. Don't you think?"

She started to laugh. "You're totally right." She
squinted at the faces, then flipped the photo over. "*Les
vendanges.* 1938. So, it's not Nico's dad, because he
was born in the '50s."

"One of these kids must be Grandpère Benoît. But who does this suitcase belong to? As far as I know, he didn't have a sister." I touched the battered nameplate, running a finger over the initials. "Who's H.M.C.?"

Heather shook her head. "I have no idea. A long-lost aunt? A disgraced daughter?"

Before I could respond, the back door flew open and Thibault hurtled inside. "Mama!" He flung himself at Heather. "We have a surprise for Kate!"

"For me?" I said.

Anna appeared at the door, and then Nico, his arms filled with bottles. "I selected some wines for a *dégustation*—to help you prepare for the exam," he told me.

"Yes!" Heather clapped her hands together. "That means we can have the three c's for dinner."

"What are the three c's?" I asked, as Nico handed me a bottle to open.

"Charcuterie. Cheese. Crudités." Heather ruffled her daughter's hair, before bending to retrieve a couple of wooden boards from a low cupboard.

"Everything you need for a balanced meal," Nico said.

"And no cooking!" she added.

Twenty minutes later we were sitting round the

kitchen table cutting through oozing cheeses, piling slivers of *saucisson sec* on sliced baguette, and heaping salad on our plates. An array of stemmed glasses stood before us.

"Now taste this one." Nico poured another white wine into my glass and watched as I swirled and breathed deeply.

"The color is pure and bright . . . yellow with hints of gold . . . ," I began. "Stone fruits on the nose—white peaches . . . and something toasty. Almonds?" I tipped a few drops on my tongue. "Yes . . . peaches. Apricots. And a lovely, long finish with notes of spice." I took another sip and sighed a little. When I opened my eyes, I found everyone watching me—Heather, Nico, the kids with their crusts of baguette held aloft in midair.

"*Alors?*" Nico raised his heavy eyebrows.

"Magnificent," I said, stalling for time.

"So? What appellation?" He spun the label away from me.

I deliberated. "Montrachet?"

He turned shocked eyes upon me. "*Mais non,* Kate. The last wine was a Montrachet. This is a Meursault. Our wine. Try it again."

The second sip revealed floral notes beneath the fruit, and something sensual—almost seductive—that

I couldn't place. My mind whirred, trying to pin it down. Where had I drunk something similar? "It's somehow—it's familiar."

"*Pas mal*, Katreen!" Nico pursed his lips together and nodded. "It is the wine of Jean-Luc's domaine. His father produced it."

"Ah. Jean-Luc's father." I swallowed a little harder than I'd intended.

"It's one of the last vintages of Les Gouttes d'Or he ever made," said Nico. "I pulled it from the *cave* so you could compare it to the others."

"Les Gouttes d'Or—Drops of Gold," I repeated. I took another sip and a memory rose, unbidden: Jean-Luc's hands cradling a bottle coated in a thick, white-grey web of cellar mold. "Les Gouttes d'Or," he had said, his eyes shining with pride. "My family's wine. This is a 1978, one of the most exceptional *millésimes*. And the first wine my father made." A wave of nostalgia hit me, so powerful the wine turned bitter on my tongue.

"Mama!" Thibault broke the silence, dropping his fork with a clatter. "I want to watch *Barbapapa*! All done!"

I pushed my glass away and hoped no one had noticed.

"I'm done, too." Anna slid from her chair.

"Wait, wait, what do you say?" Heather looked at them expectantly.

"Thank you for dinner, Mama! Please can I get down?" they chorused.

"You may," she said. "Thank you for asking."

They disappeared into the living room and seconds later the TV began buzzing in the background.

"Speaking of *les caves*"—Heather reached for her wineglass and took a sip—"Kate and I found some interesting stuff down there today."

"*Ah bon? Quoi?*" Nico reached over and speared a slice of ham from Thibault's laden plate. "A scratched Louis XV escritoire?" he said hopefully. "Or maybe a hideous painting that's really the work of a young Picasso?"

"Uh, no. More like an old suitcase . . . full of clothes. And some old photographs." She stretched, grabbed the photos from the counter, and handed them to Nico, hovering over his shoulder as he flipped through them.

"This is from one of our parcels of land," he said, pausing at the picture of the vineyards and stone hut. "My father used to take me camping out at the *cabotte*. Do you remember, Kate? I think we brought you one summer. Papa always said it was like the olden days. *Comme autrefois.*"

The memory of a dark night took shape in my mind.

A sky scattered with stars. Flickering camp light. Pork sausages cooked on sticks and, instead of s'mores, squares of dark chocolate tucked into a length of baguette.

"We used to build a fire in the middle of the hut." Nico turned to the next picture, the group shot. "Wow, the house looks exactly the same."

"It was taken in 1938." Heather snuck a cornichon off his plate. "Do you recognize anyone?"

Nico peered at the figures. "Here." He indicated the stocky man whose heavy Gallic features and dark eyes mirrored his own. "That's our great-grandfather. Edouard Charpin. He died quite young in a work camp during the war . . . it must've been just a few years after this photo was taken. And this"—his finger moved to the slender woman—"this is our great-grandmother, Virginie. And this is our grandfather, Benoît." He indicated the thin-faced child. "And the little boy is his brother, Albert. He became a Trappist monk."

"Seriously?" Heather asked.

"It wasn't uncommon back then, *chérie.*"

"Who's this?" Heather leaned over Nico's chair so that her head touched his. She pointed at the young woman in a flower-print dress. "Is she related to you guys?"

He examined the photo more closely. "She looks so much like—"

"Thibault?" Heather interrupted. "I kind of thought so, too."

Nico glanced up, confused. "I was going say that she looks like Kate. Look at her mouth."

Heather sucked in a sharp breath. "Oh my God, you're right."

I gazed at the girl in the photograph. Did she also have green eyes? Faint freckles dusting her nose? When I looked up, Heather and Nico were staring at me so intently that I flushed.

"Who is H.M.C.?" I asked, trying to change the subject. "Those initials are on the suitcase."

"I don't know," Nico admitted. "My father's the person who really knows our history. He keeps the *livret de famille*—the family record." He slipped the photos back into the envelope. "Of course, as you know, he can sometimes be . . . touchy about things like that. He doesn't like talking about the past."

I nodded, recalling Uncle Philippe's sharp features and hooded gaze. He had terrified me as a child, with his ability to silence our squabbles with a single withering glare. Even as a college student, I had found his cold formality intimidating—not to mention the way he never hesitated to correct my French so that I found myself tongue-tied around him. No, Nico was right. My uncle was not someone who would welcome questions about the past.

"It seems so sad, though." I fingered the edge of the envelope of photographs. "She's just been forgotten. Lost to time."

Across the table, Heather's shoulders drooped a fraction, before she reached out and began stacking dishes. "Honestly," she said, "couldn't that happen to any of us?"

Our days soon fell into a routine. In the mornings I accompanied Heather and the kids to their day camp and after we had dropped them off, she and I headed to the dump, located about fifteen miles outside of Beaune. Heather brought a box of homemade brownies for the manager with each load we delivered and he often helped us empty the truck, whisking away boxes and bags before we could clamber down from the cab. Our next stop was the local charity shop—always closed in the mornings—where we left our items by the back door and crept away feeling like criminals. And then we returned to the house and headed down to the cellar, where we continued sorting, bagging, and boxing. Around one o'clock, we took a short break for lunch—microwaved leftovers, which we usually ate hovering over the kitchen counter and looking at our cell phones—"Don't tell my children," Heather would mutter—and then returned to our task until it was time to pick up the kids.

At first, I had worried about spending so much time alone with Heather. I was afraid she'd be too curious about my life in San Francisco, that she'd ask too many awkward questions. Honestly, I was mostly embarrassed to admit that aside from work I didn't have much of a life. The Test consumed most of my free time and disposable income—and I'd yet to meet a guy who didn't resent playing second fiddle to my studies.

But to my surprise, Heather had been remarkably incurious—so uncharacteristically quiet I found myself wondering if *I* should start questioning *her*. Was she merely being discreet? Or was she distracted? She had a lot to juggle between the house, kids, and preparing for the upcoming *vendanges*. Still, sometimes I caught her staring into space, so lost in thought that even her bickering children couldn't rouse her attention—and I couldn't help but feel like she was hiding something.

After a week, we had opened dozens of boxes of books, sorting through outdated travel guides, multiple volumes of leather-bound French classics, and enough French-English/English-French dictionaries to outfit a convention of translators. We stared in mutual horror at an enormous oil painting of a pale young woman carrying a platter with the head of a bearded man upon it, face in pallor, eyes unseeing, bloody neck stump dripping to the ground. "Awful, right?" Heather had whispered. "It's a copy—John the Baptist beheaded—used to hang in the dining room when we moved in. Apparently your great-grandmother was *très croyante*—extremely Catholic. Artistically it's garbage, but . . . well, it's not exactly the type of thing you just throw away."

Most of the stuff we found, however, posed no dilemma. We made a bonfire from the stacks (and stacks and stacks) of newspapers, magazines, and obsolete bureaucratic forms copied in triplicate. We hauled away a bulky futon couch, permanently collapsed on one side, on which Heather and Nico had taken turns sleeping after Anna was born: "Makes me delirious just looking at it," she said. A kitchen table that Heather had painted a bilious sage green: "Martha Stewart gone wrong. Very, very wrong." A blond particleboard dresser with broken drawers that gaped like crooked teeth: "Ikea."

We had unearthed a few useful bits of furniture, too—things more salvageable than valuable, but still practical: a small desk that needed refinishing, an armchair that Heather thought she might try to reupholster. Yet, despite all our careful hunting, we had not found anything else that could help us explain the mysterious H.M.C., the suitcase, or its contents.

"Hey!" Heather's voice broke into my thoughts. "Remember this?" She brought over a stack of notebooks, the French kind, small and slim with graph paper pages and jewel-tone covers. I opened one and saw my own handwriting tumbling across the page: *Côte de Beaune-Villages, 2004. Red berries, earth, mushrooms. Soft, round. Low acid, low tannins.* I snapped the notebook shut.

"You remember our wine tasting club, don't you? Or, should I say"—she shot me a sly look—"the *nerd* club?"

I managed a smile. "It seems to have made a lasting impression on *you*."

"Are you kidding me? You guys would spend hours arguing about stuff like which *red fruits* you were actually tasting. Strawberries! No, redcurrants! No, strawberries! No, *wild* strawberries. I wanted to pour all the wines into one big cup and slug it. "

"I think you actually *did* do that."

"Did I?" She smiled sweetly, and wandered back to her area of the cellar, leaving me clutching the stack of notebooks.

The wine tasting club had been Jean-Luc's idea, proposed after he discovered I had taken a wine class in

Berkeley. "If you are in France," he had exclaimed, "you MUST learn about French wine!" Heather was less enthusiastic but by that point she would have done anything to spend more time with Nico. No, no, she didn't *like* like him—she had a boyfriend back at home. She just wanted to practice her French. (When, a few weeks later, my cousin whisked Heather to the standing section of the Opéra Garnier and pulled a split of Champagne from his coat pocket at intermission, I couldn't help but feel a little sorry for her clumsy old boyfriend left behind in Berkeley. He had never really stood a chance.)

We held the wine club meetings in my tiny attic room because I was the only one of us who lived alone—my host mother resided three floors below me in a rambling, bourgeois apartment; she rented out her former *chambre de bonne*, maid's quarters, to supplement her meager widow's income. The four of us would squash into the space, Heather and I perched on the bed, Jean-Luc and Nico on the terra-cotta tile floor. We drank out of cheap wineglasses and left the bottles of white to chill on the window ledge because they wouldn't fit in the fridge. I arranged baguette slices and a wedge of Comté cheese on a small table, along with four plastic cups.

"For *spitting*?" Heather looked almost offended. "You're joking, right?"

"We had them in my other class, and that's what professionals use."

"But that's so—*eww!*" She scrunched up her face.

"Well, it's there if you want it," I said, as Jean-Luc popped the cork from a bottle of sauvignon blanc.

No one spat. Of course we didn't. We began with small, considered sips offering up words like "flinty," "mineral," and "acidic." As the evening progressed, the wine began flowing at an alarming pace and our descriptions—scribbled with unsteady hands in our notebooks—read like entries in a bad poetry contest.

"An apple tree bows over rushing river stones, the fruit kissed by Mediterranean lemon zest, tinged with a rough bitter bile," Heather declaimed.

"Profound," Nico said with a smile that was not completely ironic.

"What?" Heather was laughing. "What?"

I couldn't resist an exaggerated sigh, and when I glanced at Jean-Luc, he wore a similar expression of exasperated amusement.

When Nico had first mentioned his friend Jean-Luc, I couldn't help but suspect he was trying to set us up. But the more time the four of us spent together, the more I realized that Nico simply liked spending time with Jeel, as he called him. Jean-Luc had grown up on a neighboring vineyard, and I remembered him from my childhood visits to Burgundy because he was the only French kid who wasn't too shy to try to speak to me in English. To my surprise, the goofy, skinny boy had become a confident young man, his brown hair verging on golden, eyes of the same tawny color with remarkable clear depths. They sparkled with relentless charm, those eyes, quick to twinkle at a joke or fill with empathy, suffused with unwavering warmth. My aunt Jeanne always said that everyone adored Jean-Luc— tiny babies, scratchy cats, the crotchety woman behind the counter at the boulangerie.

The wine club. We hardly had any idea what we were doing, but still it taught me so much. How to taste the flint and chalk that anchors the crisp charm of Champagne. The way the mistral wind can infuse a Côtes du Rhône with the scent of green peppers. How every wine tells a story—of a place, a person, a moment—a happy summer, a miserable summer, a confident winemaker, a worried one, or maybe someone in love. "The wine sleeps in the bottle, but still it is changing—evolving," Jean-Luc had told us. "And when the cork is removed, it breathes again, and comes awake. Like a fairy tale. *Un conte de fées.*" His gaze held my own.

Was that how it began? With a look, a brush of my hair, a touch of his back. Later, when we were alone, his furious blush betrayed his faltering confidence: "Every time I see you, I feel like an idiot, Kat. You are just so . . . intimidating. With your perfect palate, and that precise way you have of expressing yourself, so funny and sharp . . . I never thought you'd notice me." The sight of him so unexpectedly flustered made something inside me crack open. His lips touching mine, his cheeks rough on my face, the warmth of his body against my own, our clothes falling to a pile on the floor.

Was that when we fell in love? With long walks through narrow streets, and conversations whispered deep into the night, talking about our favorite books and music, and whether unfortified dessert wines were delicious or disgusting. All those heartfelt conversations—about my parents' divorce and their new marriages, and his family's vineyards, and the parcels of land he hoped to add one day—drawing us close, so close it sometimes felt like we had never been apart.

It was just a study abroad romance. It was merely a dreamy interlude. We were both too young to start a relationship that would last forever. But waking up one morning, his smooth and muscular body next to my own, I realized that I had never been so happy in my life. I'd had other boyfriends before Jean-Luc, but for the first time, I felt like someone saw me—not just the pretty waitress, or mediocre French major, or the lonely teen whose parents had left her too often to her own devices—but the real me. For the first time, I had fallen completely and headily in love.

And then, somehow, it was ruined.

The wine notebooks had grown damp in my hand. My left foot had fallen asleep. Across the cellar, Heather unfurled a garbage sack, shaking it so that the thin plastic snapped and billowed like a sail. I struggled to my feet, found an empty box, and placed the wine notebooks inside. It had been a long time ago. Ten years. But I could still hear his voice, whispering to me in the dark hours of the night. I could still feel his arms around me, pulling me close . . .

I grabbed a pile of moth-eaten sweaters and threw them over the notebooks, closing the flaps of the box so that it looked like all the others, ready for tomorrow's trip to the town dump. Then I pulled another carton toward me.

When I opened the new box my heartbeat returned to its normal rhythm. Smashed Christmas ornaments. Crumbling paper chains. Strings of lights ending in plugs that could easily spark an electrical fire. Chuck. I reached for the next box: more books. I glanced at the first one, a French textbook. Leafing through . . . the periodic table, ah, a French chemistry textbook. Chuck. The rest of the books were also in French, all of them from the schoolroom: history, mathematics, biology, yet another battered copy of *The Count of Monte Cristo.* Chuck. Near the bottom of the box, a thick stack of notebooks with dark brown cardboard covers—*cahiers d'exercises* filled with grammar exercises copied in a painstaking copperplate. I flipped through the first one before setting it aside with the others. Chuck.

At the bottom of the box, my fingers touched another book, large and flat. No, it was a brown leather folder, its cover embossed with a design of fleur-de-lis, and inside was some sort of document, the paper yellowed with age. A branch of pine needles bordered one side, overlaid with several official seals, and the top read: "Lycée de jeunes filles à Beaune." My eyes skimmed the script, silently translating the words:

Republic of France

DIPLOMA OF SECONDARY STUDIES

3 JULY 1940

Presented to Mademoiselle Hélène Marie Charpin

I gasped. "Hélène!"

Heather's head appeared above a stack of boxes. "You okay?" she called.

"Look! Lycée de jeunes filles!" I gabbled. "H.M.C." I waved the folder in the air. "*Hélène Marie Charpin.*"

"Wait, *what?* Hold on. I'm coming over there." Heather wove her way through the mess and took the document from me. "Hélène Marie Charpin. Born in Meursault on 12 September 1921." She touched the words with her index finger.

"She must be the girl in the photograph! The suitcase must have belonged to her. But . . ." I frowned. "Who was she? If her last name is Charpin, how is she related to us?"

Beside me, Heather sucked in a sharp breath. "Look." She pointed at the line above. "This diploma was awarded in July 1940. That was right after the Occupation started."

"Could she have died during World War II? Is that why we've never heard of her?"

"I guess . . . maybe? But why would she have disappeared?"

"Didn't Nico say the other night that great-grandfather Edouard died during the war? Maybe it's all connected."

She shrugged. "Maybe?" Her hands fumbled with the diploma as she attempted to slip it back into its folder.

"Nico said his dad would know, right? I wish we could just ask him." But even as I mentioned Uncle Philippe, I was remembering a rainy summer afternoon, long ago when we were little, maybe six or seven, and

Nico snuck into his father's office to borrow a pair of scissors. As kids we weren't allowed in there, and when his father caught him, the punishment had been swift: several sharp smacks on the bottom. Nico had shrugged it off and said it didn't really hurt. But I never forgot the sight of Uncle Philippe's white-lipped face, furious that he had been disobeyed. "Although, I suppose he's never been very, uh, approachable."

Before Heather could respond, the cellar door flew open and Nico came bounding down the stairs.

"Nico, hey! You'll never guess what we found . . . ," I started to say, but when I caught sight of his face, the words died on my lips. His eyes were dark and wide against flushed skin, and his breath emerged in gasps, as if he had been running.

"They're back," he said to his wife, and she jumped like a spooked horse.

"I thought we had another week!" she cried.

Nico shrugged. "Juan texted him the lab results. Papa doesn't want to wait another day." He took a deep breath, crossing his arms tight against his body. Heather began to chew the inside of her lip.

"What's going on?" I said, with growing alarm. "Is something wrong?"

They exchanged a glance, and turned toward me in unison. "No, no, don't worry. It is nothing," Nico said.

"It's just . . . *les vendanges*." He forced a smile. "The grapes are ready to be picked—so we will begin harvesting tomorrow."

"But is everything okay?" I pressed him. "You guys seem—"

"I've got to go to the grocery store!" Heather broke in. "How many for lunch tomorrow? Eighteen?"

"Better count for twenty," Nico said.

She nodded and started up the stairs, patting her pockets for the car keys.

"I need to start sorting the equipment. Buckets, secateurs . . . ," Nico muttered under his breath, following her.

A few seconds later, they were gone, leaving me alone in the half-lit cellar, my questions hovering like stirred dust and then settling down again, unanswered.

Meursault, Burgundy

12 SEPTEMBRE 1939

Cher journal,

I wonder if that sounds as silly in English as I think it does in French. *"Dear diary . . ."* Do other girls really write that sort of thing?

Well, I am not sure how to begin this journal, so I will start with the facts, like a proper scientist. My name is Hélène Charpin and today I am eighteen years old. I live in Meursault, a village in the Côte d'Or region of Burgundy. Papa says our family has been making wine here ever since the Duc de Bourgogne first planted chardonnay grapes on the slopes, which was at least five hundred years ago. Then again, Papa has been known to exaggerate a bit of history if it means selling an extra cask or two. Just a few weeks ago, he even told an American importer that Thomas Jefferson had brought our family's wine to Les États-Unis! *"C'est vrai!"* he said. "Les Gouttes d'Or was Jefferson's favorite white Burgundy." I'm not sure if the man believed him, but he added an extra three tuns to the order and Papa gave me a wink. After the man left, hopping in his motorcar and rattling off to another domaine, Papa threw an arm around my shoulders. "Léna, you are my lucky charm!" he exclaimed.

That was last month, August. Now that we've started the harvest, Papa's smiles have been less frequent. True, it's been a dismal summer, but I don't think any of us realized how wet or cold until they started collecting the grapes a few days ago. Half the crop is unripe, hard and green, the other half destroyed by grey rot. Papa and the other men were sorting fruit late into the night, trying desperately to make some sort of vintage from it. Last night, Albert fell asleep in the *cuverie*, and when I carried him back to the house, I was shocked to see snow dusting the courtyard. Since when does snow fall in mid-September?

I didn't tell Papa—it seems so morbid—but I fear that the bad harvest is an omen. For weeks, no one has talked about anything except France's declaration of war. Everyone is jumpy, waiting for something to happen. We're required to bring our gas masks to school and I dread turning on the radio. Papa jokes that the tense atmosphere is at least good for wine sales, but his face turns ashen whenever he opens the newspaper. How can he not worry, when he lived through La Grande Guerre that killed his two brothers and left him an only child? Thank goodness Benoît and Albert are far too little to fight.

Given the tense atmosphere, I thought everyone had forgotten my birthday today, but I was wrong. Before dinner, Papa found me at the rabbit hutch, slipping compost scraps into the cages.

"*Joyeux anniversaire, ma choupinette.*" He placed a satin pouch in my hand. Inside, I found a string of pearls, as small and white as a baby's teeth. "They belonged to your *maman,*" he said, which explains why Madame hadn't gotten her hooks into them, like all the other bits of family jewelry.

I touched the pearls, which were smooth and cold under my fingertips. "*Merci,* Papa." When I kissed his scratchy cheeks, his eyes crinkled, and for a second I felt that he missed Maman as much as I do.

"You look just like her when you smile," he said, a statement based more in nostalgia than fact, because the few photos I have seen of Maman show a slender young woman with smooth light-colored curls—not frizzy and dark brown, like mine—and a merry glint in her eye. (Madame says that my spectacles give my face a dour aspect.) Maman has been gone for more than thirteen years—so long I'm not even sure if my memories of her are real or just things people have told me. "She would be so proud of you," Papa sighed. "As your *belle-mère* and I are," he added hastily.

This was such a blatant exaggeration that I just nodded, a smile affixed to my lips. Ever since she married my father, when I was eleven, Madame has been counting the days until I leave home. I wouldn't be surprised if she crossed off each one on a calendar, like the Count of Monte Cristo. I know I have.

Papa, perhaps sensing my reticence, continued: "I know she can be particular but please try not to be too hard on Virginie. Benny's illness has caused much anguish for us all." He looked down at his feet. My half brother's frail health rules our family, like weather patterns shape the vineyards. Only Albert can soften Madame. Then again, at three years old, he is a little brown bear cub—*un petit ours brun*—who could melt the thorniest of hearts, even mine, his systematic, scientific half sister, fifteen years his elder.

Beside me, Papa took a deep breath. "Hélène." He so rarely uses my formal name that I looked at him sharply. In the fading light of early evening, his eyes had turned black. "I've decided to let you continue your studies next year."

I exhaled with a gasp. "I can apply? To Sèvres?"

"If you so wish."

"Does my *belle-mère* know?"

"I wanted to tell you first."

Neither of us voiced what we were thinking: She'll say that proper young ladies do not leave home before marriage. Even though the École normale supérieure de jeunes filles, founded in 1881, is the most prestigious women's science university in France, it is located in Sèvres, a suburb of Paris— and to hear Madame air her views about Paris, one might think she was talking about Gomorrah. I gazed down at my shoes, a pair of pale grey T-strap sandals that Papa bought me at the start of summer, even though they were outrageously expensive and Madame said I didn't need them.

"I'll talk to her," he promised, and the confidence in his voice reassured me. Perhaps Madame will view my continued education as a shrewd investment against my freckled face and gangly legs.

"We'll miss you, you know. The house already feels empty without you." A teasing smile played about Papa's lips, but his eyes remained grave.

"I don't even know if they'll accept me. It's meant to be very competitive."

"Of course they will. Though I do wonder if you should wait to matriculate. Given the current situation."

"Nothing has even happened," I protested. "I think they're bluffing. I bet there won't be a war at all." Of course, this is what we all hope.

For a minute, we sat listening to the rabbits gnaw at their lettuce cores. Then Papa brushed off his coat and said he needed to get back to work. He and the *pressoir* team will be crushing grapes well past midnight.

It astonishes me, this love my father and—I think, perhaps, eventually—my brothers have for the vineyard. Where I see sunburns, cracked hands, children working the vines when they should be in school, dirty farm equipment, and the indelible stains of vinification, they see the joy of physical activity, the satisfaction of tradition, the pride of owning the same land for generations.

I am not sure there is a place for me here, on the domaine. I'm not sure I want one, either. I've talked about finding a teaching position in Dijon if I receive my degree, but lately I have been thinking of going somewhere else, somewhere far away: Paris, Berlin, Geneva—or maybe even America? Les États-Unis . . . Would I dare?

One thing I know for certain. This house has not been my home ever since Papa married Madame. If I am offered a place at university next year, I have no intention of returning to live here ever again.

Chapter 3

A mist floated over the vines, a fine spray that blurred the distant village and heightened the color of the grape leaves so they flashed against the grey sky. It was the third morning of the *vendanges*, and my sleeves were soaked with dew, my hands cold and slick, my back throbbing as I bent and stooped. And yet, despite the physical discomfort, the beauty still bewitched me—the air, silken and pure, the crisp sounds of snipping secateurs and heels crunching on graveled dirt, the precision of orderly vines marching across gentle slopes. At this hour, before the sun rose bright and strong, the landscape was a wash of color, the pinot noir grapes fat clusters of soft violet, the chardonnay pale celadon, the broad leaves fluttering emerald, the precious soil a crumbly stroke of russet.

"*Allez, tout le monde! Ça va?*" Nico stood near the *cabotte*, a primitive stone hut. "I brought the *casse-croûte*," he continued in French, holding up a wicker picnic basket. "Let's finish this patch and we can eat before loading up. *D'accord?*"

A few calls of assent and we bent to work, the others, more experienced, moving swift and steady through the vines, while I trailed behind. Finally, I finished my row and lugged my bucket to the wheelbarrow, emptying the fruit within. The other pickers started loading crates of grapes on the truck bed as Nico stood by and noted each one on a clipboard.

In the picnic basket, I found the last sandwich—a length of baguette stuffed with a thick slice of *pâté de campagne* and a slender line of cornichons—sat down on an overturned crate, and took a bite.

"*Du vin?*" A teenaged boy appeared before me, proffering a bottle of wine.

"*De l'eau?*" I asked hopefully. After the morning's toil I needed water to quench my thirst, not wine.

"*J'sais pas.*" He shrugged. Wine it would be.

I found a plastic cup and he poured me a slug. It was young, still sharply tannic, but full of fruit, the color of rubies. I ate my sandwich in quick bites, washing it down with the wine. In the distance, a mass of clouds bruised the horizon.

Nico pushed the last crate of fruit onto the truck and walked toward me. "Storm's coming," he said, nodding at the sky. As if in agreement, a great rumble rolled across the bucolic calm. I flipped my hood over my head, expecting rain. But the sound grew until I realized it was not thunder, but an engine chugging up the slope. After what seemed like a long wait, a tractor finally appeared, grinding to a halt near the truck. The orange door opened, long legs swung down, and the gaunt figure of Uncle Philippe emerged. He surveyed the proceedings, noting the laden crates stacked in the truck, the empty picnic basket, the *vendangeurs* who stood smoking and chatting.

"Nicolas!" he called to his son, who moved quickly to his side. They spoke in low voices, punctuated by the jab of an index finger as Uncle Philippe pointed at various parcels of vineyards in the distance. Nico nodded, making notes on the clipboard. The wind gusted, shaking the grape leaves into a hiss, and I looked down at the mesh tops of my running shoes, wondering if they'd survive a thunderstorm.

"Kate." Nico beckoned, and I rose to join the two men.

"*Bonjour,*" I greeted my uncle.

"*Bonjour,* Katreen," he said with a nod. His eyes, shielded by rimless spectacles, were difficult to read.

"Listen, Kate," Nico continued in French. "Our *stagiaire* didn't show up this morning and we need help in the *cuverie*. Can you go with Papa?" His voice was casual, but—was I imagining things?—did he give an almost imperceptible shake of the head?

"Um, I, er . . . ," I faltered, glancing surreptitiously at Uncle Philippe. He was frowning at the clipboard, exuding such an air of cold formality that I felt clumsy. And yet working in the winery would give me an intimate view of the winemaking process—and wasn't that why I had come here in the first place? "*Bien sûr*," I said. "Of course."

"*D'accord*," said Nico, though he seemed antsy. "You go back to the domaine now with Papa, and I'll take the tractor to the next parcel." He turned to round up the team, but before he moved away, he shot me a look of encouragement. Or was it concern? I couldn't tell.

Uncle Philippe and I climbed into the truck. I hunted desperately for some morsel of small talk—anything to break the awkward silence blanketing the vehicle. I couldn't remember the last time I'd been alone with my uncle. In fact, had I ever been alone with him?

A blinding flash of lightning illuminated the sky, followed by a deafening crack of thunder. I gasped without thinking, my hand shooting out to grab my uncle's arm. He looked over at me in surprise. "Sorry," I croaked, clearing my throat, and removing my hand. "That just surprised me. We don't have this kind of storm in California."

He smiled thinly. "You're not scared, are you?"

"No, no, of course not," I stammered, crossing my arms. Through the windshield, I saw the other *vendangeurs* scattering for cover.

"I should hope not." He reached to turn the key in the ignition. But before he could switch on the engine, the rain began to fall, fat, heavy drops that hit the windshield with a brittle clatter, turning quickly to hail.

It was only a summer storm. Still, a shiver ran down the length of my spine.

For most of the year, Domaine Charpin's three mighty grape presses—enormous, antediluvian contraptions made of thick wooden staves circled by metal hoops—lay dormant, covered in dustcloths, surrounded by farm equipment. During *les vendanges*, they came alive, their large iron plates descending with limb-crushing strength on mountains of grapes, releasing a torrent of liquid that ran into underground vats. *The birth of wine*, I thought, crouching near the stream to fill a glass. The fresh grape must had a brisk, raw tang that would eventually mellow with fermentation, but even now, pure and untouched, I could taste the balance of acid, sugars, and tannins that heralded a remarkable year.

Uncle Philippe circled between the *pressoirs* and the *cuverie*, observing everything with a critical eye. By late morning, I was slightly regretting my offer to help him. He stalked from task to task, his narrow frame moving in a purposeful stride that precluded questions.

My mother and her brother had grown up here at the domaine, but while she had left France for college, Uncle Philippe had spent his whole life in this same place; now in his mid-fifties, he was many years from retiring as *chef vigneron*. He and my aunt Jeanne lived outside the village, in the house where she'd grown up; they raised most of their own vegetables, tended chickens and a pig. Their frugality extended to the vineyard, which sagged under battered equipment and scuffed surfaces and, I suspected, was the source of some intergenerational tension.

"May I invite you to clean *les cuves*?" Uncle Philippe tapped my shoulder and indicated a row of towering cylindrical vats. He spoke in a highly refined French, addressing me with the formal form of you—"*vous*"—which he preferred and used with almost everyone, including his own daughter-in-law. I had always been expected to *vouvoyer* him—even on those long-ago visits with my mother, when I was just a little girl with broken French struggling to keep my verb conjugations straight—until finally I gave up and started speaking to him in English (when I spoke to him at all).

"Of course." I followed him into the *cuverie*. He inserted his upper body into one of the towering steel vessels, wielding a high-powered hose with confidence, emerging with his white hair sparkling with mist. Following his example, I fitted my head and torso into the tall, narrow *cuve*—which was dark and cave-like, echoing with intermittent drips of water—lifted the hose, and sprayed the sides and ceiling. The jet of water jolted me backward.

"With enough practice, you'll get the hang of it," Uncle Philippe said, leaving me with the hose and a row of empty vats to clean.

By the time the grape presses had quieted for the lunch hour, I was exhausted. I was hoping to sit with Heather at lunch—I couldn't wait for a break from Uncle Philippe's gimlet-eyed gaze—but before I could cross the courtyard, my uncle called to me.

"Come sit next to me at lunch, please," he instructed.

I inwardly groaned, but managed to arrange my features in a pleasant expression. "*D'accord,*" I agreed.

In the kitchen, I washed my hands, scrubbing at the stubborn stains on my cuticles.

"How's it going? Can you cut some bread for the table?" Heather, flushed from the stove, bent to remove a cast-iron pot from the oven.

"Uncle Philippe invited me to sit next to him at lunch," I said quietly. "I don't suppose I can refuse?"

She pulled a face. "Probably not. Sorry. I'll try to sit down at your end."

But by the time I had helped her distribute the bottles of wine and pitchers of water, the breadbaskets, mustard pots, butter dishes, jars of cornichons, plates of charcuterie, and terrines of homemade *pâté de campagne*, there was only one seat left for me. I found myself wedged beside my uncle, with Nico across from me and members of the domaine staff filling the rest of the seats at the table.

"Do tell me," Uncle Philippe said, filling my glass with wine. "How is my sister?"

"She's fine." I fiddled with the napkin in my lap.

"Still in Singapore? I can never keep track of her."

My mother had lived in Singapore for more than fifteen years. "Yes," I said simply. "She's very busy," I added, which always seemed to be the case to me, at least. It wasn't that we didn't get along, but more that she seemed disinterested in me—her career as an investment banker, along with her second husband's charitable foundation, left little room for anything else.

This seemed to satisfy Uncle Philippe. "*Du saucisson sec?*" He speared a thin slice of salami and placed it on my plate. "You haven't become a vegetarian, have you?"

The others paused midbite, forks piled with cured meat, knives loaded with mustard, their eyes swiveling toward me.

"*Non, non,*" I assured him. "Not at all."

"You can never be sure with Americans," he said. "Last year, we even had a—what do you call it? A virgin?"

I choked on a sliver of sausage. "A *what?*"

"You know, she ate only vegetables—not even eggs or cheese!"

"Oh, a vegan!" I coughed into my napkin, stifling a laugh.

"*C'est ça. Un végan.* Can you imagine?"

"Only vegetables!" said Nico, slicing off a wobbly mass of headcheese. "Crazy! *C'est dingue!*" He shook his head in disbelief.

"Actually," I balanced my knife and fork on the edge of my plate, "a plant-based diet is a superhealthy lifestyle—not to mention good for the planet."

Everyone stared at me as if I had started to declaim a verse from the Bible.

"Such a creative spirit, *les américains.* I do admire that," said Uncle Philippe at last. "I suppose it makes up for your country's complete lack of culture. Me, I prefer Europe. Not just France—though, of course, I favor France—but Italy, Spain, Austria. Even the smallest villages are filled with charm."

"But America has so much space, Papa." Nico made an expansive gesture with his hands. "Big skies, open roads. Opportunity."

"Too many opportunities, if you ask me," his father huffed. "Americans are always trying to change things. Make improvements."

"Is that wrong?" I asked lightly.

"No, of course not. But here in France, it is tradition that we value. I make wine the same way as my father, who made wine the same as his father. Yes, perhaps we've made a few technological advancements here and there, but otherwise the domaine has remained unchanged for several generations. We don't need any *marketing*"—he threw out the word in heavily accented English—"or *design* or a *site-web.*" He gave a small shudder.

"But why not?" I responded without thinking. "Why not create a website to introduce more people to your wine? Why not redesign the labels to give them more shelf appeal? Or package the honey that you gather from the beehives in your vines? Or even start a bed-

and-breakfast here at the domaine? I know so many Americans who would absolutely love to stay at a real Burgundy winery." An image of the domaine flashed before me, freshly painted and beautifully maintained, its rooms restored to their original grace, the courtyard filled with flowering plants . . .

Across the table, Nico was staring at me, his face stricken. Beside me, my uncle heaved a sigh. I realized that I had overstepped a boundary.

"*Mais non*, Katreen. Don't you see? That is what I am trying to express." He puffed his chest with benevolent chauvinism. "We are not here for tourists. We are here to ensure that the domaine continues to another generation. Perhaps *you* do not understand, because your mother has chosen to turn away from this life. But *my* obligation is to share this with my grandchildren—this land, this heritage, this *patrimoine*."

"Along with *saucisson sec*, of course." Nico, his composure recovered, gave a wink. "Pork is also our *patrimoine*." Everyone burst into laughter, including his father.

At the other end of the table, Heather began to clear away the first course, and I rose to help her carry the lard-smudged plates into the kitchen. I found her dishing up *pot-au-feu*, frowning a little as she arranged chunks of braised beef and marrow bones on a platter.

"He's an old goat, isn't he?" she remarked conversationally.

"Stubborn." I opened the dishwasher and started fitting plates into the slots.

"You know, when we first started living here, I had a million ideas for this place. We were even going to—" A cube of meat tumbled off the platter and she bent to retrieve it from the floor.

"What?" I prompted. "You were going to what?"

"Oh, you know. Just a bunch of silly ideas. Like cleaning out the cellar. You haven't mentioned that to anyone, have you?"

"Um, no?"

"Good. Probably best to keep it on the down-low."

I shot her a confused look, but she was absorbed in piling boiled potatoes on the platter.

"Yeah, my *beau-père* threw cold water on all my ideas," she continued. "He didn't want to hire any more staff, didn't want Nico overstretched. And then I got pregnant with Thibault and I've been exhausted ever since." She smiled briefly, pragmatic. But then she heaved a little sigh that was almost undetectable.

"This place"—I ran a hand across the scratched wooden mantel—"it could be so beautiful."

"I know. So much potential, right?"

"They don't see it? This could be a gold mine."

"I do wonder sometimes . . ." She pinched coarse grey salt from a ramekin, sprinkling it over the meat. "I wonder if something happened. A long time ago. He's so reserved, Papi, so adamant that we keep our heads down, not draw attention to the family. On the other hand"—she looked up with a laugh—"I suppose he's just being incredibly *French*."

I thought of my mother, and the way she veiled her emotions. "Keep the curtains drawn."

"Exactly." She lifted one of the platters of meat. "You'll bring the other?" she asked, and headed outside without waiting for a reply.

I glanced around the kitchen again. I'd mentioned the bed-and-breakfast idea on impulse, without really thinking about the renovation involved, but the house wouldn't even need that much work—a lick of fresh paint, refinished floors, a couple of new bathrooms . . . Okay, it probably needed quite a bit of work. I pictured the shutters repainted a cerulean blue, the window frames touched with glossy white. At the other end of the kitchen, a breakfast nook with a table long enough to seat eight. *Petits déjeuners*, simple but delicious: fresh coffee, *oeufs en cocotte*, croissants, vineyard honey.

The other night I'd taken a break from studying and found Heather in the living room, absorbed in a knitting pattern and a tangle of yarn; Nico sat beside her, puzzling over a Sudoku. Was this, I had wondered, what it was like to have hobbies? It had been less than a month since I worked my final shift at Courgette, but already I missed it more than my last boyfriend. I missed my colleagues and having a routine. I missed the relationships I'd built at the restaurant, the continuous dialogue with diners, producers, and distributors. I missed the thimble of dry sherry that I poured for myself after a long day of work and night of study, when I'd finally push my books away, turn on some music, and sip the wine, suffused with the glow of self-discipline.

During these past few weeks in Burgundy, I had found myself contemplating France, America, and their differing philosophies toward work and life. Here in France, the stately, unhurried pace alternately charmed and frustrated me. Many businesses closed for a two-hour lunch break, Sundays were reserved for family not shopping, and several weeks of summer were earmarked for vacation. Most French people I knew nurtured several hobbies, tending chickens and vegetable gardens, taking photography classes or dance lessons, participating in amateur soccer leagues—even Uncle Philippe indulged his inner historian, embarking on an annual pilgrimage to various Roman colosseums.

But though the pursuit of pleasure was encouraged, ambition was considered unseemly. Hard work had to be hidden, and success needed to appear effortless, even accidental. It was, my mother always said, the thing about France she disliked the most—and the reason she had left.

Over the past few weeks, I had admired Nico's and Heather's dedication to each other, their children, and their pastimes. I thought they were happy maintaining the status quo, content to raise their family and shepherd the domaine until they passed it to the next generation. But now my conversation with Heather made me wonder if their devotion wasn't really a salve for stifled ambition. Did they, too, yearn for something greater?

15 DÉCEMBRE 1939

Cher journal,

Today was the last day of school before the Christmas holiday, which meant our teachers spent the final ten minutes of each class reading the student rankings aloud. My results were better than I expected in history, and worse than I hoped in English. But it was chemistry that found me shaking in my seat, holding my breath from the minute Madame Grenoble began reading the names, starting at the bottom and going to the top.

I could tell Madame G. was enjoying herself because every time she announced a name, she paused to make eye contact with its owner. She gave Odette Lefebvre a disappointed shake of the head, with which I privately agreed—the silly goose should have spent more time memorizing the periodic table and less time mooning over Paul Moreau.

"*Numéro trois . . .*" Madame G. paused, relishing our attention. I clasped my hands to keep myself from biting my nails. "Leroy."

From the back of the room, I saw Madeleine Leroy's shoulders sag with disappointment. Poor

Madeleine. She tries so hard, but she always manages to miss the key concept.

"*Numéro deux!*" Madame G.'s eye fell upon me and I squeezed my hands until the joints cracked. But then she was saying "Reinach," and after that I couldn't hear a word because the blood was rushing through my ears. For if Rose was number two, that could only mean one thing: I was number one. Me! I felt light-headed with joy and relief.

"*Félicitations*, Hélène," Rose said, when she approached my desk after class. I was gathering books into my satchel, my hands still a little shaky.

"It was just luck," I said with a modest smile.

Rose's dark eyes narrowed a fraction, but she gave a careless shrug. "Never mind," she said. "I'll get you next time."

"We'll see!" I replied sweetly, through gritted teeth.

Why did she have to ruin the moment? Why did she have to remind me that she's always there, right beside me, clever as a fox? Ever since primary school we have been competing for the same prizes, dividing them almost exactly between us. But now we both want the biggest prize of all: a spot at Sèvres. Our *lycée* has never sent a single girl to university, let alone two from the same class. Madame

Grenoble assures me that we both have a chance, but in my heart, I know only one of us will win admission. It seems so unfair that it could be Rose, with her pretty clothes and loving parents—she would be perfectly happy staying in Beaune near her family for the rest of her life! Whereas I—with my glasses, and horrible height, and my stepmother dressing me in gaudy offcuts of chintz—what other means do I have to escape?

I must not allow Rose to thwart my chances. It must be me. It has to be me. *Cher journal*, I am determined it will be me.

Chapter 4

The grape presses woke me just after dawn, their steady, pumping drone echoing through the *cuverie* and courtyard, reaching the furthest corners of the house. By the time I had dressed, scarfed a buttered tartine, and gulped a mug of tea, the morning's first load of fruit had been crushed.

It was the thirteenth day of *la cueillette*, the picking. Or was it the fourteenth? The days had sifted into a similar pattern: misty mornings, humid afternoons, and evenings of complete exhaustion. By now, I had learned to dress in layers, shucking off my waterproof coat and fleece jacket as the sun burned away the clouds. I had learned to bring my own bottle of water to the fields, as everyone else quenched their thirst with wine. I had learned that the sticky, black stains on my fingernails were grape tannins—and that no amount of scouring would remove them. And I had learned that hours of labor, though physically taxing, left my mind free to drift through a tangle of memories I had hoped to forget.

Everywhere were reminders of the last time I had been in France. The smell of the laundry detergent. The little tune announcing the weather interval on the radio. The color of the toilet paper, shocking pink. Even the shape of the plastic cups recalled picnics on the Champ de Mars, a blanket spread under the Eiffel Tower, everyone basking in the mild existential angst that is the right of all French people.

One day in particular still haunted me. A perfect day, a spring day—April in Paris—and the city had unfurled in the persistent warmth of true sunshine. A picnic lunch of baguette slathered with triple-cream cheese, white wine that tasted of gooseberries and river stones. Our legs stretched upon the grass, my head on Jean-Luc's chest. When he eventually spoke, the catch in his voice was so slight that I wouldn't have noticed it, except for what followed: "I was thinking," he had said, "that I could come to the California next year. For an internship in the Napa Valley. It is not too far from Berkeley, n'est-ce pas?"

"Really?" I propped myself up on my elbows.

"You'd want to do that?" We hadn't really talked about the future. Even when I was alone, I avoided thinking about my return to California at the end of the summer. I still had more than four months—still enough time to ignore it.

"*Oui,* I would want to do that because, Kat"—his voice was quiet but it jolted straight through me—"*je t'aime.*"

Without warning, tears rose in my eyes, but the words, when they emerged, came without effort, as natural as breathing. "*Je t'aime, aussi.*"

"And anyway"—he grinned—"I do think there is a lot we can learn from the California wine."

"Wow, if you're saying that, it really must be love." I leaned over and kissed his scratchy cheek.

Afterward, I would never forgive myself for not spending the night with him. I would never forgive myself for kissing him goodbye as the sky darkened, and heading home to cram for an art history exam the next morning. Because that was why I wasn't by his side when the call came in the middle of the night. The next day, I found him at our usual spot in the Jardin du Luxembourg, huddled into a metal lounge chair, arms pressed across his narrow frame, his face ashen against a backdrop of vibrant flower beds.

"What happened?" A bag of sandwiches swung from my hand.

"*Mon père,*" he whispered.

It was a heart attack, sudden and swift and fatal. Jean-Luc didn't cry until I hugged him, and even then his tears were silent, polite, as if he didn't want to trouble the other people in the park by making a scene. He was leaving on a train that afternoon, he told me, heading home to his mother and sister. "Will you come later? For the"—he swallowed—"funeral?"

"My God, yes, Jean-Luc, of course."

"I'll call when I know more details. But if I can't reach you, ask Nico. He will know. He will help."

I put my arms around him. "I will be there," I said. "I promise."

At the end of the week, Nico drove Heather and me to Meursault in a rickety Citroën that trembled at high speeds on the *autoroute.* Afterward, when I thought of that day, only a few details remained sharp: The florid scent of lilies hanging in the chilled air of the village church. The simple wreath of homegrown roses adorning the casket. The thunderous creak of the wooden pews as the assembled crowd knelt to pray. The sartorial courage of Jean-Luc's mother, with her immaculate hair and clothes, her pearls, perfume, lipstick. Only her glasses betrayed her grief, the lenses cloudy and smudged. The handshake offered by Jean-Luc's sister, Stéphanie, just a brush of trembling fingertips. The flat line of Jean-Luc's mouth as he delivered the eulogy, his eyes bright with unshed tears. Outside, the day's callous beauty—pure blue sky, rich sunshine—glancing off the casket's dark polished wood as it sank into the ground.

After the service, we followed the crowd to Jean-Luc's family's home. In the garden, he stood amid a cluster of men with weathered hands and faces. The way they gazed at the distant vineyards—with proprietary concern—made me certain they were also vignerons, winemakers from neighboring domaines, the colleagues of Jean-Luc's father. Jean-Luc's arms were crossed, his head bent as he listened to some piece of advice, but his expression held none of the stiffness that I sometimes glimpsed in Paris. Here, amid the vines, he was at home.

Later—after the neighbors and family and friends had left, after Jean-Luc's aunt and uncle had whisked his mother and sister to their home in Charolles for a few nights, after Heather and Nico had helped put away the extra food and chairs, hugging us before heading back to Paris—Jean-Luc ran down the cellar stairs and reappeared several minutes later with a bottle in his hands. "My father's first vintage," he said, wiping it clean and removing the cork. "Tonight we will drink to celebrate him." He managed a smile.

"To your father," I said, admiring the wine's color, rich and golden, like a memory of sunshine.

"Papa opened a *millésime* every spring when the vines started to awaken. He said it was an offering." He touched his glass to mine. "To a good year. My first one . . . as vigneron."

My breath caught in my throat. "You . . . you're taking over the domaine?" Even as I said it, the pieces began falling into place. Of *course* he was taking over: He was the only son, with a sister eager to escape the provinces. He had been preparing for the role of *chef vigneron* his entire life.

In the dim light of the kitchen, his face was drawn, hard to read. "We talked about finding a *viticulteur* to tend the vines," he said. "Or selling our crop to a *négociant*. But, in the end . . . well, Papa would not approve. I thought this was the best solution, and Maman eventually agreed."

I struggled to keep the shock from my face. He was only twenty-two! I was only a year younger! What did he know about running a winery—negotiating contracts, bargaining with exporters?

Beside me, Jean-Luc pressed his lips together. With

his jaw set, his face looked stern, hinting at where the lines might one day fall; his eyes, however, were filled with a confidence that was compelling in its strength. "The most important thing is keeping this land, this *terroir*, in the family. Kat—" He set down his glass and reached for my hand. "I know we talked about it . . . but I can't come to the California. Not next year . . . and probably not for a long time. And, in fact . . ." His mouth drew flat.

I crossed my arms, steeling myself not to cry. I knew what was coming next and though Jean-Luc was being perfectly sensible, I still felt like my heart was being ripped from my chest and hurled onto the tiled floor of the living room.

"This is—" He picked up his glass again but his hands shook so that wine threatened to spill over the side. "This is not how I had hoped things would happen."

"It's okay, Jean-Luc. I mean, obviously, it's not totally okay—" I swallowed hard, willing my voice back to its normal pitch. "But—"

"Kat," he interrupted me, taking my hands in his own. "*Mon amour, veux-tu m'épouser?*"

I gasped. "Marry you?" I became aware of my heart, thundering in my chest. "Are—" *Are you serious?*

We're too young! I was going to say. But something in his face made me bite back the words.

"I know, I know . . . you are thinking that we are too young. But I've thought about this constantly over the last few days. I want to spend the rest of my life with you. I want to make a family with you. Grow old together, distribute our *médicaments* for each other. When I think about continuing this vineyard, I can't imagine doing it without you."

I closed my eyes, trying to figure out what to say. Something like: *This is crazy. You're still in shock. Let's take things slow. We'll figure it out together.* But I opened my eyes and there was Jean-Luc, his long legs ending in polished shoes, his mouth unusually vulnerable, trembling somewhere between tears and a smile. A wave of tenderness engulfed me. *I want to take care of him,* I thought. *And I want to be taken care of by him.* I had never before felt that emotion, of wanting to make someone happy, and trusting with all my heart that he wanted the same for me.

"*Oui,*" I whispered.

A couple of days later, we would tell his mother and sister: "Kat has made me so incredibly happy," Jean-Luc would say, wrapping an arm around my shoulders. If his mother had any reservations, she kept them to herself, kissing me on both cheeks, and showing me her own wedding portrait, a blurry photograph snapped on the steps of the village *mairie*. I would watch her twist a thin gold band around and around her finger. "She used to fidget with her engagement ring until they sold it," Jean-Luc would tell me once we were alone again.

Right now, however, we stepped out of the house and into the damp spring night, slipping over a low fence, scrambling to the vineyards that patterned the slope in stripes. The dry soil was engraved with shallow lines, and the wire trellis frames stretched empty, waiting to support the full weight of fruit and foliage that summer would bring. Above us, the country sky extended dense and dark, a thread of woodsmoke drifting through the air.

By the light of his cell phone, Jean-Luc showed me tiny shoots emerging from gnarled vinestock, the first signs of life after months of dormancy. "Next, we wait for the flowers," he said. "And harvest will come one hundred days after that, according to the old wives' tale."

But I never saw the harvest that year, nor the next, nor the one after that. No, I left France that summer with promises on my lips, promises that I would break once I returned home to California. Now, ten years later, picking grapes on land bordering Jean-Luc's, I willed myself not to think about what might have been.

In the end, it snuck up on me. One minute I was hefting my bucket to the end of a row, dumping the fruit into the wheelbarrow, the next minute I heard the tractor horn blaring, saw lights flashing. Kevin and Thomas, the twin twelve-year-old grape pickers who worked twice as fast as me despite being two-thirds my size were pelting Nico with fruit, covering his white T-shirt in purple splotches.

"Madame! Madame!" The boys waved at me. They insisted on calling me "Madame," which made me feel a thousand years old. "Come help us!" It was a harvest tradition to decorate the tractor, they explained, to celebrate the last load of grapes.

I joined them, and together we gathered leafy branches and tiny blue wildflowers.

"But we need more flowers. Bigger flowers," Kevin said, gesturing at the endless green surrounding us.

"We passed a garden back there." Thomas pointed down the road.

"Boys." Their mother, Marianne, a seasoned *vendangeur* who had worked sixteen harvests at the domaine, shot her sons a reproving look.

"It was covered with roses! Pleeeeassse, Maman! They won't miss a few," Thomas protested.

"Ask your father," she said with a resigned sigh, glancing over at her husband, who was simultaneously smoking a cigarette, tying his shoe, and talking on his cell phone.

Nico looked up from his clipboard, where he was tallying the filled crates. He shook his head. "You mean Jean-Luc's house. His *maman* planted those flowers. No, no. You mustn't steal his roses." His lips twitched and his eyes began to twinkle. "Not unless you let me help you."

"You'd think discretion would prove difficult in a bright yellow tractor," Marianne murmured ten minutes later, as Nico parked by the low stone wall that bordered Jean-Luc's property. "Then again, it's the Côte d'Or, during *les vendanges* . . . I suppose every other vehicle on the road is a bright yellow farm vehicle."

I tried to laugh, but it stuck in my throat. At the sight of Jean-Luc's home, my heart had started skittering so that I could scarcely sit still. The house was bigger than I remembered, its roof covered in yellow and red tiles arranged in the region's traditional geometric pattern. A round turret adorned the front of the building, a stone bird on its point overlooking a wild garden of roses, lavender, and rosemary bushes.

"It's pretty, *n'est-ce pas?*" Marianne followed my gaze. "Jean-Luc turned the stables into a guesthouse a couple of years ago, but it blends in so that you'd never guess. He built it for his mother, really. And then she moved to Spain to be closer to her daughter and grandkids."

"Thomas, you take the right side. Kevin, you're on the left. I'll stay here in the tractor for the getaway," Nico was saying in French.

The blood pounded in my ears. "But, uh, nobody's home, right?" I glanced at my watch. "Six o'clock. Surely they're all still at the *cuverie.*"

"*Normalement, oui,*" Nico agreed. "But you can never be too careful. All right, boys? Ready? *Allez-y!*" He let out the last word in a loud whisper and the boys charged the house.

Marianne laughed. "MI5 they are not," she said, glancing at me when I didn't respond. "*Ça va, Kate?*"

"Fine, fine." I managed to keep my voice steady.

"Don't worry," she chuckled. "If Jean-Luc catches them, he won't mind. Likes a joke, doesn't he? I'm sure he pulled the exact same tricks when he was a kid."

I forced a limp smile to my face.

The boys ran back to us, dropping armfuls of roses at our feet. "Start decorating!" Kevin ordered. "We're getting more!" Ignoring their mother's protests, they dashed back toward the house. I moved around the other side of the tractor and began to thread roses through the cab. The blossoms were full and fragrant, the petals starting to collapse around the edges. I tried to recall the garden from my last visit, so many years ago. It had been April, too early for flowers, the buds still furled against winter.

"AHHHHHH!!!!!" The boys came pelting toward us. "*Il est là! IL EST Là!*"

I peeked over the hood of the tractor and saw Jean-Luc sprinting up behind the pair. "*Qu'est-ce que vous faîtes là!*" he roared. *What are you doing?* But he was half laughing. "Stealing my flowers, you little punks!" he continued in French. He caught sight of Nico and slowed to a stop. "Are you behind this?" he demanded.

"Behind what?" Nico said.

"You know that I can actually *see* the roses you stole from my garden."

"I don't know what you're talking about," Nico said innocently. "We just parked here for a minute to count the *caisses*. This is our last load of grapes." He clapped a hand on Jean-Luc's shoulder. "Speaking of which, Jeel, how are your *vendanges* coming along? Almost done? Or are you conceding our little bet?"

"*Pas du tout!* There's not a winner until the last

grape has been pressed. And I heard you've still got quite a back load of fruit."

"All the same, you might want to order that pig from the butcher."

"*Ah, bon?* Because I told Bruyère to give him a call."

I peeped again and saw the two of them grinning at each other, as competitive and conspiratorial as they had always been.

"Is the pig for La Paulée?" Thomas's voice piped up.

"*Ouais,* Nico and I always throw a big party after the harvest, and Bruyère roasts a whole suckling pig. You're coming to La Paulée, right?" Jean-Luc asked the boys.

"*J'sais pas.*" Thomas circled the tractor to find his parents. "Maman? Are we going to La Paulée? Maman? Papa?"

"Oh!" Jean-Luc poked his head around the vehicle and caught sight of the group of us. "I didn't see you back here!" He strode forward to greet us, kissing Marianne's cheeks, and exchanging a quick handshake with her husband, Raymond, who was still on the phone. And then his eyes fell upon me, and I heard him saying "*Bonjour,* Katherine." Our hands met, the blood rushed to my cheeks, but before I could find my voice he had moved to the other side of the tractor. A few seconds later, he returned to his truck, hopped inside, and drove away with a wave.

My knees felt so weak, they were shaking. I concentrated on twisting roses and grape leaves together, and hoped the fading light would prevent anyone from seeing the flush staining my cheeks.

"Every year I say I'm never going to roast another suckling pig. And every year I get talked into it." Heather stepped back from the wood-burning oven, her face glowing scarlet. "Is this thing hot enough? Is it too hot? Is the damn pig even cooking in there? Who the hell knows?" She squatted and stared at the flames, which were radiating enough heat to blister anything within a five-foot radius.

"*Ça sent bon!* It smells delicious," said Nico, dropping an armload of firewood on the patio's flagstone floor.

"Yeah, well, we can't eat smells. Remember last year?"

"What happened last year?" I asked.

"I started cooking too late. The pig took seven hours. Or was it eight? We ended up eating at two in the morning . . . everyone was wasted." She clutched at Nico's arm. "Do you think I should run out to the butcher to get more sausages?"

"*Chérie*, we've got ten kilos of *saucisses*." He patted her shoulder. "There's plenty of food. *Ne t'inquiète pas.*"

"Or maybe I should make another lentil salad? There's still time, right?" Muttering to herself, she headed back to the house.

"She's always like this before La Paulée." Nico watched her disappear inside with an affectionate smile. "*Alors*, Kate"—his expression grew serious—"I have been wanting to talk to you. Now that *les vendanges* are finished, we were hoping you would stay a few more weeks. To finish our special project." He lowered his voice at the last words.

I frowned. "What project? You mean cleaning out the cellar?"

"Er." He threw a glance behind him. "Yes. *La cave.*" He was practically whispering. "You and Bruyère have made such excellent progress. It would . . . it would be a shame not to see it through."

I felt guilty saying no. Nevertheless, I began to shake my head. "I really can't impose on you guys any longer."

"It's not an imposition. Having you here has really lifted Bruyère's spirits. I don't think either of us realized how isolating it can be without other Americans around."

Through the windows of the kitchen, I saw Heather at the sink. She turned to retrieve a bunch of parsley from the cutting board, then spun back around again. It was true, she had seemed more lighthearted of late, as if her momentum had finally shifted forward. But again, I shook my head. "I need to get back to San Francisco. The Test . . ." I allowed the sentence to trail off. The truth was, The Test was still several months away. But being here in Meursault made me more uncomfortable than I wanted to admit.

Nico had been listening expectantly, but now his entire body deflated. "*D'accord,*" he said. "Of course, I understand." But his disappointment was obvious— and so much greater than the situation warranted—that I couldn't help but wonder if he and Heather were hiding something. Every time I mentioned the cellar, they blanched with panic. Why did they really want to clean it out?

Against my better judgment, I heard myself saying: "My Airbnb renters did just email to see if they could stay longer. Maybe I could look into changing my ticket."

"Really?" Nico's face lit up.

"How much longer would we need?"

"Not long. Two weeks, max?"

Two more weeks in Meursault. Two more weeks

fraught with the possibility of running into Jean-Luc. But two more weeks would also give me time to visit the Burgundy vineyards Jennifer had suggested, and meet the Burgundy producers she'd contacted on my behalf. Two more weeks would allow me to taste as much Burgundy wine as I could find. What would Jennifer do? I didn't even have to ask.

By the time the guests started to arrive, the afternoon sun blazed overhead, and the pig had begun to crackle, filling the air with a succulent aroma that people exclaimed over as soon as they stepped out of their cars. The garden was soon overflowing with grape pickers and their families—I recognized my fellow *vendangeurs* from Nico's harvest; the others, I assumed, were part of Jean-Luc's team—as well as assorted friends, relatives, neighbors, and vineyard employees from both domaines. Marianne and Raymond were discussing secondhand camper vans with a Spanish couple, and Heather was whisking various platters of food to and fro. Packs of kids grazed on handfuls of potato chips before running off to play complicated games of hunt and chase.

Even as I wound my way through the crowd, I was constantly aware of Jean-Luc's presence as he chatted with the other guests. I had the feeling Jean-Luc was conscious of me, too, and for the same reason: so that we could avoid each other. Still, in little stolen glances, I saw the years had treated him kindly, broadening his shoulders, etching lines on his face that only made him more handsome. I still remembered the last time we had said goodbye: a rough squeeze at the airport, a brush of the lips. If I had known it was forever, would I have taken more care? But that was before insomnia had started driving me from bed in the dark hours of the night, before vocabulary words began running on a constant loop through my mind—*deuxième emprunt de logement* (second mortgage), *droits de succession* (inheritance tax), *publication des bans* (public announcement of marriage)—before the doubts began to dominate my thoughts: *What if we're too young to get married? What if I don't want to live in France for the rest of my life? What if it's easier for him to stay single?* I would have sacrificed almost anything for Jean-Luc. But what if the sacrifice was him? In the end, I broke it off over a phone call, a crystal-clear, long-distance conversation from California. Because I wasn't brave enough to see his face.

The afternoon was dissolving into a brilliant evening, the dark blue sky sparkling with a million stars. Heather and Nico wrestled the pig from the wood-burning oven—all crisp, golden skin and moist flesh—and when Uncle Philippe carved the first slices, everyone burst into spontaneous applause. The buffet table groaned with charcuterie and salads, a great mound of barbecued sausages, gratins of courgettes and other garden vegetables, platters of gently oozing local cheeses, and an array of homemade cakes and tarts contributed by Heather's neighbors. We ate and drank until eventually the wine gave way to *ratafia*, a home-brewed *digestif* made from lightly fermented grape juice and some sort of lethal grain alcohol. Nico and Jean-Luc lit a bonfire in a corner of the garden, and one of the neighbors produced an accordion, trilling a warbly tune and rousing a group to dance. Couples paired off to clap and stomp out the traditional steps—I spotted Heather and Nico, his sister, Chloé, and her husband, Uncle Philippe and Aunt Jeanne. A slender young woman with long, honey-colored hair pulled Jean-Luc toward the circle and together they joined the others, whirling about with linked arms. She lifted her face toward his—small foxy features, dark eyes that sparkled in the firelight— smiling at him with such warmth that I needed no one to tell me that she was Jean-Luc's girlfriend. Was she a neighbor, perhaps? Or a former schoolmate, a girl he'd probably known since they were both in diapers? She threaded through the others with the sure feet of someone who had been dancing these steps since childhood.

Not for the first time, I thought about how this life

could have been mine. I could have been the vigneron's wife, basking in the glow of my husband's smile, laughing a little as I stumbled over my own feet. I could have been savoring this respite after the harvest, satisfied with our hard work, buoyed by the hope of a spectacular vintage. Instead, here I was on the sidelines, an observer instead of a participant.

The accordionist ended the dance with a merry flourish, the couples broke apart, and everyone applauded. Jean-Luc and his girlfriend stood laughing over some joke, the light from the bonfire burnishing their flushed faces. He looked so robust standing there, out of breath, a little sweaty from the dancing, not the perfect image of my memory, but a real person who laughed, flirted, shouted, swore, who was brilliant and funny, headstrong and ambitious, and maybe a little too much of a perfectionist. For all these years, Jean-Luc had been a ghost, a specter of wishful thinking, haunting me. Now that he stood before me, I finally understood that the decisions I had made long ago had sent our lives on two separate paths, diverging too far for us to find each other again.

I walked to the patio to pour myself another drink. There was no open wine, so I reached for a new bottle, peeling away the foil and twisting into the cork with my wine key. I opened several bottles for good measure, losing myself in the familiar, soothing efficiency of the task.

"You must be Kate." It was a guy's voice, American. I turned in surprise. He had a shaggy mop of dark brown hair, thick eyebrows arching above black-framed glasses, a smile that wavered between wry and self-conscious. "Heather told me there was another somm here," he added. "Hey, I'm Walker."

"Hi." We shook hands, his grip dry and firm. "Are you friends with Heather and Nico?" I asked.

"Nah, I just met them tonight. I'm actually doing a *stage* with Jean-Luc. Staying in his guesthouse, which is pretty sweet."

I nodded without comment and grabbed another bottle of wine.

"Oh, please, let me." He removed the bottle from my hand and trickled some into my glass. "You know, a *lady* is never supposed to pour her own wine in France." He emphasized the word "lady" like it was an antiquated concept. "So are you *stage*-ing here at Charpin?"

"Um, sort of. Nico's my cousin. And I'm a Master of Wine candidate preparing for the practical exam."

"Whoa." His eyes widened. "That test is hardcore. Hats off to you."

"How about you? What brings you to the Côte d'Or?"

He sipped from his glass before responding. "Actually, I'm studying for the Master Sommelier exam."

"Ahh!" I said with mock horror. "You're one of *them.*"

"By that I assume you mean someone who's an expert on wine *and* knows how to serve it?" he said in a bantering tone.

"Actually," I teased, "I meant someone who can't hack the intellectual rigor of the Master of Wine."

"Can you even pour wine without spilling it?"

"Six wines," I said in a musing tone. "That's all you have to identify, right?"

"Look, I'll concede that the MW is more difficult if you sabre open a bottle of Champagne."

"No problem." I glanced around. "Where's the sabre?"

He held up his hands and laughed. "Truce!"

"Called your bluff, huh?" Somehow I found myself touching my hair.

"Nah, I just didn't want to see you behead one of those kids running around."

"As if." I picked up a bottle and refilled his glass. As I returned the bottle to the table, the smallest trickle of wine dribbled onto the pristine tablecloth. "Er, *anyway,*" I said as he started laughing, "did you come to work the *vendanges*?"

"I was somm-ing in New York but, man, those hours . . . they burned me out. I had some cash saved up and figured, hey, maybe I should just move to France for a while. I've got an Irish passport and speak French. It seemed as good a time as any to take off and do some traveling, finally check out the premier wine regions everyone keeps talking about. So, you know, basically, I'm yolo-ing." There it was again, that ironic twist of a smile.

Despite myself, I laughed, just as the accordion let out a sudden blast.

"Hey!" Walker nodded at the lawn, where couples were once again assembling, facing off in two lines. "You want to dance?" He whisked the glass from my hands, placed it on the table, and beckoned at me to follow him.

"I don't know the steps!" I said, growing flustered as I glimpsed Jean-Luc looming at the far end of the row.

"Doesn't matter!" He glanced over his shoulder, grinning. "We'll fake it!" And he pulled me into the swirling mass of dancers, spinning me around and around until their faces became a blur of color.

26 FÉVRIER 1940

Cher journal,

The days creep along in dreary monotony, our meals an endless rotation of roots. Carrots. Parsnips. Leeks. Potatoes. A few days ago at lunch, I expressed yearning for a stalk of rhubarb, a leaf of sorrel, a peapod, any sign of spring. Madame sniffed. "Count your blessings," she snapped. "It's wartime."

"*La drôle de guerre,*" I said, for that is what the newspapers are calling it—the Phony War. Not a thing has happened since September.

"You should be grateful you have any food at all." She slapped down a dish of pureed turnips.

"France will crush the Boches," cried Benny.

"Arrrrrh!" Albert growled.

"Enough!" Madame's voice rose. "Hélène, you are exciting your brothers. I will not have this kind of talk at the table."

"But—" I took a breath to defend myself, but Papa shot me a look.

"Come see me after school, *ma choupinette,*" he said quietly. "I want to talk to you."

For the rest of the afternoon, I worried that Papa was cross with me. After school, I hurried through my exercises for the *baccalauréat* exam so that Madame Grenoble would let me go a few minutes before the other pupils, bicycling back to the domaine as fast as my legs could pedal. At home, I found Papa alone in his office.

"*Coucou, choupette*," he greeted me absently, glancing up from his book.

"Papa, I wasn't trying to upset anyone at lunch today. It's not my fault the boys got excited."

"Hmm, did they? I didn't notice. Though we do need to remain calm around Benoît, of course," he added hastily, as if Madame might be listening. "But I wanted to talk to you about something else. About this." He pushed the book forward, its pages fluttering.

I picked it up and glanced at the cover. "*Le Comte de Monte-Cristo?*" *The Count of Monte Cristo* is Papa's favorite book, but I haven't read it since I was a little girl.

"What do you see?"

I read a few sentences and smiled. "Dantès has just been thrown into the sea by the prison guards . . ."

"No. Look closer."

My eyes skipped forward several paragraphs. "He finds an island and comes ashore?"

He gestured for the book. "Here." He pointed at a word. "And here, and here." His index finger moved down the page.

And then I saw: Faint pencil marks hovered between the lines. "There are . . . dots," I said.

"*Oui.*" He smiled. "It's a code."

Papa showed me how to place the dots over certain letters and numbers, to spell out messages. "My father taught me the same code during La Grande Guerre, right before he went to the front. My brothers . . . well, they had already passed. I was left to take care of Maman. Papa needed me to be able to send secret messages, if I had to."

"But," I protested, "nothing is going to happen."

"I know, *la drôle de guerre,*" said Papa. "Still, we must be prepared. *Dieu merci,* the situation will dissipate. But if the war begins in earnest and I have to leave suddenly . . . well, it's always good to have a private way to communicate, *n'est-ce pas?*" His voice was cheerful, but his eyes stayed on my face until I nodded.

I cleared my throat. "Have you shown Virginie?"

He hesitated. "Not yet. She has so many concerns; I don't like to add to her worries. Your *belle-mère*, she is more delicate than she looks. *Oui, c'est vrai*," he said, in response to my silent skepticism. "If I am not here, you will need to be strong for her and the boys."

"But Papa—"

"Listen to me, Hélène!" His voice was sharper than I had ever heard it. "If something happens, and I go away, I am leaving you in charge. I need you to stay here at the domaine. It's the deserted houses that will be most vulnerable to looting. No matter what happens, you must stay. Can you promise me that?"

I nodded.

"I need you to say it. Promise me."

"I promise, Papa." My voice croaked and I cleared my throat. "I will stay here and keep the domaine safe."

"Good girl." He relaxed slightly. "Now, here is what we need to do in *les caves* . . ."

We would build a wall in our private cellar, he told me, and hide our most valuable bottles behind it. As *négociants*, our family has amassed a remarkable collection of wine, not just from our domaine, but a selection of fine vintages worth a considerable fortune. "Even if we can hide just a few cases of Les Gouttes d'Or, it could be enough for your future."

"But what if they find it?"

He shrugged. "The cellars are dark and they extend for kilometers. I suppose it's possible, but I get lost down there myself sometimes!" We both laughed because it's true—a few months ago Papa went down to look for a rare *grand cru*, forgot his lamp, took a wrong turn, then another, and spent several panicked moments hunting for the stairs. Our *caves* are like a labyrinth, built by monks in the thirteenth century, the low ceilings and arches leading to strange twists and dead ends.

"No one else must know about this project. You understand? *Personne*," said Papa.

"What about my *belle-mère*? And the boys?"

"Virginie . . ." He blinked. "Yes, I will tell her. Eventually. But not the boys—they are too young. It's too risky." When I nodded, he added, "We'll work in the afternoons, after school, while there's still a little light from the windows."

I bit my lip. "I have a chemistry laboratory after school. With Madame Grenoble. For the *bac*."

"I am so sorry, *ma choupinette*." He looked down at his desk, silent and completely still, so that my heart fluttered. "Given the situation, I've decided you should wait to apply to Sèvres."

I felt like all the air had been punched from my chest. "But nothing has even happened!" I protested. "I saw a newsreel at the cinema last week and everyone in Paris was out on the street without a care in the world!" Tears pressed up behind my eyes. "Please, Papa," I pleaded. "Please let me apply." When I saw him begin to shake his head I hastily added, "Or—or, at least wait to decide. Until the examination."

I held my breath as Papa considered. "*D'accord*," he said finally. "You can continue preparing for the *bac*, if Madame Grenoble allows you to do the work early, before school."

The next afternoon, we started in the cellars. Papa showed me the portion of the *cave* that he wants to wall off—it's actually quite big, as large as the kitchen—and we began sorting through the cases of wine, setting aside the *grands crus* and rare vintages. I think we've placed about twenty thousand bottles in there. It took Papa ages to find bricks with the right kind of patina, as well as all the other bits and pieces he says he needs. We're finally going to start building tomorrow afternoon.

I have hated missing the extra chemistry lessons

after school, especially since Rose told me the other day that they got to flare up different compounds in a methanol flame. At least Madame Grenoble has been accommodating about my absences, allowing me to use the laboratory before school and encouraging me after class, and in her comments on my assignments. I pray that it's enough to allow me to qualify for Sèvres.

You see, *cher journal*, I absolutely must matriculate at Sèvres in the fall. I cannot imagine my future any other way. I know that we have declared war on Germany, and that all the young men have been mobilized, and that there's a blackout after dark, and we have to bring our gas masks everywhere, but honestly it doesn't feel like anything has really changed at all. In Beaune, people are taking coffee on the café *terrasses*, and my classmates are swapping patterns for new spring dresses, and last week Madame Laroche told me she planted seventeen new rosebushes in her garden. Is this the behavior of someone anticipating a war?

No, I simply must continue to believe that nothing will happen. Because if there is a real war, I will have to keep my promise and stay here at the domaine with Madame and my brothers. I don't believe that I am strong enough for that, I truly do not.

Chapter 5

"Shhh." Heather hobbled down the last three steps and threw a hard glare around the dim cellar.

"I didn't say anything," I protested.

"No, not you." She placed her hands delicately on the sides of her head. "When the stairs creak . . . it's just . . . agony. Is it possible to have a two-day hangover?"

"After that party? Not just possible. Probable."

La Paulée had ended just as the soft golden light of dawn began to streak the sky. I had stumbled to bed as the sun rose, waking with a splitting headache when Heather started shouting for Thibault, who was missing from his room. She eventually found him asleep in a pillow fort he'd constructed in the front hall. Later, we all ate leftover roast suckling pig for breakfast—tearing at the carcass with our hands—before embarking on the Herculean task of cleaning up the house and garden. After two days, we were still finding half-drunk cups of wine in overlooked corners, paper plates covered in crumbs—and Thibault discovered an entire apple tart tucked in the bottom of the hall closet.

"We don't have to start now," I said. "We could declare today a mental health day, and go eat poached eggs on toast and drink Bloody Marys."

"That sounds a lot like yesterday."

"Yesterday part two?"

She shook her head very gently, as if trying not to rattle the contents. "It's tempting . . . but no, no, we're finally making progress, don't you think?" She lifted a hopeful eyebrow.

I glanced around the *cave*. Piles of junk loomed in the shadows, as massive and hulking as ever. "We're getting there," I hedged.

But as I moved toward my side, I noticed that the cellar did feel slightly more spacious than when we had started. There were paths running through the mounds, and we had cleared the area around one of the windows, which allowed a glimmer of natural light to trickle into the room. I had almost tunneled through to one of the walls, and I could see the sides of a massive battered wardrobe standing against it, its doors blocked by more cartons.

"Okay. Okay," Heather muttered to herself. "Let's get started." She seemed preoccupied this morning, rearranging stacks of boxes instead of actually sorting through them.

I tore open a carton and found a pile of high school yearbooks from Nico's *lycée*. "Awww." Heather plucked one from the stack, leafing through its pages. "Look at *les garçons*." She showed me a photo of two scrawny teenagers, Nico and Jean-Luc, wearing matching top hats, bow ties, and goofy grins. "They were in the tap dancing club?" She began to laugh, raising the book to inspect the other pictures on the page. "Oh!" she sucked in a breath. "There's Louise." I recognized the foxy features of the girl from La Paulée. Despite myself, I felt a jab of jealous curiosity, sharp as a pointed stick.

"Are she and Jean-Luc dating?" I tried to keep my voice casual.

Heather lowered the book. "Yeah. I think it might be serious," she said eventually. "She owns an antique bookshop in Beaune." She raised an eyebrow. "I'm not exactly sure how she stays in business, but I suspect she gets help from her parents. Have you heard of Maison

Dupin Père et Fils? Her family owns some of the choic-
est vineyards in the Côte d'Or. I think she's had her
eye on Jean-Luc for years, but they only started dating
about six months ago."

Apparently Louise was both beautiful and rich. "Do
you like her?"

"She's okay, I suppose. She's very glossy and polished, pointy little chin. Reminds me of a hazelnut." She
bit her lip. "But . . . she makes these comments. Like
the other day at lunch, Thibault didn't want to share
the last piece of cake, and she told him, *Ne mange-pas
comme un juif*—don't eat like a Jew. I was so shocked
I almost choked. Nico didn't say anything—you know
how he is; always the pacifist—but finally I told her,
you know, *I'm* Jewish. And she just shrugged and said
I was being too sensitive. She told me, 'It's just an expression!' "

I gaped at her. I knew anti-Semitism lurked in
France, as it did everywhere in the world, but to hear it
expressed so overtly stunned me.

"I know, it's horrifying the first time you hear it,
right? These little phrases pop up sometimes, but I've
gotten used to it, I guess." She closed the yearbook
with a snap, and returned it to the box. "Obviously,
Jean-Luc's relationship is none of my business. But I
really hope he's not making a mistake."

I shifted my weight to my heels. "I'm sure he knows what he's doing," I said, smoothing the flaps of the box so that they lay perfectly flat. When I looked up again, I found her regarding me with a speculative gaze.

"Look," she began. "I don't want to pry. But can you tell me what happened between you guys? When you split up, it was so sudden . . . he kept saying you were coming here, but then you never came. And then Nico and I had Anna—she was so *colicky*—and by the time we emerged from that fog, it felt weird to start asking questions."

"He—" I cleared my throat. "Jean-Luc never told you what happened?"

She shook her head. "I kept meaning to email you. But we didn't have internet at home back then, and . . . well, I'm full of excuses, aren't I?"

An awkward silence hung between us. "It wasn't really one thing in particular," I said finally. "We were just too young." A memory flashed before me of the last night we had spent together in Paris. My *chambre de bonne* swept and clean, my suitcases by the door. Sitting on the floor, drinking Champagne, talking about our plans for the future. Jean-Luc's sudden declaration: "I don't want my wife working outside of the home. Maman has never done that."

"Your mom also makes her own jam, and bottles her own pickles. She and I couldn't be more different."

"And if we have kids?"

"I'll take time off. Or you will. Or we'll take turns. We'll figure it out."

"*Moi?* Do cooking and childcare? *Mais non*—that's the work of the women."

"Or there's the crèche?"

"And have them sick all the time?"

"It'll only be for a couple of years."

"Probably longer than that!"

"Well," I had laughed. "I guess it depends on how many kids we have."

"Four?"

"*Four?* One."

"Only one? Won't he be lonely?"

"Noooo. *She* will have all the kids in the crèche to play with." I poked him in the side.

"Hm. I think we have some negotiating to do," he said with a wink, reaching for another piece of bread. "Though I *have* always dreamed of a big family."

"You just want the free labor," I said with mock exasperation.

"Ah, Kat, you know me too well." And his face had split into a grin, before he threw both arms around me and bestowed a teasing kiss upon my mouth, a kiss that deepened as his fingers trailed delicately down my neck, dipping under my shirt, so that I quickly forgot where I was and what I had been saying.

Now, I blinked and the memory dissolved. "We were too young," I repeated, but I said it more to convince myself.

Heather reached out and put a hand on my shoulder, her eyes dark with sympathy. But I didn't want to talk about it anymore. It had happened too long ago—and I had spent too much time examining those memories—too much time wondering if I should have done anything different. "It's okay." I managed to retrieve a smile. "Doesn't matter now. It's all turned out for the best." I shrugged so that her hand fell from my arm. And then I reached for another box because I didn't want to see the hurt flash across her face.

We worked in silence. I forced myself to concentrate on the objects before me. A pile of disintegrating dustrags. An ancient box of washing soda. A set of copper jelly molds, dull and speckled with tarnish. An old book—a biography of Marie Curie. I lifted the cover and turned to the frontispiece, my heart skipping a beat when I saw the inscription written in an old-fashioned, looping hand:

Hélène
Le Club d'Alchimistes

I stared at the words, trying to make sense of them. The book was Hélène's, that much was clear. But Le Club d'Alchimistes? *The Alchemists Club?* What was that?

I lifted my head and called across the cellar: "Heather?"

"Yeah?" Was I imagining things, or did her voice sound cold?

"Check this out." Scrambling to my feet, I moved to her side and showed her the book. "What do you think it means?"

She stared at the handwriting, and then shook her head. "Honestly, I have no idea. It must've belonged to her. Whoever she is. Was. Hélène." She touched the name with her fingertip.

"What is alchemy anyway? Magically transforming metal into gold?"

She shrugged. "There's no such thing as magic. Don't be silly. That's just a medieval superstition."

"Woowwwww!" **Heather** exclaimed. "Don't you look fancy!"

Three pairs of eyes turned to look at me as I entered the kitchen. "Guys, it's nothing," I protested. "I just washed my hair."

"*And* put on shoes with heels. *And* lipstick!" Heather resumed chopping an onion. "Walker won't know what hit him."

"What do you two think?" I asked Anna and Thibault. "Do I look okay?"

Anna tipped her head to one side. "*Les jeans* are good. And I do like the shirt. But you need to tie the scarf like this." She pulled it from my shoulders, folded it in half, and looped it around my neck. "Voilà. Now it brings out the green color of your eyes."

Heather glanced up from her cutting board. "Whoa. She's actually right."

"Tomorrow, I will show you how to do a cat eye with eyeliner," Anna promised, and slid out of the room.

"Kat, will you help me build again the Lego *cave à vins*?" Thibault looked up at me.

"Oh, the Lego wine cellar . . . that was fun, wasn't it? How about tomorrow?"

"Can we make another earthquake?"

"You bet, kid," I said, and he resumed scribbling over his Minions coloring book.

"What time is Walker picking you up?" Heather crushed a clove of garlic with the side of her knife.

"Around seven." We both looked at the clock, which read ten past the hour.

"So, are you prepared for tonight?"

"Um, I guess? Why, is there going to be a test?"

"*You know.*" She raised her eyebrows. "Prepared."

"If you mean what I think you do—no! I barely know him."

"Hey, I saw you guys talking at La Paulée. There were sparks!"

"Yeah, the spark two Americans feel when they meet in a foreign country."

"Well, when's the last time you went on a date?"

"Not that long ago. Sometime in June," I hedged, shaving off a few months. "I was seeing this tech guy in San Francisco. Though I could never tell if he was really interested in me or just wanted my advice for the wine app he was developing."

"I'm just saying, keep an open mind."

Before I could respond, a car pulled into the driveway. "He's here!" I grabbed at my bag, spilling loose change across the floor.

Heather bent and collected the scattered coins, handing them to me. "Have fun! And if you want to bring him back here later, use the back staircase. The kids," she mouthed the last two words. And then she grinned.

Outside, I found Walker loping across the driveway, black canvas shoes crunching on the gravel. He was wearing a white button-down shirt, crumpled and untucked, a thin black tie loosely knotted, skinny jeans, once black, now faded to dark grey. "Hey," he called, ducking his head. I reached up to give him an American-style hug just as he leaned forward to bestow two French-style cheek kisses. Our heads collided, knocking his glasses askew. "Whoops, sorry. Hashtag expat problems," he said. And there it was again, that wry little smile, halfway to a smirk.

"So, who are we meeting again?" I asked, once we were in the car and heading toward Beaune.

"Oh right, yeah, so it's just this bunch of expats— like I said, everyone's in the wine biz, so no one will be raving about bulk chardonnay, or anything." He glanced at me and I nodded. "We've been getting together for these informal tastings. Everyone brings a bottle and the cafés have been cool about waiving any corkage fees as long as we order food. Last week Richard brought a 2001 Sauternes. It was Ah. May. Zing."

"How'd you hook up with these guys?"

He was silent for so long, I thought he hadn't heard me. Finally he said, "Uh, honestly? It was through Twitter. I know, I know—totally uncool. But I'd just arrived and I didn't know anybody and . . ." A flush began creeping along his neck.

"No, no, not at all. I'd do the same thing. I mean, hashtag wine geeks, right?" I smiled at him and he emitted a sort of embarrassed chortle.

In Beaune, we parked in the historic center and strolled to the café. I admired anew the manicured cobbled charm, the streets lined with half-timbered houses and pale stone *hôtels particuliers*. The town had flourished for centuries, I knew, it was the center of the Burgundy wine trade, home to its most prosperous merchants.

Walker paused on the sidewalk. "Here we are. Café de Marie."

I glanced up at a dirty burgundy awning, the hem hanging in tatters. "Café de la Mairie? Are you sure this is the right place?" Through the window, I saw a lone man sitting at the end of the bar, an inch of beer in the glass before him. It was the type of café that had a thin film of grease coating the tables, chairs, and plastic-sheathed menus, with toilets that hadn't seen a bleach bottle since the Mitterrand administration.

He fished a scrap of paper from his pocket. "Yep, that's what Richard said on the phone. Come on." He pushed through the door and I followed him inside, breathing in the sour smells of spilled beer and body odor. Except for a waiter and the solitary drinker at the bar, the place was empty.

The waiter looked up from his newspaper. "*Bonsoir, installez-vous.*" He waved at the empty tables and we scrambled into a booth. "*Qu'est-ce que vous voulez boire?*" he called, approaching our table.

I paused, waiting for Walker to order first. The waiter lifted his eyebrows. "What would you like to drink?" I finally said. Walker glanced at the wine bottle protruding from his messenger bag, and then at the waiter.

"Uh, *un verre d'*Aligoté?" he said, ordering a glass of local white wine.

"Me, too. *Deux.*" I offered a polite smile.

An awkward silence descended. Where were Walker's friends? Did they even exist? Or was this an elaborate ruse to lure me on a date? Beside me, Walker jiggled his foot, clearly as uncomfortable as I was. I felt a rush of relief when the waiter brought over the wine.

"So, uh . . . *santé.*" Walker raised his glass and we clinked. "What have you been up to since the *vendanges?*"

"Oh, not much. Just helping Heather clear out the *cave.*"

A spark flickered in his eyes. "Your family's wine cellars? I imagine you've got a few gems tucked away at Domaine Charpin."

"Ah, no, not *les caves aux vins*—the house cellar. And the gems are more like broken appliances and moth-eaten socks. We've been making daily trips to the thrift store, just to get rid of it all. Although we did find this mysterious high school diploma . . ." Quickly, I filled him in on Hélène, her clothes and suitcase, the book and photos. "No one has any idea who she is. All we know is that she graduated from *lycée* in 1940. Did she live through the war in Burgundy? I'm embarrassed to admit, I don't even know what happened here."

"In the Côte d'Or? During World War II?" He shook his head slowly. "It was grim. Just like everywhere in France. Occupation, deportations, executions, starvation . . . all of that. It was hellishly oppressive."

"What about the Resistance?"

"Well, the Demarcation Line was near Chalon-sur-Saône. I think that's only about twenty miles away. I'm sure there were a lot of illicit crossings to and from the Occupied Zone and Vichy France. Probably a fair amount of organized resistance, too."

"I wonder if that's how she disappeared. Hélène."

"Maybe." He fiddled with a napkin. "Of course at

this point, everyone claims they were part of the Resistance. No one was a collaborator."

The front door opened and our heads swiveled toward it, looking hopefully for Walker's friends. But it was just a grizzled old guy, shuffling in to buy a pack of cigarettes.

When Walker turned around again, his expression was more exasperated than crestfallen. "Sheesh!" He drained his glass. "Where the hell are they?"

"It's okay." I reassured him. "They probably got stuck in traffic or something."

But after two glasses of wine and a shared cheese plate, still no one had appeared. Finally, around nine o'clock, the waiter brought us the check and told us he was closing in five minutes.

"No, no—let me get this," Walker said, removing a few notes from his billfold. "Please, I feel like I owe you one. Tonight has been kind of a disaster. You must think I made those people up. I swear to you, I'm not a deranged lunatic."

"I just Googled 'signs of a sociopath' in the bathroom," I teased. Actually, I liked this version of Walker better—he was calmer, more genuine—and I felt myself relaxing a little.

We walked back to the car slowly, lingering for so long in the shadows of Beaune's medieval ramparts that I thought we might kiss. But then I moved out of step, and the moment passed. Instead, I found myself holding his hand, his palm dry and warm against my own. It was still early, but most of the shops were shuttered. The café where Heather and I sometimes had coffee after the market spilled over with light and people. I glanced at the awning: Café aux Deux Maries. Beside me, Walker gave a little start, whipping his head around to stare through the window.

"You okay?" I asked.

He dug into his pocket and produced a set of car keys. "Yeah," he said, pressing a button and unlocking the doors. "I thought I saw someone I knew. But I was wrong."

On the brief drive back to Meursault, we chatted about our favorite wine writers, and when we pulled into Heather and Nico's driveway, we made plans to visit a few wineries together, before exchanging cheek kisses. I did not invite him upstairs via the back staircase, or any other staircase.

But later, as I was brushing my teeth, something occurred to me. Café de la Mairie. Café aux Deux Maries. Had he confused the two? They sounded almost identical, especially if you didn't speak French. But Walker spoke French, didn't he?

I thought back to our conversation at La Paulée. Hadn't he mentioned it then? Perhaps he had exaggerated his fluency—perhaps he felt shy about his accent or shaky grasp of irregular verbs—perhaps Walker, despite his hipster glasses and Brooklyn pedigree, wasn't as sophisticated as he wished to appear. I could certainly sympathize—after all, I'd had my share of linguistic mishaps. I chuckled a little, remembering all the times I had mixed up the words "*salé*" (salty) and "*sale*" (dirty).

I was still thinking of Walker as I switched off the bathroom light and made my way down the long corridor to my bedroom. Climbing into bed, my mind drifted back to La Paulée and when I closed my eyes to sleep, I felt the grip of Walker's hands upon my own as we whirled around the dance floor, spinning round and round through unfamiliar steps.

3 JUILLET 1940

Cher journal,

Alors, it has come and gone, the day I have dreamed about for so many years: my graduation from the Lycée de jeunes filles à Beaune. And in the end it was not the triumphant occasion of my imagination, but rather a memory I wish I could erase. In fact, I wish I could forget the entire nightmare of the past few weeks.

Of course, we had been listening to the news bulletins on the wireless all this time—Papa, Madame, and I—our silences growing ever longer each evening when Papa clicked it off. So I knew that Belgium had fallen—oh, horrible omen—and I knew the Germans had been attacking. And yet the information was so disheartening, so conflicting and faltering, it was hard to understand the actual situation. I believed the radio commentators when they assured us that our troops were valiant. I believed that our army *was* valiant—braver, stronger, and better prepared than Les Boches. I believed that we would rest victorious, and that France—*la belle France,* our beautiful homeland—

would remain indomitable, because we, *le peuple français*, had a special role in the world. I believed all of this without question, because that is what they taught us in the schoolroom. And now I realize how foolish I was. Me, who has dreamt of becoming a scientist—how could I have accepted it all so blindly, without any analysis?

Looking back, I think my faith started to crumble when the first cherries began to appear on the tree in our garden. I remember because Albert had been pestering me to climb the tree and pick some fruit for him, no matter that it was still hard and green. Finally, I resolved to scramble up there—if only to prove to him that the cherries were as inedible up close as they appeared from the ground—and that is when I first saw them: people. Walking. From my perch in the tree, I could see the main road as it stretched into the distance, and along it a thin line of figures. They were moving slowly in small groups, loaded with large objects—suitcases and heavy sacks, I later discovered, small pieces of furniture, mattresses, more birdcages than I would have thought probable—mothers carrying small children, dragging under the merciless afternoon sun. At first it was a steady flow, but after a day or two, it had grown into a swarm, an impenetrable column of humanity choking the road, stretching for miles, trudging, trudging, trudging—and then, as German aircraft sprayed a deadly scattershot of bullets—trampling, trampling, trampling. People moved in a white panic, none faster than the fleeing French soldiers, who cast their weapons aside so they could run right through the vines when the roads became too congested.

The domaine's distance from the main road protected us from the onslaught, but still, the boys were terrified. Truthfully, we all were. Only Papa remained calm. To those who made the detour to our house, he offered water and wine, a bowl of soup, clean rags to bandage bloody feet, shelter in our barn. For the sake of Madame and the boys, he tried to muffle the panicked whispers of defeat, humiliation: "the Maginot Line, pierced"; "the French army, in retreat"; "Paris has fallen"; "they're coming." *They're coming.*

"You cannot flee? You will remain here?" a young mother asked when I refilled her jug with water. When I nodded, her dry lips moved in a grim whisper: "*Dieu vous bénisse.*"

"God bless you, too," I responded automatically. She shot me a look as if I was not quite right in the head. Then she and her three children limped back toward the road to continue their journey south.

I can scarcely bear to write about what happened next. The Germans swept in like angels of death, ripping through the Côte d'Or on tanks and motorcycles, hard sunlight glancing off their goggles. A small unit tore into Meursault at lunchtime and in the space of an afternoon they had established a village checkpoint and gathered us at the *école* to verify our papers and announce everything "*verboten*." We are forbidden to go outside after nine o'clock at night. We are forbidden to keep firearms, to listen to foreign stations on the wireless, to allow even a pinprick of light to escape our blackout curtains after dark, to help or shelter *any* enemies of Germany, but *especially* English soldiers. Of course we are forbidden to refuse any German demand. We are expected to collaborate with the German authorities, faithfully.

The lieutenant in charge is a thin-lipped man who speaks hideous, broken French. As he shouted his commands I felt Madame stiffen, even as Papa placed a hand upon her arm. She had feared the worst, but it appears that we will not have to face the indignity of hosting a German soldier in our home—not yet, anyway. I had been steeling my-self for the news—our house is one of the largest in the village, and one of the most beautiful—and when the lieutenant announced that he and his men would remain based in Beaune, *for now*, my limbs shook like aspic.

Madame alternates between passive acceptance of the present and frantic preparation for the fu-ture. At the table, she gabbles with relief. "At least this time we will be spared the horror . . . I still remember La Grande Guerre like it was yester-day . . . I lost a cousin, you know . . ." (At these words, Papa's face turned stony.) During the day, she scurries about the house in a panic, hiding all her treasures—the silver and linens, books and bits of jewelry, the antique porcelain vases flanking the mantelpiece, smoked hams and crates of jam, even the fine copper jelly molds from the kitchen—all tucked away under lock and key.

Amid the shock of these events—grimly capped by news of the "Armistice"—the *baccalauréat* exam in March had begun to seem like something from another lifetime. When the results arrived, I delayed opening the envelope, not because I was afraid I had failed—I hope this doesn't sound boast-ful, but I had been studying quite diligently these past few months—but because the world had been turned upside down. Everything that had been so important to me—the *bac*, escape from Madame's critical eye, the dream of studying and living away from home—now seems completely ridiculous. Frivolous. I am repulsed by the idea of living so close to Paris, with the Boches crawling over the city and its suburbs like dirty cockroaches. I would be terrified to be so far from Papa's protection.

I held the sealed exam results in my lap, and before I opened them, I forced myself to admit that the dream of attending Sèvres next year is impossible. Not next year, and maybe not ever. Then I sliced the envelope and read the results. They made me cry even more than if I had failed the entire thing.

And so, we arrive finally at today: *la cérémonie de remise de diplômes*—our "Commencement Exercises," as they say in English (am I allowed to even write in the language of the enemy of the state?). This morning, Papa hitched Pépita to the farm cart and drove us to Beaune. In the end, it was just the two of us, because Madame had a nervous attack and took to bed, insisting that the boys remain with her. Upon arriving at the *lycée*, I found only a handful of my classmates—the others had stayed home, or fled south with their families, I don't know which. But Rose was there with a fetching pink cloche pulled over her dark curls and a nosegay of magenta peonies in her hand, and I was glad I'd worn my new green silk day dress. After Madame Grenbole presented me with the Science Cup, Rose squeezed my arm and pressed the flowers into my hand, and whispered she would have been sick with envy were it not for the absolutely pathetic selection of prizes (a few paltry classics and a vast assortment of volumes penned by belovedly Vichy authors). "How does one choose from this bounty?" I murmured, gazing at the array. And then we both giggled. I admit, at times the competition between us has been cutthroat—but now it doesn't matter at all. Rose will matriculate in September, and I will remain here in Meursault.

Our headmaster, Monsieur Leconte, gave an awkward speech—he seemed to have excised any reference to "the future" from previously prepared remarks—and then he picked through the diplomas and handed them to the scant few of us there. After this, instead of a reception, we simply milled about until it felt too uncomfortable to stay any longer.

Perhaps wishing to lift my spirits, Papa suggested we have lunch in Beaune, but my head had started to ache, and so we returned home. Despite the bright summer heat, the day had started to feel portentous, especially with Monsieur Leconte's speech full of pointedly innocuous literary references, and the school choir forgoing "La Marseillaise" for the rather less rousing "Maréchal, nous voilà!" (sung in honor of our dear new leader, Maréchal Pétain, of course). I began to wish Leconte had simply sent us our diplomas by post, instead of this half celebration, which felt more ominous than anything else.

And yet . . .

Writing this account tonight has reminded me of the refugees who hobbled to our door. I think of those poor souls with their bloodied feet and bewildered faces, with their homes—their entire lives—left behind them, and my self-pity seems preposterous. They are homeless now, their possessions limited to what they can carry, many of them separated from the people they love most in the world. When I think of being separated from Papa and my brothers . . . I am weeping as I write this. And yet, here is the truth that I have not admitted to anyone since I climbed the cherry tree: I am afraid.

Chapter 6

Sunday lunch at Uncle Philippe's house was a weekly tradition. But on this Sunday morning, Heather was so frazzled it seemed like she had never before dined at her in-laws' table. She clattered around the kitchen throwing jars of tapenade and bottles of wine into a voluminous wicker market basket, wrapping a pear frangipane tart in parchment paper for transport, swiping her eyelashes with mascara, tying and retying the belt of her wrap dress until it fell just so—all while barking orders upstairs.

"Anna, I hope you're wearing the dress I put out for you! No, not the leggings! Mémé already thinks we're slobs—let's not prove her right by showing up in athleisure wear." This last part was muttered under her breath. "Thibault! What happened to your shirt? Well, what were you doing with the ketchup? No, it's *food*. You can't use it for fake blood . . . yes, you have to change. *Just go and change.* Nico, are you dressed yet? Nico? *Nico!* We're going to be late!" She spotted me waiting by the kitchen door with my coat on. "Well, at least *somebody* listens to me. Thanks, Kate. But you might want to make yourself another cup of coffee, or something." She sighed and glanced at her watch. "At this rate, we won't be leaving until next Tuesday."

"Actually, I came down a little early, because"—I lowered my voice—"I wanted to run something by you."

"Hmm?" She fiddled with the back of her earring. "What's that?"

"I was thinking," I said slowly, "that today might be a good time to ask Uncle Philippe about Hélène. Remember Nico said he keeps the family records?"

"No!" Heather's eyes widened. "We can't tell his father about what we found. Because he'll want to know why we're cleaning out the *cave*, and—" She bit back the end of her sentence.

I watched as her face turned various shades of mottled red. "But don't you want to know who she is?" I demanded.

Heather fingered a button on her coat. "I guess I'm curious, yeah. But we can't ask your uncle."

"What if we told him one of the kids is doing a genealogy project for school?"

She shook her head. "Thibault did one last year. It
was a big deal and everyone's grandparents were invited for *goûter*. Unfortunately, the family tree only
went back one generation." She stared out the window
for several seconds. "If we could just check the *livret
de famille*—the family record book—we could find out
how Hélène is related, and when she died."

"If she's dead."

"She graduated from *lycée* in 1940. If she's still alive,
she'd be in her nineties. I mean, I guess it's possible.
But unlikely."

"True." I chewed the inside of my lip. "Do you
know where they keep this thing?"

Her shoulders drooped. "No. And obviously we
can't just ask to see it—Papi would be suspicious."

Before I could respond, Nico and the kids appeared
with combed hair and shining faces, looking as if butter wouldn't melt in their mouths.

"What are you two whispering about?" Nico asked.

"Oh, we were just reminiscing," Heather said, not
untruthfully. "You guys look great! Let's go!"

Once we were strapped into the car, Heather
switched back into instructive mode. "Remember—
don't speak too loudly at the table," she said, swiveling

around from the front seat to fix her children with a steely glare. "Don't take more than two helpings from the cheese plate, or Mémé will think you didn't like her cooking. Do be patient—remember lunch at Mémé and Papi's house takes a very, very long time. Do use your knife and fork the French way—don't cut off a bite and switch your fork from hand to hand, like Grammy taught you. Mémé *hates* American table manners."

Wedged between Anna and Thibault, I felt like another one of the kids, being prodded into good behavior.

"Please eat everything Mémé serves you today," Heather continued. "Even if you hate it, don't say anything—just take tiny bites, and chew and swallow really fast."

"Even if it's *blanquette de veau?*" Thibault asked. "The mushrooms . . ." He shuddered.

"*Oui, même la blanquette de veau,*" Nico broke in. "It's part of your heritage."

"It won't be *blanquette de veau,*" Heather reassured him. "Mémé made veal last week."

Beside me, Thibault's little chest rose and fell with a gulp.

"If it's really, truly awful, give it to me," I whispered to him. "I love *blanquette de veau.*" He turned huge, dark eyes on me, and nodded, grateful.

My aunt had positioned a long table in the garden, angling it under an old oak tree so that dappled shade fell in artful patterns over a fine blue linen cloth. Sunlight glinted on the antique silverware and china, and a light breeze ruffled the sprigs of lavender tied to each napkin. Uncle Philippe poured *crémant* into delicate flutes and handed them around.

"*Santé*," he said, raising a glass, and we echoed him. While we sipped our sparkling wine, Nico rotated tiny lamb chops on the gas grill.

"*Bonjour, tout le monde!*" called a fluting voice and my cousin Chloé—Nico's sister—sashayed into the garden, small and slender in grey trousers and a matching dove-colored sweater. She embraced her parents, then sought out each person to exchange cheek kisses, trailing a musky cloud of scent behind her. "*Venez, les enfants! Donnez des bises!*" she commanded, and three tiny dark-haired children appeared, two girls and a boy dressed in matching smocked rompers with pristine Peter Pan collars. They dutifully pressed their cheeks to everyone present, even to Thibault and Anna, even to me—a virtual stranger. I was beginning to understand why Heather dreaded Sundays.

"Where's Paul?" Nico asked, feeding desiccated rosemary branches into the barbecue fire.

"*Au boulot.* Next week's fashion week," Chloé said, and I remembered that she and her husband owned a boutique publicity firm that represented young designers. She ran a hand through her thick, dark hair. "The children and I are taking the train back to Paris immediately after lunch."

"Would you help me serve, Bruyère?" Aunt Jeanne appeared with a vegetable terrine, cut into slices so that the layers of eggplant, tomatoes, basil, and goat cheese gleamed like jewels. Heather began distributing a piece at each place setting, while Nico followed with the wine bottle.

"*Juste quelques gouttes pour moi,*" said Chloé, and Nico obligingly poured her only a few drops. I eyed my cousin. Was she pregnant again—for the fourth time?

"Are we expecting someone else?" Nico asked. He counted the place settings. "Five kids and seven adults, *n'est-ce pas?*"

"*Huit adultes,*" corrected his mother. "Since Kate's here, I invited Jean-Luc." She turned to me. "You two knew each other in Paris, didn't you? I thought it would be festive."

I examined her face, but found no intrigue there. "How nice!" I said, as cheerfully as I could.

Uncle Philippe appeared at the French doors that led from the house to the garden, with Jean-Luc trail-

ing behind him. "I found this *jeune homme* snooping
in my bookshelves," he said, clapping a hand on Jean-
Luc's shoulder and drawing him forward.

"I was looking for last year's *Guide Hachette des
Vins*," Jean-Luc explained. "I wanted to photocopy
our listing for the press kit."

"*Bien sûr, bien sûr.* I'll find it for you after lunch,"
Uncle Philippe said.

"Hey, Jeel, *ça va?*" Nico greeted Jean-Luc with a
kiss on each cheek and I considered, not for the first
time, the differences between French and American
culture and their perceptions of manliness.

"Is, er, Louise joining us?" Heather asked, deliber-
ately casual.

"No, she's at her parents' house. *Bonjour.*" Jean-Luc
greeted me, stepping forward to touch his face to mine.

"Hi." Our eyes met, and I looked away, burned by
the cold politeness I found there. His rough cheeks
scratched my own and then he moved to greet Chloé.

"*Allez!*" called Aunt Jeanne. "*Tout le monde, à
table!*"

At the sound of their grandmother's voice, the children ran to their chairs. Heather nudged me to the seat
beside her, with Uncle Philippe across from us. Aunt
Jeanne fluttered from the kitchen to the garden, ferry-
ing baskets of bread, pitchers of water, a platter of grilled

baby lamb chops scattered with rosemary flowers that she'd snipped from her herb garden seconds before.

"The terrine is delicious, Mémé," said Heather. Did she ever feel silly calling her in-laws by the same pet names her children used? "Mémé" was short for "*grandmère*," and "Papi" for "*grandpère*," the French equivalents of "granny" and "grampy." Then again, I supposed it was better than addressing them with a vague "*vous*"—like she used to do before Anna had been born.

"*C'est très simple*, Bruyère," Aunt Jeanne replied. "First, you cook the tomatoes in a slow oven for twelve hours." She continued detailing the recipe, which seemed to involve more steps than the *pas de deux* in *Swan Lake*.

I glanced at the children's end of the table where Anna and Thibault sat with their three cousins. "*J'ADORE l'aubergine*," said Chloe's youngest daughter, Isabelle, gobbling eggplant. How old was she? Three? Next to her, Thibault had picked a lamb chop clean, but eaten only the cheese and tomatoes from his half slice of terrine. He caught his mother's eye and placed a piece of eggplant in his mouth, gulping it down with a slug of water. The basil leaves he dropped on the ground, where they blended into the grass.

My aunt rose from the table and moved toward the

house. A few seconds later, Chloé popped up and began stacking plates. "*C'est bon, c'est bon,*" she said, waving at us to remain seated.

The men began discussing the upcoming visit of an American exporter. "But do you know who else he's meeting?" Jean-Luc asked, and the three launched into intense speculation.

Aunt Jeanne reappeared with a large tureen in her hands. Chloé followed with a dish of boiled potatoes. "Mmm . . . *ça sent* . . ." Heather's voice trailed off as Aunt Jeanne whisked the lid off the tureen.

"*Voilà! Tripes à la mode de Caen!*" she proclaimed.

A savory aroma wafted toward me, leeks and carrots heightened by the sharp tang of dry cider . . . and lurking underneath, the dark scent of tripe, unmistakable.

"*C'est la recette de ma grandmère,*" said Aunt Jeanne proudly.

"Her grandmother's recipe," Heather repeated faintly.

"She was from Normandy!" boomed Uncle Philippe.

"Oh, how . . . nice!" I said. "What is it?"

"Beef tripe braised in cider for hours and hours, until it's so tender it just melts under the fork," said Nico.

"Ohh, Madame C.! You're spoiling us," said Jean-Luc in French.

Aunt Jeanne spooned a portion onto my plate, the

thin sauce puddling around sliced carrots and pale squares of tripe. I added a few potatoes.

"You must have been preparing this for days," Jean-Luc was saying to my aunt. "What a treat!"

She let out a girlish trill. "I know you miss your *maman*'s cooking," she said, giving him an extra scoop.

Uncle Philippe raised his glass. "*Merci, chérie,*" he thanked his wife. "This looks delicious." She shrugged off his praise, while managing to simultaneously appear pleased. "*Bon appétit!*" Everyone clinked glasses.

I picked up my cutlery and began sawing through a square of tripe so rubbery it seemed to actually repel the blunt edge of my knife. When I managed to slice off a small morsel, I popped it into my mouth. The first bite tasted bright, the cider's tangy sweetness masking the offal's unsavory whiff. But not even hours of slow braising could soften the tripe's elasticity. It bounced like rubber bands between my teeth. The unbidden image of a cow's stomach appeared in my mind's eye—a dingy white flap of spongy, honeycombed flesh—and with it came a wave of disgust. I tried to bat it away, averting my eyes from the plate, forcing myself to take another bite, then another. Eventually, with several strategic sips of wine, I managed to choke down most of the food. Tripe, no matter how carefully prepared, was not for the faint of heart.

"Katreen, *encore un tout petit peu?*" Aunt Jeanne gestured at the tureen.

"*Oh, non, merci.* It was delicious, but"—I summoned up a bit of politesse learned in college—"*je reserve.*" I'm saving room.

She nodded and bent toward Heather, speaking in a slight undertone. "Did you want to put your tart back in the oven for a few minutes? Or did you mean to serve it a little pale like that?"

The muscles in Heather's throat moved, as if she were swallowing something whole. "Yes. A few more minutes in the oven." She pushed her chair back. "I'll go do that now."

"Kate," Chloé caught my eye from across the table. "Nico says you're here preparing for an important wine exam?"

I nodded. "The Master of Wine."

"There are so *many* wine competitions these days," Jean-Luc said in clipped tones. "Master of Wine, Master Sommelier, the Court of Master Sommeliers, Best Sommelier in the World . . . it's hard to keep track of them all."

Beside me, Uncle Philippe snorted. "*Les américains!* They have to make everything a competition. Wine should be studied for the knowledge and pleasure of wine itself."

"Well, actually, the Master of Wine program is British," I said.

"*Les anglais,*" he snorted. "Even worse."

Chloé ignored her father. "Has your time in Burgundy been helping your studies?"

"Oh yes! I'm starting to meet with local winemakers next week. Everyone has been incredibly generous."

"I've been testing Kate," Nico broke in. "She could use more practice . . . but she can get by." *Elle peut se débrouiller.* From a Frenchman, it was a compliment of the highest regard.

"I wonder if Bruyère needs help turning on the oven," Aunt Jeanne murmured, turning to peer fretfully at the kitchen windows.

"I'm sure she's fine, Maman," Nico assured her, mopping up sauce with a crust of bread. "Is there any more tripe?"

She beamed at him and whisked the lid off the tureen. "I used the cider we bought in Normandy last summer. Your father says he can't tell the difference, but I think it gives a delicate aroma, almost flowery, don't you?"

Nico bent obediently to his plate. "You know, I do smell—" He stopped. "Is that smoke? *Smoke? FIRE!*"

A harsh, acrid cloud was billowing from the kitchen windows. I shoved my chair back, but the others were swifter than me. They sprinted toward the house,

Nico, Jean-Luc, and Chloé first, with my aunt and uncle panting behind. Before I could follow, I felt a tug at my sleeve.

"Kate. Kate," said a voice. I looked down and there was Thibault holding a heaping plate of tripe. "You said you would help me. Can you help me?" He gazed up at me with enormous eyes.

I gulped. "That's a lot of tripe, sweetie."

"*Ouais,* Anna, *mes cousins, et moi.*" He gestured at all the kids. "We combined all of ours together. I told them what you said." He whispered: "They hate tripe, too." I glanced at their end of the table. Four kids were staring at me, wearing expressions of pure hope.

I surveyed the yard. Maybe I could hide it? Bury it? Aunt Jeanne's garden stared back at me, unforgiving clipped box hedges and immaculate flower beds—even the vegetable patch contained pumpkins and late tomatoes as perfectly uniform as the produce in a Japanese department store. "Okay," I finally conceded. "Give it to me." I took the plate from his hands, shocked by its weight.

"*Merci,* Kate!" He skipped back to rejoin his cousins.

I set the plate down and poured more wine in my glass—I'd need it. Then I looked around to make sure no one had seen me commit the sin of serving wine to myself.

"Hungry?" Jean-Luc was striding toward the table with the others trailing in his wake. He raised an eyebrow at the pile of offal before me.

"I didn't think I was, but somehow this appeared." I gestured at my plate. "Is everything okay?"

"Everything's fine. It smells worse than it is." Heather slid back into her chair. "I thought I was turning on the oven, but I accidentally lit the broiler instead. When I put the tart in, the parchment paper caught fire. Smoke started pouring everywhere."

"I always keep a close eye on the oven—at least for the first few minutes," clucked Aunt Jeanne.

"Mama, can we have cheese now?" piped Thibault.

"No, love. Not until you're done with the *plat*," she responded automatically.

"All done! Cheese, please!" he sang, and the other kids joined the chorus: "*On a terminé! Fro-mage, s'il vous plaît! On a terminé! Fro-mage, s'il vous plaît!*"

"*Attendez les adultes,*" Chloé admonished them with a stern look.

"Another little bit of tripe, anyone?" Aunt Jeanne rested a hand on the lid of the tureen.

"I didn't realize you were such a tripe enthusiast." Heather nodded at my plate as her mother-in-law served seconds to Chloé and Uncle Philippe.

"Me neither. It crept up on me," I said, eyeing the

rubbery squares with their dull color and peculiar rough texture. When I looked up again, I saw Jean-Luc studying the children's empty plates with a thoughtful expression.

"Actually"—he rose halfway in his chair—"Katreen has *my* plate." He reached over, removed the dish to his place, and began to apply himself to the food.

Across the table, Uncle Philippe was staring at me. I felt his gaze of appraisal traveling over my face, but when I tried to meet his eye, he glanced away.

"If you little monkeys like cheese so much," Jean-Luc said to the kids with a teasing lilt to his voice, "tell me—what's your favorite kind? *Jeune homme?*" he asked Thibault.

"Comté!"

He turned to the girls. "*Et vous, les filles?*"

"Comté!" shouted Isabelle. Soon, all the kids were talking about different types of cheese—goat, sheep, cow—*chèvre, brebis, vache*—and making the noises of their favorite animals. Their cries were so joyful, I didn't have the opportunity to thank Jean-Luc. In any case, his attention was so resolutely focused on the children, I suspected that my gratitude was the last thing he wanted to hear.

I sank back in my chair. This lunch—the wine, the stress, Jean-Luc's icy demeanor, followed by his unexpected kindness—all of it pressed upon me until I felt my chest constrict. Mumbling an excuse, I pushed back my chair and headed toward the house.

Inside, the living room dimmed before my sun-dazzled eyes. I waited for them to adjust, listening to the tick of a clock, breathing in the smells of smoke and lemon oil soap. Eventually, the details began to take shape, familiar from my childhood visits. A brass clock gleaming faintly in the diffused light. The mantelpiece of pale stone, carved with bunches of grapes and leaves. Two deep leather sofas flanking the fireplace. A pair of Turkish rugs softening the tiled floors. Above, beams of dark polished wood ran across the entire ceiling, casting the room in a somber pall. My heels clicked on the floor as I moved toward the powder room in the front hall. Here, the light was tinted pale green from the ivy that grew on this side of the house, covering the walls and shading the windows. I shut the bathroom door and leaned against it, closing my eyes.

My cousins had grown up in this house, I thought, and their mother before them, and one of her parents before her, and back, and back, and back to the very first ancestor who had planted a stake at this spot. What would it be like to spend your whole life in the same small village, on the same patch of land, surrounded by the same people and things? I hadn't lived with both my parents since I was twelve, when my mother's bank promoted her to vice president—dependent upon transfer to Singapore. She'd hopped on the next flight to Asia, leaving my father to raise me. My parents sold their house in the Marin County suburbs and split the proceeds in their divorce. They both had new families now—a young wife and baby boy for my father and, for my mother, a silver-haired attorney to match her high-powered banking career, and a passel of grown step-children who lived in New York, conveniently halfway around the world from her.

I had spent enough time in France to know that the words "*chez moi*" meant something a thousand times more profound than one's current home. "*Chez moi*" was the place your parents came from, or maybe even the region of your parents' parents. The food you ate at Christmas, your favorite kind of cheese, your best childhood memories of summer vacation—all of these derived from "*chez moi.*" And even if you had never lived there, "*chez moi*" was knitted into your very identity; it colored the way you viewed the world and the way the world viewed you.

Where was my *chez moi*? Northern California, I supposed—I'd spent my entire life there—though, be-yond my friends and colleagues, I didn't feel a particular affinity for the place. I liked to eat take-out Chinese food at Christmas, my favorite kind of cheese was aged Gouda from the Netherlands—where I'd never set foot—and the best vacation I'd ever taken as a kid was a three-day pioneer camp in Yosemite with my eighth grade class. We had chopped wood, square-danced, and slept under the stars on burlap sacks stuffed with pine needles—no arguing parents allowed. At this point, my "*chez moi*" was more a space within myself—the dreams and ambitions that I carried with me—rather than any tangible place. For years I had been proud of this self-sufficiency, this minimalism—the ability to shape-shift into new jobs and new restaurants, or to pack up an apartment and move within two days.

But ever since I'd arrived in Burgundy, I had felt unsettled. Something about being here in the land of my ancestors, ensconced among the layered souvenirs of several generations, made me feel small and vulnerable. Alone. Maybe it came from cleaning out the neglected cellar—the dust of melancholy hanging over items no longer beloved. Maybe it was the effort of communicating in my faded French. Maybe it was the strain of forging a new normalcy with Jean-Luc. Or maybe it was the constant reminder of what I'd given up all those years ago: not only love, but also a home.

A sharp breeze banged the window against its frame, bringing me back to the present. I flushed the toilet, just in case anyone was outside, and washed my hands with cool water and lavender soap. But when I opened the door, I found the front hallway empty, and through the tall windows of the *salon*, I could see everyone still seated at the table outside. I lingered inside for a moment longer, standing before the bookshelves, steadying myself with a few deep breaths. Just another minute to clear my head.

My eyes drifted along the rows of books, wine guides and atlases, a set of encyclopedias, a row of French classics that included all the usual suspects: *Madame Bovary, Les Misérables, Le Comte de Monte-Cristo* . . . At this last title, I smiled. *The Count of Monte Cristo.* How many copies did one family need? I pulled the book from the shelf and opened it to the title page, peering at the inscription, which was written in an old-fashioned hand: "Benoît Charpin." It was my grandfather's book—though I found it hard to match my memories of the stern-faced, white-haired authoritarian with such a flamboyant tale of adventure. I leafed through the pages, breathing in the fusty smell of unaired paper. A slender pamphlet fell from the center, and as I bent to retrieve it, the cover caught my eye.

République Française

VILLE DE MEURSAULT

LIVRET DE FAMILLE

ANNÉE 1933

My breathing grew shallow. And then, before I could stop to consider what I was doing, I opened the booklet and turned its yellowed pages, squinting at the copperplate handwriting. It was a family record of sorts—a booklet issued by the French government. I scanned the first section, filled in by hand and marked with official stamps.

MARIAGE

Entre: Monsieur Charpin Edouard Auguste Clément . . . Né le 18 juin 1902 . . . Profession: Vigneron . . . Veuf de: Dufour Marie-Hélène . . .

Et: Mademoiselle Bonnard Virginie Louise . . . Née le 18 février 1908 . . . Profession: Néant . . . Veuve de: Néant . . .

Délivré le 3 mars 1933

Le Maire,

I thought back to the photograph Heather and I had found in the basement, of the proud vigneron and the beautiful, doll-faced woman standing beside him. "Our great-grandparents," Nico had said. "Edouard and Virginie." But wait. I examined the booklet once more, peering at Edouard's details. "*Veuf*"? That meant "widower." Had Edouard been married before?

I flipped to the next page, marked "*Enfants.*" Yes, here was the record for Benoît, born in 1934, and Albert, 1936.

The last page was labeled "*Décès des Époux*"— spouses' deaths—and there was Edouard, dated simply "*Printemps* 1943"—Spring 1943. The rest of the book was blank, as if someone had stopped filling it in.

Had I missed Hélène? I flipped back to the front and scanned the pages again. No, her name wasn't listed anywhere. But again, the word "*veuf*" leapt out at me. Did anyone know Edouard had been married twice? I reread the name of his first wife: Marie-Hélène Dufour. Hélène Marie was the inverse of Marie-Hélène— was that a coincidence?

I was so absorbed in the document, I didn't realize someone had entered the room until a voice spoke behind me. "Ah, here you are. We were getting worried." Uncle Philippe stepped from the shadows.

Almost instinctively, I slid the pamphlet behind my

back. "You have so many interesting books on your shelves," I said, holding up *Le Comte de Monte-Cristo* with my other hand.

He moved closer, reaching for the book. "Ah. This was my father's favorite novel." He turned a few pages. "Have you read this?"

"Um, yes, a long time ago," I stammered, wondering how I could return the *livret de famille* without his notice. "In translation, of course."

"Of course." He smiled faintly. "And you recall the story?"

"More or less?" I tried—and failed—to keep the question mark out of my voice.

"Edmond Dantès is falsely accused of treason and imprisoned for many years," he prompted me.

"And he escapes and becomes fabulously wealthy."

"And exacts terrible revenge on those who wronged him."

"Yes, that's right."

"But do you remember why?" He tapped the book with a finger. "Why was Dantès imprisoned in the first place?" Before I could respond, he supplied the answer. "His friends set him up. They were jealous of his good fortune. And Dantès . . . well. He trusted the wrong people." He snapped the book shut. "I do hope, Katreen, that our trust has not been misplaced."

"Your trust in *me*?" I began to lift my hands, before remembering to keep them behind me. With a swift, desperate motion, I managed to slip the pamphlet into the waistband of my skirt. "*Moi?* No, of course not!"

He challenged me with a stare, but I kept my gaze steady. "*D'accord*," he said eventually. "Well, shall we rejoin the others?" He gestured broadly, inviting me to go first.

Ignoring his penetrating glare, I maneuvered behind him so that he was forced to walk in front of me. As we stepped into the garden, I tugged at my sweater, making sure the *livret de famille* was completely hidden.

"We saved you some cheese," Heather called as we made our way down the path, single file.

A wooden cheese board sat in the center of the table, its contents ravaged. I served myself, trying hard to maintain the original shape of each cheese.

"*Qui veut du café?*" Heather asked. "Coffee? Tea? I'll go put the kettle on."

"I'll do it," Aunt Jeanne said hastily, rising from the table. A few minutes later she returned bearing a pot of coffee and a gilt box of chocolates. "I almost forgot that Chloé brought us these."

"Chloé! These are like tiny works of art." I admired the colorful designs painted on each shell.

"Hmm?" My cousin looked up from her phone.

"Oh, *les chocolats?* They're just from the boutique down the street from our apartment. *C'est pas grande chose!*" she chirped, though I was sure that box had probably cost about half the GDP of Montenegro.

"What's on the bottom layer?" Heather nudged a finger underneath.

My uncle's hand shot out. "Don't go poking around too much." He snatched the box away. "You might not like what you uncover."

9 OCTOBRE 1940

Cher journal,

It happened today in Beaune. I was on the place Carnot when two German soldiers stopped me and demanded to see my papers. I had never before been stopped while alone, and my hands started shaking as soon as I opened my handbag to find the documents. They spent ages scrutinizing the dates and stamps, checking and double-checking everything in minute detail. The whole time my heart was pounding so hard I feared they could hear its thundering beat. It's sickening to have to submit to inspection by these people, to dread the sweep of their icy gaze, to be treated with such suspicion even when you have nothing to hide! I despise living this way, cowering like a beaten dog, yet there I was, barely able to squeak "*Merci*" when they gave me back my identity card.

Madame had sent me to Beaune to buy sugar. I used to love going into town, but now my visits are so rare, each time I am shocked afresh by the Germans swaggering everywhere—the cafés are heaving with them, the newsstands stacked with their papers, their flag hanging above the Hôtel de Ville, their pink, pork-fed faces crowding the train station. Oh! The mere sight of them fills me with such a revulsion, I fear it is seeping into my very soul.

At least I am usually too busy to obsess about this cancer of shame that is eating us alive. Our *femme de ménage*, Vieille Marie, retired in August and no one has come to replace her. Instead, Madame and I, though largely *moi*, it must be said, do all the cooking and cleaning, the washing, ironing, and shopping—*ouf*, the shopping alone could fill our days, calculating the allotment dictated by those horrid ration cards, standing in endless queues—collecting and chopping firewood for the stove, not to mention feeding the chickens and rabbits, and cleaning their hutches. Benoît and Albert sometimes help with the latter—when Madame judges them hale enough, which is not often.

In the weeks following the "Armistice," I feared Madame was on the verge of a nervous collapse. She had virtually stopped eating and spent most of her days in bed, her forehead covered with a damp cloth (that is, when she wasn't secreting away her "treasures," moving them from one place to another, until even she couldn't remember what she had concealed where). But a few weeks ago, Madame Fresnes invited her to attend a meeting of the Cercle du patrimoine français—some sort of French heritage society—at the Musée des beaux-arts in Beaune. We are all a little afraid of Madame Fresnes—even Papa!—because her husband presides over one of the oldest *négociant* houses in Burgundy, and there are rumors that one of her relations is close to our "dear leader," Maréchal Pétain. So Madame forced herself to bathe and dress and off she went to town, drenched in perfume and wearing a violet silk day gown that billowed at her waist, she's lost so much weight.

Well! She returned several hours later with a gleam in her eye, chattering about the *authentic* traditions of France, creating an *ideal* French village, and the *strength* of this new France under Vichy, a France that had been *revitalized* by her ordeal. Papa let her talk for a while, and then he quite calmly told her that he could not tolerate further praise for Vichy under his roof. Madame flushed and replied that we needed to work together with the Germans, that collaborating was the only way we would survive, and that if he would only accept the situation, he would see the Occupation wasn't even that terrible for us here in the Côte d'Or.

"Those of us who make wine, we are lucky!" she insisted.

And how did Papa respond to this defiance? (Because, trifling though it was, it was undeniably defiance.) For a moment, he slumped in his seat, deflated. Then he pushed his chair from the table and stalked away, muttering something about letters to write. In short, he did nothing.

As far as I'm concerned, these Cercle du patrimoine meetings have rather proved to be a boon. Ever since she started attending them a few weeks ago, Madame's spirits have improved—she hums around the house, she teases the boys. In fact, she has been rather pleasant—no, strike that. Madame could never be pleasant. But she has softened toward me slightly, as if trying to apply the spirit of cooperation within her own home. Yesterday she even thanked me for cleaning the WC! And today she shooed me off to Beaune, saying *she* would prepare the evening meal. "It'll do you good to have a change of scenery after so many weeks cooped up here—*ça fait du bien!*" she trilled.

Papa, on the other hand, has been distracted and forgetful of late, quiet almost to the point of silence, fretful with worries that I can only guess are related to the domaine. We had another dismal, cold summer, and this year's harvest was disastrous—even worse than the last, the grapes so sparse and green it took us only three days to pick them. Even if Papa had wanted to chaptalize the must to encourage fermentation, there was no sugar to do so, and goodness knows how we'll clarify the wine with our limited supply of eggs. If things continue in this manner, we'll scarcely have any wine to sell to that portly German Weinführer who seems so eager to buy it.

The stress of all this has rapidly aged Papa. In the past six weeks, his hair has gone greyer and he appears to have shrunk within himself. He disappears for hours in the afternoons. When I asked him about it, he told me he was pruning the vines. I expressed surprise—because pruning season doesn't usually start until the winter—and he snapped at me and told me to mind my own business. He stormed from the house and about a quarter of an hour later, I saw him amid the vineyards walking back and forth. Pacing, pacing. I have absolutely no idea what he was doing.

Yesterday I was chopping wood behind the house when Papa appeared. His shoulders were stooped in that peculiar manner that has become so familiar, and his entire face blanched, even to his lips. When I paused to fetch more logs, he picked up the axe and began to wield it, splitting the dry wood with far more force than was necessary. I crept up behind him and heard him muttering between blows: "It is they who have taken leave of their senses . . . not I. Them. Not I. Them. Not I. Them." After he had chopped for several minutes, he threw the axe to the ground and strode off toward the stables. I didn't see him until the next morning when he appeared after breakfast with a grizzled face, reeking of stale drink, his grim expression forbidding any questions or exclamations of concern.

Frankly, I am worried about Papa. At times he seems hollow, callow with shame, utterly defeated; at others he crackles with suppressed fury. Meanwhile, Madame holds her tongue until he disappears—she does not have to wait long—and then prattles endlessly about the charming ladies she sees at the Cercle du patrimoine, women of such beauty, elegance, and wealth (according to her descriptions), they could rival Helen of Troy. Truthfully, of late, I have found Madame's attitude more tolerable than that of Papa. At least she swallows her fear for the sake of the boys. Yes, she needles us into submission, but the end result is that she maintains some semblance of a routine. And that helps us stumble through this purgatory of uncertainty.

Oh! There is Papa, listening to the wireless in his office. There are the four gloomy beats of Beethoven's Fifth Symphony, the faint murmur of words—"*Ici Londres. Les français parlent aux français*"—so that I know it's Radio Londres, the BBC's French service, which is forbidden. I must tell him to lower the volume—even from my room upstairs I can hear it.

Chapter 7

"We've made progress, don't you think?" The light flicked on and Heather began clomping down the stairs.

"What is this, *Groundhog Day*?" I teased, following her into the cellar.

"Oh, come on, I don't say it *that* much." She turned with one hand on the stair rail. "Do I?"

"At least every morning. And usually after lunch, too."

"Well, if I do, it's only because it's true. Look, I can do this now!" She jumped off the last step and turned to face me, stretching her arms out on either side. "See what I'm touching? Nothin'!"

I laughed. "Okay, so what's the plan for this afternoon? Should we finally tackle the armoire?"

Our gazes traveled to the behemoth standing against the far wall: a hulking carved wardrobe, about six feet high and almost twice as wide. How anyone had squeezed it down the narrow cellar stairs was a mystery that defied spatial logic. Yet there it stood, dominating the wall that ran perpendicular to the windows, its dark wood covered in a thick layer of dust and cobwebs. We had avoided touching it because all five of its mirrored doors were shattered, the cracks radiating like cobwebs.

Our reflections in the broken mirrors showed our faces refracted into a Cubist specter. "Yeah, I guess." Heather repressed a shiver. "That thing spooks me."

"Is it the million slivers of sharp glass? Or something else?"

"It's probably nothing." She collected herself and glanced at her phone. "Oh, wow, it's getting late. Look, I'll help you get started . . . and then are you okay working on your own this afternoon? Nico's taking the kids to Dijon this afternoon to buy new shoes . . . and I thought I'd use the time to stop by the *mairie* in Meursault. They keep the *registres d'état-civil* for our village."

"The . . . what? The civil register?" I frowned, puzzling over her words. Suddenly, it dawned on me. "Are you going to look for Hélène?"

She flushed. "I know it's sensitive—Papi made that much clear at lunch on Sunday. But . . ."

I pressed my lips together. "He's only made me *more* curious about Hélène."

Her eyes flashed. "Honestly? I'll be damned if Papi thinks he can tell me what to do. And now that we have Great-grandfather Edouard's *livret de famille*, it'll be easier to do some digging. Now let's pull these boxes away from the armoire."

We quickly cleared the space around the armoire so the doors could open. After about thirty minutes, Heather peeled off her work gloves and stuffed them into the pocket of her jacket. "You're sure you're okay down here alone?" she asked.

"Yes! I'm fine! You're the one who keeps seeing ghosts, not me."

"Okay, well . . ." Despite her earlier flash of spirit, she now seemed reluctant to leave. "I should be home for dinner. Nico and the kids are eating at the *crêperie* in Dijon for a special treat, so . . ."

"Avocado toast?"

"You read my mind." She grinned. "Text me if you need anything, okay?" And with a bounce of her dark curls, she leapt up the stairs.

I touched one of the armoire doors with the tip of my work glove, wary of the broken shards of mirror. But they remained intact, so I eased the doors open and waved a flashlight inside, finding more old clothes hanging from an interior rod, a rancid odor drifting from the stale fabric. Wide-leg trousers. Men's suits of tweed and corduroy. Rough clogs with thick wooden soles. I began pulling the clothes from their hangers, pausing only to remove my gloves, which made my fingers too clumsy to unfasten the buttons. I stuffed everything into yet another black plastic sack.

In the center compartment, I found shelves holding stacks of worn linens: faded bedsheets, fine tablecloths riddled with cigarette burns, bath towels, their nap worn threadbare, air-dried to a rough scour. In the drawers below, a heap of mismatched ladies' gloves in stretched kid, loose threads dangling at wrists once fastened with pearl buttons. I snapped open another garbage bag and swept it all inside.

I moved to the third—and last—section of the armoire, another compartment with double doors that matched the first. As I reached for the filigree latch, something scrabbled near me, a frantic, clawing scratch, followed by a flash of grey fur skittering across my feet. I shrieked and jumped, losing my balance and hitting my hand against the doors. The creature darted around a stack of boxes, and disappeared on the other side. A mouse, just a mouse. My heart pounded in my ears and I took several deep breaths and reached again for the latch. A gasp escaped me when I saw my hand covered in blood.

The cut was on the tip of my thumb, a clean slice from the broken glass, not deep enough for stitches, but bad enough so that the blood flowed steadily. I pressed a thick wedge of paper towels against the wound, hard enough to numb any feeling, and watched a crimson stain seep immediately through. *Don't worry,* I told myself. *It'll stop.* But a minute later, the bleeding hadn't slowed. Should I call 911? Did I even know how to do that in France? I struggled to snuff my rising panic. Somewhere the words from an emergency training seminar came to me. *Apply pressure. Elevate.*

I lifted both hands above my head and closed my eyes, remembering the day of that first aid training session. The restaurant had forgotten to tell us they'd scheduled it and I'd had to cancel coffee with my friend Anjali at the last minute. The entire staff had been annoyed and we'd pretended the CPR dummy was the head manager while practicing the Heimlich. I laughed a little, recalling our vigorous abdominal thrusts. It was barely two months ago, but already it felt like another life.

I looked up at my hands, lifting the paper towel away so that I could inspect the cut. Yes, the bleeding was slowing, though a red thread still welled up steadily along the edge of the wound. With my hand still elevated, I moved closer to the window. And that's when I saw it. Above the armoire, near the ceiling, a jagged crack ran across the brick wall. Heather hadn't mentioned any structural damage in the cellar. I squinted a little in the dim light. The wall looked uneven, built from bricks that were almost the same size and color, but not quite. Or was I imagining things?

The throbbing pain in my thumb reminded me that I needed to dress it. Upstairs in the kids' bathroom, I washed the cut with cool water, sprayed it with something that I hoped was antibacterial, and wound a bandage around the middle. A goofy, bucktoothed snowman grinned from the top of my finger. Before I returned to the cellar, I stopped by the broom closet for a ladder.

Maybe Heather was right, maybe we had made progress with our cleaning, because it was easier than I'd have thought to move the ladder through the cellar. I opened it next to the wall, close enough to the grubby window to absorb a trickle of light. Yes, from this perch, I could see that the bricks were slightly different, the top rows longer and narrower than the rest. Someone had tried to fill in the gaps, but the mortar had split, leaving a curious crooked line that ran horizontally along the wall.

I reached to touch the bricks. But raising my arm caused the ladder to wobble on the uneven floor, and I clutched at the wall as I scrambled to steady myself. Without warning, a few bricks gave way beneath my hands, tumbling to the ground. "Jesus!" I gasped. The last thing I needed was a trip to the emergency room. I forced myself to breathe deeply until my heart had slowed. Then I inspected my thumb, which seemed fine—the bleeding hadn't started again—before turning to examine the wall. A patch of bricks had tumbled in, leaving a small hole. But what was on the other side? I pulled the flashlight from my back pocket and waved it around, but the beam picked up nothing, not an object or gleam of glass. I stuck my hand through the hole and felt a puff of air—cool, but no colder than the rest of the cellar.

I climbed down slowly, backing away from the wall so I could gaze at it from a distance. Even in the poor light, did I spy the outline of an arch near the ceiling? Like a doorway that had been bricked up? I hadn't noticed it before because the armoire covered most of the wall. Was the armoire there for a reason?

I reached for the latch of the armoire's third compartment, holding my breath as the double doors swung open. But the interior was identical to the first, more old clothes hanging on a metal rod. Repressing a sigh, I cleared away the garments, exposing another set of swan-necked hooks, the same horizontal boards at the back.

My thumb throbbed. I was beginning to feel silly. Heather would be home soon and I hadn't made half as much progress as I'd hoped. And, anyway, what was I looking for? A secret cellar? The Count of Monte Cristo's hidden treasure? A door in the wardrobe leading to Narnia? This was the stuff of fairy tales. I gave the back of the armoire a hearty shove, if only to prove it to myself, and to my disbelief heard a faint but audible *click*.

Gripping my flashlight with one hand, I pushed at the back of the wardrobe with the other, summoning all my strength as the four center boards began to move as a hinged unit, creaking to reveal a small panel cut into the back of the armoire—and through the wall. The opening was just large enough for a person to pass through.

Testing the strength of the frame, I swung myself over the ledge, dropping down on the other side. The space was bigger than it first appeared, filled with large, dark furniture. Upon closer inspection, I saw they were wooden wine racks, filled with bottles lying horizontally and covered in masses of fluffy mold. Unwilling to disturb anything, I peered at one of the bottles without touching it. My flashlight picked out the number "1929"—an exalted vintage in France, and one I always remembered because of the American stock market crash of the same year. I scanned a few other bottles, spotting other distinguished vintages from the 1920s and 1930s.

What was this place? A secret cellar? I had read stories about them, of course—they were legendary in Burgundy—of *les caves* sealed off during World War II, the walls built to hide precious wine from the Germans. But the war had ended more than seventy years ago—surely all those cellars had been uncovered, the wine happily reclaimed? Why would this one have remained hidden for so long? I edged around the space, my flashlight sweeping over a fallen slate sign, a mass of cobwebs. In the corner, a wine rack screened off a small encampment: a foldout bed covered with a rough blanket, a small desk with an oil lamp, a basin, and a pitcher. Wrenching open the top drawer of the desk, I heard a rattle, and my fingers touched the hard chill of an old-fashioned key. My eyes landed on the lock punctuating the bottom desk drawer. To my surprise, the bolt turned sweetly.

The drawer was empty but for a sheaf of tracts with titles like "*33 Conseils à l'occupé*" (33 Hints to the Occupied) "*Vichy fait la guerre*" (Vichy wages war) "*Nous sommes pour le général de Gaulle*" (We support General de Gaulle) and a handful of stickers proclaiming in large type: "*Vive le général de Gaulle!*"

I stood still for a moment in the cool, moist cellar air. I didn't need to examine the armoire's clever carpentry, or disturb the narrow bed, or read the defiant words of the political tracts, to deduce that this was a secret lair. The message was obvious: "*Vive le général de Gaulle!*" The Resistance had hidden here.

A thrill shot through me, racing to the tips of my fingers and toes. I knew it! My family had been part of the Resistance movement during World War II! It explained so much about the intrinsic secrecy of my mother and uncle, their consistently careful demeanor. If their father, my grandpère Benoît, had been a *résistant*, they would have learned from an early age to keep their own counsel, to nurture suspicions. As a child of the Occupation, Benoît would have remembered too well the consequences of indiscretion: Deportment. Concentration camps. Execution.

I glanced around the cellar with growing excitement. Had this been a safe house for Jewish refugees? Or maybe Allied servicemen had hidden here while waiting for escape? Or both? I'd never heard anyone talk of it—but then again there were a lot of things my family never spoke about. I fanned quickly through the political tracts, hunting for a name, a date, an address—any clue, no matter how small. But the papers yielded not a single detail and the reason came to me unbidden: It was too dangerous.

Someone long ago had thoughtfully placed a step stool beneath the opening in the armoire and I climbed it now, scrambling through and then hopping down on the other side. The panel at the back of the armoire swung on its hinge, and I closed it by pulling one of the swan-necked coat hooks until the latch clicked shut.

With its doors closed, the armoire appeared as ugly as ever. Who could have guessed the sophisticated cabinetry within? It must have taken weeks, if not months, to build. I thought about the wine hidden behind the wall—even from a cursory glance I could tell those bottles were worth a fortune. And with a burst of pride, I considered the defiant resistance that had taken place just a few feet away—and all the lives my family must have saved, despite the enormous risk to their own. I remembered what Walker had told me last week—we were only miles away from the Demarcation Line that separated the Occupied Zone from Free France. The domaine must have played a crucial role in helping people escape across the border. Suddenly, everything made sense: The complete absence of information about Hélène. Her sparse belongings. A suitcase packed so she could flee in an instant.

Upstairs, a door slammed. "Kate? Hey! *Kate!*" Heather called, and then her feet began running down the stairs.

"Oh my God, Heather!" I shouted. *"Guess what?"*

"What?" She rounded the corner and appeared before me, placing her hands on her knees, leaning forward to catch her breath.

"You won't believe what's back here . . . I cut my hand and found it . . . secret cellar . . . thousands of bottles of wine . . . worth a fortune! *Look!*" I grabbed her arm and pulled her to the armoire, opened the center set of doors and climbed inside to show her the panel at the back.

She sucked in a sharp breath. "What is this?"

I explained about the cellar hidden behind the wall. The racks of vintage wine. The hideout in the corner. The Resistance literature. "I think it must have been a safe house during the war."

"You mean during . . . World War II?" She stared at me in disbelief.

"Yes, of course, World War II. Hélène must have been a *résistant*—or maybe a spy—and that's why we can't find any information about her. It all makes perfect sense."

Her words sliced across mine. "You're wrong."

I laughed. "I know it sounds completely fantastic, but I promise you—I'm not making this up. There is actually a secret cellar on the other side of this wardrobe, and it has a hideout in the corner."

Heather brushed a strand of hair away from her face with an impatient gesture. "No, not that. It's Hélène. She couldn't have been a *résistant*. Because I just found a photo of her in the library archives. From September 1944. And her head was being shaved."

I shook my head. "I don't get it. Are you saying she was ill?"

"No," she said sharply. "September 1944. After the Liberation. *Her head was being shaved.*"

"But what does that mean?" I crossed my arms, completely mystified. Next to me, Heather's face had turned to stone.

When she finally spoke again, her voice was like ice. "It means Hélène was a Nazi collaborator."

PART II

Chapter 8

I stood completely still, my eyes fixed on the cellar's rough floor until it grew blurry. Somewhere in the darkness a series of sharp clicks popped, followed by the roar of the boiler flaring to life. Heather shifted her weight, found a tissue in her pocket, and dabbed at her eyes. The naked bulb dangling from the ceiling cast her face in a wan light.

"A Nazi collaborator? But"—I shook my head, bewildered—"how? What exactly did you find at the *mairie*?"

Heather took a deep breath and began explaining. She had started at the local registrar's office in the village, requesting the *actes d'état civil* for Hélène Marie Charpin. But the woman behind the desk had

taken one look at the year of Hélène's birth—1921—
and refused, saying that unless the documents were
over a hundred years old, she could only release them
to a direct descendant. Undeterred, Heather asked to
see the records for Edouard—my great-grandfather,
born in 1902—and the woman had produced his
acte de naissance, or birth certificate. "Most of the
information we already knew," Heather told me.
"But when I took a closer look, I saw notes written
in the margins—the clerk called them '*mentions
marginales*'—apparently they're pretty common,
a way to reference other documents." In Edouard's
case, these lines recorded his marriages—including
his first, in 1920, to Marie-Hélène Dufour—as well
as the product of their union, a daughter, Hélène
Marie Charpin.

"So Hélène was our great-aunt?" I asked.

"Technically, she was your great-half-aunt. Benoît
and Albert were her half brothers . . . it's confusing,
I know. Look, I scribbled this little family tree to help
figure it out."

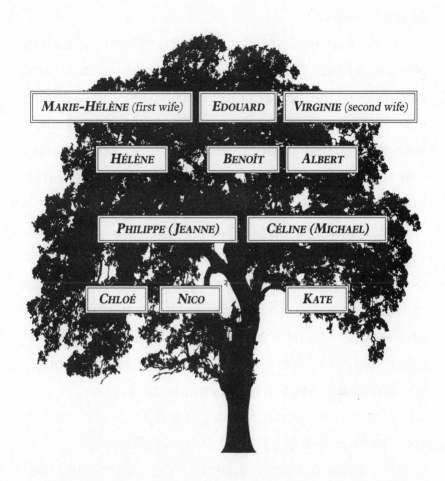

MARIE-HÉLÈNE (first wife)   EDOUARD   VIRGINIE (second wife)

HÉLÈNE   BENOÎT   ALBERT

PHILIPPE (JEANNE)   CÉLINE (MICHAEL)

CHLOÉ   NICO   KATE

"But what does any of this have to do with"—I could scarcely utter the word again—"collaboration?"

"When I returned the *acte de naissance*, I told the clerk I was disappointed that I wasn't allowed to see any other documents. She was very correct and firm, but I think she felt a little sorry for me, because she suggested that I try searching the archives at the library in Beaune."

At the Bibliothèque municipale de Beaune, Heather started sifting through the microfiche of the local newspaper, but information was sparse, and almost certainly censored during the war. "At this point, I was getting really frustrated," she said. "So I started just trying any old search—Edouard Charpin. Marie-Hélène Dufour Charpin. Edouard and Marie-Hélène. Edouard and Virginie. Finally I typed Hélène's name into a database for academic journals. And this article popped up. Here, I printed a copy." She pulled a wedge of folded papers from her bag and handed it to me. The article, titled "The Punishment of Guilty Female Collaborators After the Liberation," was from a scholarly journal and written in dense, academic French.

"Look." She pointed to a paragraph. "The authors refer to Hélène and her trial for collaboration."

My hand crept to my mouth. "She was put on *trial*? For *collaboration*?"

Heather crossed her arms. "I only had time to skim it—the language is very dry—but, yes, it was an ad hoc trial right after Liberation. And there're these pictures . . . she's here."

Even in grainy black and white, the village square

looked the same. Two women were seated amid an angry crowd. They had thick black swastikas smeared in greasepaint on their foreheads, downcast eyes, and grim expressions; behind them, two men in white barber coats brandished razors, sneering as they shaved all the hair from the women's heads.

A surge of horror washed over me. I had formed an impression of Hélène from the items in her suitcase—a serious girl who hid a sentimental streak—but the photograph in front of me depicted a savage young woman with a hard set to her mouth.

Heather's voice shook with barely controlled fury. "I just can't believe it, Kate. I feel completely sick. She was a *Nazi*. Do you realize what that means? This family—*they're anti-Semites*. This blood is running through my husband . . . and my children . . ."

And me, I thought. Instead, I said: "But people aren't genetically predisposed to be bigots or xenophobes. We don't know anything about Hélène or the circumstances that surrounded her choices. Not that I'm defending her," I added quickly. "What she did was unforgivable. All I'm saying is that we're not doomed to repeat her mistakes."

"I guess." But Heather looked unconvinced.

"And isn't that what you and Nico are here for? To teach Thibault and Anna a moral code—to give them an ethical conscience—so that nothing like this ever happens again?"

She crossed her arms and sighed, but I could tell the point had hit home.

"Of course," I said slowly, the thoughts still forming. "Now it's obvious why no one in this family has ever spoken of Hélène. Why they've kept her a total secret."

Even as I spoke, I was remembering a rare visit to my mother's office when I was about ten years old. Her coworker Midori asked about our summer vacation and I told her we were going to visit my grandfather in France. "He lives in Burgundy. He's a winemaker," I said in response to her questions.

Later at home, my mother pulled me aside. "Never say that Grandpère Benoît is a winemaker," she said quietly, as if she didn't want my father to hear. "Americans don't understand what that means. It sounds pretentious."

"What should I say?" I barely knew what a winemaker was, let alone a long word like "pretentious." But I knew I wasn't supposed to lie.

"Say he's a farmer." She shrugged. "After all, that's the truth."

For years I had puzzled over this exchange, wondering why my mother always avoided personal questions.

Was her coldness part of her genetic makeup? And did I carry it, too, this instinctive evasiveness? But now that I knew about Hélène, I was beginning to suspect that my mother's reluctance to talk about her family history was, in fact, a practiced skill, something she and Uncle Philippe had perfected as children. Now that I knew about Hélène, the truth was obvious.

They were ashamed.

The next morning, I found the kids alone in the kitchen, a spray of multicolored frosted loops scattered across the wood counter.

"Maman is out doing *le jogging*," Anna informed me, pushing her brother's hand away from the cereal box. "And Papa is in the *cuverie*."

"Who's taking you guys to school?" I filled the electric kettle and rummaged in the cupboard for a tea bag.

"Kate!" She giggled. "It's Saturday!"

"Oh, right." I lifted a hand to rub my forehead. "I guess I stayed up too late last night."

Thibault turned huge brown eyes upon me. "Fur of the dog," he said.

"Hair of the dog," I corrected him automatically. "Wait, *what?*"

"Air of the dog. That is what you eat when you have a pain in the head, *n'est-ce pas?*"

"Sort of." I swallowed a laugh. "Anyway, I don't have a headache. I just stayed up too late reading."

"*Ouais*. That's what Maman usually says before she mixes a Bloody Marie." He licked his index finger and turned a page of his Tintin comic.

Waiting for the kettle to boil, I leaned my elbows on the counter and gazed out the kitchen window, noticing for the first time that autumn had crept across the vines, the leaves of bright green fading to soft russet. I'd slept with an extra blanket last night, and this morning I had warmed the bathroom with a space heater before steeling myself to undress for the shower. There was no doubt about it. The seasons had turned, and soon it would be time for me to return to California, reclaim my apartment from the Japanese professors on sabbatical at San Francisco State, find a new job, rejoin my Master of Wine study group, register for The Test—in short, free myself from this increasingly complex web of family secrets and resume my real life.

The kettle churned angrily, and I poured scalding water over my tea bag, hoping the hot drink would chase away my fatigue. Last night, Heather and I had eaten a quick dinner of toast before she retired, pleading a migraine. Meanwhile, I'd stayed up far too late untangling a thicket of academic prose with only the help of a dated French-English dictionary. As far as

I could tell, the article that Heather had found discussed the treatment of female collaborators after the Liberation in 1944. This period saw the *épuration sauvage*, or wild purge, a spontaneous and violent movement motivated largely by revenge, which sought to punish collaborators. Some of the most humiliating public punishment was reserved for "horizontal collaborators"—women who had slept with the enemy—their heads shorn in outdoor public spaces before they were forcibly stripped and painted with swastikas, the vitriolic crowds jeering and spitting as the women were marched about town.

"The punishment of head shaving," the authors wrote, "which dates back to the Bible, when it was considered a purification process, was used in France throughout the twentieth century. In 1918, French women who consorted with German soldiers had their heads shaved; the Nazi party also shaved the heads of German women who were having relations with non-Aryans or foreign prisoners. In short, there is a long history of these *femmes tondues*"—shorn women—"as well as the practice of female shearing as punishment for sexual infidelity."

The authors cited Hélène midway through the article. "Women accused of horizontal collaboration were punished by the vigilante justice of the *épuration sauvage*," they wrote. "Horizontal collaborators were often prostitutes, although there were also many teenage girls who acted out of bravado or boredom, young mothers desperate to feed their hungry children, or women who simply worked for German soldiers, as is the case of one cleaning woman at a German military headquarters. Female Gestapo informers like Hélène Charpin, Marie-France Gaucher, or Jeanne Petit were more vulnerable scapegoats than their male counterparts, whose punishments were meted out during the *épuration légale*"—legal purge—"conducted from 1944 to 1949 . . ." I skimmed the rest of the article looking for more information about Hélène, but found no other mention of her name.

Now, as I removed the sodden tea bag from my cup, I felt again the shock of revulsion. Though the authors of the article had been generally sympathetic toward these horizontal collaborators—pointing out that the humiliation they'd suffered post-Liberation had been largely motivated by sexism and repressed fury stemming from France's emasculating defeat—Hélène's crime was far worse than sleeping with a German soldier. She was an informer. A traitor. I struggled to connect the ugly words on the page with the items we'd found—the girlish clothes, the biography of Marie Curie, the *lycée* diploma. My hand slipped on the handle of my mug and hot liquid splashed on my wrist. "Ow!" I reached for a paper towel and bent to mop up the puddle.

"You okay, Kate?" Thibault slipped from his chair and carried his cereal bowl to the sink, a tidal wave of milk threatening to slop from the sides.

"Sure, sweetie—ooh, be careful with that!"

"No problem!" he said as his bowl clattered into the sink. "I'm-going-to-play-now-see-you-bye!" And with a soft pounding of bare feet, he was gone.

"Should I be worried that he's up to no good?" I asked no one in particular. The family cat, Chaussettes, appeared from nowhere and began lapping drops of milk from the floor.

"Probably." Anna glanced up from the glossy pages of *Elle* magazine. "But Maman got rid of all the matches last week." She winked and returned to reading an article headlined "How the Stars Wear Denim!"— complete with a photo of a leggy Gisele Bündchen "*en jean.*"

I found myself hesitating outside the cellar door. I hadn't wanted to upset Heather by poking around down there this morning—but if she was out maybe it was a good time to look for more information about Hélène. "If you need anything," I called to Anna, "I'll be in the *cave*, okay?"

"*D'accord!*" She flipped the magazine over and

pulled another from the stack in front of her. There were no sounds emerging from Thibault's preferred play area—the front hallway—(though maybe that was a bad thing?) so I headed downstairs.

Now that I knew about the secret chamber behind the armoire, I wondered if someone long ago had created the disarray on purpose. My foot brushed against a heap of old clothes. In the excitement of the day before, I had left them piled on the floor, and now I knelt to stuff them into a plastic sack, knotting the top so we could take it to the dump later.

Sudden anger bloomed within me and I kicked the bag, spilling half the clothes across the floor. They were so guarded—my mother, my uncle—protecting these nasty secrets. *Gestapo informers like Hélène Charpin . . .* I shuddered, and the armoire's broken mirrors turned my horrified face into a hundred fragments. *Oh, Hélène,* I thought. *How could you? Why did you?*

A bang from the door caused me to start. "Heather?" I called to the nimble feet that were running down the stairs.

"Kate?" It was Nico, his stocky figure winding through the boxes. "How are you doing? Bruyère told me everything before she passed out last night. And she woke up angrier than I've ever seen her—she actually went running. That hasn't happened since my father told her women shouldn't pursue advanced degrees . . . before Thibault was born." He smiled briefly.

At the sight of my cousin, tears pricked my eyes. "I'm having a hard time accepting all of this," I admitted. "How are you?"

"Pff." He puffed out his cheeks. "Fine." But his face had clouded over. "It seems impossible," he said eventually. "Our family, we are good people. I just can't believe it's true. But then I keep remembering little things. Like Grandpère Benoît—he never, ever wanted to talk about the war. Do you remember?"

I shook my head.

"Chloé and I used to beg him for stories about his childhood, but he would turn silent and tell us he preferred not to think about it. '*Ce n'était pas heureux*'—it wasn't happy." Nico frowned and his face fell into deep lines so that I caught a glimpse of him in twenty years' time. "And of course this is all so much more painful because Bruyère is Jewish." His chin dropped to his chest.

Silence fell between us, hanging heavy in the chill, moist air. Upstairs, something small and hard fell with a clatter and rolled across the floor. Beside me, Nico had shifted his gaze to the armoire. "So, this is it?" He extended a tentative hand. "There's really a *cave* hidden behind here?"

"Oh, right, the secret cellar!" In the aftermath of yesterday's discoveries, I had forgotten everything except the horrific revelations about Hélène. Now, as we turned toward the armoire, I sensed my cousin's curiosity and my own spirits lifted a fraction. "You must be dying to see it. Look, it's this last compartment—no, the panel at the very back. Push right here. See?" He leaned through the opening and then, with a hop, he was up and over to the other side. "Do you need a flashlight?" I called. "Here." I thrust mine through the window.

Several minutes later, he came barreling back through, breathless. "*C'est incroyable,*" he gasped. "Unbelievable. Who could have built this? The hideout in the corner . . . do you really think it was used by the Résistance?"

"I thought so at first, because I found those pamphlets. But now I don't know."

"And the wine! Obviously I didn't have time to examine each bottle, but from the little I saw, I swear that I've never seen such a collection of vintages . . . some of the most exceptional *millésimes* of the twentieth century . . ." His voice faltered. "It is, at the same time, both horrible and wonderful. This could be—" He shifted his weight, staring at the floor. "Kate," he said finally, "I don't know how much Bruyère has told you about our concerns."

"She hasn't told me anything," I reassured him. Was he finally going to reveal why they'd been acting so cagey?

"We have made some bad investments. Bad decisions. Refinancing at the wrong time." He winced. "I'm sure you've been wondering why we're cleaning out the cellar. The truth is, we are hoping to open a bed-and-breakfast—nothing too elaborate, just a simple endeavor to bring in a bit more income. After all, we have this huge house, and we're rattling around in it . . . and Bruyère likes to cook, and have visitors . . . and we both want the kids to be exposed to people from different places."

"It's a perfect plan," I said with genuine enthusiasm.

"Except for my father." Nico sighed. "He's dead set against the idea. But Bruyère and I thought that if we got everything prepared to start renovations . . . well, it would be very difficult for him to say no."

It was all starting to make sense—Heather and Nico's reticence, their rush to clean out the cellar— and especially their horrified silence when I'd suggested this exact idea to Uncle Philippe. "You guys should've told me!" I exclaimed, slapping a hand to my forehead. "I would have been more discreet."

"Yeah." Nico scuffed a foot on the floor. "We . . . well, we felt embarrassed. Honestly, we've been struggling for a while, trying to figure out a way to keep the domaine." He swallowed. "This wine—it could be the miracle we need."

"It might be worth a lot of money," I agreed. "But it's hard to judge without knowing the exact contents of the cellar, and examining the condition of each bottle."

"You know about rare wine, *n'est-ce pas?*"

"I'm not an expert. But, yes, I've studied it for The Test. And, as you know, I'd like to work at an auction house one day, dealing with vintage wine sales."

"So you can help us? You can create a cellar list—an inventory of this *cave*—so that we know exactly what is inside?"

I instinctively took a step back. "But that could take ages! I have to go home, back to San Francisco. Get ready for The Test and actually take it."

"But this would be wonderful preparation for The Test!"

"What about Heather? She was so angry last night, I thought she might burn this house to the ground."

"Ehzaire doesn't care about the wine. She just wants

to get rid of it. She detests the idea that we might profit in any way from the collaboration." His eyes pleaded with me. "But the thing is, Kate—the domaine—it is in danger of repossession. We could really use this money. I thought that if you stayed and talked with Heather, and were able to give us a proper estimate for the wine, well"—he glanced away—"maybe she might change her mind."

I took a deep breath, but before I could say no, the image of the hidden cellar flashed before me—not the piles of antique wine bottles swathed in mold, but the hideout in the corner—the desk and its contents. The Resistance literature. Who had left it there? I had spent half the night racking my brain, but still none of it made sense: How on earth did those things end up in the same house as a known Nazi sympathizer?

"Okay," I found myself saying. "I'll see if I can change my ticket again. But only if Heather agrees. And only for a few weeks."

"*Mais bien sûr*, I understand." His face had begun to relax. "*Merci*, Kate—*merci infiniment*. I can't express to you how much help this is. Above all, I know you'll be discreet, because you're part of the family. You're one of the few people who understand how sensitive this situation really is."

A blaze of late-autumn sunshine transformed the fading vineyards into a bank of dancing flames. I lingered behind the others so that the sound of their voices drifted to me on the breeze, relishing the sun soaking through the dark fabric of my coat, the strength of my stride as the terrain steepened. And then, nearing the top of the slope, a view of golden vines tumbling to a toylike village—a white steeple piercing the cluster of buildings—and, even here, the faint clang of church bells chiming the hour. Sunday in France, I thought, was forever an idyll.

Ahead of me, Heather slowed and separated from the group, lifting a hand to shade her eyes.

"You okay?" I asked when I caught up to her.

She was staring at the view, her expression difficult to read. "It's so beautiful," she said. "I almost never walk up here, so I forget. But the way the vineyards ripple across the landscape . . . it's gorgeous. It almost makes me forget about the other stuff." She pressed her lips together. "Almost."

A gust of wind shook the leaves with a silken whisper, raising a chill across my back. "At least we got out of family lunch today," I said.

"I know. Nico was so relieved when he remembered Papi and Mémé were taking the kids to the circus in

Dijon. At this point, I think he's afraid of what would happen if Papi and I were alone in a room together."

In the distance, the others paused to turn and wave at us. "*Allez, les filles!*" Jean-Luc called.

"Do you want to head back to the house?" I asked.

She shook her head. "Let's catch up to them. Nico said he wanted to go to the *cabotte*. After all these years, can you believe I've never been inside?" We set off at a brisk pace, steadily closing the gap between us and the four figures in the distance.

Shortly after lunch, Jean-Luc's truck had appeared in the driveway, the tires spraying gravel before he popped out to invite us on a Sunday afternoon hike. Louise was with him, greeting us with considerably less enthusiasm; Walker completed the trio, his usual, quirky, inscrutable self.

Heather and I scrambled up the slope, the steady, upward climb preventing conversation. The autumn colors were lavish even as they crisped brittle around the edges—nature's last spectacle before winter stole away the vineyard's vibrancy. We reached the others as they paused to admire the view. A small, oval hut appeared to float on a sea of undulating leaves, a dash of stony white capped by a slightly domed roof.

"Isn't it adorable?" I drew out my phone and snapped a photo. "You see these *cabottes* all over Burgundy, but

I've always thought ours was the prettiest." Ever since we'd camped here as children, the hut had enchanted me. I still remembered the stories Uncle Philippe had told us, tales of the tough old vignerons of yore who relied on these *cabottes* in the days before cars, tending the vines until dark, sleeping inside, and waking at dawn to continue their labor.

"How'd they keep warm?" Heather asked.

"You build a fire right inside, in the middle," Nico said. "Just move the roof tiles apart to make a hole for the smoke to escape—sort of an ersatz chimney." He nodded at Jean-Luc and me. "Do you guys remember? Papa used to let us build the fire when he brought us out here. Come on," he strode ahead. "I'll show you."

We quickly covered the remaining downhill stretch, and then the *cabotte* was before us, strangely smaller up close than it appeared from a distance. The entrance was simply a hole in the stone wall, with no door to close against the elements, the frame built low so that we stooped to enter. Inside, the room was close and chill, with streams of wind and sun coursing through the entry, and needles of cold air piercing the dry stone walls. In the center of the small space, a charred black heap hinted at a hearth.

"Look, Bruyère," Nico beckoned to his wife. "I left

my initials here." He pointed at the letters chiseled into the stone. "And here's Papa."

Heather knelt by the wall. "Who's this?" She pointed. "B.Q.C."

Nico squatted beside her. "That's my grandfather. Benoît Quilicus Charpin. And A.U.—that's his brother—Albert Ulysse. And here . . . hmph." He pointed at another set of letters that read A.U.C. "That's strange. I guess this must be Albert again, *le petit insolent!*"

"It's a good thing Nico didn't insist on family names for our kids," Heather said to me drily.

Louise was craning her head around the cramped interior. "But where do you sleep?" she asked, her brow creasing into a charming little frown.

Jean-Luc shrugged. Anywhere. "*Là, ou là, ou là . . .*" He began pointing at various spots on the dirt floor.

"It is so very . . . rustic!" Louise's enthusiasm seemed to be dampening.

"We didn't come here for the luxury." Jean-Luc smiled.

"I'm starving!" Heather announced. "Shall we have our *goûter* in here? What do you guys think?" She threw a doubtful look around the *cabotte*. "Or maybe outside is better?"

"I should have brought the camp kettle—we could have made tea." A wistful note crept into Nico's voice.

We trooped outdoors, finding a sheltered spot against the side of the *cabotte*. Heather began rummaging through the backpacks, handing out various items—a picnic blanket, which Nico and Walker unfurled, bottles of water and lemonade, bars of chocolate, boxes of shortbread cookies, a heavy brick wrapped in foil that turned out to be a *quatre-quarts*—a homemade buttery pound cake.

"When did you have time to do all this?" I asked her, reaching for the cake.

"Me?" She brushed crumbs from her lap. "I didn't do it. It was him." She nodded at Jean-Luc, who was pouring lemonade.

"*He* baked a cake? No way. He doesn't know how to cook."

"Before she left for Spain, his mom taught him to make a few things. She insisted—said otherwise he'd be living on Mac-Do and pasta. Actually, he makes a pretty mean *boeuf bourguignon*."

I bit into the cake—which was moist and rich, flecked with vanilla—and regarded Jean-Luc as I chewed. "Personally, I prefer the vanilla from Tahiti," he was saying to Louise, who was sitting cross-legged beside him, her knees pale and slender through the holes in her jeans. "It has a more floral note." Was this the same guy who had once declared cooking and childcare *le travail des femmes*—women's work?

"*Du fruit*, Jeel!" Louise held up a banana, her sharp features brimming with laughter. "To eat after the cake. You promised!"

He grinned and grabbed it from her hand, demolishing it in three bites.

"Now let's go look for wild blackberries. I thought I saw some over there in that sunny patch." She scrambled to her feet and the two of them wandered away.

"Come on." Heather noticed me watching them, and sprang to her feet, her shadow falling across my lap. "Let's check out the *cabotte*."

Inside the stone hut, Heather found a stick and poked at the pile of scorched logs. "I have to admit, I'm finding it a little hard to see the charm of this place. It kind of reminds me of . . . I don't know, a medieval prison? Just add some iron bars on the door." She swept a hand out, indicating the uneven stone walls, the rough dirt floor, the hobbit-size entry gaping like a missing tooth. "Did you really *camp* here?"

"It's not so bad at night, with a fire."

"Out here completely alone? In the dark?" She shivered. "*Non, merci!* I'm going to clip some sprays of vine branches. Don't you think they'll be pretty on the dining table?" With a dramatic duck of her head, she stepped outside.

I picked up the stick she had dropped and raised it to the ceiling, attempting to displace the roof tiles like a vigneron from another century. Sure enough, with a bit of persistence, the flat stones spread apart. As I mentally filed away this arcane bit of knowledge in case it happened to show up on The Test, I became aware of voices drifting through the hut's interlocking stone structure. I recognized Louise's fluted French tones: "She wants me to move to New York with her."

Jean-Luc's response was an indistinguishable murmur.

"*Mais non . . . j'adore* New York! But obviously, my work is here—I can't just abandon my little bookshop. And . . ." She sighed. "*Franchement,* it's not just my work—it's my family. I feel a responsibility to remain close by."

"Your sister doesn't feel the same way?"

"She says it'll just be for a year, maybe two, *au maximum.* But I know that once she sets foot in Brooklyn, she's never coming home."

"Perhaps because she knows she can rely on you. It's

easy enough to move halfway around the world when someone else is picking up the pieces. I've been in that situation and—well . . . trust me, it's a thousand times harder being the one who stays behind. Don't get me wrong—I like your sister—she's extremely funny and fun to be around. But the qualities I admire most are dependability and loyalty." Jean-Luc's voice deepened on the last word. "Like these tough old grapevines. Any other plant would die in this hard, rocky soil. But they love it here—they don't mind the work. They actually *thrive* on it. Nope, these vines will never let you down."

Louise fell silent. Frankly, who wouldn't after that speech? I heard the crunch of their footsteps, moving closer to the door of the *cabotte* and froze. What if they caught me in here? But to my relief the sound of their steps turned in the other direction, toward the dirt path.

I let out my breath slowly, staring straight up at the scrap of blue sky shimmering through the hole in the ceiling. Yes, I deserved it: the eavesdropper's proverbial fate. And even though I hadn't heard any words directly against me, there was plenty to cause me pain. Clearly Jean-Luc's opinion of me was abysmally low. And, sure, I deserved it. But still, it hurt.

"Hey." Walker spoke from the doorway, causing me

to jump. He ducked and entered the *cabotte*, raising his face to the hole I'd made in the ceiling. "Whoa. I knew it was primitive, but this is kind of like the Stone Age."

I laughed. "I was just thinking that I could see this appearing as a question on The Test." I affected a pompous tone: "*Describe the physical aspects of the Burgundian* cabotte, *its history and role in nineteenth-century winemaking.*"

He laughed and ran a hand along the stone wall. "Speaking of The Test, did you get my email with those MW practice exams?"

"Oh my gosh, yes. Sorry—I forgot to write back. The last few days have been kind of crazy."

"Yeah? How's that? You find any more skeletons in the basement?"

The stick slipped from my fingers, falling to the ground. I quickly knelt and retrieved it. "What makes you say that?"

"Actually, I was joking. But—" He moved closer, lowering his voice. "Why? Did you find something?"

"No," I said quickly, hoping he couldn't hear the strained note in my voice.

"Well, if you do find something, you should definitely tell me. I know people who deal in vintage wine. Even if it's just a couple of bottles, I'm sure they'd be eager to work with Domaine Charpin. There are rumors, you know."

"Oh, really?" I struggled to keep my expression neutral. "What kind of rumors?"

"Your family used to own one of the wealthiest *négociant* houses in the region, back in the 1930s. Apparently your great-grandfather was some sort of genius businessman. Did you know that?"

I shook my head faintly. My mother had never mentioned Great-grandpère Edouard's business acumen—of course she hadn't—but it did explain her own successful banking career.

"Things started heading south after he died," Walker continued. "According to local legend, the family could have survived for decades just by slowly selling off their collection of rare wine. Except, by the end of the war, all of it had disappeared."

"Disappeared? How is that possible?"

"It's a mystery. Either he hid it—and died before he could tell anyone where. Or"—Walker spoke in hushed tones—"he sold it to the Germans."

"Really?" My voice rose to a squeak.

"Oh, yeah, it used to happen all the time. Hitler was crazy for French wine—not to drink, mind you—he was a teetotaler. But the Third Reich sold it at a huge profit on the international market to help pay for the war."

"Yes, but if my great-grandfather sold the wine to the Germans, we'd have the money to show for it," I pointed out.

He shrugged. "Maybe he sold it at a loss? Honestly, at this point, who knows? It wasn't a glorious time for Burgundy. A group of winemakers actually gave a parcel of vines to Maréchal Pétain as a gift. Part of the Hospices de Beaune, some of the best land in the region. Like I said—there weren't a lot of heroes coming out of the Côte d'Or." He shoved his hands into his pockets. "More than seventy years after World War II, and the Resistance has been so glorified, hardly anyone remembers that the majority of French people were cheese-eating surrender monkeys."

I blinked. Even just a few days ago, I would have argued with him. But right now I couldn't muster the enthusiasm to defend France. Instead, I lifted my chin so that the wind bit my cheeks.

"In any case, if you do happen to find something in the cellar, you should tell me." Walker continued. "Like I said, I'd be happy to put you in touch with the right people—and I'm sure there'd be an extra finder's fee in it for you, too. Just keep it in mind."

"Guys?" Heather called, popping her head through

the doorway. "We should probably start heading back. The sun's already starting to go down."

Outside, I found the others packing up. Nico was gathering trash, and Jean-Luc and Louise were stuffing the picnic blanket into the narrow mouth of the backpack, which involved much squealing and giggling on her part. We began walking home, the narrow path forcing us once again into a single file. Aside from the sound of our shoes scuffling on the dirt path, and the never-ending birdsong that twittered from some unseen perch in the foliage, the vineyards radiated with a majestic silence born of centuries of doting care. Soon, I thought, the thinning vine leaves would fade to brown, and an army of viticulturists would attack the bare branches, trimming them for winter, burning piles of clippings at the sides of the road. I dropped behind the others, kicking my feet into their shadows. The beauty of this land still took my breath away, but now I was acutely conscious that it was merely a shell, hiding the rot within.

Cher journal,

The thing I never realized before this winter is what a nuisance the cold is, a steady drip, drip, drip, until suddenly the proverbial vase has overflowed. Take, for example, this morning. I had every intention of leaping out of bed and starting the kitchen fire before the others came down to breakfast. But when I awoke, I found it snowing—again—and the courtyard and garden heaped with indistinguishable white, icy mounds. My apron was frozen—as usual, because it's always wet from the washing up when I take it off at night—and frost covered the toes of my clogs. My housedress is wilted with grime. It has been at least three weeks since we last washed our clothes. The effort of heating the water, and then wringing and drying the wet laundry—immense on even the mildest of summer days—has proved gargantuan in this bitter weather, with our hands permanently swollen with cold. Instead, we have simply readjusted our limits of tolerance.

For a minute, I considered diving back into

bed—still faintly warm—and staying there for a few more minutes. Then the image of Albert swam before me—those enormous eyes the color of burnt sugar, that peaky little face—and I forced myself to dress in the stale clothes, so that he wouldn't have to face another school day without at least a warm drink in his tummy.

Of course when I got downstairs and tried to light the stove, I remembered why my shoes were frozen. I had gone into the courtyard last night to bring in some logs so that they could dry overnight. Unfortunately, the recent blizzard, along with the temperatures that creep up and down below freezing, mean the woodpile is soaked through; even after hours inside, the logs were still damp this morning. Madame would not be pleased, but I had no choice. I threw a wet log onto the dying embers where it hissed and filled the kitchen with smoke, so that when Madame came down she already had a scowl on her face.

This winter has been the worst I have ever known. Add to this the coal shortages, the ever-niggling problem of rationing—clothes, fuel, food, all of it unattainable—and I sometimes wonder if I'll first freeze from the outside in, or starve from the inside out. Supper yesterday was two rutabagas each, adorned with the *thinnest* sliver of ham. I can't remember the last time we had calf's foot jelly or a bit of plain sole to offer Benoît—once the poor boy's entire diet. Madame counts every mouthful that passes his lips, so fretful that he will grow thin and take ill again. We have bread on only the most special of occasions. Butter? Jam? Those are merely fond memories of yore. Oh, if only I was warm, I could bear the hunger. If only I was full, I could bear the cold.

Madame maintains a purposeful appearance for the boys, but indulges her misery by throwing me black looks and sharp words when she thinks no one is looking. The Cercle du patrimoine is on hiatus because of the glacial temperatures and without this bracing outlet, Madame's resolve has weakened. This morning at the breakfast table, I saw her poking at a clammy boiled potato and if I could guess her thoughts, I would hazard they were the same as my own: How long can this go on?

I was teasing the last translucent scrap of skin from Albert's potato—we've begun to peel them cooked because it wastes less flesh—when Papa appeared. He looked so awful—eyes glassy with fatigue—that I immediately poured him a cup of the barley coffee we're trying to accustom ourselves to drinking. He sat and sipped it, staring into the distance.

"Do you want anything to eat?" Madame asked.

"*Non.*"

"Where have you been?" Her voice was controlled, but suspicion leached through the surface.

"Pruning."

Cher journal, it was obvious he was hiding something for there has been a meter of snow covering the vines for at least a week.

I think Madame observed the same, for she replied: "It's snowing again."

"For Christ's sake, do you think of nothing but the weather?" Papa shouted. He shoved his chair back from the table so that our "coffee" slopped from the cups and he stomped from the room. Albert started to cry and Madame let him climb into her lap at the table, which is usually forbidden.

After I had bundled up the boys and walked them to school, I lingered in the village hoping to buy some food—a scrap of meat or bread, a few grams of sugar—anything to help cheer this miserable day. We have a fistful of ration tickets but the shops are always empty. How are the people in cities surviving? Without the vegetables stored in our cellar, our chickens and rabbits, I am certain we would starve.

When I returned, the house was quiet. I knew Madame was out at the chicken coop because I could hear the hens squawking as they fought each other for crumbs. The door to Papa's office was closed. I came up here to my room to finally scribble a few lines to Rose—she had written me from Sèvres, a few days ago; a brief letter, but fascinating, all about her coursework—and I wanted to respond quickly. I opened the top drawer of my desk to retrieve my fountain pen and right away I saw the unfamiliar piece of paper—a mimeographed leaflet titled "33 Hints to the Occupied." I dare not copy any of them here, *cher journal*, but suffice it to say I gulped the text down as if I'd been dying of thirst, and then read it several more times until tears of relief stung my eyes.

Who had placed it in my desk? Obviously it wasn't Benoît or Albert—they are much too small. Vieille Marie quit nearly six months ago. We haven't had any other visitors to the house for weeks. That leaves only my stepmother or Papa. I've been considering them both.

My initial impulse is that it cannot be Madame. After all, she is an enthusiastic member of the Cercle du patrimoine and her regular praise of Vichy's values—"*travail, famille, patrie!*" (work, family, homeland!)—appears abundantly sincere. Recently, however, the new deprivations have soured her. She joked the other day that the only genuine information printed in the newspaper is the announcements about rations, which detail how many coupons we need for various food items— everything else is censored or false, even the death notices. Except it wasn't really a joke because her laugh was so cold it sent chills down my spine. Yes, the persistent hunger and cold are certainly turning Madame against our jailers. But still. Distributing Resistance tracts? Honestly, I don't think she has the nerve.

That leaves Papa. Papa who has remained in a distant fog ever since the surrender in June. Papa who seethes with anger and shame. Papa who disappears for hours without ever providing a plausible explanation of his whereabouts. Papa who listens to the BBC service every single night.

Yes, I am certain it was Papa who put the leaflet in my drawer. But why did he do it? Perhaps it was just a *petit bonjour*—a small gesture to raise my lagging spirits. We all do it from time to time—call the Germans by nasty little names—Les Fritz, Les Boches, Les Doryphores (the latter because they've ravaged the potato harvest, like the gluttonous beetles they resemble)—or just happen to dress in the *bleu-blanc-rouge* colors of our beloved flag. Yes, of course it was my dear Papa.

But this makes me wonder about another possibility, so frightening that I scarcely dare to speculate about it. Is Papa one of them? Could he be working with the movement . . . la Résistance? Oh, see how my hand trembles as I write these words. Calm yourself, Hélène. Calm. There is an enormous divide between circulating one mocking little article and actually joining the Resistance. And Papa has never breathed a word about these activities to me, either in support or criticism. As far as I know, he continues to passively wait out this war—like all of us in this family, silently enduring.

Later
This idea still eats at me. I cannot sleep. Instead, I have spent these last hours analyzing all my recent interactions with Papa, scouring them for clues. There are so many discrepancies, so many occa-

sions when I thought he was fibbing, but I couldn't understand why. Truthfully, I thought he was hiding so that he could drink in secret. Now I am not so sure. Oh, please, please let Papa be safe. I admire what that group does, but if something happens to Papa, my heart will completely break in two.

Even later

Still awake. It occurs to me that I have just endangered all of us by recording these thoughts so plainly. I must find a better hiding place for this journal.

Chapter 9

After we found the secret cellar, Heather stopped coming downstairs to help me. She said she'd lost her heart for the project, and I didn't blame her. Still, it was lonely down there without her, and—even though Nico had run extension cords through the wardrobe, plugging in a pair of high-watt, halogen work lamps—it was spooky, too. Here in this hidden space, which had remained untouched for so many years, the air breathed sharp with a persistent edge of mold. Shadows pooled in the corners, and gathered along the walls and below the wine racks, magnifying shapes and sounds, faint scratches and scrabbles that hinted at mice, spiders, roaches. I threw boxes of poison in the corners and tried not to think about it. And, anyway, once I started working with the wine, I stopped thinking about anything else.

Because the wine . . . oh the wine! Even enclosed within glass it bewitched me, this potion lying in fairy-tale slumber, waiting for a spell—the twist of a corkscrew, a breath of air—to make it vibrant once again. The heavy bottles lay on their sides, covered in thick, fluffy grey clouds of mold, a product of microbes and moisture that thrived in cool, damp conditions. At first, I worried that almost eight decades of neglect had ruined these bottles but after inspecting several, I found them still perfect, the corks intact and lightly bathed in liquid, which prevented any oxygen from penetrating and spoiling the precious vintages. After all, I reasoned, the ancient walls of these cellars had been built for this very purpose—to preserve wine.

Though we still didn't know who had hidden the bottles, the one thing I knew for certain was that an expert had selected them. The collection took my breath away: La Tâche, Clos de Vougeot, Chambertin. The spectacular years: 1929, 1934, 1935, 1937, the stratospheric vintages, as Jennifer would have called them. And it was alive, this wine. Even trapped inside the glass, it would continue to change and evolve until the moment it was drunk. Any of these bottles would be worth a fortune, valuable even at the beginning of its life, but decades of aging had transformed them into something almost sacred.

I tried not to touch the bottles too much as I counted and catalogued them, recording the numbers by hand in a notebook and later transcribing the information into a spreadsheet on my laptop. I was afraid of disturbing the liquid—wine doesn't like movement—and, more than anything, I was afraid one of them would slip through my fingers and break. But by the end of the third day, I had catalogued only a tiny portion—maybe a thousand bottles—and I estimated there were at least ten thousand more stored in the secret *cave*. Ten thousand precious bottles resting like so many sleeping beauties.

"Big. With Minions. And a yellow cup. But mostly big. He claims one of the kids at school pulled out a hot slice of pizza during lunch."

"From a *thermos?*" I started to laugh.

"Thibault swears it's true." Heather maneuvered the shopping cart around the corner of an aisle.

We gazed at the ravaged shelves.

"Not much choice," I observed, picking up a lunch box covered in rainbows and unicorns.

She sighed. "Bad mom. I waited too long. All the good moms came to Carrefour three weeks ago. Now there's a 'rupture' in stock, and even though they say they're reordering, there won't be any new thermoses until next August."

"Aw, poor Thibault," I clucked. "Denied hot pizza from a thermos. Just remember—childhood trauma makes for a compelling life story. This is all great material for his memoirs."

"Ha ha. Very funny." Suddenly she stiffened, teetered up on her toes and snatched something from a high shelf. "Yes!" She brandished a thermos adorned with small bug-eyed creatures. "But the question is"— she unscrewed the yellow top and peered inside—"can I get a slice of pizza in here?"

"You've got competition," I murmured, nodding at the woman beside us—skinny jeans, chunky boots, smoky eye makeup, the works—who was ogling the thermos like a cat eyeing a fishbowl.

"I swear, shopping in this country is a blood sport," Heather muttered, throwing the thermos into her cart and making a sharp turn to the refrigerated section.

"This *entire* aisle is yogurt?" My jaw dropped at the small containers, stacked five rows high and stretching for several yards.

"Come on, you've been to the grocery store in France a million times." Heather placed two twelve-packs of plain in her cart.

"Yeah, but I've never shopped for dairy products before. This is hardcore." I snapped a photo on my phone and posted it to Instagram, where it was immediately liked by Walker.

Heather paused to complete some mental calculation and slowly reached for a package of yogurt mousse. "I guess after a while you start to forget the stuff that's weird. Like why can't you buy canned chicken broth? Why is the baking sugar flavored with vanilla? Why are the peanuts and potato chips always in the booze aisle?"

We wheeled to the next aisle and sure enough, nestled by the bottles of wine were jars of salted nuts and packets of potato chips boasting flavors like cheeseburger and roast chicken. I inspected a few of the wines, grocery store labels, most of it produced in mass quantity, a world apart from the rarefied appellations of Burgundy's Côte d'Or.

Heather plucked a bottle of Sancerre from the shelf. "Eek, don't look," she said, placing it in the cart. "Sometimes I just want to drink something crisp and light, you know?"

"Don't be silly. Wine doesn't have to be expensive to be delicious. It all depends on the right situation. Like on a hot summer day, I'd definitely prefer a glass of rosé with ice cubes to the finest vintage Champagne."

She added a couple of glowing pink bottles to the cart and we both laughed.

"Hey, at least you have options. I was glancing at the domaine's old account books and back in the day the family used to set aside a couple of barrels of *vin de table* once a year—and that's all they drank . . . ," I faltered, remembering too late Heather's feelings about the secret cellar and everything related to it.

We started moving again, more slowly now, past a section labeled États-Unis, the shelves filled with American products like Tabasco, peanut butter, and marshmallows, all at vastly inflated prices. "It's okay, you know," she said. "You can talk about the *cave*. I was really angry, but I'm coming to terms with it. As Nico pointed out, we don't even know how much his father knows—and I'll never know unless I ask him. And I'm definitely not ready for that conversation." She pressed her lips together.

"Yeah, me neither." I shivered at the thought of Uncle Philippe's formidable demeanor.

"But if I separate my own feelings from the *cave* . . . well, this is obviously the most exciting thing that's ever happened at the domaine. And the domaine is Nico's life—so of course I want to be a part of it."

She mustered a smile, and I gave her arm a squeeze,

admiring not for the first time my friend's loyalty. "Nico's a lucky guy," I told her.

"Believe me," she said, "it's taken me a while to get here. I've been doing a lot of thinking about responsibility and what one generation owes to the next."

"What do you mean?"

"What if Anna and Thibault blame me and Nico for what Hélène did all those decades ago?"

"But that's completely unfair!"

"So you see? I can't blame my father-in-law for what Hélène did—only for keeping it from us."

I glanced away. "You're right," I said finally. And I was surprised to find I meant it.

We wheeled toward the checkout area, joining a queue that snaked halfway up the pet food aisle. I sighed and crossed my arms, shifting my weight from foot to foot. "You don't think . . ." I frowned. "We didn't miss anything important in Hélène's stuff, did we?"

"Nah. There was nothing in the suitcase except the clothes and photos."

"What about that other box?"

"What other box?"

"The one with her diploma? Didn't you find that in a different box?"

"Yeah, that was just a bunch of old schoolbooks, notebooks, stuff like that. Nothing interesting."

"But now we know about the secret *cave*." I chewed the inside of my lip. "What did we do with that stuff anyway? Did we get rid of it?"

"I can't remember."

"Was it charity shop? Or dump?"

"Not sure."

The line inched forward. "I think probably charity shop," she said eventually.

I tried to picture the contents of the box. Biology textbooks. Chemistry. Physics. Had there been a copy of *The Count of Monte Cristo*? A stack of notebooks with thick, brown covers, the pages filled with copperplate handwriting. I remembered flipping through the first one, finding row after row of grammar exercises, and setting the others aside.

"The notebooks." An odd feeling began scrabbling in my chest.

"Yeah?"

"There was a stack of them in the box. But I only looked at the first one." I crossed my arms, and uncrossed them again. My skin had begun to prickle. "What time does the charity shop close?"

"Five? I think?"

The clock on my cell phone read 4:26.

"We can see if they're still open on the way home." She gave me a reassuring smile and pulled out her grocery list, mentally checking off the items.

"Heather," my voice emerged, strangled. "I think—we need—this is going to sound crazy, but can we just go there *now*?" For some reason that I couldn't explain, a weird feeling had started crawling up my spine.

"*Right now?* This very minute? What about the groceries?"

"We can come back for them. Please. I just have this . . . *feeling*."

She must have seen the panic on my face, because her smile disappeared. "I would just leave, except for the thermos. There's no way it'll still be here when we get back—and Thibault'll be crushed if I come home empty-handed."

"Can we hide it somewhere?" I looked wildly around me. "Like on that shelf behind the kitty litter, or something? No, wait. We can hide it in that aisle with the American foods. I'd bet my hat that no one ever shops there."

Heather reversed out of line, snatched the thermos from the cart, and we raced over to the États-Unis section, still as empty as it had been ten minutes earlier.

"Here, I'll do it. I'm taller," I said. She handed me the thermos and I stretched to the top shelf, tucking it behind a row of blinding-yellow taco kits emblazoned with the words "Old El Paso" that appeared untouched by human hands since the day they'd been stocked.

"You're sure it's safe here?" Heather said anxiously.

"Come on." I shot her a sly smile. "When's the last time you heard of a French person eating tacos?"

We ran to the car. Heather peeled out with a squeal of tires, pushing the speed limit all the way to Beaune, where she squeezed into a parking spot right outside the charity shop. We flew to the door, just in time to see a silver-haired woman flip the sign to "*fermé.*" Spying us through the glass, she shrugged and pointed at her watch.

Heather peered through the window. "There are people in there! She still has customers! What time is it?"

I checked my phone. "Four forty-six."

Heather rapped on the door. "*Bonjour? Bonjour?*" She twisted the knob and it opened. I followed her into the store.

"*Mesdames. Mesdames! On ferme.*" The silver-haired woman appeared before us.

"There're still fourteen minutes until you close," Heather said in French, smiling at her sweetly. "And you have other customers."

"Yes, but they're just paying," she protested, throwing a glance to the back of the shop, where two people were squatting over some open boxes.

"Oh my God," I whispered to Heather. "It's Walker . . . and Louise."

Heather dodged around the woman and walked toward the pair. "Hey, guys!" she called.

Louise's head jerked up. "Oh, Bruyère! Katreen! *Quelle surprise!*" She appeared slightly rattled.

"Hey!" Walker greeted us with a smile, bright and bland.

"Find anything good here?" Heather loomed above them.

"Just a bunch of old books." Louise closed the flaps of one of the boxes and stood. "How much for all these?" she asked the silver-haired woman in French.

"*Attendez*—mind if we have a look?" Heather knelt on the floor and reached inside one of the boxes. She pulled out a French-English dictionary and caught my eye. I shook my head as subtly as possible.

"*J'sais pas.*" The silver-haired woman puffed out her cheeks. "*Trente?*"

Louise fished into her pocketbook and pulled out two twenty-euro notes.

The woman pulled a face. "You don't have any change?"

"Do you have a ten?" Louise asked Walker.

He patted his pockets. "Sorry."

"*Putain,*" Louise swore under her breath. "I'm going to have to go to the café." Clutching her handbag, she darted out the door.

Heather dug into another box and held up a red-and-white striped candle. Again, I shook my head, noticing too late that Walker had seen me.

"What are you guys planning to do with this stuff?" I asked him.

"I dunno. Louise wants it for something."

Heather found a third box and held up a notebook with a brown cover. My heart quickened and I gave her a nod.

"Madame." Heather approached the silver-haired woman, who was rather pointedly dusting a large brass clock as it chimed the hour. "We'd like to buy this box."

The woman frowned. "I don't know—your friend was interested in it."

"I'll give you thirty euros." Heather said firmly.

"I'm only a volunteer here."

"Forty."

"I'm not sure we're allowed to bargain."

I stole a glance at Walker, who was watching the interaction with a frown.

"Don't you donate all your profits to charity? Think

how many hungry children this could feed." Heather offered her most persuasive smile, just as Louise burst through the door.

"*Mon dieu!* Everything was closed!" she said, breathless. "I had to go all the way to the place Carnot!" She caught sight of the money in Heather's hand. "What is going on here? *Mais non*, Madame, this box is mine. We had an agreement, *n'est-ce pas?*"

Madame lifted her shoulders in an elaborate shrug.

"Actually," interjected Heather, "if we're really splitting hairs, the box is mine. We've been cleaning our *cave*, and I accidentally threw away some family memorabilia. My husband was terribly upset. You understand how personal these things are, Madame, *n'est-ce pas?*" She paused significantly. "And of course I'd be delighted to offer a donation to your organization, in appreciation for all the wonderful work you do."

"I'll give you fifty euros." Louise crossed her arms. "Fifty for everything."

"Sixty," countered Heather.

Louise heaved a sigh. "Seventy."

Heather's eyes narrowed and I caught a flash of the girl I'd known in college, the one who hated to lose so much, the other junior year abroad students had proclaimed a fatwa against playing cards with her.

"A hundred euros," she said, gazing at her nails with an expression of deep ennui.

Louise scorched us both with a withering glare. Then she held up her hands. "*C'est bon. C'est bon.*" She forced a smile to her face, turned, and swept from the shop, trailing Walker in her wake.

"I'll call you," he mouthed at me, miming a phone at his ear.

While Heather counted out a sheaf of euro notes at the cash register, I scooped up the box and checked the contents. Yes, Hélène's notebooks were there, as well as the textbooks. The clamp on my chest began to loosen.

In the car, I clutched the box in my lap, unwilling to release it.

"Sheesh, can you believe Louise? My God!" Heather's eyes flashed. "Why the hell was she so desperate to buy that stuff? She can't possibly suspect anything about the secret *cave*. You haven't said anything to Walker, have you?"

"Of course not." I thought back to the day of our hike, and the conversation I'd had with Walker. I'd been discreet—hadn't I? Unless Walker was a mind reader, there was no way he could know about the secret cellar.

Heather buckled her seat belt and jerked the car away from the curb so that my head whipped back.

"Hey, what's the hurry?" I asked. "We already got the box, remember? We can breathe easy."

She gunned the engine through a yellow light. "Are you kidding?" A little glint had crept into her eye. "We've gotta get back to Carrefour to buy that thermos! Mama's on a roll!"

Soft afternoon light fell across the kitchen table and the house seemed to sigh. Nico and Heather had taken the kids to the *fête foraine*, a seasonal fair in Mâcon that promised carnival games, spinning rides, and *barbes à papa*, which was what Anna and Thibault insisted on calling cotton candy.

"You sure you don't want to come?" Heather had asked me, shoving slip-knotted plastic bags into her purse. I looked at her quizzically, and she explained: "For emergencies. If the spinning cider bowls don't make them puke, it'll be that ride with centrifugal force—never mind. Of course you don't want to come!"

"I was hoping to have a quiet afternoon."

"That sounds like complete and utter bliss," she said with a wistful sigh.

"And I might look through Hélène's stuff," I added.

"Ah," she said. "That sounds less blissful." Suddenly, Thibault slid across the floor on socked feet, slamming a hard stop into her thigh. "Ow! Thi-bault!" She bleated his name, two notes of warning.

"SORRY!" he yelled without a shred of remorse. And then he threw his arms around her legs and gave her a giant hug.

"Monkey pants." Heather lowered her face to his head and covered him in a hundred kisses.

Now, alone in the house, silence rang in my ears, broken only by the birds twittering in the garden. I reached into the box and pulled out one of Hélène's *cahier d'exercices*. The cover read "La chimie"— chemistry—and the pages were covered with notes that looked like gibberish to my untrained eye: chemical formulas sprawling like spiderwebs, composed of letters and numbers of which I recognized only the most basic—H_2O. Hélène's writing was loose, almost illegible. Perhaps Nico would be able to decipher it? Even though I didn't think it held any secrets, I left the notebook splayed upon the table, pushed to one side.

Next "L'histoire"—history—filled with detailed notes on the Hundred Years' War, *le roi* Henri IV, and various kingly decrees. After that, "La littérature" and a series of essay responses on recurrent themes in Voltaire. An enormous yawn escaped my lips but I doggedly looked at every page before reaching into the box again.

My fingers brushed against satin, and I pulled out a

thin stack of envelopes addressed to Hélène Charpin, Domaine Charpin, Meursault. Ahhh—letters? Had I finally found a relic of Hélène's personal life? Now, this could be interesting! I slipped the ribbon from the packet, and pulled out the first letter, squinting to decipher the round, French hand. The stationery was brittle and yellowed, and the ink had begun to fade.

27 octobre 1940
Sèvres

Chère Hélène,

You had asked for books on thermal expansion and I finally had a chance to ask Professor de la Haye. He recommends Maxwell's own study, *A Dynamical Theory of the Electromagnetic Field*, though I'm not sure it can still be found at the library. I do think it's interesting that his paper on control theory is still considered central to the field, given that he died in 1879 . . .

The rest of the letter continued in a similarly scholarly vein, devoid of any personal questions or other bits of information. It was signed: "Amicalement, Rose."

Rose? Was she a classmate? I turned to the next letter, and the next, but all of them were of a similar nature, written in a friendly, affectionate tone, full of academic vigor but free of any news or gossip that would indicate a girlish friendship. Whoever Rose was—and judging from her writing, she seemed intelligent, energetic, and extremely scholarly—she revealed nothing about Hélène's inner life. Sighing, I stacked the envelopes into a pile, retied the ribbon, and set them aside.

I pulled the last notebook from the box, opening to find it filled with French grammar exercises. I was beginning to form a picture of life in the 1930s schoolroom and it was even duller and more rigid than I'd suspected. The writing blurred before my drooping eyelids: *L'étude m'a toujours semblé une sorte d'égérie désintéressé . . .* Red pencil slashed across the last word. Licking my index finger, I turned to the next page, and the next, until I reached the middle of the notebook, where the writing abruptly stopped. A blank page. Another. A third. And then, carefully drawn lines, columns, and rows—it was some kind of chart. I sat straight in my chair.

The headings read "Appellation," "Année" (year), "Quantité" (quantity). As I scanned the page, a line leapt out at me: "Les Grands Epenots, 1928, 35."

I shoved my chair back from the table, startling

the cat, who leapt down with a yelp. Sprinting across the kitchen and up the stairs, down the long hallway to my room, I snatched up the notebook on my desk. "Come on, come on," I muttered, flipping the pages until I found the scribbled line I'd been looking for: *Les Grands Epenots, 1928, 35 bottles—check???*

"Oh my God," I breathed. Had I just discovered an inventory of the secret cellar's contents—a record of all the bottles stored there? My legs shook all the way to the kitchen. When I compared Hélène's notes with my own, I found that the appellations, vintages, and quantities matched almost exactly. I hugged Hélène's notebook to my chest, resisting the urge to press my cheek to its pages. For some reason that I didn't fully understand, I felt close to tears.

Half an hour later, I was still examining Hélène's cellar list, comparing it to the information I'd gathered on my own, when I heard a sharp rap at the back door. "*Coucou!*" Jean-Luc stepped into the house. "Oh. Hi, Katreen," he said, glancing away from me.

"Hi." I resisted the urge to cross my arms.

He shifted his weight, looking as discomfited as I felt. "I stopped by to see Nico. Is he around?"

"They're at the *fête foraine* in Mâcon," I told him. "They won't be back until tonight."

"Ah. I guess I should've texted before I came over."

"I'll tell him you stopped by."

Silence washed over the kitchen—even the birds had stopped singing—and, glancing out the window, I saw the afternoon had faded to dusk. I reached behind me and switched on the lights. Should I invite Jean-Luc to sit down? Offer him a drink? I felt suddenly conscious of the situation—alone with him, after so many years. I fidgeted with my pen.

"You are studying?" he asked, impeccably polite. His eye fell on Hélène's notebook, which I'd left splayed on the table. "Whoa!" he exclaimed with genuine surprise, peering more closely at the page. "You have to make *bouillie bourguignonne* for your exam? That really *is* serious."

I blinked. "What?"

"*Bouillie bourguignonne.* Burgundy mixture." He pulled the notebook closer. "See?" He pointed at a scribbled line that read "$CuSO_4 + Na_2CO_3$." "Copper sulfate and sodium carbonate. We learned about it at the *école de viticulture*. They sprayed it on the vines to treat fungus." His long fingers trailed down the page. "But, see, these quantities—that's quite a big batch, if you're just experimenting with the stuff. Maybe start with one hundred grams of copper, not ten kilos. And be careful of the sulfuric acid. Make sure to have lots of sodium bicarbonate on hand to neutralize, because it can burn a hole right through you."

My mind was churning, trying to make sense of this new information. How did it fit together with everything else I knew about Héléne? "It's a fungicide?" I said, stalling for time.

"Yeah, it used to be very common, especially before the war." He turned the page. "These aren't your notes, then?"

I hesitated. Should I tell him about Hélène? He and Nico were so close, I felt sure it was only a matter of time before he learned the truth. "It's—" To my surprise a flood of shame bottled the words within me. "A friend," I said eventually. "They belong to a friend."

With this, something shifted in the atmosphere. Jean-Luc gently closed the cover of the notebook and said goodbye. After I heard his truck pull out of the driveway, I sat for a long time in the yellow light of the kitchen wondering if I had done the right thing.

By the time Nico, Heather, and the kids came home, I had brought my laptop downstairs and started combing the internet for information on Burgundy mixture. The kids burst through the back door, their cheeks dabbed with face paint—butterflies for Anna, turtles for Thibault—with Heather and Nico trailing wearily behind.

"Kate! *Kate!* I went on the giant roller coaster four times and Anna won a fish!" Thibault galloped up to me.

Anna held up a clear plastic bag filled with water, a flash of orange darting from side to side. "I think I will name it Taylor," she said. "Or maybe Swift."

Heather was taking in the table scattered with splayed notebooks and scribbled sheets of paper. A side plate smeared with melted butter and toast crumbs stood by my elbow. "Have you even moved from this spot?" she said, but there was a twinkle in her eye. "Thibault, Anna—time to get ready for bed. Upstairs—teeth and jammies, please. It's late." She clapped her hands.

"What about Swifty? I have to find her a bowl!" Anna cried.

"Not fair!" Thibault shouted. "Why does *she* always get to stay up late?"

"I will find a bowl for the fish," Heather declared. "Now, go. *Up.*"

"Aw, Mo-om!" they chorused, but nevertheless they trooped out of the room and up the stairs.

"I'll be there in ten minutes to tuck you in!" Heather called after them.

"*Quoi de neuf?*" Nico opened the fridge and removed a bottle of fizzy water.

"Yeah, what's up? Did you find anything juicy in Hélène's stuff?" Heather handed him a couple of glass tumblers, then squatted to open a low cupboard and began removing vases and other vessels. "This one'll work for now, right?" She held up a cube vase and eyed the goldfish.

"Oh, nothing big—just an inventory list of the secret cellar!" I said. I slid the notebook toward them.

Nico started choking on his glass of water. "*Putain,*" he swore, when he had finally stopped sputtering. "A cellar list? Are you serious?" He picked up the notebook. "How in the hell did you find this?"

Quickly, I told them about discovering the list in Hélène's *cahier d'excercises* and comparing her information to my own. "I mean, obviously I haven't yet inventoried the entire *cave*—but the numbers I do have match up almost exactly."

"*C'est incroyable!*" Nico shook his head in disbelief.

Heather shivered. "And to think Louise almost got her hands on it."

"Yeah, well." I pushed forward the other notebook. "As it turns out, there's also something else."

"*Burgundy mixture?*" Heather read. "Do you know what that is?" she asked Nico.

"Copper sulfate with sodium carbonate," he said. "I remember it from the *école de viticulture*. Of course it's rarely used anymore, with all the synthetic compounds now available."

"Apparently, it's relatively easy to make," I added. "Forms these beautiful blue crystals." I pushed my laptop toward them, open to a page titled "How to Create Copper Sulfate."

Heather moved behind me to check out the screen. "Sodium carbonate," she said. "That's washing soda."

"Yeah, it says here that sulfuric acid is really corrosive, but sodium bicarb neutralizes it."

"No, not sodium bicarbonate. Sodium carbonate." Her hand gripped my shoulder. "Don't you remember? We found an entire case of it downstairs—the washing soda." She gasped. "The holes! On the skirts of Hélène's dresses. I thought they were from moths, but obviously moths don't eat cotton. You guys, I think those holes were from sulfuric acid. What if Hélène was making the Burgundy mixture herself?"

"A young girl? During that era?" Nico scoffed. "Would she even know how?"

"But these *are* her notebooks," I pointed out. "So obviously she knew the formula." I thought for a moment. "Maybe she had a passion for chemistry. There's a packet of letters from a school friend, all about thermal expansion. And there was that biography of Marie Curie in her suitcase."

"Well, I suppose it's possible," Nico conceded.

"No," said Heather thoughtfully. "The question isn't *if* she made the Burgundy mixture. She definitely did make it—I am positive. The question is how. And where."

"And why," I added.

The three of us stared at each other, equally mystified, until a small voice floated down the stairs.

"Mamaaaan! *Tu es oùuuuuuu?* Come tuck me in noowwwwww!" called Thibault.

"Keep thinking about it," Heather said, as she started toward the stairs. "I bet the answers are staring us right in the face."

13 FÉVRIER 1941

These are the places I have hidden this journal: In a hatbox on the top shelf of my armoire. In the bottom drawer of my desk. Beneath a pile of stockings in my dresser. But still I am unsatisfied. All these places are too obvious—if the Boches ever search our home, surely my armoire, desk, or dresser would be the first places they'd look? Oh, who am I kidding—the Boches? It will more likely be Madame who ransacks my room—I feel sure she snoops when I am not home. I must keep looking for a safer hiding spot.

15 FÉVRIER 1941

There is a loose floorboard in my room, near the window, and I have settled on keeping this notebook in the hollow below. My only worry is that it creaks so volubly whenever anyone steps there, I fear that I'll give it away as I obviously tiptoe over it. But I moved the carpet a meter to the left and, visually at least, the spot looks unremarkable, just a bit uneven, which you can scarcely discern unless you know what you're looking for.

3 AVRIL 1941

Cher journal,

Forgive my trembling hand. I should not be writing this. I am bound to silence—I have promised not to tell a soul. If this diary is found it will mean dire consequences for him—and probably me as well, for keeping the secret. But if I don't tell *someone*, I will burst, and so I scribble the words here: *Papa is a* résistant.

I don't think he would have told me, except I found them this morning. I was halfway to Beaune on my bicycle when I realized I'd forgotten the boys' ration books. I immediately turned back to fetch them. Benoît and Albert are entitled to additional quantities of milk and meat, and Madame—who was at a Cercle du patrimoine meeting—would have boxed my ears if I hadn't brought their extra food home. I pedaled back furiously, banging the door as I entered, and to my shock, I found Papa sitting at the kitchen table with two strange men.

"*Ma choupinette!*" Papa exclaimed, and his cheeks drained of color, though he forced a smile. "I wasn't expecting you! I just ran into some old friends and we were sharing some lunch!"

Cher journal, it was ten o'clock in the morning and Papa had no plate before him. The other men looked up from their boiled potatoes—which they were supplementing with two tins of potted meat, a hard-boiled egg each, and a generous handful of radishes and spinach from the garden—and nodded at me. "*Bonjour*, mademoiselle," said the younger one—blue eyes, brown hair, and a striking flame-colored beard. From his accent, I immediately deduced that he was not French—and was, in fact, very probably English. The men returned to their food, devouring it in seconds, and Papa peered into a pot simmering on the stove, spearing them each another potato.

"I forgot the ration books," I announced, and fetched them from a tin on the mantelpiece. "*Au revoir*," I said politely and left the house before anyone could respond. As I was mounting my bicycle, Papa came out the door.

"Léna," he said quietly. "You surprised me. I didn't think you'd be home until later this afternoon."

"What are they doing here?" I whispered as fiercely as possible. "Why are you helping them? Papa, surely you must know how dangerous this is? We—*you*—could be arrested, or worse!" My voice shook.

"We will talk about this later," he said firmly.

"For now, I must request that you do not mention this to anyone. Do you understand?"

"Yes, but—"

"Good." He cut me off. "Now, you should be on your way to Beaune. It's best if you're not here right now. We'll talk later."

I cycled to Beaune, and stood in the ever-interminable lines—ninety minutes outside the *boucherie* for a morsel of steak, forty minutes at the cobbler only to learn that the soles of Benoît's shoes will need to be replaced with wood, because leather is simply no longer available. The whole time, I fretted over what I'd seen in the kitchen. How had Papa met those men? Were they the only people he had helped—or would there be others? I was so worried, I skipped the line at the *boulangerie* and pedaled straight home to find Papa before Madame returned.

He was in the *potager*, clipping asparagus, which have been shooting like mad. "Ah, you're back," he said. "Any luck today?"

"A bit of steak for *les garçons*."

"Good, good. Your *belle-mère* will be pleased." He snipped gently at a stalk.

"Papa, what I saw this morning—those men— who are they? I am frightened." I tried to keep my voice steady.

"*Moi aussi*," he said quietly. "Yes, don't look so surprised. I, too, am afraid, *ma fille.*" Silence, broken by the clipping of his secateurs. "But do you know what I decided?" He turned from the asparagus and our eyes met. "I decided that I am more afraid of becoming rotten inside than I am of imprisonment—or even death. I thought I was going mad, literally mad, for not doing something, for not reacting somehow. Now at least I have some semblance of self-respect."

"It is true, then?" I swallowed. "You are a . . . *résistant?*" I mouthed the last word, even though there was no one within earshot.

He set the shears gently on the ground. "I am a *passeur.* Do you know what that means?"

"*Non.*"

"As you know, there are often . . . *people* . . . who need assistance on their journey . . . *south.*"

South. That means only one thing. The Demarcation Line. La France Libre. And beyond—England, the United States. Freedom.

"We give them a bit of food, a safe place to rest, until we can help guide them to the next stop on their journey. We are a small network, but I cannot express to you the relief of working together with these like-minded comrades—" He bit back the rest of his sentence. "Well. I mustn't tell you too many details."

"A safe place to rest," I repeated. And then his meaning dawned on me. "You mean *here*? At the domaine? But where?"

"The wall that we built in the cellar—I made some modifications."

I waited for him to continue, but after several seconds, I hazarded another question. "So there have been other . . . guests?"

"*Oui.*" His face was grim. "And as long as I am here, there will be more."

I fell silent, considering this information. The expression on his face told me I needed to tread lightly. "Does my *belle-mère* know?"

"Absolutely not. She would not look favorably upon this endeavor." His mouth drew into a hard line but his next words were soft. "Léna, I am not asking you to join me. But I am asking for your discretion. No one can know about this."

I noticed how thin and haggard his face had become, and I wondered if he had been skipping meals so that he could sneak his portions to his guests.

"Can you promise me?" he asked.

Cher journal, of course I promised him. But already I am regretting it. I am terrified that Papa will be carted away. That is what happened to the older brother of my classmate, Laurence. Of course we all suspected he was a *résistant*, but one day he simply vanished, leaving his family in an agony of silent speculation. What if that happens to us?

18 AVRIL 1941

Now that I know the truth, Papa's secret seems so obvious. When he disappears for hours without explanation, I know he is in the hidden *cave*, or at a meeting of his fellow *résistants*. When food vanishes from the larder, I know he has taken it for his guests. When he appears in the mornings grey-faced and exhausted, I know he has spent the previous night shepherding his charges—and at this point, after several weeks of observation, I even know that if a night sky is filled with clouds, he will be dropping with fatigue the next morning.

These covert comings and goings terrify me. I wish Papa would stop. If I speak to him, will he listen? Is it worth risking his anger?

21 MAI 1941

Jacques—Papa's apprentice—has run away. No warning, no explanation. Yesterday he simply didn't show up for work and no one has any idea what happened to him. (When I expressed my concern aloud at the dinner table, Papa gave me a sharp look, so I actually do have *some* idea of what happened to him.) As a result, I am to help Papa in the vineyards.

Of course, with Jacques's disappearance I am more worried than ever that Papa will also vanish. But when I try to raise the topic, he steers the conversation firmly in another direction. I'm beginning to feel like his secret work is the only thing that brings him peace. I'm not sure there is anything I can say that will make him stop.

22 JUIN 1941

Today is the first anniversary of our "Armistice" with Germany, which Maréchal Pétain commemorated with a speech: "You were neither sold, nor betrayed, nor abandoned," he declaimed. "Those who tell you so are lying, and throwing you into the arms of Communism. You are suffering, and you will continue to suffer for a long time, for we have not finished paying for all our faults." Papa snapped off the radio, and I felt disgust rising within me, swift enough to choke, as bitter as bile. Pétain's accusations are atrociously unjust—how could we *deserve* this suffering?

For the first time, I have been questioning

my restraint. Is Papa right? Have I allowed fear to influence my actions? But when I consider the alternative—active resistance—well, that also feels wrong. Sometimes I see boys in Beaune, strutting about with an air of bravado, decked out in *bleu, blanc, rouge,* or some other silly display of defiance, and it seems so unnecessarily dangerous, so utterly pointless . . . and I wonder, is there a way to endure this war quietly—yet honorably?

30 JUIN 1941

The bitter, wet winter has become a hot, humid summer and as a result our vines are covered in black rot and *oïdium*—powdery mildew. "We need to spray," Papa keeps saying. "*Mais, il n'y a plus.*" The Boches have requisitioned every last bit of metal and without any copper sulfate, the fungicides are no longer available, "Not for love or ration cards," as Papa likes to say. (And each time, he chuckles a little at this display of "war humor.") We steel ourselves for yet another dismal harvest.

7 JUILLET 1941

Cher journal,

Something noteworthy happened today, to break this miserable monotony: I ran into Rose in Beaune.

I didn't recognize her at first, she has grown so thin (as, I suppose, have I—as we all have), but her face broke into a smile when she saw me and I immediately knew her voice, calling "Charpin" in a singsongy imitation of Madame Grenoble, our old chemistry prof.

"Rose!" I moved to the back of the *boulangerie* queue so we could chat while we waited. "What are you doing here?"

"Waiting for bread, *comme tout le monde*," she replied with a little shrug.

"But why aren't you at Sèvres? Or has the semester already finished?"

"*Non.*" Her tone did not invite questions, and so I changed the subject, asking her about thermal expansion, which she had mentioned in her last letter. Thanks to our discussion, the queue passed more quickly than usual. After we had collected our dense, dry, brown crusts, she suggested we go to the park, a few blocks away.

"It's so pretty here—I forgot," she said, gazing at the muddy waters of the river Bouzaize flowing past our feet.

"I don't think I've come here since our last school picnic. Has it only been a year? So much has happened since then."

"*C'est vrai,*" she said softly. "Everything before I went to Sèvres seems like a dream."

"Can you tell me why you left? Was it because your parents wanted you back home? I don't want to pry, but . . . Sèvres." I sighed wistfully.

Her mouth tightened. "It wasn't my choice." She turned her head and in her expression I was shocked to see something that looked like fear. "Hélène." She took a deep breath. "I was required to leave the university—because I am Jewish."

"Jewish? What do you mean? We sit behind your family at mass every Sunday. We took our First Communion together."

"Yes, my family attends church. But my mother's family is Jewish, bankers from Frankfurt; they moved to Paris at the turn of the century. My father's mother was Jewish, too, from Alsace, though he grew up with the church. Maman converted to Catholicism when she married Papa."

"But then you are Christian."

"Not according to . . . them." Her lips thinned. "Three Jewish grandparents—it is . . . enough."

"But they are brutes! Clumsy stupid louts! Who cares what they think?" Even as the words left my mouth, I knew how foolish they sounded. We are forced to care what Les Boches think because that is the price of Occupation. "Anyway," I continued, "what does being Jewish have to do with your place at Sèvres? How could they force you to give it up? After all your hard work? It's not fair!"

"Are you living under a rock, Hélène?" Her voice sliced across my own. "The Statut des Juifs excludes Jews from universities and most professions. I'm actually one of the lucky ones. My uncle is a doctor in Paris and he was ordered to close his office. There are many others—lawyers, architects, *fonctionnaires . . .* all forced to quit."

The injustice of it flashed through me, a wave of anger so violent that it left me shaking. "But we can't just allow this to happen! It's not right. *C'est pas correct!*"

She looked at me, startled. "What can we do, Hélène? They defeated us. We are powerless. We have no rights as individuals—or as a nation."

Suddenly, I understood what Papa has been enduring for the past year—the helplessness, the fury—the shame. I wanted to tear at my hair, scream with rage, beat a German soldier in the face until he was bloody. But I could do none of those things. I could do nothing.

"What do your parents say?" I finally managed to ask.

She sighed. "They're arguing all the time. Papa thinks we should find a way to leave France—he believes the situation will only worsen. But Maman doesn't want him to sacrifice our family's *négociant* business—and besides, our home is here. We are French. Or, at least, I thought we were." She stared at the river, the waters moody under grey skies, and suddenly there were tears spilling down her cheeks. "I feel so selfish saying it," she cried. "But I regret the loss of my studies so very bitterly. At this point, I have no hope of ever earning a degree."

"Don't say that—the Allies will come."

"Sure, when chickens have teeth."

We gazed at the water. Clouds of algae bloomed just below the surface of the river, and it seemed astonishingly cruel that anything could flourish in this current state of misery. The world is so ruthless, I thought.

"I miss it, too," I confessed. "The laboratory. Madame Grenoble's lectures. The periodic table, like a secret code. Most of all, I miss that feeling of certainty when you finally understand why a chemical reaction happens. No mystery, or intrigue— just pure science."

"I keep thinking about the experiment I left behind at Sèvres," she said. "My copper sulfate was starting to develop crystals—beautiful blue shards, they looked like jewels."

"If only you could have brought them home as a *petit souvenir.* Papa was just saying the other day how desperately we need copper sulfate to treat our vines."

"If we had any hope of finding enough copper, we could make it ourselves. It's actually not that difficult."

There were a thousand reasons why I should have pretended I had misunderstood her. But my anger was still simmering and entertaining a subversive plan against the Germans pleased me. I fell silent, dissecting the idea, examining it from different angles. "I know where we could find a few bits of copper," I said, thinking of the locked storeroom where Madame keeps all her treasures squirreled away. "What else would we need?"

"Sodium carbonate."

"*Pas de problème.*" It's all we have to wash our clothes these days.

"And sulfuric acid. From an old car battery, perhaps?"

"Trickier, but not impossible. What else?"

She began listing other items: earthenware pots, shallow ceramic baking dishes, protective gear like aprons and safety goggles. "And of course we'd need to create some sort of laboratory—nothing fancy, but some place well ventilated and fairly isolated. The initial solution releases noxious fumes, and then it must evaporate over several days, or weeks."

"Ah." My shoulders sank. "That *is* a problem."

"*Ouais*," she agreed.

"Well, it brightens my spirits to even consider such a thing." I flashed a grim smile. "Though I suppose it would have been terribly risky, considering what they do to *résistants*." We've all heard stories of torture; they streak through the village, passed along in dark whispers of warning. "And especially given your situation . . ."

Rose sighed, but she nodded in agreement. "I'm sure you're right. It's much safer to do nothing."

16 JUILLET 1941

Rose and I had made plans to meet in the park again this afternoon, but she was late—so late, I had only a few minutes before I needed to fetch the boys from the neighbor's house.

"*Désolée*," she said mechanically when she finally arrived, and as she drew close, I saw her face was pale, blank with shock.

"What is it? What's happened?" I grabbed her arm and forced her to sit.

She stared down at her lap. "They came," she said in a quiet voice.

Sudden fear forced the breath from my chest. Of course I knew who had come—the Boches. "Are you all right? Did they hurt you?"

She shook her head. "They ransacked the house. Maman's silver, the jewelry she'd forgotten to hide away, the portrait of great-grandfather Reinach, our *caves* . . ." Her mouth set into a thin line. "They were so furious when they discovered the cellar nearly empty, they went on a rampage, bludgeoning the walls. Eventually they smashed through and discovered the bottles Papa had been hiding." Her voice dropped to a whisper. "They took all of it."

"But how? What did they say?"

She shrugged. "The head officer claimed it was his duty to"—she assumed a tone of mock pomposity—"*eliminate all Jewish influence in the national economy.*"

A wave of fury scorched me. "Those dirty Boche bastards."

Rose gave a start of surprise. "Oh, *non, non, non,*

Hélène, they weren't German," she said. "They were Vichy."

"They were *French?*" I gasped.

"*Oui.*"

"But your family—they are also French! How could they do this? How can we do this to each other?" I cried. "We have to do something. We can't allow this to continue."

Rose shrugged, and something about her pale resignation brought me close to tears. "We've been over this before, Hélène. There's nothing we can do."

I closed my eyes against the sun, the light beating red through my lids. The truth is, ever since that day in the cherry tree, fear has controlled almost all my actions—and I've tried to use it to control others, too, especially Papa. But after my recent conversations with Rose, my fear has been replaced with a white hot, burning rage. "An act of subversion would be so very, very satisfying," I said recklessly.

Before she could respond, the church clock started to chime the quarter hour. I leapt from the bench and snatched up my bicycle, well aware that I'd have to pedal hard to reach the boys on time.

Still, as we exchanged cheek kisses, I suggested that we meet again at the end of the week. "*Bon courage*," I said. "And who knows?" I attempted to lighten her mood with a joke. "Maybe by then I'll have found a place for a secret laboratory."

"If you do," she said, surprising me, "I will help you make the copper sulfate. I'm serious. I have to do something, Hélène—or I fear I will go . . . completely mad." Her voice dropped, but when her eyes met mine, they were defiant.

I cycled back to the village, my mind so full of our conversation that I scarcely noticed the familiar landscape of dry red earth and scraggly vines, the distant *cabotte* floating on a sea of leaves . . . *la cabotte*. Our little stone hut amid the vines. It's about ten kilometers from the domaine—very primitive— and no one ever goes there.

The idea hit me as I jolted over a pothole so deep it nearly sent me flying over the handlebars. *La cabotte*. Could there be a more perfect place for a secret, makeshift laboratory?

18 JUILLET 1941

At first, Papa dismissed our idea. "*Absolument non*," he said. "Under no circumstances. It's too dangerous. And, anyway, what could two young girls know about making copper sulfate?"

"But, Papa," I told him, "that's the beauty of our plan. Even if they do catch us, why would they ever suspect the truth?"

He laughed, a quick, sharp bark. And then his fingers began drumming the kitchen table. "It might just work, *ma choupinette*, you know that? It might just work."

With a bit of persuasion, Papa has convinced Madame to part with a surprisingly large box of copper jelly molds "*C'est pour le vignoble, chérie, et nos fils*," he said in dulcet tones. *It's for the vineyard, darling, and our sons.* Apparently, she had "forgotten" to turn over the box to the Germans, which—frankly—makes me wonder what else she has salted away in those mysterious cupboards of hers. Papa also gave us an old car battery, a final relic of his dearly departed Citroën, which he had tucked away in the stables. Rose and I began our project today with a minor mishap—I splashed acid on myself when removing it to the clay pot, but Rose was quick with the sodium carbonate and I escaped with only a hole in my skirt—a rather large hole, but better on my clothes than eating away at my flesh! We have agreed to take turns bicycling to the *cabotte* to check on the evaporation.

25 JUILLET 1941

The liquid is a beautiful, unnatural blue, the color growing steadily deeper. Only another day or two, I think, before we mix it with water and sodium carbonate, and spray it on the vines. I am bursting with pride! Rose, ever pragmatic, has also pointed out that though our first attempt has been successful, it's been very modest. She estimates that we'll have created enough fungicide solution for only about a hectare of vines—which means we need to somehow find more copper if we are to continue. More copper. A leg of lamb would be easier to obtain. A cone of pure white sugar. A pair of fine kid gloves. But Rose says her brother has a friend who deals in scrap metal on the black market, and we plan to make contact next week. I am to ask Papa if he is willing to barter some wine in exchange for copper scraps.

To think a few scarce months ago, it frightened me to read a Resistance newsletter (not even passing it along, mind you, merely *reading* it). And now I am poised to meet with a professional black marketeer. On the other hand, even Madame—or, perhaps, especially Madame—has been known to bring home a slab of butter, a tube of lipstick, an extra packet of cigarettes, obtained from some slippery source. And I must admit that sticking it to the Boches is awfully satisfying.

Indeed, my fear has given way to anger. And anger has made me bold.

Chapter 10

"Oh, Kate! It's absolutely remarkable," Jennifer said for about the thirtieth time. She spun around and whacked me in the arm. "Oops, sorry, darling. I didn't realize you were there behind me. I'm a bit overexcited. I just can't get over it. The armoire! That door! These bottles!" She waved her arms and the beam of her flashlight slashed through the gloom. "Is it very different now from how you found it?"

I rubbed my arm where she'd hit it. "I've tried to disturb it as little as possible."

"Well done." She nodded her approval and moved between two wine racks, stooping for a closer look.

I had forgotten all about Jennifer's semiannual trip to France until her email had appeared in my inbox two days earlier, announcing her imminent arrival and inviting me to join her meetings with winemakers. She and I had spent the entire day together, and in between appointments I filled her in on the discovery of the secret cellar—though I had carefully omitted details about Hélène and her sordid history. I had also extended Nico and Heather's invitation to have dinner at the domaine—"And maybe you could come early and check out the *cave*?" I asked—and she had eagerly agreed.

"You know," Jennifer said now, training the flashlight on a bottle of Pommard Rugiens. "I'm no expert on rare wines—and I dislike making broad generalizations—but I think someone put a fair amount of thought into this selection. These are some of the very top prewar vintages—they weren't just chosen at random." She closed her eyes, breathing in the cool, damp air. "And obviously the conditions down here are perfect for storing wine—even with decades of neglect." She moved further along the row. "Have you found any of Les Gouttes d'Or?"

"No, not yet, though according to the cellar list, there's a small stash."

In fact, Les Gouttes d'Or covered just a single line of Hélène's notebook, only one vintage—the 1929, widely considered one of the best *millésimes* of the twentieth century.

"You should start looking for it. This collection

alone is worth a fortune, there's no doubt about it. But with Les Gouttes d'Or, it would be an enormous fortune. Like a tell-your-frenemies-to-go-to-hell type of fortune."

We lingered in the cellar, companionably poking around in a desultory search for the missing Gouttes d'Or. Every so often, Jennifer emitted small gasps of astonishment as she glimpsed various labels—"Sorry, sorry," she always apologized. "It's like seeing a celebrity"—but we found no sign of the elusive white wine.

"Jennifer, what did you think of the *cave*?" Nico said a few minutes later as we emerged from the cellar door, blinking like moles in the bright light of the kitchen. He handed us each a slender flute of *crémant*, the sparkling wine's bubbles shooting to the surface.

She placed the glass on the counter and raised both hands to her cheeks. "Amazing," she said. "In all my years in the wine industry, I have never seen anything like it. I've never even *heard* of anything so completely and utterly extraordinary."

"What would you say our next steps should be?" asked Nico.

"Well, after the inventory is complete—and you've spoken to the rest of your family—you could think about contacting the major auction houses."

They began discussing the pros and cons of New York versus London, and I moved toward the oven to check on a tray of chicken *vols-au-vent* that was filling the kitchen with an irresistible buttery aroma.

"Thanks again for doing this," I said to Heather, who was arranging lettuce leaves in an earthenware bowl.

"Hmm? Oh, don't be silly—I love having people over. Anyway, you did all the cooking."

"Ah, you mean *Picard* did all the cooking." Earlier in the afternoon, Nico and I had gone to a nearby branch of the French supermarket chain, filling a cart with the most elegant frozen food I'd ever seen—tiny squares of brioche topped with truffled foie gras mousse, filets of beef slathered with mushroom duxelles and wrapped in puff pastry, dainty chocolate éclairs and raspberry tarts—all of it ready to be baked, microwaved, or merely left on the counter to defrost.

"Oh, yeah, Picard. Love it." Heather absently fluffed the salad greens.

"Are you okay?"

"I'm fine. Why?"

"Nothing—it's just that usually any mention of Picard sends you into a rapture." I examined her more closely. Her eyes looked tired, pinched at the corners.

"I'm *fine*," she insisted.

Before I could question her further, Jean-Luc stepped through the back door, followed by Louise and Walker.

"I still can't believe you invited them!" I whispered to Heather under the flurry of introductions.

"I didn't have a choice!" she hissed back. "Nico said Jean-Luc really wanted to meet Jennifer, and you know Louise sticks to him like shampoo with conditioner. Besides," she said, wrinkling her nose, "you're the one who asked Walker."

"I know, I know! But like I said, we ran into him at Picard and he seemed really apologetic." In fact, he had expressed his complete bafflement at Louise's behavior in the charity shop. I still wasn't sure if I could trust him or not, but he had looked so wistful gazing at the contents of my shopping cart—"Having a party?" he had asked—that I had softened, inviting him to join us.

"Hey," Walker said a few minutes later, sidling up to the counter, where I was opening wine for dinner. "You need any help?" He spoke without a trace of his usual irony.

I cradled a bottle, showing him the label. "Do you think I should decant this?"

He whistled. "Aloxe-Corton, 2008? Nice. And, yes, absolutely, it needs air."

I peered through the thick glass at the dark liquid within. "Are you sure? I don't think it's throwing a lot of sediment."

"When in doubt, decant—at least, that's always been my philosophy."

"And an excellent philosophy it is." Jennifer appeared beside us. "Hello." She nodded at Walker.

"Ms. Russell," he said. "It is an honor to meet you. I'm such an admirer of your work."

"And which work is that?" Jennifer, ever wary of sycophants, fixed him with a gimlet eye.

"Your blog at Cost Club's website," he said without skipping a beat. "I always tell people that's where the best wine tips are. Forget Robert Parker!"

"Oh gosh, I don't think anybody reads that old thing." Jennifer said with a girlish trill.

"Not true! I've made a point of subscribing so that I never miss a post. I particularly liked your analysis of the Portuguese market." He launched into a recital of the finer points as Jennifer nodded with an intense look on her face. Neither of them noticed as I moved into the dining room to search for a decanter.

In the end, the puff pastry crusts of the individual beef Wellingtons took a lot longer to bake golden brown than the box had indicated, so we were all very jolly by the time we finally sat down to eat.

"Nico, this wine is delicious," said Jennifer, breathing from her glass. "And Kate, the pairing is beautiful,"

"Thanks." My knife slid into the meat. "But you can't really go wrong with beef and red Burgundy, can you?"

Out of the corner of my eye, I saw Louise take a sip and make a face.

"*C'est le* 2008?" Jean-Luc craned his head toward the sideboard, where I'd left the bottle.

I nodded, my mouth full.

"You decanted it," he observed.

I finished chewing, and swallowed. "Yeah, I wasn't sure if I should, but . . ."

"I always decant," Walker spoke up beside me. "Obviously, the older reds need it because of sediment. But I really think the aeration benefits any wine, young or old."

"*Ah bon?*" Jean-Luc frowned as he balanced his knife and fork on the edge of his plate. "I actually find that decanting can make a wine fade too fast. You get plenty of exposure to oxygen simply by swirling in the glass."

"So you *never* decant?" The incredulity in Walker's voice suggested that Jean-Luc had just revealed he'd cryogenically preserved a long-lost pet hamster.

"Well, no, not *never.*" Jean-Luc spoke with an edge.

"Obviously, like you said, sediment can be a problem for aged reds, and decanting is necessary. But I do think a lot of sommeliers decant too aggressively, without any consideration for the delicacy of the wine."

"Yeah, we're such brutes, us somms," Walker said with a mocking lilt.

"I wouldn't have put it quite so bluntly, but . . ." Jean-Luc picked up his cutlery and sliced through an artichoke heart.

Louise, who was sitting next to Jean-Luc, cleared her throat and placed a possessive hand on his thigh just as Heather slugged the remaining liquid in her glass, stood, and announced: "Looks like we could use more wine. No, no"—she waved us all back in our seats as she moved around the table—"*I'll* do it." She grabbed a bottle off the sideboard.

"Oh, *chérie*, that's just a simple *vin de pays*," Nico protested. "Why don't we open something more special?"

"Nope." Heather ripped off the foil and dug in the corkscrew. "I officially proclaim the wine club adjourned for the evening." She yanked the cork from the bottle and splashed wine into the nearest empty glass, which happened to be Jennifer's.

My mentor took a large swig. "Perfect!" she declared with a twinkle in her eye.

Heather moved around the table pouring wine for everyone. Only Louise placed a hand over her glass. "*Non, merci,*" she said, with an almost indiscernible twist of her lips.

"Louise drinks nothing less than premier cru," Walker explained in dry tones.

I thought he was joking until Louise gave a careless shrug and said without a hint of embarrassment: "Anything else gives me terrible headaches."

In the end, Heather's distraction served its purpose. By the time we were passing around the miniature éclairs and berry tarts, our guests were chatting with renewed cheer. Heather and Louise finally found a subject of mutual interest—the market fishmonger.

"Have you *seen* him fillet a *daurade*?"

"Smo. King. Hot."

Jennifer and Jean-Luc had their heads bent over a lunar calendar for grapevines, which he had whipped from his pocket, and she was asking how it differed in the southern hemisphere. Nico and Walker were debating with great animation the best route for driving across the United States. I seized the opportunity to sneak into the kitchen and put the kettle on for coffee.

Heels clicked across the wood floor, then Jennifer spoke behind me: "Such a lovely evening, darling!"

I turned from the cupboard, where I'd been rummaging for the French press. "Thanks." I saw she had her coat slung over one arm. "Are you leaving already?"

"Afraid so. I've got an early start to Bordeaux. You know how these trips are—death march travels. But this has been a wonderful respite. I shall go forth completely fortified to endure six more days of excruciating small talk."

"I'm really glad you had a chance to meet Heather and Nico."

"Me, too." Jennifer eyed me. "And you, Kate? How are you doing?"

"I'm fine." I flushed under her gaze. "You were right. I've made progress here." There was so much I wanted to tell her—about Hélène, and all the horrible family secrets that I wished we had never uncovered. But when I opened my mouth, I found myself unable—or unwilling. Instead, I stepped forward and hugged her. "Thank you for coming." I gave her a quick kiss on the cheek.

"My dear, it was a pleasure."

"And I'm sorry about that weird interaction between Jean-Luc and Walker earlier," I added.

She patted my shoulder. "They're both very loyal to their principles. I admire that."

"I guess I didn't realize that decanting was such a divisive topic."

"Oh, Kate." Her face creased with mirth. "My dear girl, that was never about decanting."

"Désolée, mesdames." The woman behind the counter shook her ash blond head. "I cannot help you." Her regret was evident—as was her determination not to transgress the official regulations by a single millimeter.

"Please," I pleaded in French. "I know I don't have my birth certificate with me, but I swear that I am a direct descendant of the Charpin family. Are you sure you can't release the file of my great-aunt?"

"Her mother was born right here in Beaune," Heather added in her most persuasive tones.

"*Mesdames.*" The clerk's voice sharpened. "As I said, I would love to be able to help you. But without the proper paperwork, I can do absolutely nothing. *Désolée. Merci. Bonne journée!*" Her message was clear—we were dismissed.

"Stuffy old *fonctionnaire.* Stupid French bureaucracy," Heather huffed as we exited onto the *mairie* steps.

As if in response, a bolt of lightning cracked the sky, followed by a clap of thunder, and then rain began bucketing to the ground.

"Shit!" Heather shouted above the deluge. "We forgot the umbrella."

"Should we wait it out?" I yelled back.

She slumped into her coat. "Looks like we don't have a choice."

We huddled beneath the portico, watching the rain cascade into oceanic puddles.

"We knew it was a long shot," I pointed out.

"Still, everything is so impossibly rigid in this damn country. It's a wonder anything ever gets done at all," she fumed. A gust of wind blew straight into our faces, and the rain shifted suddenly to hail.

Beside me, Heather fingered the strap on her handbag. "I've been doing some reading about France after the Liberation," she said. "I ordered a couple of books online. The punishment of these horizontal collaborators—it was absolutely brutal. And not just the head shavings—that was only the beginning. These women were stripped half-naked, smeared with tar, marched around town, kicked and beaten, spat upon. It was complete misogyny. Yes, a lot of them were prostitutes. But some of them were raped by the Nazis. Some of them were forced into liaisons so they could get food or medicine for their children. And some of them were falsely denounced out of petty jealousy. At least twenty thousand women had their heads shaved—it happened in pretty much every single town and village in France. Women used as scapegoats." Her voice had risen with the storm so that she was practically shouting. "And do you know what happened to the men who collabo-rated? Nothing! In fact, do you know who usually did the head shaving? Men! A lot of them were just trying to divert attention away from their own collaboration during the war!" A blast of wind tore the words from her lips.

But before I could respond, a deep voice boomed from overhead. "*Who was collaborating during the war?*"

My head whipped around, and my heart began thundering in my chest. For there, looming on the step above us, was Uncle Philippe. He wore a black rain jacket, its deep hood pulled over his head so that his face was cast in shadow.

"*Bon—Bonjour,*" I stammered, glancing at Heather. She had snapped her mouth shut, as if she didn't trust herself to speak.

"*Bonjour,*" he said shortly. "What, may I ask, are you girls doing here?"

Quickly, I tried to gather my wits. "We could ask the same of you," I replied, even as my mind spun. Had he followed us here? How long had he been there? How much of our conversation had he heard?

"I was dropping off the renewal of my car's registra-tion," he said. Was I imagining things, or did his eyes flicker?

"Soccer club," Heather croaked. She cleared her throat. "I was registering the kids for soccer club."

Uncle Philippe descended a step, so that he stood directly above us. "I thought, Katreen," he said, "that I had made myself clear the other day. But I forgot that your mother spent too much time in America. Clearly, she neglected to teach you to respect your elders. Or to respect the past!"

"I do respect the past," I insisted. "But I also have the right to know about it."

"I don't think you understand," he said icily, "that for my generation, the Second World War is always present; it is touching every aspect of our lives. You will never comprehend what it was like to grow up in its shadow. Do you have any idea how easy you have it? How ridiculous your problems are in comparison? How trivial? Whatever you and my daughter-in-law are doing here, I am telling you now to stop. Leave it alone! There are things you do not need to know. Things that are better left forgotten." His eyes bored through me, dark pools of fury. "Do you hear me?"

I crossed my arms so he wouldn't see me shaking. "*Oui—Oui*," I stammered.

"Good." He descended the rest of the steps and, with a final glare, disappeared around the corner of the building.

"How much of our conversation do you think he heard?" I asked Heather several minutes later. We were in her car with the heat blasting, having finally made a run for it through the abating storm.

"Seems like it was just the tail end."

"I hope so." I chewed the inside of my lip. "So what do we do now? It seems impossible to continue."

She turned to me, her face filled with astonishment. "Are you joking? We have to keep going now."

"But what about everything he said about respecting the past, and—"

"Don't you get it, Kate?" Her voice collided with mine. "I have to know the truth. If she was a collaborator, how far did it go? What if she got people sent to the gas chambers?" She took a deep breath, and I saw that she was steeling herself against crying. "I have to know," she said more calmly. "You understand that, right? Because it could have been my family. It could have been me."

Even as she spoke, I felt a weight settling upon my shoulders. For weeks it had been hovering above me, this cloak of family responsibility, heavy with unanswered questions of obligation. I had tried to sidestep it, but now with Heather's anguished eyes upon me I realized the consequences of this truth reached far beyond my own conscience. I had told her that our family's past would never repeat itself, but now I knew there was only one way to ensure that it never would: sharing the truth. All of it.

I shifted in my seat, pressing a hand against my heart, which was beating with a strange rhythm. Taking a deep breath, I spoke as calmly as I could. "We will find out the truth," I promised.

3 AOÛT 1941

Cher journal,

The scrap metal dealer is called Bernard, but I don't know if that's his real name or a *nom de guerre.* Our first meeting was at a café in Beaune, an establishment with dirty windows where no one seems to make eye contact. If I had to guess, I would say Bernard is a couple of years younger than I—his cheeks are spattered with acne—and he speaks in boastful tones that remind me of the boys at the *lycée.* Though Bernard appears full of swagger, Rose's brother swears he is trustworthy, so against my better judgment, I proposed the exchange of wine and copper. He has made two deliveries to the *cabotte.* Both times, the burning wood of the gazogene engine wouldn't fuel his car up the slope, so we had to get out and push. I almost had a nervous breakdown for fear that the Boches would stop and search us, but thus far we have escaped notice. I have not asked where he obtains the copper scraps, nor what he does with the wine I give him. I take care that our bottles go unlabeled.

21 AOÛT 1941

For five weeks we have been spraying the vines with our homemade Burgundy mixture. Dare I say that the plants are responding? Even Papa agrees that the leaves appear stronger, healthier, no longer dusted with a sticky white web of fungus.

"I can't believe it," Rose said, then sighed. "It's like a miracle." We had met at the *cabotte* to check our solution and eat an ad hoc picnic. I raised my tin cup to hers and we toasted our success with the last splash of apple cider.

"Not a miracle." My voice sharpened. "It's science."

"Still," she marveled. "Who would have thought that some boring old copper wiring could save your grape harvest? You said yourself that your father had completely lost hope."

"And now he thinks that even Les Gouttes d'Or will be worth bottling."

"Les Gouttes d'Or," she said thoughtfully. "Why's it called that?"

"No one really knows." I brushed crumbs from my lap. "I like to think it's because the wine's color resembles drops of gold."

"So in a way"—she cocked her head—"we turned metal into gold."

I laughed. "I suppose we did."

"That's more than chemistry. It's alchemy."

"Alchemy." The very word sounded like a secret. "Alchemy," I repeated, delighted.

"That's us." Her smile broadened. "The Alchemists Club."

22 SEPTEMBRE 1941

Another birthday come and gone: a week ago, I turned twenty years old. We didn't celebrate—we were in the full midst of the *vendanges*, all of us dropping with fatigue—though Albert did gather a little *panier* of late blackberries for me, which we ate with a scrape of sugar.

And so, another harvest has ended. Our grapes this year were not the most spectacular, but we had more bounty than others, and for that we were grateful. I give thanks that all of us—Papa, the boys, our neighbors, and I—brought them in together.

21 OCTOBRE 1941

I was in town today at the pharmacy—Benny has a cough and Madame sent me to try to buy a tincture for him—when I glimpsed Bernard outside. I hadn't seen him for a few months—not since the last time he delivered scraps to the *cabotte*, which was mid-August at least. We passed each other on the street as strangers, not even making eye contact. Still, I noticed he was limping.

This war has created strange friendships. A few months ago, I would have never guessed I'd be concerned about a shifty-eyed boy with a tongue too fast for his own good. But here I am, unable to sleep, worrying over how he got that limp.

5 NOVEMBRE 1941

Tonight we twisted the radio dial at least thirty times, desperate to find the voices from London. The Germans have become adept at jamming the signal, but with enough persistence we finally caught it. What a relief it was to hear those four notes of Beethoven—to think I once thought them gloomy! A few weeks ago, they began broadcasting snippets of coded messages, strange and unnerving sentences that dangle like severed limbs. *Lisette is well. I like Siamese cats. It always rains in England.* They sound so silly, it's hard to believe the Allies would announce an invasion in this manner. But as we listen, I discreetly watch Papa's face, trying to discern if they mean anything to him.

9 DÉCEMBRE 1941

I heard them talking last night—Papa and Madame—their voices sending vibrations of fury through the walls of the house.

"*Non, c'est pas possible!* Not in my house," Madame hissed. It's astonishing how far her whisper can carry.

The issue, I eventually grasped, is Papa's clandestine activity, not his work as a *passeur*—which Madame suspects, but cannot prove—but rather the sheltering of people in our cellar. Apparently she found a heap of dirty rags by the bottom of the cellar stairs and was shocked to discover it was the tattered uniform of an English airman. "A uniform of an *anglais*! Covered in blood! How on earth did it get there?" By this time, she had given up the pretense of whispering.

At first Papa vacillated—"*C'était rien, chérie,* just some old rags"—but then Madame confronted him with the missing food from the pantry: "Two kilos of potatoes, three tins of sardines, and a jar of cherry preserves! I think Hélène is stealing from us and selling on the black market!" That's when Papa admitted that he'd taken some of her stock "for a few friends."

"What friends?"

"Friends who need help."

"Who needs help more than your own family? Your growing sons? If you continue giving away food to these good-for-nothings, we won't have anything left!"

"They're not good-for-nothings," Papa objected. "May I remind you, Virginie, that we are at war?"

"And may I remind you," she said shrilly, "that you have two small children? Benoît could fall ill again at any time! That food is his strength!"

"It will hardly do Benoît any harm to give up a few spoonfuls of cherry jam. Believe it or not, *chérie*, there are actually people who need it more than our son."

"Who?" she insisted. "*Who?* One of those sweaty English slabs of roast beef? You think I don't know what you've been up to in the cellar? You think I haven't missed the linens from the closet? Didn't see the disgusting rings left around the bathtub? The dishes washed like a slattern, piled wet upon the shelf? I'm not an idiot, Edouard—I know you've been hiding people down there. But it has to stop! Do you understand? It will stop."

"*Chérie*, please, you're overreacting. I'm being very cautious."

"So it's *true*?" She broke into unbridled sobs, which continued for several seconds, even as Papa remained silent. Finally she seemed to collect herself. "Edouard," she said in a steadier tone. "I beg of you, please stop. Joséphine Fresnes says the Gestapo shoots *résistants* on the spot, just like that. And for what? This struggle—it's not worth it. We should keep quiet, mind our own business, be patient, wait out the end of the war. Joséphine says—"

"Joséphine Fresnes?" spat Papa. "Do you think I care about anyone from that stupid, spineless Cercle du patrimoine? Circle of Nazis is more like it."

"We are protecting our heritage," insisted Madame.

"You are cowards!"

Silence. I imagined them at opposite corners of the room, Madame cast in sulks, Papa with his arms crossed, defiant. Despite my near constant anxiety, I was proud of him.

Finally Madame spoke. "I'm sorry, Edouard," she said in a soft voice. "It was wrong of me to get angry. Of course it's not my place to tell you how to behave. And I admire you for doing what you believe to be right. But I also have a duty—to my children. *Our* children. I want you to know that I will be listening. I will be watching. And if you do not stop sheltering strangers in our home, the next time I hear someone down in the cellar, I will turn them in."

"Report me? Your husband? You wouldn't dare."

"Noooo, perhaps not. But an English pilot? I could say he broke into the domaine. He'd be gone like that." She snapped her fingers. "Taken to a POW camp." I could practically hear the gears grinding in her mind.

"Why, Virginie?" Papa shouted. "Why are you doing this? Don't you care about our freedom?"

"*Non,*" she replied. "I care about our safety."

A shrill wail rose from the boys' room, followed by another—my brothers awakened by their parents' argument, now frightened in their beds. I heard Madame open her bedroom door and run to them, the murmur of her voice soothing the boys as they cried, the sound of their tears covering the quiet sobs of our father.

3 FÉVRIER 1942

Cher journal,

The cold is ravaging us like a pack of wolves. I have vowed not to complain in front of my brothers, but we are constantly frozen, constantly hungry. I thought last winter was the most bitter of my life, but this year is worse, with even less food and fuel. My fingernails are brittle and yellow, my legs covered in bruises that refuse to fade, my hair thinning. Yesterday we each ate a single potato, and then Albert and Benny fought over who would get the transparent scraps of skin.

This morning I cycled to Beaune to visit the shops once again but, honestly, I had no hope of finding any food—I simply wanted to escape the house. Papa rarely emerges from his office—I think he's started sleeping there. Madame has become unbearable, with a permanent toothache that swells her face so that her insults emerge slurred and almost incomprehensible. At the *boulangerie*, I happened to meet Rose, but it was too cold to queue outside and after a few minutes I said so.

"Are you going home?" Rose asked.

"Where else? There is nowhere to go these days."

"I have an Italian lesson," she said. "Are you interested in learning Italian?"

"You're studying Italian? Why?"

"I thought you might want to learn a few words. It's a beautiful language."

"No, thank you." But as I turned to leave, a patrol group sauntered toward the bakery—they weren't even German, but French police, those *collabo* bastards—demanding papers from everyone in sight. I recognized one of the *gendarmes*, a pale, blond boy, tall and thin. It was Madame's nephew, Michel; he and I used to play hide-and-seek together in the vineyards. I handed him my documents, unsure of what to say. Should I greet him as a friend? Pretend we'd never met? I decided on the latter—I would wait for him to acknowledge me first. "*Merci, mademoiselle*," he said, handing back my papers without a flicker of recognition. The pair turned to Rose, staring for a long time at her identity card. Michel's eyes shifted between the two of us. "You are together?" he asked me. Yes, I told him, we are friends from school. "Be careful of the company you keep," he said to me in an undertone.

"How dare he," I hissed under my breath when they had moved down the street.

"It's because I'm Jewish," she said faintly. Her hands were shaking so that she could hardly return her documents to her pocketbook.

I swallowed my outrage and squeezed her hand. "Are you all right?" I asked.

She nodded but her grip indicated otherwise. "Come on," I told her. "I'll walk you to your lesson."

I accompanied Rose to a building on the place Marey, where we ascended two flights of stairs and knocked on a door. After several minutes, a man cracked it open, his face half-covered in a beard. "*Bonjour, mon cousin,*" Rose said, and he opened the door further and we stepped into a small reception area furnished with a desk and two chairs for visitors. Through a cracked door marked "*privé*" I glimpsed a large room filled with enormous machinery.

"Your cousin?" I hissed to Rose as we lingered in the vestibule. "I thought you had an Italian lesson."

"*Si, so parlare l'italiano,*" the man said. He jerked his head at me. "Who's she?"

"A friend. She's one of us," Rose said.

He crossed his arms and examined me, eyes dark blue and hostile. He was younger than I'd initially thought, though his beard, coupled with the shadows under his eyes, aged him. He shook his head. "*Non.*"

"We can trust her," Rose insisted. "She made the copper sulfate with me. Bernard can vouch for her. Please."

"*Non.*"

"*S'il te plaît,*" Rose said again. "She is the daughter of—Avricourt."

Her words shot straight through me. Papa's Christian name is Edouard, and Rose knows that—just as I know her father's name is Marcel.

"His daughter?" Flint Eyes was looking at me with a sliver less of suspicion.

Rose nodded. "She is a brilliant chemist—and I need her help."

My help? With what? Panic circled me like a vise. "Wait," I whispered. "What's going on? I never said—"

"She was with you at Sèvres?" demanded Flint Eyes.

"We were at *lycée* together. She knows the laboratory better than I do, and Madame G. was always very fond of her."

"A *lycéen?*" He snorted. "She doesn't even have proper training." He moved to open the door.

Despite my rising fear, I was beginning to feel rather indignant. "I won the Science Cup," I informed him haughtily. "I would be at Sèvres if not for this stupid war."

"I'm sure." He smirked.

I drew myself to full height, which is as tall as

most Frenchmen, though still—I was chagrined to find—half a head shorter than old Flint Eyes. "Disbelieve me if you wish." I kept my voice cold. "But at this point, I doubt you'll find anyone more qualified than I, nor anyone more loyal to France, and that is the God's honest truth. I never lie."

After a pause, Flint Eyes simply laughed. "Does she have a bicycle?" he asked. When Rose nodded he conceded, "*D'accord.* She can come to the meeting on Thursday. And you—if you're going to join us, you better learn how to tell lies."

God help me, *cher journal.* It seems, somehow, I have joined a circuit of the Resistance.

25 FÉVRIER 1942

We meet at various locations in Beaune: A barrel maker's workshop on the rue des Tonneliers. The modest home of a sympathetic wine merchant on the rue de l'Arquebuse. The address on the place Marey, which is the atelier of an Italian printer who returned two years ago to Bologna. Flint Eyes—Stéphane (though that's not his real name, of course)—is related to the printer somehow. Or perhaps that's his cover? I don't ask too many questions. He uses the printing equipment to produce tracts and create forged documents. They call me Marie—I chose the name in honor of my beloved Madame Curie. So far, I've attended three meetings, sitting next to Rose at the edge of the group. Each time, there have been five or six people, and I was not terribly surprised to find Bernard among them. They discussed distribution of newssheets and movement of hidden weapons. Stéphane leads the meetings. Now that he and I have met a few times, I am less affronted by his initial suspicion of me. Like all Resistance circuits, ours is extremely vulnerable to infiltration and betrayal—a mere slip of the tongue, either accidental or prompted by a beating from the Gestapo, and everything could be lost.

Today I listened as they threw about outlandish proposals of theft and sabotage. How can we break into the ammunitions depot at the Château du Clos de Vougeot? How feasible is it to steal a shipment from one of the region's smaller train stations? How long can a man hide inside a wine barrel? Stéphane considered each of these ideas with more patience than I would have thought him capable. How difficult is it to create explosives? At this last question, everyone turned to Rose—or, rather, I should call her Simone—and suddenly I understood our role in the circuit. "We're considering several possibilities," Rose said. Stéphane nodded his approval and moved on to the next topic.

I spent the next ten minutes in agony, so terrified I saw black spots floating before my eyes. Create explosives? Of course I had read about it. But where would we find the materials? The equipment? And what if we were caught? The threat of imprisonment in some squalid cell—or, worse, the horror of an impromptu execution—makes me sick with fear. I had just resolved to tell Rose and Stéphane that I could not continue with the group when the meeting came to an end. Unlike last week when the group dispersed without even a farewell, today Stéphane beckoned all of us closer. "*Venez nous rejoindre*," he said—"come join us"—and noticing that I hung behind, his hand closed upon my own, his grip gentler and more reassuring than I would have suspected. Bowing his head, he began to sing "La Marseillaise," and the rest of us joined in, not a rousing chorus, but a whispered, defiant refrain. "*Allons enfants de la Patrie, le jour de gloire est arrivé!*" It had been over two and a half years since I last sang those words. Glancing at the other faces in the group, I saw that I was not the only one moved to tears. And suddenly I knew—as sure as the laws of chemistry—that remaining passive is no longer prudence. It has become cowardice.

2 MARS 1942

Rose sent me to talk to Madame Grenoble—"She's always liked you," she said, though I'm not sure that's true—so this afternoon I cycled to our former high school. I found Madame G. in her classroom grading exam papers. She seemed surprised to see me, greeting me with a distracted smile and hovering above her desk as I lurched through the pleasantries and into my request. I wanted to keep abreast of my studies, I told her. I was hoping to use the school laboratory for special sessions, as I had done two years ago when I was preparing for the *baccalauréat*.

"You always were my most diligent student," she said with a smile. "It's such a shame that your studies had to be interrupted by this . . . situation." She brushed an invisible speck of dust from her sleeve, her hand smooth and white, the nails painted pale pink. "Yes, I do think something could be arranged."

"Oh, Madame, thank you!" A smile stretched across my face, even as I strove to keep an appropriate level of excitement in my voice. "I can't tell you what this means to me. I've been feeling so despondent these past few months. "

But she waved away my thanks. "What course of study are you planning to follow?"

"Well, Rose still has her textbooks from Sèvres and we thought we would use the same syllabus."

"We? Rose?"

"You remember Rose Reinach, *n'est-ce pas*? My rival?" I said, only half joking.

"*Bien sûr.* I remember her very well." Madame's eyes were suddenly veiled, her smile thin. Or was I imagining things?

"We meet sometimes to go over our books. She's as eager as I am to continue working."

"Didn't Mademoiselle Reinach get expelled from Sèvres for moral turpitude?"

I flinched and hoped she hadn't noticed. "That's an unfair rumor," I said.

She hesitated, the muscles moving delicately in her throat. "You know, technically I can only allow students access to the laboratory—not even other faculty members are permitted."

I sensed the window of opportunity closing, and moved quickly to stop it. "*S'il vous plaît*, Madame," I pleaded. "We are only asking for a spare hour here or there, and we won't waste your time, or any supplies. We simply hope to deepen our knowledge of science." I spoke in my most earnest schoolgirl tones.

"Well . . ." Her face softened. "Let me think about it."

Rose was waiting for me in the churchyard, three streets away. "We're in," I told her.

Chapter 11

A trio of poached eggs quivered on the plate before me, nestled atop a puddle of meurette sauce, rich with wine, laced with bacon. With the tines of my fork, I pierced a yolk, and used a spoon to scoop up a luxurious bite.

"How is it?" Walker was watching me from across the table.

"Oh my God." I closed my eyes to finish chewing. "How're the escargots?"

"The snails are kind of rubbery but the parsley-garlic butter is amazing." He dabbed a morsel of baguette into one of the hollows dotting his dish.

Walker had called three days ago—not an email, not a text, but an actual phone call; I'd almost fallen out of my chair—to invite me out to dinner.

"Oh, is your wine group meeting up?" I had asked a little warily. I still hadn't managed to join one of their tastings, and was beginning to suspect they didn't exist.

"No, no. I've been hearing good things about this restaurant—Chez Pépé? I'd like to try it. With you," he added, without a shred of irony in his voice. When we agreed on Thursday night, he said: "It's a date!"

I froze, unsure of my response. Was it a date? Did I want it to be? I had no idea, so I settled for a cheerful "See you then!"

Chez Pépé's walls were lined with wine racks, the room lit with spotlights that cast a soft bright glow. The crowd was about half local, half tourist—the latter were inescapable in Beaune, any time of year—and our waiter, with his scraggly moustache and sleeve of tattoos, would not have been out of place in a Brooklyn beer garden. He had taken one look and addressed us in English, an assumption that had annoyed me—albeit unjustifiably—though Walker had happily complied. The two of them spent an inordinate amount of time discussing the wine list—even given our profession, even given our location in the heart of Burgundy—engaging in the type of oenophiliac one-upsmanship that made my eyes glaze over.

"So"—I speared a butter-crisped crouton with my fork and swirled it around the yolk-enriched sauce—

"what've you been up to lately?" In fact, I'd been wondering for some weeks what exactly Walker did with his time.

He blinked. "Did I tell you I've been working with Louise?"

I assumed this was a rhetorical question—he had not told me and we both knew it—but still I shook my head.

"I've been giving her a hand with the bookshop. Just sorting and shelving, that sort of thing."

"Oh, wow!" I said politely.

"I needed some extra cash." He shrugged. "She's got an awesome collection of antiquarian wine books. She spends a lot of time at estate sales and secondhand stores hunting them down. That's why she was so eager to buy all that stuff at the charity shop. Remember that afternoon we saw you and Heather?"

My mouth was full of poached egg, so I nodded.

"Actually, it's something I've been meaning to bring up for a while." He broke a baguette slice in half. "I know Louise still feels weird about it, but honestly, her intentions were innocent. She only thought those boxes might have some stuff for her shop, that's all."

There was something disingenuous about his explanation, but he spoke so naturally—with a faint twist of his lips, slightly embarrassed—that I decided not to pursue it. "I think Heather and I were a little surprised, that's all," I said. Our waiter removed our empty plates, returning a minute later with the main courses—*steak-frites* for Walker, and *salade aux gésiers* for me, the lettuce leaves topped with sautéed chicken gizzards. "But it's not a big deal."

"Okay, cool." He took a deep breath and exhaled. We both picked up our cutlery. "As long as we're being honest"—he paused to slice into his meat—"what's the deal with you and Jean-Luc?"

My fork scratched across the plate. "What do you mean?"

"Every time I see you two together, he's got a scowl on his face. Do you guys have some sort of history?"

"Not really."

He shot me a look of disbelief.

"Well, sort of," I amended. "We knew each other in college and there was . . . something. But that was a long time ago."

"Louise is convinced he's in love with you. It's breaking her heart." He clocked my skepticism, and shrugged. "Whatever you may think of her, she really does love him."

"I'm certain Louise's heart will be fine," I said. It came out sounding harsher than I'd intended, so I added: "What I mean is that I'm sure Jean-Luc cares a lot about her, too." With a slash of my knife, I sliced through a beautifully seared chicken gizzard. "Is it weird to be talking about hearts and eating them at the same time?"

Perhaps he recognized my joke for what it was—a feeble attempt to change the subject—for he smiled and speared a french fry. For several minutes we ate without speaking, listening to the rise and fall of voices at the other tables.

"What about you?" Walker said suddenly, staring at a fixed spot on the table. "What about your . . . gizzards?"

"Oh, they're delicious—" I began to say, when he covered my hand with his own.

"Kate," he said. "I like you. You have a weird proclivity for offal, but I still like you." He reached across the table and brushed something from my chin. "A crumb."

"*Fromage? Dessert?*" Our waiter dumped a heavy chalkboard menu onto the side of our table.

Walker squinted at the board. "Do you want to do cheese, then dessert? Let's do that," he declared, without waiting for me to respond. "*Époisses et crème brûlée?*" The waiter scribbled our order on a notepad and hurried away.

I gulped some wine without tasting it. Walker *liked*

me? What did that even mean? I gazed discreetly at his hands—strong fingers, the backs threaded with dark hairs—and tried to imagine them touching me. The thought was not unpleasant. Then again, it had been a long time since I'd been touched by anyone. Without warning, an image of long fingers flashed before my eyes, Jean-Luc's hand entwined with my own, his tawny eyes darkening as he leaned toward me . . . *No, no, no.* I forced myself back to the present. "I hope you're going to share that crème brûlée," I said, giving him a sidelong glance.

At the end of dinner, Walker rebuffed my credit card. On the street, our hands brushed together until our fingers entwined, his palm hot and dry against my own, my wrist twisting at an uncomfortable angle. Would it seem aloof if I pulled away? Before I could decide what to do, our steps slowed in the shadows of the Hospices de Beaune, and then we were kissing. It was a soft kiss, sweet, but even as his hands touched the nape of my neck, I was too conscious of the situation, my mind skittering from thought to thought: *Am I getting lipstick on his face? Can he feel the mole through the back of my sweater? Is that unappealing? My neck kind of hurts.*

"Kate," he sighed, when we drew apart. "I just can't get enough of you."

I settled for a noncommittal "Mmm."

"Do you want to go somewhere?" he murmured near my ear.

I leaned into his chest, breathing in his scent, which was dark and spicy, and unfamiliar. An image of Jean-Luc and Louise rose unbidden, the two of them laughing over some private joke. I shoved it away. "Sure." I was just tipsy enough—and uninhibited enough—to agree.

He looked uncertain. "I'm still staying in Jean-Luc's guesthouse. But he's probably asleep by now."

Though I suspected he was right, I shook my head. "No." It came out more forcefully than I'd intended.

If he noticed any vehemence on my part, he didn't remark upon it. "Okay, well, how about your place?"

I spoke without thinking. "Only if we use the back staircase."

"Let's use the back staircase." His lips brushed my neck, and a shiver crept down my spine. "We'll tiptoe up in our socks, like nineteenth-century servants. It'll be just like a costume drama." His grin went crooked and when I laughed, he bent and kissed me again.

Back at the domaine, the downstairs windows were filled with light and I saw Heather moving around the kitchen. Walker parked at the far end of the driveway and we crept across the gravel, moving slowly to muffle the sound of our steps, edging closer to the side door just a few feet away. Suddenly lights blazed down upon us. I'd forgotten about Heather's security spotlights, set off by the motion detector. Before I could dart into a shadow, the back door flew open.

"*C'est qui?*" she demanded. "Who's there?" She caught sight of me and Walker in the glare. "Ohh!" Her voice arched. "Hey, guys! How was dinner?"

"Good, good," I mumbled.

"Looks like it! Hello, Walker!"

"Hey," he said, ducking his head. "What's up?" His face had turned bright red.

"Such a chilly evening! Cozy!" She wrapped her arms around herself and grinned.

"*Chérie*, is everything okay?" Nico appeared behind her, then caught sight of us. "*Bonsoir, vous deux.*" He gave us a polite nod and shot Heather a look of mock disapproval. "Come on, *chérie*. Stop embarrassing them."

"Don't do anything I wouldn't do!" Heather called.

"*Bonne nuit!*" said Nico, firmly. And with a little wave, he closed the door.

I raised my hands and covered my cheeks, which were aflame. Beside me, Walker had begun to laugh. "This is like being in high school, but with the world's nosiest and most permissive parents."

Somehow we made it to the third floor without further commotion. Walker waited in my room while I went to the bathroom and when I returned he was standing by the desk, wearing a thoughtful expression. Through his eyes, I saw afresh my barren quarters—the narrow bed with its thin blanket, the bentwood coatrack holding my clothes, the scuffed desk with my laptop, wine books, and notebooks scattered across the surface. I closed the door behind me, threading the hook through its latch.

"It's a little Spartan," I admitted.

"A *little*? This is like a nunnery."

"You get used to it after a while."

"Come here, Sister Kate." He drew me close with a wicked grin. "Let's ratchet up some sins."

I wasn't quite sure what I'd been expecting, but in the end, it was all a little more awkward than I had anticipated. The vintage bed squeaked mercilessly—I had known it, but forgotten—so we ended up on the floor, which was harder and colder than I would have guessed, and in need of a good sweeping. Walker was attentive, but there was a dust bunny near the left side of my head and I kept worrying that it would drift toward us and get tangled in my hair. Still, our encounter was pleasant, if not particularly passionate and, as we put our clothes back on—the hardwood floor impeded cuddling—I felt good, attractive, and confident. That was nice, I thought. Nice. But bloodless.

Unaware of my thoughts, Walker's head emerged through the neck hole of his sweater, his hair ruffled. He caught my eye and at his self-conscious smile, I felt an unexpected pinch of sympathy. As it turned out, Walker was a good guy. It was too bad we had almost no chemistry.

For a few minutes we sat side by side, very still on the edge of the bed. I considered how I could extricate myself gracefully from the situation. More than anything in the world, I wanted to put on my pajamas, drink three glasses of cold water, and go to sleep without worrying about waking him up in the middle of the night when I went to the bathroom. In the end, he spoke first. "Hey, did you ever look at those MW practice exams I sent you?"

"I did!" I said, a little too brightly. "I've been working on the essay questions, but some of them are pretty tough. I keep meaning to ask Jennifer to take a look."

"I could read them," he offered. "If you want."

"Really? Would you?" It had been so long since I'd had a peer review my practice essays that I jumped at the offer.

"Of course," he said.

I shifted my weight and the bedsprings emitted a bloodcurdling shriek. "Um, I would invite you to stay over, but I'm afraid this bed would massacre us in the dark."

"Oh." Did a flicker of disappointment cross his face? He reached out a hand, smoothing the tiny strands at my hairline. The bedsprings protested with a shrill squeal. "Jesus, I think you might be right."

From the depths of the house, a small voice called: "Mama! *Mama! What's that noise?*"

"That might be my cue to go." Walker rose and the bed released a screech of fury.

"*Mamaaaaaaa!*" Thibault cried.

Walker grimaced, slipped his jacket on over his sweater, and picked up his messenger bag. He hovered by the desk. "I can take the essays now if you want me to look at them. The bookshop's closed tomorrow so I have some free time."

Was he looking for an excuse to see me again? I felt it again, that little squeeze of sympathy. "Well, if you're sure it's not too much trouble. They're in the green notebook on my desk," I said, and he slid it into his bag.

I sat motionless on the bed as he drew close and kissed me a final time, a soft brush of the lips. "I'll text you tomorrow, okay?" he said. And then he was gone, closing the door softly behind him. As carefully as I could, I collapsed onto my pillows and exhaled.

"Well, well, well! Look who we have here!" Heather caught sight of me at the kitchen table and beamed.

"G'morning." I mumbled into my coffee cup.

"Is it? A good morning?" She began to fill the kettle at the tap. "Wait." Her head snapped around. "He's not still *here*—is he?"

"No! Are you crazy? He left last night."

"Phew." She exhaled. "I mean, it's not a problem if he stays over—we can tell the kids he stopped by for breakfast, or whatever."

"Actually," I gulped some coffee. "I don't think we'll need to worry about it."

She raised an eyebrow and straightened a spoon and fork on the counter, until eventually I fell prey to her silence.

"No chemistry," I explained.

"Yikes." She winced. "Was it bad?"

"No. It was, uh, nice. But it was like . . . married people sex. No offense."

"Hey, don't underestimate married people sex," she said with a little twitch of her lips. "But," her voice rose over the kettle's whistle, "if you ask me, Walker looked pretty devoted last night."

I stared at the bottom of my mug. "I think maybe he felt weird, too—and we can just pretend none of this ever happened."

But several minutes later, when I ran up to my room to retrieve a hair tie and my phone, which I'd left charging, I found three texts from Walker.

The first one said: *Hey.*

The second was an emoji of a hand—a wave, or a high five?

The third said: *Hope it's not completely uncool to text you so early! Thanks for last night. I'm going to Paris for a few days, but let's hang out when I'm back.* 🎉 🍸 😎

I gazed at his texts with mild consternation. Had I misjudged his feelings? I smoothed a finger across the screen and considered my response. Then again, maybe responding too quickly would give the impression that I felt similarly keen. I slipped the phone into my back pocket and began to prepare for the day's work, gathering a flashlight, a couple of pens, my notebook.

But my notebook wasn't in its usual spot, on the top corner of my desk. I searched through the stack, and then below the chair and bed, all around the floor, even as a sick feeling crept into the pit of my stomach. Had Walker taken it? I thought back to his hasty departure the night before. I had told him to take the green notebook—but there, in the middle of the desk, sat the green notebook. He must have taken the red one, the one where I kept the cellar list. Which begged a single question: Had he done it on purpose?

I snatched my phone out of my back pocket and tapped out a message, my hands shaking so that it took much longer than it should have: *Hi! Good to see you, too! Thanks again for a great evening. Did you by any chance take the red notebook instead of the green?*

My hand hovered over the keyboard, but in the end I decided to skip the emojis for some good old-fashioned punctuation: *? ? ?*

I sent the text and it instantly marked itself "delivered." A few seconds later, three little dots appeared in a bubble. Walker was typing a response. And then they vanished.

Silence.

For the rest of the day, a tight band of stress squeezed the side of my head and neck, twisting into a sickening ache. I kept hoping Walker would return my text but my phone remained blank—and when I finally tried to call him, the number went directly to voice mail. How could I have been so stupid? I was embarrassed to tell Heather and Nico what I'd done, and so I avoided them, working through lunch and waiting until they had left to pick up the kids from school before stepping outside for a walk.

I'm going to Paris for a few days, Walker had written in his text. But he hadn't mentioned it last night. Had he been planning the trip all along? Or was this an unexpected visit based on the contents of my notebook? Had he seduced me so that he could steal it? Did he somehow know about the *cave*? As I sped toward the village, I examined every aspect of the situation in minute detail, until I felt hollow with despair.

In Meursault, I circled the central square and continued up the rue de Cîteaux, a pretty little street lined with vigneron cottages. I was so absorbed in my thoughts that the cemetery appeared out of nowhere, the headstones tucked beyond a low stone wall, and I was jolted from my thoughts. Why hadn't it occurred to me before: If Hélène was buried anywhere, surely it must be here.

The memories swooped upon me as soon as I stepped amid the gravestones. I had been here once before, long ago—the day Jean-Luc buried his father. My head turned involuntarily in the direction of his father's plot, and I gave a start as a tall figure rose from a bench and waved. It was Jean-Luc.

"*Ça va, Kat?*" he said, walking over to greet me.

Both of us performed a sort of awkward jig, so that we managed not to embrace.

"I'm sorry," I apologized. "I didn't mean to disturb you here."

"It's okay. I was just getting ready to leave."

"Do you come here a lot?"

He flushed. "It's my father's birthday. I woke up this morning thinking about him. He would have been sixty-seven today." He spoke simply, but his grief was palpable.

"I'm so sorry, Jean-Luc."

"Yes, well. *C'est comme ça, alors.*" He shrugged. "And you? What brings you here today?"

I hesitated. "I'm, um, trying to learn more about my family's genealogy." I gazed out at the rows of headstones. "Though I guess I'm not really sure where to look. This place is bigger than I remembered."

"I think your family is over there." He pointed toward a far corner, shaded by a chestnut tree. "I can show you, if you like."

I followed him across the cemetery, trying not to stare at his long legs striding on the path.

"Here it is." Jean-Luc indicated a modest mausoleum in grey stone. The plaque on the front read "CHARPIN" and the pointed roof was capped with a prominent cross.

"We have a mausoleum?"

He shrugged. "Your family has been here a long time."

The structure's sides were covered with rows of plaques commemorating Charpins from two centuries past, dating all the way back to Jean-Pierre Auguste, who died in 1865.

"Are you looking for someone in particular?" Jean-Luc asked.

"My great-grandparents. Well, not my great-grandfather, Edouard. He died in a work camp during the war and the family never recovered his remains. But I thought maybe my great-grandmother . . ."

Jean-Luc touched a plaque. "Here? Marie-Hélène? Beloved wife of Edouard. Born in 1903, died in 1926."

I swallowed a gasp. "What about . . . do you see anyone named . . . Virginie? Or, Hélène? Or my grandfather? Benoît?"

"Hmm. *Non*." He stepped back from the crypt and began examining the surrounding markers.

My thoughts were churning so fast I felt dizzy. Where was Virginie? Where was Grandpère Benoît? I knew my great-grandmother had died after the war, and I remembered my grandfather's passing when I was twelve. But why were some members of my family here, and not others? None of it made any sense.

"Hey!" Jean-Luc called from beside the chestnut tree, waving at me.

When I reached him he pointed me to a bench with a simple silhouette, its dark blue paint cracked and flaking. On the back, a memorial plate bore the inscription:

Hélène Marie Charpin
12 Septembre 1921–4 Novembre 1944

"Was this what you were looking for?" Jean-Luc asked.

I drew a shaky breath, blinking away tears that had gathered with surprising force. "I guess it was." It had seemed impossible that she had survived, but now the certainty was like a punch in the gut.

"Poor girl. She died just a few months after the Liberation." He touched the dates with his index finger. "Was she a relation?"

I nodded. "My great-aunt. She was . . ." I considered the best explanation. *She was a collaborator. She was a shorn woman. She was a disgrace.* But the words stuck in my throat, and I found myself mute. Instead, I allowed the sentence to dangle in midair, as awkward as a broken bough on a Christmas tree.

Beside me, Jean-Luc's expression had darkened. "What?"

I winced at the flatness of his tone. But before I could form a response, he continued: "You know, I was just being polite. Expressing interest. That's what friends do, *n'est-ce pas?*"

My cheeks were growing hot. "I wasn't trying to imply that you were prying. But this is complicated," I said, more sharply than I intended.

"Why did you come back here, Kat?" he challenged me, and I knew from his tone that he didn't mean the cemetery—he meant Meursault. Burgundy. France. "Did you ever stop to consider what happened after you left? You just disappeared." He snapped his fingers. "Without a single concern for anyone left behind, least of all me."

"That's not true," I protested. "Anyway, I'm sure you now see it was the right decision. Look at how well your domaine is doing."

"No." A muscle moved in his cheek. "Now I see that I was an idiot to think that love was enough to make a relationship last. Now I see that it takes compromise. Sacrifice. Commitment. All the things you were unable to give me."

"*Me?*" My voice rose. "What about you? You're more attached to this place than anything or anyone, least of all me. To the *terroir*," I spat the last word.

He shook his head in disgust. "If you still can't understand that, then nothing I say will ever explain it."

I stared furiously at the horizon. The days were growing short, and the sun had already begun its creeping descent. "You know what? Forget it. I need to get home before dark and this is pointless."

He opened his mouth to continue arguing, but watching me button my jacket, his expression softened. "Let me give you a ride home, at least," he said.

"I prefer to walk."

"C'mon, Kat. It's far. You won't make it home before twilight."

"Don't underestimate me," I snapped, turning on one heel and marching briskly away.

About one thing, at least, Jean-Luc was right. By the time I reached Heather and Nico's house, the sky had deepened to cobalt and the first stars glimmered. In the driveway, I saw my friends' parked cars, and squared my shoulders for yet another difficult conversation. My argument with Jean-Luc had temporarily distracted me from the situation with Walker. But now I knew I had to confess my mistake.

Opening the kitchen door, I heard the kids arguing about the best shape of pasta: "Spaghetti!" "No, spaghetti's totally stupid!" "Mo-ommmmmm, she called me stupid!" "Owww!" Their voices faded as they raced to the living room.

Heather's face lit up at the sight of me, and I felt a fresh stab of guilt. "Kate, hey! We haven't seen you all day!"

"Hi!" I busied myself hanging my coat and bag on a hook.

"Kate!" Nico slid into the kitchen on socked feet. "We missed you at lunch!"

I flushed. "Yeah, I got caught up in the *cave* and decided to skip it."

"Ahh!" He brightened. "Find anything good? Les Gouttes d'Or, *peut-être?*"

"Not yet." I bit my lip. "I have something to tell you," I said quietly. "I completely screwed up."

Heather lowered the orange she was holding to the counter. Nico crossed the kitchen and placed a hand on my arm. I took a deep breath and, as quickly and accurately as possible, told them about Walker and the missing notebook. "It's totally my fault," I finished. "I am so sorry this happened." I forced myself to meet their gazes.

"Did he hurt you?" Nico demanded. "Because if he did, I swear, I'll—" He balled his hands into fists.

"No, no, it wasn't like that," I said. "Honestly, I'm still not sure if he took it on purpose."

Heather slid past her husband and put her arms around me. "Like you said, you don't know the full story. It might have been an accident." She patted my back with a gentle rhythm.

"Bruyère is right," said Nico. "Don't speculate until you've talked to Walker again. Do you need the notebook to continue downstairs?"

"Not really." I stepped away from Heather and swiped a finger under each eye. "I've been transcribing the information into a spreadsheet. Like we talked about."

Nico heaved a sigh, visibly relieved. "Then we will worry about Walker when the time comes." Opening the fridge, he produced a bottle of wine. "Here." He reached for a glass and poured me a slug. "This'll make you feel better."

And the funny thing was, after a few sips of chilled chardonnay, I did feel a little better.

"I should start dinner," Heather said, opening a cupboard. "Pasta?" she asked, staring listlessly within.

"I'll help you." I moved toward the sink and began to fill a pot with water.

"We need to tell Kate what we discovered," Nico

said, lifting a sagging bag of trash from the can. "We went to the *mairie* this afternoon and looked up Hélène's documents. Unfortunately, the clerk couldn't find her *acte de décès*. Apparently there was a fire in the '70s, and they lost a lot of records."

Heather chimed in: "So, it might even be possible that she's still alive!"

I shook my head. "No. I was at the village cemetery this afternoon. I saw Hélène's memorial. She died in 1944, soon after the Liberation."

"Ah. Too bad." Heather shrugged.

"Hélène's mother is there, too," I added. "But the weird thing is, none of our other relatives are buried there. Not Virginie, and not Benoît either."

"*C'est vrai*," Nico said. "Grandpère Benoît died when I was twelve and he was buried in Mâcon—next to his mother, Virginie. I still remember the funeral procession. Hours in a hot car, and Maman wouldn't let us roll down the windows."

"Grandpère Benoît . . ." I rubbed my eyes, remembering. I hadn't gone to his funeral. My mother had come back for it alone.

"The other day," Heather said musingly, "you said Benoît never talked about the war, because his childhood was so unhappy. But did he ever mention Hélène?"

Nico shook his head. "Never. Did your mother?" he asked me.

"No."

The three of us fell silent. In the background blared the sugary voices of children's television.

"I suppose"—Nico reached for the bottle of wine and poured a small glass for himself—"we could ask my father."

"Yeah, right." Heather laughed. "Because our last conversation with him went so well."

Nico ran a hand through his hair and frowned at the cellar door. "Actually, I think the time has come to tell the rest of the family about the secret *cave*."

It took me a long time to fall asleep that night and when I did I dreamed of The Test, that old recurring nightmare in which the tasting glasses multiplied every time I started answering a question. "Bordeaux, Right Bank," I scrawled and when I raised my head to swirl and sniff the sample, five more wines had appeared on my desk, then there were ten, fifteen, thirty, sixty. The hands of the clock sped round to the hour as my frantic swirling became swilling, drops of wine scattering across the test papers. On the desk, my cell phone vibrated with a text from Jennifer: *It's Bordeaux, Left Bank!*

Sweat prickled across my palms. Why was my phone out? Had the proctor seen it? Was he going to accuse me of cheating? The phone pulsed with another message; Jennifer again: *Hint: C'est pas Graves!;)* I snatched it off the desk and shoved it into my back pocket, but it hummed with messages, so that I could scarcely concentrate. *Buzz, buzz, buzz!* Would she please just stop? I squeezed my eyes shut. *Jennifer*, I thought. *Stop. STOP!*

BUZZ BUZZ, BUZZZZZZZ!

I awoke, soaked with sweat. The sound of my pounding heart filled my ears, so loud it took me several seconds to realize that some of the noise was actually coming from my cell phone, which was vibrating on the bedside table. I picked it up and pressed the button to illuminate the screen.

Missed call from Walker.

Missed call from Walker.

Text from Walker:

Hey—Sorry, didn't see this til now. I just looked and think I do have the wrong notebook—no MW essays inside. WHA'?! Not sure if it's green or red because . . . did I mention that I'm color-blind? 🙈 I can drop it off as soon as I get back from Paris. More soon!

Color-blind? Was he being honest, or covering his tracks? For a long moment, I stared at his words, the screen burning artificially in the dark room, and then I pressed a button on the phone until it went black and silent. Flipping my pillow over, I smoothed my cheek against the cool cotton. I tried to go back to sleep, but my thoughts kept returning to the events of the day, first Walker's duplicity, and then that confrontation with Jean-Luc. I tossed and turned, and when I closed my eyes, strange bright shapes floated before them. Without even knowing why, I found my face wet with tears.

Cher journal,

Saltpeter. Charcoal. Sulfur. Just three things, but when combined in the proper proportions, they need only a flicker of fire to cause destruction. Rose and I decided to make gunpowder because of her romantic attachment to it. "It's the earliest known chemical explosive!" she said. "The Chinese had it in the ninth century!" But truthfully, it was also the simplest.

We had initial success with a tiny quantity and, looking back, I think that was the problem—it gave us too much confidence. Madame Grenoble had granted us small amounts of various common elements and compounds, among them sulfur and saltpeter (which she insisted on calling by its scientific name, potassium nitrate). And while she never left us completely unattended in the laboratory, there was the odd moment when she stepped away to chat with another teacher or collect papers from the main office. At these opportunities, Rose and I leapt into frantic activity, weighing out precise quantities of sulfur and saltpeter, tapping the powders into glassine envelopes. Later, at the *cabo-tte*, we used my *belle-mère*'s mortar and pestle to grind a lump of charcoal, saving the black dust in a small tin box and weighing it out during our next laboratory session. All told, given the constraints of time and equipment, it took us three weeks to produce a lump of gunpowder the size of a sugar cube. We tested it one afternoon in a clearing behind the *cabotte*: Rose touched a match to the wick, and both of us ran to a safe distance. The sparks shot high enough to make us leap onto our bicycles and pedal like fury—for fear the Boches had seen them, too, and were sending a patrol to investigate.

After this, our problem became not "if" but "how." Specifically, how can we obtain enough sulfur to produce a useful amount of gunpowder? Somehow, Stéphane had gleaned saltpeter from a local *charcutier*, a disgruntled man who has little use for his supply now that there's scarcely any meat left to cure. Our success rested in finding the sulfur.

"We could try stealing the key to the supply cabinet," I said one day as we were walking toward the *lycée*.

"Impossible," Rose moaned. "She never lets it out of her clutches."

It's true. Madame G. holds on to that key like a warden at Fresnes, the prison where the leaders of the *Résistance* are locked up to rot.

"Anyway," Rose said, "have you noticed how she has to record every single thing she removes from the cupboard? Down to a tenth of a gram? If we steal anything, she'll get in trouble. It's hopeless."

"It's not," I insisted through clenched teeth. But we couldn't find a way around it.

Though Stéphane was initially pleased with our progress, in the past few weeks, he has grown more impatient. A number of problems have beset our circuit—a series of cloudy nights that we hoped would be clear, a set of forged papers gone missing, and, most distressing of all, Bernard's arrest. Yes, Bernard, my black marketeer. He was last seen two weeks ago, led from his mother's apartment in handcuffs. Ever since, we have been on a knife edge for fear that the Gestapo would torture him into informing on us. So far, nothing has happened, *Dieu merci*. But our group has turned jittery. Irritable. All of us, but especially Stéphane, who has hatched an elaborate plan to help Bernard escape from the local prison—one that centers on a gunpowder bomb.

"Just steal the sulfur," Stéphane commanded us. "We need to act before he's sent to Drancy, or worse—Poland." Everyone shuddered. Poland means work camps. Poland means death.

And yet, what about Madame G.? Every time she left the laboratory, I checked the door of the supply cabinet to see if she had left it unlocked. Always, the answer was no—she was meticulous with the key.

Yesterday afternoon we arrived for our regular laboratory session, but as soon as we entered the room, I knew something was wrong. Madame G. was behind her desk, staring intently at a piece of paper, barely glancing up when we walked in. Rose and I began arranging our equipment; we had decided to experiment with hydrolysis of salts.

"*Mince!*" Rose swore. "We need ammonium for one of the weak bases." She glanced uncertainly at Madame G.

"I'll ask." I slid off my stool and moved toward our professor. But so absorbed was she that even when I was a meter behind her, she didn't notice me. My eyes slid to the sheet before her, a letter of some sort.

We, the undersigned teachers of history, literature, and science who believe it our duty to instill in

our students a love of freedom and tolerance, hereby
state that we consider it unworthy of our mission to
take our students to the film Le Juif Süss . . .

Before I could read further, she thrust a notebook over the paper, her head whipping around to
fix me with a glare.

"Uh, *excusez-moi*, Madame. We were hoping
for some ammonium from the supply cabinet?"

"*J'arrive*," she said in an irritable tone and I
sidled back to my seat.

A couple of minutes later, Madame rose and I
joined her at the cabinet, waiting at a respectful
distance as she unlocked the doors. She had just
placed the bottle in my outstretched hand when
Madame Bernard, our former literature professor, popped her head through the door. "Eugénie,
did you have a chance to read the petition—" She
caught sight of me standing next to the cupboard.
"*Pardon, je m'excuse*," she apologized. "I thought
you were alone. I'll come back later."

"*Non, non, c'est bon*," Madame G. snatched the
paper off her desk and hurried after her colleague.
"Let's talk in your classroom." I heard their voices
hissing down the hall.

"It's a letter of protest," I told Rose quietly. "Refusing to take their students to see that horrible anti-Semitic propaganda film." But she was stabbing the air with her index finger.

"The cabinet," she said urgently. "*She left it unlocked.*"

For a second I couldn't move. Then I forced my limbs into action, easing open the door, searching frantically among the shelves in search of the bottle marked "*sulfate.*" Where was it? Finally, near the top, I spotted a jar half-filled with a chalky powder the jaundiced color of egg yolks. I snatched it up, but before I could return to my desk and slip the bottle in my bag, I heard Madame G. in the hallway. "*Merci!*" she called. The slam of a door. The click of her heels returning to the laboratory.

"*Vite!*" Rose hissed, her eyes enormous. The sound of Madame G.'s footsteps grew louder. Rose raised her arms. Without thinking, I tossed the jar, an underhanded lob that arched up, up, up over the Bunsen burners before falling down, down, down—so poorly aimed, Rose was forced to lunge for it. She held it triumphantly aloft, whisking it behind her back just before Madame G. swished through the door. My legs were shaking so that I could hardly stand, but I managed to cross my arms and slouch against the wall in an attempt at nonchalance.

"Is something going on here that I should be aware of?" Madame G.'s voice cut through the air.

"*Non*, Madame," we replied in a dutiful chorus.

Her eyes darted toward my hands, which were empty. Before she could look at Rose, I kicked over a stool. "Oh!" I gasped. "Sorry—I'm so horribly dizzy all of a sudden." I staggered forward and Madame G. dashed over and caught me by the arm.

"Sit down for a moment. Do you want some water?" She guided me to a chair.

A few seconds later, Rose was by my side. "Did you eat lunch?" She fanned me with a notebook. "I know, the hunger, it's so terrible—*c'est affreux*. I also get taken with these spells from time to time."

"I'm fine, *ça va*." I closed my eyes and willed my heart to slow. When I opened them, they were both staring at me. "I'm fine," I repeated, as I stood and moved slowly toward our workstation.

For the rest of our time in the laboratory, Rose and I spoke to each other in murmurs as we worked. Madame G. graded exams at her desk, slashing her pen across the pages. Focusing on the experiment calmed me, so that by the time Rose and I had finished and tidied away our equipment for the day, the jaws of terror gripping the nape of my neck had loosened.

Before we left, we paused as usual before Madame G.'s desk to say goodbye. "*Merci*, Madame. *Au revoir.*"

"*Au revoir,*" she replied without looking up from her stack of papers.

We had almost left the room when her next sentence came hurtling toward us like an arrow. "You know, I will get in trouble if anything is missing," she said.

We froze in the doorway, but Rose turned back and I forced myself to follow. Madame G. put her pen down and stared at us. My conscience grabbed me by the throat and squeezed so that I couldn't breathe. Madame Grenoble, who has always been so generous with her time, so willing to offer extra help—how could we endanger her? The silence stretched long and wobbly before I saw Madame's eyes move to the star that Rose now wears sewn to her coat. I remembered the petition I'd seen on her desk and a flash of fury coursed through me.

I arranged my features into an earnest expression. "Of course we wouldn't take anything," I said sweetly. "You know you can trust us."

"*D'accord.*" She nodded slowly, but her face was still clouded.

We forced ourselves to walk slowly out of the classroom, strolling down the hallway as if we hadn't a care in the world. I kept expecting to hear running footsteps or the crack of Madame G.'s voice, to feel the clap of a hand on my shoulder. But we were out the door, then moving across the courtyard, reaching for our bicycles, bidding each other farewell, pedaling away. Rose's satchel was slung across her back, the bottle of sulfur an indistinguishable lump through the thick canvas.

But still, I worry: Did we really get away with it?

22 JUILLET 1942

I am frantic with fear. Where is Rose? I haven't seen her for a week, nor received word. She didn't appear at the laboratory—Madame G. was deeply suspicious when I claimed she was unwell—and then she missed the circuit meeting, where previously she had missed none. The others also have no news of her and we dare not go to her house. Though he tries to hide it from us, I sense Stéphane is concerned, enough to put out discreet inquiries with his contacts at the prison. But surely we would have heard if she had been arrested?

I keep wondering if she was detained for taking the sulfur. Did Madame G. turn her in? But, then, wouldn't I also have been questioned? These thoughts go round and round in my head, tormenting me, so that I can barely keep an even keel. Today I was so distracted I dropped an entire bowl of porridge on the floor. It crashed in a heap of steaming mush and shattered crockery and Madame very nearly tore my head off while the boys sobbed with hunger.

I feel the walls of this war closing in on me, not only fear, starvation, deprivation, but endless uncertainty—and guilt. How long can this go on before I crack?

24 JUILLET 1942

I received word to meet Rose at the usual spot, in the park on the banks of the river Bouzaize. I waited for an hour and no one came. Today, I returned at the same time, waited and waited until someone finally appeared: Stéphane.

"What are you doing?" I asked, as he threw his arms around me.

"Pretend we are lovers," he whispered, and bent his head. His cheek scratched mine and he kissed me, softly at first, growing to an intensity that took me by surprise. When we pulled apart, I clung to him until my legs had stopped trembling.

"*Viens*," he murmured, leading me to the bench and wrapping an arm around me.

"Where is—Simone?" Just in time, I remembered to use Rose's code name. "I've been distraught. I keep asking myself why we stole the sulfur. We should never have taken such a risk." As I braced against his shoulder, my emotions spilled from me—a flood of anxiety combined with the headiness of the unexpected kiss—so that I found myself weeping.

"*Tiens.*" He felt in his pocket and handed me a handkerchief, surprisingly spotless. "Simone and her family are safe."

"Oh, thank God." I could have sobbed with relief, but instead I blew my nose and thus composed myself.

"We got a tip last week and managed to get them into hiding before the Gestapo turned up." He stared straight ahead. "But you are right. It was the sulfur that raised suspicions. Your *professeur*—did you know she is involved with a German officer?"

"Madame Grenoble?" I gasped. "But what about her husband?"

"War breeds strange indiscretions." He

shrugged, matter of fact. "*Écoute*, Marie, listen. Simone and her family are safe for the moment, but we've got to get them out as soon as possible. You know about the Vel' d'Hiv roundup a week ago?"

"But that was in Paris." The BBC had reported on the thousands of Jews who had been taken in the middle of the night—not only men, as before, but also women and children—shuttled by bus to the Vélodrome d'Hiver, an indoor racing track in Paris. They were held for days in squalid conditions before being transported to internment camps. Papa and I had listened in horror, though very few details were available.

"They're coming here. The roundups. Not only for men, now everyone—entire families." Stéphane's arm tightened across my shoulders. "We have a source who says they will start in a few days. Simone and her parents, her brother—their names are on the list, and this accusation from your professor makes their situation even more precarious. We're trying to assemble forged papers for them to escape south."

I twisted the handkerchief around my fingers until the tips turned white. "South?"

"Simone's father has family in the United States. If they can reach Portugal, they'll have the chance of passage to New York. Frankly, they should have left months ago—years ago. But right now they need another safe house, a place where they can wait indefinitely until their documents are ready."

"You mean the domaine," I said slowly.

"Your father made it clear that he needed to stop his activities for a while. But these circumstances seem extenuating."

"Of course they must stay with us," I said with as much confidence as I could muster, even as my stepmother's hard face flashed before my eyes. "Don't worry, I'll see to it." I gazed at the river, studying the algae blooming in great green clouds beneath the surface of the water, remembering the afternoon Rose and I had first sat here plotting and planning. Could it have been only a year ago? It seems like five lifetimes have passed.

"*Merci, ma chère* Marie, always so thoughtful of everyone else." His arm around my shoulders relaxed, but he didn't pull away.

"You know, you could have just asked my father," I said. "He would have said yes. You didn't have to take the risk of meeting me here."

"I wanted to see you. I know you've been desperate with worry."

"Who told you that?" I frowned. I've only

shared my concerns here, *cher journal*, not with anyone else, not even Papa.

"I didn't need anyone to tell me. It's been eating me alive, and I guessed you would feel the same." He rested his cheek on my head and this time it didn't feel like playacting. For a fleeting moment, I closed my eyes and pretended that we were the young lovers we appeared to be—that this was an ordinary summer day, and I was an ordinary girl with lips tingling from her first kiss. But it was too dangerous to linger, so I pulled away before such frivolity brought us to peril.

29 JUILLET 1942

They are here, all four of them. In the end, it was easier than I had anticipated because Papa and I agreed that we simply would not tell Madame about Rose and her family hiding in the basement. Yes, God forgive us, we will deceive her until our noses fall off, if it means safe passage for the Reinachs.

On Sunday morning, I told Madame I was feverish and would stay home from church. Papa, who never goes to Mass anymore, drove out in the donkey cart and returned with the Reinachs covered over in the back with burlap sacks. We snuck them downstairs before Madame and the boys re-

turned for lunch. My "*grippe*" has proved a useful excuse for skipping meals so that I may save
my portion for the four refugees. I slip below with
food, fresh water, linens, and other assorted items
as often as I dare.

Though her parents and brother remain stoic,
I am worried about Rose. She has a bad cough—
which is surely exacerbated by the cold, damp
cellar—and too often I catch her doubled over with
the effort of trying to suppress it. She assures me
her strength is returning, but I fear for the journey
ahead—so many arduous kilometers to Spain, and
then onward still to Portugal, and from there a ship
across the ocean. Even in the best of circumstances,
it seems Herculean, and we are in far from the best
of circumstances.

This morning, when I collected the eggs from
the henhouse I slipped one into my pocket. I plan
to boil it with our dinner, and bring it down to Rose
later tonight. She will say it's too much, but I know
the truth—that it is not enough, and that there will
never be enough.

27 AOÛT 1942

I began this journal as a record of facts, and so I
report them now, even though I can scarcely bear

this documentation. And yet I keep going over the events in my mind, over and over again, examining each terrible moment, wondering what I could have done differently.

Of course we knew our risk was increasing with each day that Rose and her family remained at the domaine. But four sets of forged documents are not easy to obtain—and so the days turned into a week, and then crept into a second and then a third, the Reinachs moving silently about the secret *cave*, emerging for light and air only when Madame and the boys had left the house. By the time we received the papers, the moon had grown full and bright. We decided to wait two more weeks for it to wane, so that Papa could guide them to their next stop under cover of darkness.

After more than a month, Papa decided that the Reinachs *must* be offered baths again. "They absolutely cannot look like refugees while in transit. It would be be a dead giveaway," he said firmly. We waited until the boys had gone to the neighbor's house, and Madame had departed for one of her infernal Cercle du patrimoine meetings (yes, *cher journal*, I, too, cannot believe they still continue—at this point, what heritage does France have left?). Down in the cellar, I invited the Reinachs upstairs to bathe and they gathered a change of clothes before clamoring out of the wardrobe and trooping to our bathroom on the second floor.

Madame Reinach went first, then Rose, Théo— when each was done, they joined the rest of us around the kitchen table. Papa poured wine—"For nourishment," he said—and I began preparing a simple lunch of boiled potatoes, coddled eggs, and a salad of dandelion greens. By the time Monsieur Reinach was finished with his bath, we were all quite cheerful. I had left the back door open so that a light breeze blew through the room, stirring the tablecloth, and setting adrift the scent of ripe peaches from the bowl on the windowsill.

What a stupid idea it was, to leave that door open.

She saw us before we spotted her. Our merry conversation obscured the sound of her footsteps, so that Madame watched us unobserved through the gaping door for several minutes. She stayed still—quiet, listening—and none of us knew she was there until her slender frame filled the doorway. Her shadow fell across the table, and the room turned airless.

"Oh, *chérie*! You're back early. How lovely!" Papa forced a smile to his lips. "Do come join us! Please!"

Madame stepped into the kitchen. There was a peculiar look on her face—one I'd never observed before, in all my years of observing Madame—a fixed fury as hard and cold as marble.

"You remember Rose, *n'est-ce pas?*" said Papa. "She and Hélène were at the *lycée* together. And these are her parents, Monsieur and Madame Reinach, and her brother, Théodore. We were just having some lunch. Léna"—he turned to me— "set a place for your *belle-mère.*"

"Edouard." Madame practically spat Papa's name. "I will talk to you in the *salon.* Now." She stalked from the room, not pausing to see if he was behind her.

"Of course, *chérie. Pardon.*" Papa offered the Reinachs an apologetic smile and followed her to the next room.

It was hard to breathe, all of a sudden. I glanced at the Reinachs and saw their faces blanched to a deathly pallor. "Come, have some more wine," I urged them. "The potatoes are just ready." Quickly, I tossed the salad, removed the potatoes to a bowl, and started coddling eggs. "Let's start before the food gets cold. Papa won't mind." Truthfully, I wanted them to eat a good meal, in case Madame threw them out of the house.

From the sitting room, I could hear their voices, a low murmur of repressed rage.

Madame: "What are these people doing here? Why are they in *my* kitchen? Why are they eating *my* food?"

Papa: "Virginie, where is your mercy? These people are your daughter's friends. You would turn your back on them? How can you call yourself a Christian?"

Madame: "My daughter? She is *not* my daughter. And, yes, these people—how can you allow them in our home? How can you welcome them? Edouard, I know I turned a blind eye once before—but at least those other men weren't *Jewish*." With this last sentence, Madame dropped the pretense of politesse, screaming the words in a crazed frenzy. I turned away from the table so that I didn't have to see the look on the Reinachs' faces.

"They must leave this house," Madame declared at full volume.

"*Chérie*, of course they aren't staying here permanently. We're waiting for the moon to wane. As soon as there's a dim night—"

"They must leave this house," Madame repeated, more quietly. "Or I will go see Michel at the station and tell him to come and remove them.

I hope you haven't forgotten that my nephew is a police officer."

My head grew light and spots swam before my eyes, until I realized that I had forgotten to keep breathing. Madame Reinach, too, looked like she might faint, the color drained from her cheeks, her dark eyes huge and panicked.

"Just give us a few days—it's not safe otherwise. Please, Virginie, just another day or two until the moon is not so bright," Papa pleaded.

"No." Her voice rose, hysterical. "*They will leave tonight!*" There was the pounding of heels up the stairs and the crash of a slammed door, and the conversation was over.

At this point, none of us had any appetite, but I dished up the food and urged the Reinachs to eat. "You don't know when you'll have another hot meal," I told them, and they forced down a few mouthfuls and then went downstairs to prepare their things. As soon as they left the table, I began boiling more potatoes and eggs, before ransacking the cupboards for any scraps of food that I could pack up and send along with them.

Full darkness descended at nine o'clock, but Papa waited until midnight before setting out. I begged him to let me come, too, but he convinced me that they would be safer without me. "You don't know the route, *ma choupinette*," he pointed out. "If we need to run or hide, it will be easier if I don't have to worry about you."

We said goodbye in the cellar so that our voices would not wake my brothers, who were sleeping upstairs. I embraced Monsieur Reinach first, then Madame Reinach—two formal cheek kisses for each of them—a hearty squeeze of the arm for Théo. Finally Rose and I exchanged a hug.

"When this is all over, you'll come to New York," Rose said. "I'm going to finish my degree at an American university, and I expect you to join me."

"Les États-Unis!" I exclaimed. "I'll never be able to speak English well enough."

"Pff, *c'est facile*," Rose scoffed. She affected an American drawl: "'Ow DEW yew DEW?" We giggled a little hysterically.

"We need to go." Papa pulled a dark cap on his head, buttoned a black jacket to his chin. "The patrol changes shifts at midnight and we must take advantage."

We made our way to the kitchen, silent as they adjusted their clothes one last time and heaved packs to their shoulders.

"Don't worry, *ma choupette*," Papa whispered to me. "At this point, I've made the journey a hundred times. *C'est rien.*" He wrapped an arm around me and dropped a quick kiss on the top of my head. "I'll be back by breakfast. Save me a cup of that terrible barley coffee, *d'accord*?"

I forced a smile and nodded.

Papa motioned at me to switch off the kitchen light, then opened the back door and one by one the five of them slipped into the damp night, their feet muffled by the shaggy grass in the garden, so all I heard was the chirp of crickets. Moonlight streamed like a silvery beacon, cascading over the landscape. Even though they tucked themselves in the shadows, I could see their little group walking out into the vineyards until they disappeared over the slope.

I was far too restless to sleep. My hands worried over some knitting—the first few rows of an oiled wool sock—but I dropped so many stitches, I finally unraveled the whole thing and cast on again. Eventually, my nervous energy burned out and I placed my arms on the table and lay my head upon them, closing my eyes. If Papa returned early, I would be here waiting for him.

The boys woke me with shouting, their usual morning squabble about who was to wash first.

A dull ache throbbed in my neck, and my hands prickled as the blood returned to them. Behind the blackout curtains, milky light trickled through the trees in the garden; the living room clock began to chime seven o'clock. Breakfast was in half an hour. Papa would soon be home.

I fetched some logs from the woodpile, stirred the stove's embers to life, filled the kettle, and set a small pot of semolina simmering for the boys. It was a relief to busy myself with these familiar tasks, to distract myself from the thoughts running on an endless loop in my mind. Above, I heard thumps and more shouts, and I ran upstairs to help my brothers get dressed for the day.

"Léna, *j'ai faim!*" cried Albert when he saw me.

"You're always hungry, *cochon!*" Benoît stabbed an index finger into his brother's stomach.

"Boys, stop that right now! I have porridge on the stove—it'll be ready in a few minutes." I glanced at Madame's door, surprised to find it open. She was standing before the mirror pinning up her hair, already clad in a day dress of violet silk, high heels, and, instead of silk stockings, a painted line running down the back of each leg.

"Oh, good, Hélène, there you are. Can you watch the boys this morning? I'd like to breakfast with Edouard." She raised her arms to adjust her hair and I caught a whiff of perfume—Chanel No. 5—floating through the air like an exterminator's cloud.

Madame must be feeling guilty about yesterday, I thought as I wrestled a pair of socks onto Albert's feet. "Of course," I replied.

"*Merci!*" she chirped.

By the time I had dressed the boys, run downstairs, and saved the simmering semolina right before it stuck and burned, brewed a weak pot of barley coffee, and set the table for breakfast, it was eight o'clock. I kept one ear cocked as I scraped out the meager bowls of porridge and watched my brothers eat. Madame drained the coffeepot, and I made another without complaint, placed the dishes to soak, drew on my shoes, and walked my brothers to the neighbor's house to play. All the while, I told myself: "Papa will be home when I get back. Papa will be home when I get back." But when I returned, Madame was in the *salon*, draped elegantly over a velvet *chaise longue*, and Papa was nowhere in sight.

Ten o'clock. Eleven o'clock. No Papa.

At lunch, I forced down a cold potato and took my bicycle to the vineyards. I rode up the same hill that Papa and the Reinachs had walked several hours earlier, but if the vines knew their where-abouts, they kept it secret. I returned home in the late afternoon, bursting through the kitchen door, certain I'd see Papa sitting at the table, crumpling up pages of the newspaper and shoving them into the stove.

At the sound of the door, Madame came running down the stairs. Her face fell when she saw me. "Oh, it's you."

I, too, was disappointed not to find Papa, but for once I managed to keep my voice even. "Sorry." I lowered my head and slid from the room.

"Hélène." She followed me to the hall and gazed up at me on the stairs. "Where is he." It was not a question.

I shook my head and climbed another step.

"Don't tell me you don't know. I know you know everything—you two are thick as thieves, always whispering behind my back!"

"Virginie." I turned toward her. "I'm worried about him, too. If I knew where he was, I would tell you." Despite myself, my voice began to shake.

"But he's always come home before this! He's never not come home. It's because of those people, isn't it? I told you, they should never have come here. He was helping them, and now the worst has happened. I'm left completely alone!" She covered her face and began to sob.

I stared at her, and even sick with worry, I felt filled with disgust for this woman, so myopic she lacked a shred of compassion for anyone else.

Madame lowered her hands, her eyelashes spiky with tears, and looked at me beseechingly. "What are we going to do?"

We? I thought. "The only thing we can do," I said, turning back up the stairs. "Wait."

Two days went by—two fraught, agonizing days in which my heart leapt every time I heard heels crunching on the driveway or the creak of the back door. But Papa did not return. By this time, Madame had taken to her bed, lying on the covers with a damp cloth across her forehead, screaming at me if the boys made any sound above a whisper. By the end of the second day, it was almost a relief when Michel arrived at the domaine.

I opened the door to his knock—the boys were in the garden, and Madame was, of course, in bed— but if he was surprised to see me, he gave no indication. "*Bonsoir,*" he said, stone-faced. "Is my aunt at home?"

"Edouard? Is that you?" Madame ran down the

stairs in slippered feet. Two days of nervous crisis had left her face sallow, though I saw she'd taken the time to comb her hair into a knot and pull a few soft tendrils around her forehead. "Oh, Michel! What a surprise!"

"*Ma tante, bonsoir.*" They exchanged cheek kisses.

"Can I offer you a tisane?" she asked. "A glass of wine? Hélène"—she threw me a sharp glance—"prepare a tray for my nephew."

"*Non, non, c'est bon,*" he declined. "Is there somewhere we can go to speak privately?"

Her eyes widened, but she spoke steadily. "Of course! Come, we'll go into the *salon.*" I heard her opening the curtains and plumping cushions, the rise and fall of their voices.

Why had he come? Did he know something about Papa? I had to hear the words from his lips—I could not depend on Madame to relay the information. Slipping off my wood-soled shoes, I crept to the open door of the *salon* and stood to one side, just out of their line of sight.

"Tatie, I have bad news, I'm afraid," Michel said. "Your husband—"

"Your uncle," Madame demurred.

"Edouard was picked up two nights ago by one

of our patrols. He claimed he was out for an evening stroll, but we believe he was helping a group of Jews cross the Demarcation Line."

Madame gasped. "*C'est pas possible.*"

"Did you have any idea that he might be planning something like this?"

"*Non,*" Madame said immediately.

A long silence while I held my breath and waited for Michel's response.

"Where is he now?" Madame said at last. "At the prison in Beaune? Can I go see him?"

"I'm afraid not." Michel cleared his throat. "As I said, he was picked up with several Jews. They were sent immediately to an internment camp—and Edouard along with them."

"But he's not Jewish! This is a terrible mistake! He must be released immediately."

Michel's shoes scuffed the floor. "The authorities will sort it out, Tatie. But even when they discover he's in the wrong place . . . well, there are other places to send him. He won't be returning home."

Madame burst into noisy tears, as my heart began thudding again in my chest.

"But how will we survive without him? We can't survive!" Madame moaned.

I didn't hear Michel's response, and anyway I

was desperate to be alone. In my socked feet, I crept up the stairs to my room, where I sat at the desk and watched the light fade from the afternoon sky. Papa was gone. Rose was gone. Théodore, Madame and Monsieur Reinach, all of them as good as dead.

Eventually, I heard footsteps in the foyer, and a few minutes later I watched Michel ride away on his bicycle. My head dropped to my arms and I wondered if I'd ever see my father again. Tears came streaming down my face, choking me with their strength, until every part of my face ached—my eyes, my teeth, my jaw.

I was so caught up in this torrent of emotion that I didn't notice Madame until she spoke from the door of my room. "I gather you overheard my conversation," she said. In her hand were my clogs, which I'd left in the hallway.

I nodded and tried to swallow my sobs. "Papa . . . *Papa.* I'm so afraid, Virginie, I'm so desperately afraid."

Her face was white, tight-lipped, her eyes burning lumps of fury. "I suppose you should have thought of that before you let those people into our house," she said acidly.

I stared at her blankly, unable to process her words. "Those people? *I* let them in?"

"*You* brought them to our home! *You* put us all in danger! And now look what has happened to my home and my husband. Are you happy with yourself, Hélène? *Are you happy?*" She was screaming at the top of her voice. "Because this is all your fault. *This is entirely your fault!*" And before I could shield myself, she threw the shoes at my face, one after the other, striking first my forehead, and then my nose, leaving a stream of blood to mingle with my tears.

Three days have passed, *cher journal.* The first three days of the rest of my life. I've managed to continue because of the boys. My little brothers still demand to be fed; they show their fear by fighting with each other and shoving me away when I try to intervene, even as they creep to my bed in the middle of the night. This entire time, I have not seen Madame emerge once from her room, though late at night I hear her sobbing. I am not sure if she is crying because she misses my father—or his protection.

23 SEPTEMBRE 1942

Last night I snuck down to Papa's office and twisted the radio dial until I found the BBC. I listened carefully to the news, and then sat through every one of the personal messages even though they were gibberish to me. *Jean has a long moustache. Yvette likes big carrots. Paul has some good tobacco.* Even though I know it's impossible, I couldn't help but wonder if one of those messages was for Papa. Was there was some way he was listening, plotting an escape?

Eventually sorrow took hold of me. I switched off the radio and came upstairs to bed, hoping to find the sleep that has eluded me for so many weeks. The moon was full and bright in the sky, and I left my blackout curtains open a crack so that I could take comfort in its steady presence. Eventually I drifted off, waking several hours later to a low rumble. Thunder? No, it was a steady drone, the buzz of an engine. By the time I peeped out the window, the aircraft was far in the distance—and a thousand leaflets were fluttering from the sky.

What was it? I had to know. Heedless of the curfew that pens us in our homes from dusk to dawn, I slipped through the house, to the back door, and out into the vineyards. The rocky soil tore at the bare soles of my feet, but I scarcely felt a thing as I ran to the nearest paper, snatching it from the ground.

It was a poem called "Liberté." No, not just a

poem—an ode. To freedom. To strength. To hope. I didn't so much read the words as absorb them, returning to whisper them aloud again and again until they began to imprint themselves on my heart.

Is it a sign? A reminder—an instruction—a prayer? Reading the poem over and over, I hear Papa's voice reciting the lines, my papa who has refused to allow his moral strength to falter.

Papa, are you out there?

Chapter 12

Three o'clock in the afternoon in France is the hour for tea and biscuits. Today, the tea was lapsang souchong, dark amber with smoky depths. The biscuits, buttery discs with pale gold centers and crisp bronze edges, broke with a delicate crumb. Not even this toothsome pairing, however, could tempt the small group gathered in Heather and Nico's living room. The Charpins sat on the edge of their chairs, spines stiff, feet crossed at the ankles, not a morsel passing their lips.

From my spot next to the fireplace, I watched Heather and Nico circling futilely with laden trays. On the couch sat my aunt Jeanne, fresh from the *coiffeuse*, hair fluffed to an apricot pouf, and Uncle Philippe, grey and stern-faced, arms crossed. Chloé perched on the arm of the sofa like a sleek, dark bird. Her husband,

Paul, sat on a nearby chair, swiping at the screen of his smartphone with thinly veiled impatience.

Only my mother had been unable to come at such short notice. Her response to my email had been typically swift and succinct: "Sorry, Katherine, I'm swamped. P.S. I advise you to steer clear of family politics." I had spent a few extra minutes puzzling over her message, wondering why she was warning me about family politics when I hadn't mentioned them at all.

At last Nico strode toward the fireplace. "Thanks for coming today, everyone," he said in French. "I know you're probably curious about why I asked you here, so I won't go around the pot." He drew a deep breath. "A few weeks ago, Kate and Bruyère began to clear out *la cave*—the cellar beneath the house." I glanced at Uncle Philippe, whose face remained stony. "After several weeks of work, they discovered something astonishing. In a corner of the *cave*, there is an old armoire, and at its back a secret panel." He went on describing the hidden cellar, "an Aladdin's cave," and the trove of wines within—"some of the greatest *millésimes* of the twentieth century."

Chloé gasped. "How long has the wine been down there?" she asked.

Nico hesitated. "Several decades. We can't be sure of the exact date, but since the 1940s, perhaps?"

"You think it was hidden during World War II?"

Again, a brief hesitation. "*C'est possible*," Nico said.

Chloé's forehead folded into an adorable gamine pucker. "*Mais c'est incroyable!* We've been sitting on this treasure for over seventy years, with absolutely no idea. How is it possible?"

"It must have been during the war," said Aunt Jeanne. "There are so many legends from that period. I was just reading an article about a Renoir that was found hidden in an attic in the Dordogne."

"Well, *obviously* it's from the war," huffed Paul. "The question is—*who* hid it?"

"Grandpère Benoît?" suggested Chloé.

"But he was just a small boy back then," said Paul. "It must have been your great-grandparents who hid the wine."

Chloé considered this idea. "Our great-grandfather died in a work camp," she said. "So it would have been before 1942."

"Actually"—Heather cleared her throat—"we were wondering if it could have been—"

"*Enough!*" exploded Uncle Philippe. "You are all gossiping like a bunch of old hags. Have you no respect for your great-grandparents' memory? Have you no regard for the integrity of this house?" He glowered at us before rising from the sofa and striding in front of the fireplace so that Nico was forced to move beside him. "Listen. Obviously this is an interesting discovery. I'm sure some of you are relishing this small spark of excitement. But as the *patron* of this domaine, it's my duty to safeguard its legacy—and that means proceeding with caution. I wish I had been told immediately about this alleged *cave secrète*." He shot Nico a dark look. "But since I was not, I must insist that we end this discussion until I can familiarize myself with the details. We will organize a meeting at a future date. *Merci*." He uttered the last word briskly, dismissing us with a nod.

Without argument, Chloé slid off the arm of the couch and began putting on her coat. Paul stuffed his iPhone in his back pocket and wrapped a scarf around his neck in a single fluid gesture. Heather started rearranging teacups on a tray, and Nico moved to help her. Aunt Jeanne rummaged through her handbag. Only I remained motionless, curled onto a stool by the fireplace. As I sat there, witnessing their mute acquiescence, a rising fury began to burn within me. Yes, Uncle Philippe was the family patriarch, but still, what right did he have to issue directives like an autocrat? Without thinking, I sprang to my feet. "*Attendez, tout le monde!*" I called. "Wait—just a moment, everyone, please!"

"What is it, Katreen?" Uncle Philippe did not bother to disguise his displeasure.

I took a deep breath. "Uncle," I said in placating tones, "you know how much I admire you." I lowered my head. "But in this case I must—respectfully— disagree." I paused, twisting my fingers together. "I believe everyone has a right to know more about this secret *cave*—and we all have a right to decide how to proceed *together.* We are all descendants of Edouard Charpin, which means this heritage belongs to all of us."

"Of course it does. I agree with you, and so would any French court," snapped Uncle Philippe. "But surely I also have the right to review my property."

"Our property," I said mildly.

Uncle Philippe's face hardened. "Did it ever occur to you that I might be trying to protect you?"

Chloé turned to her father. "Did you know about this *cave*, Papa?"

My uncle shook his head. "I had absolutely no idea. It's not the *cave*, it's . . ." But the words stuck in his throat.

"Is it because of Hélène?" Nico asked.

"Who's Hélène?" Chloé and Paul spoke almost in unison.

"She was our great-half-aunt," Nico explained, throwing his father a pleading look. Uncle Philippe remained grimly immobile, his eyes fixed on the edge of the carpet where a bit of fringe had been torn away.

It was so silent I could hear the floorboards creak as I shifted my weight from one foot to the other.

"Excuse me, everyone—Papi—*je m'excuse.*" Heather stepped forward from the back of the room. "I'm sorry, but there's a reason you never talk about her. Hélène. A terrible reason, *n'est-ce pas?* At the end of the war, she was accused of being—" She hesitated, then plunged ahead: "*A collaborator.*" Her voice was low, but her eyes flashed with suppressed anger.

Paul's head snapped up. Chloé gasped. Aunt Jeanne stared at the floor.

"Papa," Chloé demanded of her father, "is this true?"

"*Oui.*" His shoulders sank. "It's true. After the Liberation, Hélène was accused of being a collaborator. She died shortly afterward."

"Why didn't you tell us?" Chloé's face had drained of color, except for two flaming spots in the center of each cheek. I'd never seen her so distressed.

"I—" Uncle Philippe coughed and cleared his throat. When he spoke again, his eyes were hooded. "My father never talked of Hélène."

"But you knew about her," Nico persisted. "How?"

My uncle crossed his arms against his chest, but not before I saw that his hands were shaking. "I must have been about ten or eleven. There was a group of boys at school, an angry, tough gang who used to taunt me and Céline." He nodded at me. "Your mother hated them. They called us *collabos*—said we had an aunt who was a Nazi whore. I told your mother to ignore them, but she insisted on telling our father. At first, Papa told us to forget them, said they would lose interest and stop. But it didn't stop and when we complained to him again, he told us to never *ever* speak about Hélène. He said she had brought shame upon our house. For years the taunts continued and our father never did anything, never said anything. And that was how we knew that it was true."

My mother's entire childhood, I thought, had been shadowed by this family ignominy, this indelible stain. Finally it made sense why every visit here had been so wracked with tension, why she had no desire to return. Finally I understood Uncle Philippe's aversion to the most trivial things—his reluctance to open the domaine to visitors, his refusal to create a website. And yet by trying to hide the truth, our family had prevented itself from ever moving forward into the future.

I stole a look around the room. Heather was fiddling with a tea strainer, her face pinched and tired though, also, perhaps, relieved. Nico was moving toward her, about to slip an arm around her waist. Chloé was gulping shallow breaths, her chest heaving. Paul stood with his arms crossed, head bowed to the floor. My aunt and uncle were motionless, guilt etched upon their features.

A crash from the fireplace broke the spell—a disintegrating log releasing a shower of sparks—and Nico sprang forward to reposition the screen. When he stepped back again, he glanced around the room at our gloomy faces, his eyes coming to rest on his father's wracked figure. "Should we . . ." His expression softened. "Let's open some wine for everyone, shall we?"

Uncle Philippe visibly relaxed. "*Bonne idée*," he said, moving toward the cabinet that held the wineglasses.

"I'll fetch some bottles from the cellar," Nico said. "What do you think—the 2011?"

"A bit older, I think," said Uncle Philippe.

Nico raised his eyebrows. "The 2009?"

"Older."

"1985?"

"*Mon fils*"—Uncle Philippe clapped a hand on his son's arm—"this evening we will drink the 1945."

I repressed a gasp—1945 was considered one of the most exceptional *millésimes* of the twentieth century. "Are you sure, Uncle?" I asked. "That's really generous."

He squared his shoulders. "I am absolutely sure," he

said. "We will drink the 1945, to honor the end of the war, and all those who suffered. And we will drink to Hélène, our aunt. For too many decades, we have kept her hidden, indulging our shame." His eyes sought Heather across the room, and he gave a nod. "It is time for us to acknowledge the truth, and our mistakes, both past and present, so that we may put them behind us. And also time to discuss the future, and the discovery of this secret *cave*. I hope, Katreen," he turned to me and bowed, "that you will give us an overview of what you've found."

"Of course," I said immediately.

Heather offered her father-in-law a tiny smile. "*Merci*," she said.

I would never have thought it possible, but after spending so many hours in the *cave*, I had grown fond of the place. Whereas once the shadowy, underground chamber had seemed ominous, creeping with many-legged creatures, devoid of light and air, now its darkness felt peaceful—quiet and still. Each morning I descended the stairs and breathed in the atmosphere, appreciating anew the damp chill that was as much a part of the wine as the grapes, the sun, the soil.

This morning I got to work straightaway, losing myself among the bottles, completely absorbed in counting and logging quantities in my green notebook, which Walker had finally returned to me. Yes, Walker stopped by the domaine a few days ago, and we had a brief exchange—he was sheepish and apologetic, I was brittle and skeptical—and while I wasn't certain of his true motives, I decided to pretend to take him at face value while secretly nurturing a healthy suspicion.

By the time I realized I was hungry, it was four o'clock, and there was just one more rack of bottles left to inventory. Wait a second. Only one more? In the whole cellar? After two months of work, was it finally possible? I walked carefully through the cave, inspecting the rows and double-triple-quadruple-checking my notes. But it was true—just one final rack and my inventory of the secret cellar would be complete.

Holding my breath, I turned to the final bottles, my last chance to discover the precious cache of Les Gouttes d'Or. I plucked one from the rack and wiped it clean with a rag, angling it toward the light. At the sight of the first word—"*Les*" in ornate Gothic font—my heart caught in my throat. I swiped at the label to read the rest.

Les Caillerets. Not Les Gouttes d'Or. Wherever those bottles were—hidden? stolen? sold?—they were forever lost to us. I sighed deeply, frustrated, stirring tufts of mold on the bottle in my hand. But then I looked down at it—Les Caillerets—and softened. It was still one of the greatest wines in the world, a legendary parcel of vines cultivated since the Middle Ages. In any ordinary circumstance, a rare cache of Les Caillerets would be an amazing discovery.

In less than a week, I would fly home to San Francisco. I would reclaim my apartment from the visiting Japanese professors, and my rattletrap thirdhand Volvo from Jennifer's driveway. I would spread the word among my former colleagues until I found a new job, in a new restaurant, once again working the floor as a sommelier. In a few months, I would take The Test and cross my fingers that the results would launch me to the next step in my career. I would miss Heather, Nico, and the kids, miss the crumpled, crumb-strewn affection of their household. Now that I'd found them again, I didn't want to lose their friendship. But I would lure them to visit me in California with promises of Alcatraz tours and Ghirardelli chocolates. I knew I couldn't come back to Burgundy. I had too many memories associated with this place, the specters of shame and ghosts of lost happiness swirling into a melancholy fog.

I made my final notes, closed the notebook, and lingered in the *cave* for a moment, breathing in the combination of moisture, mold, and secrets. I had come to Burgundy to immerse myself in its wine, to finally understand what had eluded me for so long. But I feared the past weeks had only widened the gaps in my knowledge. After tasting and studying so many different appellations, the wines still seemed remote: elegant, supple strangers. I had hoped this time here would make me understand this place—at least enough to pass The Test. But now I knew there hadn't been enough time. There would never be enough time.

PART III

Chapter 13

"Hey, Chef added an artichoke lemongrass carpaccio to the tasting menu." Becky—or was it Betsy?—thrust a menu sheet in my hands. "Is that still cool with the wine pairings?"

"Um, no," I said, repressing a groan. "I'm going to have to redo them."

"Mmm'kay, well, service starts in five minutes—so you'll take care of it now, right?"

"Sure," I said, and she flounced off.

It was my third day at Pongo y Perdita, a new "Thaitalian" small plates café that had just opened at the Ferry Building. It was a completely different scene from Courgette—loud, flashy, and cheffed by a reality cooking show winner who thought food paired best with Johnny Walker Red—although I had to admit a fondness for the kaffir-lime-green-curry-red-snapper cioppino.

I'd been home in San Francisco for about two months—long enough to stop mentally translating everything into French before I spoke, but not enough time to lose my taste for unpasteurized cheese, whose soft, salty, lingering perfume I still craved after every meal. I had thrown away the open jars of condiments from the fridge, and unearthed the wineglasses from under the sink. I had gotten a library card and checked out a stack of books about occupied France and World War II, hoping they could add context to my recent experiences. And, at Jennifer's urging, I had registered for The Test in June—only six months away. "If you're not ready then, you'll never be," she had said. And though I didn't feel ready, not even close, I knew she was right. It was time to take The Test, to face my destiny: glory and success or failure and reinvention.

Service tonight jerked along in a left-footed quickstep. The restaurant had been open for only three weeks and the front of house staff still had a lot of rough edges to smooth before we achieved the gliding waltz of Courgette. By the end of the evening, the effort of avoiding my colleagues' jostling elbows and trodding heels had left me more exhausted than usual. I stashed my clogs and apron in my locker and headed home, not stopping for a post-shift drink with my colleagues, even though Becky had told us to start "team building." I'd pay for it later.

The night was cloaked in a salty fog that bathed my cheeks and frizzed my hair. I shivered on the walk to my car, and when I climbed into the driver's seat, the windows immediately clouded from the inside. I switched on the engine and blasted the fan, scrolling through my phone as I waited for the mist to disappear, smiling when I saw a long email from Heather.

"Hi, Kate! How are you?" she began. I could almost hear her happy, high-pitched voice through the glowing screen. She wrote of Christmas: "For the first time ever it was just the four of us. We went skiing in the Alps—it was FAB!" Anna's newest obsession: "She begged Père Noël for a sewing machine. I can barely thread a needle . . . is she seriously my child?!" Thibault's latest accomplishment: "He can ride a bike! A two-wheeler! What's next? A studio apartment?!" Nico's recent fitness craze: "He's taking a yoga class at the *mairie*, and greeting everyone with '*namaste*.'" Even Jean-Luc got a mention: "He came over on New Year's Eve and made us baked Alaska. The kids were so excited." There was, I noticed, no mention of Louise—presumably Heather was trying to spare my feelings.

"The biggest news," she continued, "is that we are

moving ahead with the B&B!" She and Nico had plans to overhaul the kitchen and install a couple of bathrooms upstairs; they were starting to file for permits. "Papi referred us to a couple of architects," she wrote. "He'll never admit it, but I think he's secretly happy to see us breathing some life into this place. Of course, none of this would be possible without your discovery."

Uncle Philippe, Nico, and I had been in touch as we made quiet plans to sell the hidden cellar's collection of wine. "As you know," Heather wrote, "Jennifer's contacts have been super helpful. If the auction takes place in London maybe you can come over! Oh, and you'll be amused to learn that Walker—believe it or not—is still staying at Jean-Luc's house, but reportedly moving to a *chambre de bonne* in Beaune this weekend!"

The atmosphere in the car was suddenly stifling. Glancing up, I saw the windshield had cleared, so I switched off the heater before scanning the final paragraphs of Heather's email.

"One last bit of news," she wrote. "It's hardly anything, but you're the only person I know who'd understand. Do you remember those letters we found in the box with Hélène's schoolbooks?"

I summoned up the memory of a thin packet of envelopes tied with a faded pink satin ribbon. Sent to Hélène by someone called Rose, they had revealed nothing more than a friendship between two girls who shared an interest in science that was ahead of their time.

"I decided to find out more about Rose," Heather wrote. "I thought maybe I could contact her family— maybe they still had the letters Hélène wrote to her. As it turned out, I didn't have to dig too deep, because she and Hélène were classmates." Her full name, Heather reported, was Rose Sara Reinach, and she graduated from the Lycée de jeunes filles in 1940, a small, slight girl with dark curls, according to the photograph in the *annuaire*. But something about her name felt significant to Heather. "Sara isn't a common French name, unless you're Jewish . . . well, given the time frame, I was nervous. I searched online, and nothing came up. But then I found the website of the Holocaust Museum, which included a database of Jews deported from France. When I typed in the name, two pages of Reinachs popped up. Rose was number seven. All her info was there. Date of birth: 3 Mar 1921. Place of birth: Beaune. Convoy number: 18. Date of convoy: 9 Sep 1942. Convoy destination: Auschwitz."

I thought back to Rose's letters, recalling brittle stationery covered in round, girlish handwriting, and a lot of scientific talk about spontaneous combustion, or something. The letters hadn't painted a very clear picture of her, but she had seemed clever and intense.

And young. How horrifying that her life had ended so cruelly, her promise snuffed out and forgotten. Had Hélène known about Rose's fate? Or . . . an awful thought emerged unbidden: Had Hélène turned her in? I had feared making a discovery like this, and now it appeared to be true. Despite the heat choking the car, a chill ran down my spine. For a few seconds, I stared out the windshield at the fuzzy halos of light surrounding the street lamps before returning to the email.

I bit my lip as I read the rest of her message: "I'm starting to understand why Papi warned us about the skeletons in the closet. I know I was the one who pressed to learn more about Hélène, but the truth is, the implications are so awful, I'm losing my nerve. Don't get me wrong—I don't think Hélène should be a secret. I still feel we have a responsibility to tell Anna and Thibault about her when they're older, just as they have one to tell their children. All the same, I'm ready to close this particular chapter of family history. At least for now."

She ended the email with a flurry of questions— "How are you? How were your holidays? How's your new job?"—and signed off with a line of XOs.

I dropped the phone into my lap, its light ebbing away, and rested my head on the steering wheel. I had dreaded a revelation like this one, but nothing could have prepared me for the way it twisted in my gut: My ancestors—they were anti-Semites. No, worse. They were Nazis. A bitter taste rose in my mouth, and I opened the car door and leaned outside, retching as if that could eject the poison from my family's history. How could we ever move forward from something like this? I forced myself to breathe slowly, allowing the marine fog to cool my cheeks, and it occurred to me that we had the example of an entire nation before us: You just never talked about it.

25 OCTOBRE 1942

Cher journal,

Vichy is censoring Radio Paris so heavily, people go about humming a little tune: "*Radio Paris ment, Radio Paris ment / Radio Paris est allemande*" (Radio Paris is lying, Radio Paris is lying, Radio Paris is German). The only reliable news of France comes via *Radio Londres* on the BBC, but the signal is blocked more and more. Last night I spent ages hunting for it, until finally I admitted defeat and crept to bed, deprived of one of the few bright spots of my day. Obviously, the newspapers are also filled with rubbish. Any military action is always favorable to the Germans—they are always saying things like "this withdrawal is a way to gain new impetus"—so we must read between the lines and guess at the actual situation.

Papa has been missing for eight weeks and three days. We have had no news—neither from Stéphane and the circuit, nor from Madame's circle of spineless collaborator friends—and so we are left to wait. Wait, and wend our way around the signs of Papa, which are everywhere. His place at the table, empty. His winter boots in the hall, empty. His hat on the hook, empty. Only his grapevines are overfull—in desperate need of winter pruning, but I can't manage it on my own. As for this year's *vendanges* . . . well, with Papa gone, I couldn't manage the harvest, either. We sold the grapes to Monsieur Parent up the road, and for the first time in the domaine's history, someone else made wine from our fruit. Papa will be horrified, but given the summer's meager sunlight, this year's vintage is sure to be mediocre at best.

3 NOVEMBRE 1942

Madame's *crise de nerfs*—if that's what you call never leaving your room—continues. For several weeks, she has spent most of her time in bed with the curtains drawn, emerging only at night, when the house is still. In the morning, I find bits of food missing from the larder, crumbs scattered across the table.

The atmosphere in this house is oppressive to the point of being unbearable, so that I have thought of leaving a thousand times. Another *réseau* has tried to recruit me—they need *passeurs* to guide people to and from the region's hidden airstrips. I could live in a safe house with other *résistants*, speak my mind freely among them, fight openly for our cause. Yes, it would be dangerous—but oh, I would be free! Free from the responsibilities of this house! Free from Madame's accusing glare! Only two things keep me here. First, the boys. Who would care for them? Madame flies into a rage at the slightest hint of fractiousness, so that they have learned to cower before her moods. If I were to leave, I fear they might go completely neglected. Second, there is my promise to Papa. I haven't forgotten that I swore to stay and protect the domaine, no matter what happens—and with Madame unable (or unwilling) to shoulder any responsibility, this vow seems more important than ever. No, I am stuck here until Papa returns.

The clock has just chimed quarter to four. I must go and fetch the boys from school. And then we will return home, and I will cobble together something for their supper, chivy them through an evening of minimum noise and squabbling before all of us collapse in our beds, exhausted from the hunger that can never be satisfied.

7 NOVEMBRE 1942

Terrible circuit meeting today in which we learned that one of our messengers, Agnès, disappeared two days ago. Stéphane said she was stopped outside the *pharmacie* with the lining of her satchel stuffed with Resistance tracts. Her position looks very, very bad, but Stéphane assured us that Agnès is bold and fearless, that we can count on her not to talk, and that she will emerge more or less unscathed. I pray he is right, but when I think of her a cold, hard stone settles in the bottom of my stomach.

Aside from the horrible danger of Agnès's circumstances, her loss also leaves a great hole in our organization. In the past six months, our numbers have dangerously dwindled, and we have only one messenger to do the work of three. I've been laying low ever since Papa's arrest, but now it makes sense for me to take over a portion of the route, delivering orders and information around the countryside on my trusty bicycle. "If you get stopped, say you are out collecting food for your rabbits," Stéphane instructed me. I left the meeting with a stack of messages slipped into the lining of my coat, and instructions to collect as much paper and ink from my contacts as I deliver.

1 JANVIER 1943

New Year's Day today, though there is nothing to celebrate. Another day without Papa. Another year of this eternal war. The ration has been cut again, only 1,160 calories a day, a laughable amount. There are no potatoes, no milk—not even for children. Not a lump of coal to be found, and we've taken to washing with cold water to conserve our woodpile. At home, Madame screams at the boys for shouting too loudly while they play. Benoît has had a cough since Toussaint; Albert's legs have turned to spindles. Even the news from the circuit is bleak—we haven't had a meeting for three weeks, and Stéphane left word in one of the circuit's secret mailboxes that I should start collecting messages at the *boulangerie.*

More and more often I have found myself asking: How much longer can we endure? Where are the Allies? When will they come? (Or, more horribly, what if they *never* come?) These thoughts chase each other, nipping and snarling like a pack of rabid dogs until—having worked myself into a panic—I try to reassure myself, closing my eyes and reciting the litany of our faith: The Germans are weakening. The Eastern Front will destroy them. The Americans are coming. We just need to survive this winter.

Only one more winter.

Only one more winter.

Only one more winter.

Dear God, please, only one more winter.

10 MARS 1943

Two days ago, I received word to meet at one of our usual spots, the barrel maker's atelier, but when I rang the bell, no one answered. Mindful of our precautions, I returned today at the same time, and rang again. Across the street, a slender girl hurried down the sidewalk, her heels tapping. Was it Emilienne? I thought I recognized the wispy curls of my fellow circuit member, but she didn't turn to acknowledge me. I rang the bell again, waited and waited, until finally I left. Fear makes me sleepless tonight.

23 MARS 1943

In line at the *boulangerie* this morning, I saw a tall figure slipping into the courtyard of the *hôtel particulier* across the street. The tattered coat and hat were unfamiliar but there was something about the set of the shoulders that made my heart skip a beat. After I had collected my bread (a quarter loaf today!), I wheeled my bicycle past the building's heavy set of doors—the once-glossy blue paint now dull and flaking—and a rough voice whispered: "Café des Tonneliers. Fifteen minutes."

My legs were shaking so that I couldn't mount my bicycle. I walked it over to the café and went straight to the back room, catching the eye of the proprietress, Madame Maurieux, who is well known to our crowd. She brought me a tisane, and I sat stirring the steaming liquid with an empty spoon (there is nothing sweet to add these days). Eventually, a tall figure bounded up the cellar steps and slid into the chair across from me. His face was covered by a black beard—dyed, he later told me— but I recognized the dark blue eyes as soon as I saw them, for haven't I been looking for them every-where? It was Stéphane.

"Marie." He nodded and crossed his arms as if to warm himself even though, surprisingly, the stove was dispelling a faint suggestion of heat from the expired coals.

"How are you?" I asked, staring at the shadows under his eyes. He had lost weight, his cheekbones angular beneath the beard.

"I wanted to see you before—" A peculiar gri-mace seized his face and he started to cough, a rough, dry hack that went on for at least a minute.

I pushed my untouched cup toward him and he took a long sip. "What? Before what?" I asked, when he had recovered.

"I am joining the Maquis," he said. "Underground."

A hollow feeling engulfed me. Ever since last month, when the law was passed, the newspapers have been full of the Service du Travail Obligatoire, which deports French men to work in Germany. Many have refused, choosing instead to disappear and join the underground Resistance—and it doesn't surprise me that Stéphane plans to do the same. But until I heard the words from his lips, I hadn't known how much I depended on him—even just *imagining* him in that drafty old print shop gives me so much comfort. The hope of glimpsing him on the street, or receiving word to meet—these are the small sparks of joy in my dreary existence. A horrible sob of self-pity rose to my throat but I managed to catch and swallow it.

Stéphane had been watching me across the table, and now he touched my arm. "Look for my messages," he said. "I will write to you."

9 AVRIL 1943

Strange events afoot. This morning Madame Fresnes came to the domaine to see my stepmother. I think she must have been driven in a car and dropped off just before the driveway, for she looked impeccable as she clipped across the gravel, not a hair out of place, her face pale and smooth with fresh powder.

"*Bonjour*, please tell Madame Charpin that I am here," she announced at the door, addressing me as if I was a servant girl.

"Is she, er, expecting you?" I stammered, conscious of Albert hovering behind me.

"I am certain she will see me" was the reply.

Sure enough, when I went upstairs to inform my *belle-mère* of her visitor, she said she'd be down shortly. "Show her into the *salon*," she instructed me.

"A cup of tea with lemon. *Merci*," said Madame Fresnes, as I opened the windows of the *salon* and tried to air the room.

I choked on a speck of dust. Tea? Lemon? What war was Madame Fresnes living through? "*Désolée*, Madame," I said. "It's been many years since we've had such luxuries."

"Ah, well." She looked a little discomfited, but soon recovered. "Bring me a glass of water. You *do* still have water, I suppose?" An eyebrow twitched.

Before I could reply, my *belle-mère* appeared wearing a housedress, the only one without patches,

her hair hastily combed. "Joséphine! What a surprise!" The pair embraced, and I went to fetch the
water—if only so I could eavesdrop as I delivered it.

In the kitchen, I filled a pitcher from the tap and
placed it on a tray with two clean glasses, whisking
the ensemble to the doorway of the *salon* as quietly
as I could. Only a few words were intelligible from
the low murmur of voices. "*Choquée . . . navrée . . .*
no news . . . completely alone . . . *completely alone!*"
And then the familiar sound of Madame's sobs. I
waited a few seconds for her to stop before knocking
and entering.

"You must be strong for your sons," Madame
Fresnes was murmuring. "It'll do you good to start
seeing people again." She glanced up, saw me, and
frowned.

"Water!" I announced, sliding the tray onto the
low table before them.

"Thank you, you may go," instructed Madame
Fresnes. "Close the door as you leave."

Reluctantly, I left the room, and they resumed
their conversation. Half an hour later, Madame
Fresnes swept out of the house, and my *belle-mère*
spent the rest of the day humming and pinning up
her hair. What is she up to?

10 AVRIL 1943

Madame just left for the afternoon. "I shall be with the Fresnes," she announced. A few minutes later, they came to collect her in a car. *A car.* Only the most craven collaborators have access to a car these days. Papa will be livid when he hears of this betrayal. A noxious cloud of Chanel No. 5 fills the front hallway; I can still hear the click of her heels as she flounced out the door. How can she do this? Never mind the ignominy her betrayal will cause us in the village. How can she stand to be in their company for *even one second*? My disgust for this woman engulfs me, choking me, choking me.

8 JUIN 1943

Cher journal,

Life has formed into a strange pattern. Madame still spends her days in bed—but that is because she stays out all night. Past sunset, past curfew, sometimes past even the first light of dawn. In the mornings, when I go downstairs to start the fire, I find her evening wrap heaped on a kitchen chair, reeking of forgotten luxuries: cigarettes, scent, brandy. This morning I found two tins of sardines on the table, and that was not all. A packet of ham, its paper wrappings transparent with fat. A loaf of fine, white bread. An entire Époisses cheese releasing a mouthwatering perfume. At first, these items aroused a violent rage within me. I wanted to smash them, burn them, grind them into the dirt with my heel. But when the boys saw the food, their faces grew luminous. Benoît fell upon the cheese, cutting an enormous wedge and cramming it into his mouth. Albert, bless his heart, looked at me, waiting for my permission before he snatched up the ham and ripped open the paper, gobbling half the slices in one bite. Even as I vowed not to let a crumb pass my lips, I knew I could not deny my brothers.

"Oh, good, you found the treats I left for you." Madame floated into the kitchen in her dressing gown, beaming at her sons. She was up early—or maybe she hadn't gone to bed. "*C'est bon? Mangez bien, mes puces.* Eat well." She reached out and caressed Benoît's limp curls.

The boys were so absorbed by the food, they scarcely acknowledged her. Madame watched them with an indulgent smile before her gaze fell on me. "You're not eating, Hélène," she said, her voice as sharp as vinegar.

"I'm not hungry," I lied, even as my stomach rumbled a low, disloyal growl.

"Now, now, I can hear that's not true. One meal

won't kill you, will it? I won't tell anyone you ate the enemy's cheese." Her lips twitched.

"*Non, merci.*" I turned toward the sink, away from the table of food, and began to fill the kettle.

Madame moved close to me, her words a low hiss in my ear. "You're as pathetic as your father," she said. "The two of you would cut the noses off your faces just to spite me."

I didn't respond, for what could I have said but to agree?

26 JUILLET 1943

I found it wrapped around the quarter loaf of rough bread I brought home from the *boulangerie*: a note from Stéphane. It is unsigned, but I'd know his handwriting anywhere.

Ma chère professeur,

A word of greeting from the brush. My friends tell me you have been looking peaky. Courage, chérie, and a word of caution: the hen is laying rotten eggs.

Bisous.

I spent a long time puzzling over this note. "*Ma chère professeur*"—that is me, a reference to my *nom de guerre*, Marie (Curie). "The brush" surely refers to the Maquis, both a rough, wild scrub plant and the Résistance group. But "the hen is laying rotten eggs"—who is that? I've considered and discarded a thousand possibilities, but in the end I keep returning to one: Could it possibly be *Madame*?

What does he mean? What are the rotten eggs? Is she doing something worse than socializing with our Occupiers and bringing home their largesse? Oh, dear God, what could she be up to?

4 AOÛT 1943

I know it's silly, but lately I've taken to carrying Stéphane's note in my pocket. Whenever I'm feeling low, I pull it out and touch the last word with my finger. *Bisous.* Kisses.

10 SEPTEMBRE 1943

This morning, I found the following on the kitchen table:

2 TINS OF PÂTÉ

1/2 CONE OF SUGAR

1 ENORMOUS LUMP OF BUTTER

1 PACKET OF RICE

4 BARS OF CHOCOLATE

The boys are beside themselves.

22 SEPTEMBRE 1943

When I stopped at the Café des Tonneliers today, Madame Maurieux told me she had no tisane to serve me. "A cup of barley coffee then," I said, smiling and heaving a mock sigh.

"We're out of that, too," she snapped, and turned her back on me to polish wineglasses.

I stood stock-still at the counter, trying to grasp the situation. Madame Maurieux has always been so friendly with me, exchanging a good gripe about the idiotic ration regulations or a juicy bit of gossip—what happened? "Have I done something to upset you, Madame?" I finally asked.

She took her time arranging glasses on the shelf before turning back to me. "I do hope," she said in a low, tense tone, "that you and your brothers have been enjoying all that delicious food. While the rest of the nation *starves*." The last word escaped in a snarl.

I tried to swallow, but my mouth was so dry, I choked. "What do you mean?" I asked, disingenuously.

"You think we haven't noticed your *belle-mère* in the car of that German lieutenant? Creeping from his quarters at the Hôtel de la Poste? Laden down with a basket of provisions—ham, sugar, jam, things we haven't seen in years? We see everything, mademoiselle. Even the walls have eyes."

"Lieutenant?" I stammered. All of a sudden, the food made perfect sense—forbidden food, luxurious food, the food of an officer.

Madame Maurieux tapped the side of her nose. "She picked the one in charge of the local supply office, didn't she? No fool, your stepmother."

A cold-fingered dread tightened around my neck, until my head grew light and spots danced before my eyes.

"If you're going to faint, at least have the courtesy to go outside," Madame Maurieux said without a shred of sympathy.

I clutched at the zinc counter. "Madame, please, you have to believe me when I say that not a crumb of that food has passed my lips. *Je vous jure.* I swear to you. I would rather starve to death . . . *S'il vous plaît,*" I begged her. "You know who I am—what I believe—my father . . ." I drew a ragged breath. "Please."

She crossed her arms, but her face had softened. "You need to stop her, mademoiselle. People are beginning to talk. She's making enemies. Do you understand?"

I nodded, but kept silent. What could I say? I am the last person she would listen to.

Later

I've spent the entire afternoon fretting over my conversation with Madame Maurieux. A German lieutenant? A romantic attachment? It's absurdly dangerous. Surely Madame is not that stupid. Is she?

19 OCTOBRE 1943

The days are growing shorter. The light and warmth of summer made my work for the circuit so much easier, and I dread the frigid months ahead. If only I could fatten myself like a bear, curl up in a cave, and hibernate through the winter.

News from the circuit is mixed. Our numbers continue to shrink, even as the group of farmers hiding stockpiled weapons grows. As a result, my bicycle journeys have grown longer and riskier. The Boches have taken to setting up surprise checkpoints—this morning Madame Maurieux told me of one outside Beaune, so I had to push my bicycle through the vines in order to avoid them. I am wary about bringing any Resistance material into the house, which means I must make regular detours to the *cabotte* instead of cycling straight

home. I have a constant, nagging undertone of paranoia, like the unrelenting throb of a toothache that I
am constantly testing with my tongue.

2 DÉCEMBRE 1943

Sick with worry. Three days ago Benoît began com-
plaining of a sore throat. Of course Madame flew
into a panic, insisting he stay in bed, and even sug-
gesting that we slaughter a chicken (!) to make him
a nourishing broth. I thought she was overreacting
like she usually does, coddling Benny through one
of his phantom ailments. Just because he was a frail
baby, she treats him like fragile glass. In fact, given
his new diet of cheese and meat, my stepbrother
has recently seemed more hale than half the kids in
the village. I wasn't concerned.

But things took a turn this morning. When I
went in to wake the boys for school, I found Benny
curled in a corner of his bed, teeth chattering. I
touched his forehead and it was dry and hot—
shockingly hot. Worse, when I brought the lamp
close, I saw a rash creeping from his torso to his
neck, bright red, rough as sandpaper. I gasped
aloud and Albert heard me and started to wail.

"What? What is it?" Madame came dashing
into the boys' bedroom, her threadbare nightdress

floating as she ran. When she saw Benny, her eyes grew enormous.

"Maman," Benny croaked and she sat on his bed and put her arms around him. "*J'ai froid . . .*" He shivered uncontrollably.

"Don't worry, *mon coeur, Maman est là . . . J'suis là . . .*" she crooned before turning to me and hissing: "Hélène, for God's sake, go put the kettle on."

Somehow I managed to get Albert dressed, fed, and off to school, and to steep a tisane of thyme leaves for Benny, which he scarcely touched. "It hurts!" he moaned, and indeed his jaw and throat were swollen. Madame piled more blankets over him and eventually he drifted into a restless sleep.

3 DÉCEMBRE 1943

Benoît's condition is unchanged, or—if anything—worse. His eyes are glassy, and he shakes with chills. The rash has swept across his upper body, red and blistering like sunburn. We force him to drink liquids, of which he takes only tiny little sips. Madame holds the cup to his lips, trying to hide her hysteria when she sees the effort it takes him to swallow.

"We need a doctor," she said this afternoon, as I was leaving to fetch Albert from school.

I buttoned up my cardigan, and then pulled a second sweater on top of it, hoping it would stop the cold seeping through the holes in the elbows of my coat. "A doctor?" We haven't had one in the village for years, not since old Docteur Gaunoux passed just after the War began. And now that our men have been sent to work in Germany, there's no one left in Beaune, either. "Where on earth would we find a doctor?"

Her face closed over, secretive. Before I could press her, the clock in the hall chimed four o'clock and I was obliged to rush out the door.

4 DÉCEMBRE 1943

Oh, God, oh God. Benoît is worse. His breathing has become very shallow, and he is delirious from fever, crying out for Papa, and sometimes for Pépita, our dear, fat cart horse requisitioned months ago to the Eastern Front. Madame kneels on the floor next to his bed, her lips moving constantly in prayer. It is very late, past midnight; Albert is curled up in my bed—the poor darling cried himself to sleep—and I sit at my desk, scribbling this in the dim lamplight.

What if the worst happens? What if Benoît . . . No. I cannot bring myself to actually write the words. And yet, without a doctor, what hope do we have?

Later

Very, very late. The clouds are thick tonight, and the darkness so dense it seems as if even the moon and stars have abandoned us. I woke with a start a few minutes ago, for I think the idea came to me in a dream: Stéphane. Could he help us? The Maquis network must have a doctor, *n'est-ce pas?* I know Stéphane loathes Madame but surely he would not deny a child?

Voilà, here is my plan: After I drop Albert off at school, I will go to the boulangerie in town, and beg the woman behind the counter to help me get a message to Stéphane. I will . . . Wait, wait. What is that?

A car is in the driveway. Wheels crunching on the gravel. Peeping through the blackout shades I see twin slivers of light from shaded headlamps. . . . Is that Madame stepping from the back seat? Did she slip from the house when I was sleeping? Who is watching over Benoît?

They are entering the house. Now there are voices in the hallway. Madame and a man. No, no, there are two men. They are following Madame up the stairs. Through the keyhole of my bedroom door I can see their polished boots reflecting the hallway lights. "*Merci d'être venus,*" Madame is saying, close to tears.

"Come, come, Virginie, you should have called me earlier." He speaks in a light, youthful tenor, his French fluent but unmistakably accented.

"I didn't want to bother you . . ."

"Darling girl, I hope you know that I am always at your service."

I strain to catch a glimpse of their faces as they pass my door, but they move too quickly and the angle through the keyhole is bad. Then I hear the rough, uneven footsteps of someone stumbling. "*MEIN GOTT!*" cries a different man's voice, rougher, older.

"*Herr doktor!*" says the younger man, followed by a question—I can't understand the words, but the tone implies concern.

"*Ja, danke schön,*" says the older man. Then a few quick words, of which the only one I recognize is "*gut*"—good. The party proceeds down the hall-way and into Benoît's room.

Germans. There are Germans in this house.

Still later

They were in Benny's room for about an hour, emerging just as the first streaks of light appeared in the sky. I stayed upstairs until I heard their car moving across the driveway. When I went to the kitchen, I found Madame arranging various bottles on the table. "He needs two of the small pills every three hours, and one of the large pills every four. Can you remember that?" she asked without greeting me.

"Where did you get all of this?" I asked, feigning ignorance of our wee-hour visitors.

"His fever has broken," she murmured, as if she hadn't heard me. "*Dieu merci*, his fever has broken."

Chapter 14

"Are any of these gluten free?" The customer flicked her gaze to me, then to the wine list, tossing back a hank of magenta hair. She was in her midsixties, clad in leather trousers as tight as a second skin, though they—along with the eccentric hair dye—did little to counteract the lines furrowing her face.

"Yep! All of them!" I said with false cheer.

"Are you absolutely sure? Because I've got a severe gluten sensitivity—"

"Mo-om!" her daughter—midtwenties, slim, heavily mascaraed, and exasperated—broke in. "*Please.* If you're not celiac, you shouldn't say you can't have gluten. It just makes things worse for people who really do have it."

"Honey, I ate a sandwich last week, and I was bloated for three days. We can't all be toothpicks like you."

I waited for her to select a wine, carefully maintaining a pleasant expression. Internally, however, I couldn't stop myself from contrasting her concerns with the plight of Rose Reinach. Though a couple of months had passed since I'd received Heather's email, Rose's tragic death still haunted me. I found myself scrutinizing my thoughts, wary that I would discover some ingrained bias, some inherent prejudice, some evidence that I was genetically predisposed to moral weakness. And I often considered what Uncle Philippe had said that afternoon on the *mairie* steps. Our problems were frivolous in comparison. My uncle had been right, I understood that now, but he had been wrong, too—for this was life, no less meaningful than generations past, and though our problems were trivial that made them no less real.

"So"—the customer glanced up at me again—"you're saying *all* these wines are gluten free?" She leaned toward me slightly, tilting her face up with a broad smile. "We're celebrating my one-year anniversary of beating breast cancer," she said conspiratorially. "I just want to keep feeling as good as possible."

"Of course," I murmured. "In fact—" I took a deep breath, ready to gently explain that all wine was naturally free of gluten—along with vodka, tequila, rum, and every other spirit—but before I could finish my sentence, out of the corner of my eye I caught sight of the hostess leading a customer to table 12. Something about his shape—tall, thin, with a loping stride—made my heart move to my throat. "Um, actually, Chef is very sympathetic to gluten sufferers. Have you decided on a wine? The Russian River chardonnay? I'll bring it out to you right away. And two glasses of Champagne to start. On the house," I added, smiling as they shrieked with delight.

I raced from the dining room through the kitchen, and straight into the walk-in cooler at the back of the restaurant, leaning against a metal shelving unit and gulping cold air. The refrigerator's engine hummed, and the fluorescent light overhead bleached color from the shelled English peas, turning them sallow in their clear quart containers. Why was Jean-Luc here? I hadn't spoken to him since that day in the cemetery when we had argued. Now, the sight of him was unleashing a flood of adrenaline so intense I found myself clenching my jaw to keep myself from shaking. My hands fiddled with the strings of my apron, tying, untying, tying, untying.

The door of the walk-in flew open. "Oh, *there* you are." It was Becky, with a face like thunder. "I just covered you on table 3, and now 24 wants you. Get your ass back out on the floor." She slammed the door behind her without waiting for me to reply.

I crossed the dining room, ignoring the customers at table 24 waving at me and calling "Somm! Somm!"

"Kat!" Jean-Luc exclaimed as I approached, and he half rose to greet me.

"Please, sit," I said, as he hovered over the table. He was halfway through a glass of wine, I noticed, and the screen of his cell phone displayed an online French-English dictionary.

"*C'est délicieux!*" His eyes had followed mine to the glass. "Round, deep, beautiful *malolactique* notes . . . a wonderful example of the California chardonnay."

"What are you doing here?" The words burst from me. "Sorry, that came out wrong. I just . . . didn't expect to see you."

His smile faltered. "I had a meeting with my American distributors. Bruyère told me you were working here." He gestured at the menu. "What's green papaya carbonara?"

"It's a warm salad of slivered green papaya with guanciale and a coddled quail egg—you know what? Skip it." I lowered my voice. "The food here is bizarre. Not in a good way."

"*Non, non,*" he insisted. "*Je veux bien essayer.* I want to try this California cuisine I have been hearing so much about. Please, I will take the carbonara *papaye verte,* and then . . ." He frowned at the menu.

I looked up to see Becky shoot me a murderous glare. "I'll just have them bring out the papaya," I said to Jean-Luc in a rush. "I get off at ten—we can grab a bite to eat then. Can you wait that long?" Becky was striding toward me. "I've got to go. Meet me out front, okay? *Dix heures.*"

"*D'accord,*" he nodded, surprised, and I hurried off to attend to table 24.

We got slammed around seven o'clock, the customers piling three-deep at the bar, their eyes shifting like sharks as they watched hopefully for a positive sign from the hostess. I had been counting the seconds to ten o'clock, but in the heat of service, time disappeared until, finally, on my fortieth trip up the cellar stairs, I was surprised to see that the restaurant had almost emptied, with just one last table lingering over small glasses of Chef's special-distilled Mekhong grappa.

Amy, the bartender, stopped me as I was heading to the kitchen. "Have you seen anyone using the coffee machine when I'm not around?" she demanded, swiping behind the heavy equipment with a striped rag.

"Sorry, no. Why?"

"They've been leaving spilled coffee grounds all over. Slobs." She frowned and lowered her voice. "Do you think it's Becky?"

"Hmm. Seems unlikely?" I liked Amy, but she enjoyed gossip far too much for me to trust her.

Amy shot a dark look in our manager's direction, then threw the rag into a sink of soapy water. She leaned across the counter, plucked a bottle of Austrian Riesling from the ice bucket, and dangled it before me. "The usual?"

"No, thanks. Can't tonight."

"*You* got plans?" She emphasized the "you"—as if I never had plans!—raising an eyebrow so that the light overhead glanced off her piercing. "Wait, lemme guess. Is it that hot guy from table 12 who was in earlier?"

"Um, what?" I lifted the strings of my apron over my head, feigning a nonchalance I did not feel.

"It IS! You sly dog, Elliott." She laughed. "Don't do anything I wouldn't do!" she called after me as I backed away from the bar.

Polishing. Scrubbing. Mopping. It was ten thirty by the time I clocked out. I went out the back door so that my colleagues, relaxing at the bar over their shift drinks, wouldn't notice me sneaking away. Jean-Luc was leaning against a bench in front of the restaurant, hands shoved into his pockets, a cotton scarf wrapped loosely against the night's chill. We touched cheeks, exchanging a brief hug.

"You hungry?" I asked, leading Jean-Luc to my car, which was parked a few blocks away.

"*Ouais, j'suis crévé!* It's breakfast time in France." He glanced at his watch. "Where are we going?"

I buckled my seat belt and put the car in drive. "You wanted to try real California food, right? I'm taking you to the best spot."

By some miracle, I found a parking spot right outside the restaurant, squeezing in between a Prius and a pink moped. Fluorescent light spilled from the windows, and twin blasts of steamy air and loud music greeted us as we opened the door. For a moment Jean-Luc stood in the entry, silently taking in the red Formica tables, the tipsy crowd, the sombreros dangling from the ceiling, the smell of cumin, onions, and sizzling meat permeating the air.

"We order there!" I raised my voice above the din. "The menu's up there."

His face tipped up toward the sign on the wall, frowning over the list of unfamiliar words. "Uh . . . what are you taking?" he asked.

"I'll order for both of us, okay? Why don't you grab that spot by the window." I pointed at a table covered with litter-strewn trays. "Beer okay?"

He nodded and moved to the table, clearing the debris to a trash bin. I placed a double order for my usual, along with a couple of Sierra Nevadas. At the table, I sat across from Jean-Luc, handing him one of the icy bottles of pale ale.

"*Cin!*" he said, and when our eyes met, my cheeks began to flush. "I'm very happy to see you, Kat. But—"

"*Fifty-seven!*" boomed a voice from the loudspeaker and both of us jumped. "*Fifty-seven, your order is ready.*"

"That's us." I pushed back my chair. "I'll get it."

When I returned with our trays, Jean-Luc stared at the food, craning his head to inspect it. "Um, how do you . . ." He mimed using a fork and knife.

"Just use your hands. Look." I pinched the top of the taco and scooped up the bottom with my other hand, angling it toward my mouth for a bite. The crunchy fried shell contrasted with creamy refried beans, followed by the punch of hot salsa. "Mmm, so good," I mumbled.

Jean-Luc's eyes widened with mild shock but he followed suit, lifting a taco to his lips, and unleashing an avalanche of shredded iceberg lettuce onto his lap. "*Ohh!*" he said thickly. "*C'est shshhehsh!*" He continued chewing, making appreciative sounds. "Mmm. What's this thing called again? *Le tay-ko?*"

I laughed. "It's a taco. Well"—I glanced at the menu on the wall—"this is actually a super vegetarian taco."

He took another large bite, then chased it with a swallow of beer. "The California is amazing! You can eat with your hands . . . you can drink out of the bottle . . . no one cares! I think I love it here!" He grinned at me, and then suddenly yawned, covering his mouth with both hands. "*Désolé!*" he said quickly. "I didn't mean to do that. It's the jet lag."

"When did you arrive again?"

"Yesterday morning . . . I think? Seems like a week ago."

I picked at the label on my beer bottle. "How's everyone?"

He wiped his mouth with a paper napkin. "Heather has told you about the . . . how do you say? *Les chambres d'hôtes?*"

"The bed-and-breakfast, yes. I'm really excited for them. I think it's going to be a huge success . . ." I trailed off, wanting to inquire about Heather's emotional state, but uncertain of how to bring it up. "Have you seen her recently?"

He nodded. "I was at their house for dinner a few nights ago."

"And she seemed . . . okay?"

He picked up a plastic fork and began transferring shredded lettuce back into his taco shell. "They told me. About the secret *cave*. And about Hélène. Don't worry, they swore me to secrecy," he said, as I looked away. "Kat," he continued gently, "I am sorry about that afternoon in the cemetery. If I had known . . . well, I wouldn't have brought up any of that stuff."

"It's okay." I thought back to that day, remembering what he'd said about his father. "*C'est comme ça, alors,*" I added with a shrug.

He meticulously positioned a cilantro leaf on top of a black bean. "Bruyère is fine," he said after a pause. "She is not often talking about Hélène, but I think she is always thinking about her. Sometimes we can be having a conversation about—*par example*—the best *boulangerie* in Beaune, and suddenly she will burst out with a question about the war—like 'Were there German soldiers occupying this house?' She asked that the other day. Questions we have no answers to."

"Can you blame her? Hélène's story has particular meaning for her."

"*Mais bien sûr!*" Jean-Luc's face creased with empathy. "It is awful. A period of black shame for our country. And for Bruyère—well, her situation is particularly complicated."

I stared down at the table. "Yes. It is."

"What's, ah . . . what's a boo-ree-toh?" Jean-Luc asked several seconds later, and when, glancing up again, I found him squinting at the menu on the wall, I felt suffused with gratitude.

"You'll love it," I assured him, reaching for the hot sauce. "You want to split one? The carne asada is really good here."

"Sure!" His face lit up. "I'll get it," he added before I could rise, returning a few minutes later with a heavy, foil-wrapped cylinder and another round of beers.

"So, did Heather and Nico show you the secret cellar?" I asked, sawing through the burrito with a plastic knife and transferring half to a paper plate.

He nodded. "*C'est incroyable.* Like something out of a film. And Nico was saying that you have no idea who hid the wine?"

"I think it must have been Edouard. My great-grandfather. But I suppose we'll never really know. At least we found a cellar log, so I was able to double-check the quantities. Not a single bottle was missing—except for Les Gouttes d'Or."

"Nico told me." Jean-Luc chewed thoughtfully. "Too bad. The collection is superb, of course, but with Les Gouttes d'Or it would be truly magnificent."

"Yeah, well, at this point I'm pretty convinced those bottles of Les Gouttes d'Or are just a myth."

"Have you asked your mother?"

"She doesn't care. And Uncle Philippe said their father forbade them from ever talking about the war."

"There is no one else to ask? Your grandfather, Benoît—he was an only child?"

I thought back to the photographs we had found in Hélène's suitcase, to the pair of scruffy little boys pictured in some of them. "No, he had a brother. Albert. He became a monk."

"Have you tried looking for him?"

I lifted my hands, the palms facing up. "Don't they have to take a vow of silence or something?"

He laughed. "Not all of them."

"Well, it seems pretty unlikely we could find him. If he's even still alive he'd be in his eighties."

"He's just a monk, Kat, not vanished from the face of the earth." But the glimmer of a smile softened his words.

I picked up my half of the burrito. "How do you like the carne asada?" I asked, gesturing at his plate.

But Jean-Luc didn't respond. He was staring somewhere over my shoulder, his mouth drawn into a frown. "You know," he said musingly, "Louise had a meeting at the Abbaye de Cîteaux a few weeks ago."

"Oh, really?" I couldn't imagine a more unlikely visitor to a monastery. "Well, I'm sure that was just a coincidence. I distinctly remember Nico saying that Albert became a Trappist monk."

He gave a cough so sharp, I feared he was choking. "Oh, Kat," he said. "Trappists and Cistercians—they're the same thing."

A familiar, panicky feeling buzzed within my chest, as angry as a wasp. "What was her meeting about? She doesn't know about the secret cellar, does she?" I asked.

"I—" The heat was rising in his cheeks. "Maybe. I didn't tell her," he added quickly. "But the other day, she was asking strange questions about Nico and his father, and how your family survived the war. It didn't mean anything to me at the time, but . . ."

The feeling in my chest was growing more and more uncomfortable. Across the table, Jean-Luc was watching me with concern. "If Albert is still alive . . ." I took a deep breath. "Damn it! I wish I wasn't so far away."

"Can you come back to Burgundy? I probably have enough airline miles to get you a ticket." Jean-Luc leaned his elbows on the table.

I could still smell the cellar's moist, moldy air, feel its chill touching my face and bare arms. I had left without uncovering all its secrets and still they beckoned to me. For a moment, I hesitated, tempted. But no—with all my obligations, it was impossible.

"But, ah, of course, you cannot leave right now." Jean-Luc's tawny eyes were watching me. "Your responsibilities must be keeping you here in San Francisco. The exam for the Master of Wine, it is only a few weeks away, *n'est-ce pas?*"

"Two weeks," I said, touched that he had remembered. "Although another trip to the Côte d'Or probably wouldn't be the worst idea, at this point." I had performed so dismally at the last practice session with Jennifer, she had pointedly remarked it was difficult to believe I had ever spent time in Burgundy at all.

"And your work at the restaurant, as well. You're extremely talented at your job, Kat. I saw tonight how much they are relying on you." He smiled at me with something that looked like pride.

"Er, I don't know about that." I coughed awkwardly. "Although it *is* true that I can't afford to piss them off. I'll need that job if I don't pass The Test." It was the first time I had admitted the possibility out loud.

"*Ne t'inquiète pas,*" he reassured me. "You will succeed." His nod was so firm, his confidence so certain, that, for a tiny sliver of a moment, I felt sure of myself, too. It caught me off guard, this feeling of hope. "Thanks," I said. Without thinking, I reached over to squeeze his arm—but I had forgotten that my hand was still greasy from the tacos, and my fingers left oily smudges on his clean sleeve. "Oh! I'm so sorry!" I said, snatching my hand away, knocking over his beer in the process. Liquid cascaded across the table, flowing into his lap. "Oh my God, I am *so* sorry!" I cried.

"*C'est bon—ça va.*" Jean-Luc blotted at his trousers with a napkin. He stood to fetch more napkins, and I saw that he was completely soaked.

"Maybe I should take you back to your hotel," I said.

He opened his mouth to respond—and suddenly a yawn engulfed him, followed by another, and another. "*Désolé,*" he apologized, forcing open his drooping eyelids, blinking several times. And then, after a pause, "*Ouais*—I should probably get some sleep. I have a long flight back tomorrow."

"Sure." I slid back my chair and stood, swinging my bag over my shoulder with a jaunty gesture in an effort to dispel a pinch of irrational disappointment.

Twenty minutes later I deposited Jean-Luc at his hotel, bade him farewell with an awkward hug from the front seat, and watched him stagger through the glass doors to the lobby. Then I drove home and went straight to bed, exhausted. But in the last quiet moments before sleep, I thought about our conversation, and when I finally drifted off, it was on a raft of conviction that made me feel calmer and more clear-headed than I had in weeks.

I slept late the next morning, pulling the covers over my head to block out the muted light of another cloudy day. My phone rang a couple of times, but when I saw it was Amy, I ignored it. My coworker was no doubt calling for gossipy details about my evening with Jean-Luc, and even though absolutely nothing had happened, I still felt reluctant to talk about him with anyone.

It was almost noon when I finally emerged from the duvet and began moving around the apartment to the soothing sounds of NPR. I brewed coffee, showered, and popped the last pieces of bread in the toaster. I'd have to go to the store before work; I should make a grocery list . . .

BZZZ BZZZ. My phone vibrated against the counter, and I swiped at the screen with a finger, accidentally smearing it with peanut butter. My smile faded when I saw a text from Amy.

HEY LADY! WHERE ARE YOU? I tried to call but you're probably still with Frenchie. SO guess what? The Health Dept. came by this morning.

SURPRISE! Remember those weird coffee grounds all over the bar? Turns out it's COCK-ROACH SHIT. Long story short, we FAILED the inspection. Chef is PISSED and Becky's ass is FIRED. Restaurant has to CLOSE for 5 days for treatment. Chef will call everyone next week about a staff meeting and reopening. Perfect timing for you, right?;) Have fun with Frenchie! CALL ME!!!

I placed the phone back on the counter. The restaurant was *closed*? Was this some sort of sign? I took a deep breath, picked up the phone, and tapped "Hotel Lombard San Francisco" into Google. Seconds later, I was speaking to a receptionist, and then the sound of ringing filled my ear: once, twice, three times, four, five . . .

"*Allô?*" said a groggy voice.

"Jean-Luc?" I said. "*C'est moi,* Kat. *Je veux t'accompagner.* I want to go with you."

Chapter 15

I was tucked between crisp sheets, the comforting weight of a down-filled duvet draped across my body. Under my head I had arranged two pillows, perfectly fluffed, and yet they kept collapsing. I plumped them, shaking them to fit into the hollow of my neck. Again my head crushed the pillows. Again. Again. *Again.* If I couldn't fluff the pillows correctly, I wouldn't be able to sleep. And if I couldn't sleep, how would I be able to concentrate on The Test the next morning? I punched the pillows into the proper shape and lay down again. My eyes fluttered shut, my mind began to drift . . . suddenly, with a sharp jerk, my head snapped forward, my eyes flew open, and there was Louise, snatching the pillows away. "*Mine,*" she said. "Mine. Mine. Mine."

"Kat. Kat. *On est presque là.*" Jean-Luc's voice broke into my dream.

My eyes flew open, the dream shattered. We were in Jean-Luc's truck, speeding along the motorway. The dull ache in my neck testified to the awkward position in which I'd been sleeping.

Jean-Luc and I had been traveling for almost twenty-four hours. First, there was the flight from San Francisco to Paris, and then—after picking up Jean-Luc's truck from the long-term parking garage at Charles de Gaulle airport—the drive from Paris to Beaune, which on this three-day weekend of Lundi de Pentecôte lasted seven hours instead of the usual four. Needless to say, we had made several stops for coffee.

I swallowed a yawn and looked out the window. I'd last seen this landscape six months ago, just as the fiery blaze of fall foliage had started to fade along the slopes. In my absence, the vines had slept and awoken again, sending out tender fronds, tightly furled, and glowing green in the distance. From the rushing car, I couldn't see the hard clusters of unripe fruit sheltered beneath the verdant canopy, but I knew they were there, just as I knew the sun would sweeten those grapes and draw color to their skins.

We passed a sign that read "Route des Grands Crus," and then another for Beaune, skirting the town before we turned west toward Meursault. "I should probably give Heather a call," I said, digging in my bag for my cell phone. "I feel really bad that I didn't get in touch earlier to ask if I could stay."

Jean-Luc glanced at me, and then returned his eyes to the road. "*Ils sont en plein travaux*," he said. "The house is a complete wreck—they're living out of three rooms, with a hot plate. I was thinking you'd be more comfortable staying with me."

"Sure!" I said quickly, before an awkward silence could descend. "Thanks—I completely forgot about their renovation." We continued a few miles, the landscape growing increasingly familiar as we passed the garden center, the Carrefour shopping complex, the gas station. It felt strange being here without Heather and Nico, but then I thought back to her email of a few months ago: *I'm ready to close this particular chapter of Charpin family history*. Maybe it was best to spare them this fresh round of amateur sleuthing—or at least investigate its merit before dragging them back into the mire of emotions.

The truck was climbing now, nearing the top of a slope, and Jean-Luc was looking out the windshield and frowning at his rows of grapevines, which seemed meticulously tidy and vibrant with health. A few minutes later, we were pulling into his driveway, the front garden a profusion of peonies, early roses, and wild lavender beds, the rough walls of the old stone house shimmering in the afternoon heat. I hesitated a moment before following Jean-Luc to the side door, our feet crunching on the gravel.

Within the thick walls, it was dark, quiet, cool. I stood in the mudroom, breathing in the smells of musty fleeces and waxed raincoats draped along the walls, the laundry detergent drifting from the machines in a side room. I hadn't been inside this house for nearly ten years, but it appeared unchanged. How many times had I inadvertently pictured the kitchen's beige laminate countertops and scuffed oak cabinets, the linoleum floors, clean but worn, the large round table tucked into the nook of the bay window? How many times had I thought about the warmth radiating from the old cream-colored Aga standing against the wall? I sidled up to it, holding my hands above the burners. It was stone cold.

"Ah, I let it go when Maman moved to Spain." Jean-Luc said when he saw my face. "If I'm going to make pasta or something, it's easier to just use the electric cooker."

"Makes sense," I agreed. But without the stove's steady warmth, the kitchen seemed to have lost some piece of its soul.

"I thought you could stay in the blue room," Jean-Luc was saying. "First door at the top of the stairs. The *femme de ménage* came while I was away so the sheets should be clean." He moved back toward the mud-room. "I'll bring the bags inside. If you want, you can have a little rest before we decide what to do first."

The wide stairs creaked under the thick carpet. I peeked into the bathroom—same flowered curtains, same *eau-de-nil* toilet and sink, though Jean-Luc had replaced the cracked tub with a shower—and continued to the blue room. Two narrow twin beds greeted me, covered in blue-and-white toile duvets. I collapsed onto the closest one, closed my eyes, and fell into a deep, dreamless sleep.

I woke at dusk, eyes dry and burning, heart racing. Slowly the pieces returned to me: Burgundy. Jean-Luc's house. My great-uncle Albert. Had Louise met with him at the monastery?

I struggled from the bed and moved to the bathroom, where I brushed my teeth and threw cold water on my cheeks, and then headed downstairs to the kitchen. I found Jean-Luc hovering over the electric stove with a wooden spoon in one hand. A colander of chopped broccoli sat on the counter, and the smell of browning garlic perfumed the air.

"Oh, hi!" He looked surprised to see me. "Did I

wake you?" I shook my head. "Are you hungry?" He waved the spoon in the direction of a bubbling pot. "I'm making some pasta."

"*You're cooking?*" The words, steeped in incredulity, escaped me. I saw a flush creep across Jean-Luc's face. "Sorry." I cleared my throat. "I mean, wow, you're cooking! Pasta sounds great. *Merci*," I said, as he handed me a glass of white wine.

We ate at the kitchen table—the site of so many other meals together, the site of our ill-fated engagement—both of us sitting in different seats than we had ever used before.

"This looks delicious." I gazed at the shallow bowl of penne and broccoli florets. "Thanks." I ate a noodle, surprised to find it subtly infused with chile.

"I thought we needed a hot meal," he said, proffering a dish of grated cheese.

"Mmm, no, thanks—it's perfect." Suddenly ravenous, I began eating more quickly.

"While you were napping, I called the Abbaye de Cîteaux," Jean-Luc added, sipping his wine. "No answer."

I stabbed at my food with my fork. "Is this a wild goose chase? We don't even know if Albert is there. And with my luck, all the monks are probably cloistered away in some special silent retreat."

"Guided visits start at ten-thirty tomorrow morning," Jean-Luc said in calmer tones. "It takes about forty minutes to get there, so I think we should leave at nine."

"We?" I perked up in my chair.

He looked surprised. "Of course, Kat. You didn't think I'd abandon you now, did you?"

Flat farmland surrounded the Abbaye de Cîteaux, pastures of interlocking green that left the plain buildings vulnerable to the elements. A gust of wind pierced my coat, and I shivered as we entered an immense stone building with cavernous vaulted ceilings, enormous arched windows, and not a shred of heat.

"The abbey was founded in 1098, when a group of monks came to this remote spot hoping to follow a simple lifestyle, as indicated in the teachings of the Gospels," said our guide, a surprisingly young novitiate who had introduced himself as Frère Bernard. "This room is the scriptorium, where medieval scribes copied, illuminated, and bound books." He lifted an arm to indicate the vast space. "As directed by the rule of Saint Benedict, their work occurred mostly in silence—though a vow of silence is not required by our order. Today there are about thirty brothers in the community, and we strive to speak only when necessary; idle chitchat is discouraged, and any talk that leads to mockery or derision is considered evil—which means, of course, we don't use social media." He smiled at us all benevolently.

Jean-Luc and I both laughed, but the other visitors on our tour, a gaggle of spry retirees, appeared unmoved by this show of hermetic humor.

"Please, take a look at the exhibit, and then we shall visit the cloisters, which offer an early example of Romanesque architecture." Frère Bernard moved to the side of the room, and I darted beside him, anxious to engage him before any of the others could ask a question.

"Is it ever possible to make contact with the brothers here?" I asked, trying not to shiver in the draft that flowed from the thin-paned windows.

"We offer silent retreats for those on a spiritual quest," he said automatically, and I had the feeling he had been asked the question before. "Seekers of God, or peace, or those at a turning point in their life." He peered at me more closely. "Is that what you mean?"

I flushed under his gaze. "No, not exactly." I paused, considering my words. "I am looking for my great-uncle. I have reason to believe he joined the community many years ago. Please, can you tell me if there is a Frère Albert among you?"

Frère Bernard frowned, fingering the cloth belt wrapped around his waist, its edges so frayed I suspected this was a nervous habit. "What brings you in search of him?"

Again, I hesitated. What should I say? Here, amid this atmosphere of rigid aestheticism, the idea of hunting down a cache of rare wine seemed horribly craven. I thought of Hélène, and of the turmoil and destruction she had wrought on so many. "I am hoping to find peace," I said quietly. "I am hoping to forgive."

His eyes softened. "Stay behind after the tour," he said in an undertone, as the others began to drift toward us. "I will see if anything can be done."

"Is Albert here?" Jean-Luc asked in discreet tones when I had rejoined him.

"Frère Bernard only said he'd see if anything can be done."

"Hmm. Ambiguous."

We continued the visit, traipsing to a plain chapel, the austere refectory, and a cutting-edge *fromagerie*— where the monks silently produced a delicious, creamy cheese called fromage de Cîteaux—and finally ending at the gift shop. Jean-Luc and I waited for Frère Bernard, nervously filling a shopping basket with jars of honey and jam, a wheel of cheese, and other Trappist delicacies. Jean-Luc added a box of chamomile tea to the basket and we headed to the cash register, where a young woman began ringing up our purchases and placing them in a bag.

"That'll be a hundred and seventy euros," she said, and my jaw dropped to the floor.

Jean-Luc gave her his credit card, laughing at the expression on my face. "I know, it's crazy, right? These monastery gift shops are more expensive than the Harrods Food Hall."

"Mademoiselle?" Frère Bernard's robed figure appeared from a door leading out the back of the gift shop. "Would you like to follow me?" He beckoned, his invitation clearly precluding Jean-Luc.

"I'll meet you at the car," Jean-Luc said. "Take your time."

Frère Bernard led me outside and across the abbey grounds, our heels sinking into the grass. I began to search my mind for some banal topic of idle small talk before I remembered that the brothers spoke only when necessary. In truth, the silence was restful.

Rounding a long building, we entered a kitchen garden marked carefully into planting beds brushed with spring growth. An elderly monk knelt in the earth, clad in the order's garb of a sleeveless black tunic over an off-white robe, belted with a leather strap. Strands of white hair did little to protect his pink scalp from the sun, though his generous white beard perhaps compensated.

Beside me, Frère Bernard gave a little cough. The monk looked up and my breath caught in my throat, for there, set into his lined face, were my mother's eyes—my eyes—dark green, the edges deepening to brown. "*Bonjour,*" I whispered.

He leaned back on his heels and held out a hand. "My child," he said. "I have been hoping you would come."

As Frère Bernard bowed and slipped away toward the main path, I moved forward to clasp Albert's hand, kneeling beside him in the dirt. "I am your great-niece," I told him in French. "I am Benoît's granddaughter."

"Do you like peas? Benoît likes peas," he said, handing me a trowel.

"I do," I assured him, my heart sinking. Was his mind slipping? I pulled at a plant, hoping it was a weed. "Frère Albert," I began, "I was wondering if I could talk to you about your childhood."

"Benoît was very delicate. Always very poorly. Maman gave him calf's foot jelly, but I had to eat the rabbit."

"And what about . . . Hélène?" I winced, bracing myself.

"Ahhh, Léna." To my surprise, his voice grew tender, and he smiled. "She used to sing me to sleep . . . *Fais dodo, Colas, mon petit frère . . .*" He hummed a few bars of the lullaby. "Of course, it was brutal—the war years. *C'était absolument affreux.* But Léna tried to protect me and Benoît from the worst."

"She protected you? What do you mean?" My voice rose in astonishment.

"She rescued me from the cherry tree. She can climb like a boy. When it's warmer, she's going to take me camping at the *cabotte.*" His face darkened. "It's not true, you know. I don't care what everyone says. Something was twisted around. There was a mistake."

My breath caught in my throat. "What was a mistake?"

"Hélène can't be a *collabo,* and when I'm older, I'm going to investigate. I'm going to find out the truth. Maman says I should let the dead rest in peace, but that's because she prefers to pretend that Léna never existed. No, no! That's a beet seedling!" He stilled my hand with some alarm.

I leaned back on my heels, and Bernard patted the earth around the beet plant, nestling it back into the ground. As he gazed tenderly at the delicate leaves, I sensed the window of opportunity closing. I hunted fruitlessly for a way to draw him back into the conversation, but just as I thought it was too late, he spoke again.

"She's been looking for it." In the crook of his smile, I saw the mischievous boy he'd once been. "All over the house, in the cellar, taking the books from the shelves, tearing through the cupboards. Maman doesn't know where Léna hid it, but I do. Oh, yes"—he tapped his nose—"I do have an idea! I think she left a clue in Papa's favorite book—I saw it on her desk. But that's a secret." His eyes grew suddenly anxious. "You won't tell anyone, will you? Don't tell Maman."

"I won't," I promised.

He squeezed my arm. "We keep silence here; we only speak when necessary. I need the silence to purify my soul." His eyes shifted away. "I have sinned. I didn't stop them. After the war . . ."

"Stop who?" I pressed him. But his mouth drew into a hard line. "Is that what brought you to the abbey?"

"That other girl didn't respect the Rule of Saint Benedict."

"What other girl?" There it was again, that strange scratchy feeling in my chest.

"She came a few weeks ago. She asked a lot of questions." He heaved a sigh. "What was her name?" He eyed me. "What is your name?"

"Katherine."

"Yes!" he exclaimed. "That's it. She was my great-niece, Katreen. Benoît's granddaughter. Benoît likes peas. Do you like peas?"

I pressed a hand against my heart, trying to slow its strange beat. "*Oui*."

He reached out and lifted my chin, searching my face. "You look so much like Léna," he said, his voice suffused with wonder. His eyes met mine and for an instant they were perfectly lucid, before clouding over again. "There hasn't been a day of my life that I haven't thought of you and asked for your forgiveness."

I swallowed hard against a lump in my throat. "Frère Albert, I am sure she has forgiven you," I said.

His face crumpled in bewilderment. "Who?"

I drew a shaky breath. "*Je te pardonne*," I whispered. "I forgive you."

His hand crept up and clasped my own and as my tears fell to the soil below, I saw that they mingled with those of my uncle.

"It was so horribly sad," I said several minutes later, as pastures flashed through the windows. "Tragic, actually. He has obviously spent his entire life wracked with guilt."

"But over what?" said Jean-Luc.

"I'm not sure. Something happened with Hélène.

But I couldn't figure it out." I chewed the inside of my lip.

We were in the truck on the way back to Meursault. I had already told Jean-Luc about my conversation with Albert—and yet I couldn't stop thinking about that fleeting moment when my great-uncle's eyes had turned perfectly clear and sharp.

"He was confused," I said. "I'm pretty sure he has dementia. He thought I was her."

"What did he say when you told him you were Benoît's granddaughter?"

"He, er—actually, he thought I was talking about someone else." A full minute passed, during which time I counted seven cows. "I think Louise went to see him at the monastery and pretended to be me."

"Seriously?" Jean-Luc sounded skeptical. "That seems a little far-fetched. Would Louise really do something so dastardly?"

Yes, I thought with irritation. But there was no point trashing Louise. "Although if she did meet him," I said in a reasonable tone, "I can't imagine their conversation being any more informative—*oh my God.*" I sat forward so quickly the seat belt locked against my chest.

"What?" he asked. And then, when he saw the expression on my face: "*Quoi?*"

"Papa's favorite book—his father's favorite book! Albert said Hélène left a clue in it. Monte Cristo. *The Count of Monte Cristo*." I hesitated, struggling to connect the pieces. "Uncle Philippe told me that was his grandfather's favorite book. When Heather and I were cleaning out the *cave*, we found so many copies. We thought it was just a coincidence. But what if Hélène had planted a secret message in one of them?"

"*Attends*, I am having trouble understanding." Jean-Luc frowned. "You think Hélène left something in *Le Comte de Monte-Cristo*?"

"Not just something," I said, impatient. "Information about where they hid the bottles of Gouttes d'Or."

"Where is the book now? Is it with Nico and Bruyère?"

"I think we took it to the charity shop, so it must be . . . oh shit." I knew where the book was, with unerring certainty. "It's with Louise."

"Ah." Several kilometers passed. "You know, she keeps unsorted books in the back office of her shop," Jean-Luc said at last, blandly. "It's a mess—cartons piled everywhere."

"Yeah, but how would I get into her private office?"

Ahead of us, red brake lights bloomed around a stalled vehicle. Jean-Luc downshifted and the truck slowed. "Maybe"—he tapped his fingers on the steering wheel—"I could ask Louise to lunch tomorrow. She's been talking about wanting to go to Le Jeu de Paume."

My eyebrows shot up almost of their own volition. Le Jeu de Paume was one of Beaune's most celebrated restaurants—recently awarded two Michelin stars, with the prices to match. "Wow! I've heard that place is really . . ." I hesitated, searching for the right word. Expensive? Romantic?

"Slow," interjected Jean-Luc. "*Oui*, I expect lunch will take at least a couple of hours. Four courses, wine, coffee. It should be plenty of time for you to hunt around her office while she's out."

"Wait," I said, a tiny spark of hope igniting within my chest. "Hunt around her office? But if she's not there, how will I get in?"

"I imagine Walker will be there, minding the store. Perhaps you may not find it so very difficult to distract him? That is, only if you agree, of course."

"Of course," I said, fighting to keep a grin from spreading across my face. "I agree."

"Good." He smiled. "*Alors*, here is what I have in mind . . ."

With a small spoon, I stirred the murky demitasse of coffee for the twentieth time. Half an hour ago, Jean-

Luc had dropped me off at this café in Beaune before zooming off to meet Louise for lunch. By now, they had probably finished their Champagne and *gougères*, and moved on to the *entrées*—chilled crab, perhaps? Shaved white asparagus in truffled vinaigrette? Glasses of chilled Meursault before a bottle of Gevrey-Chambertin? I pushed away the limp remains of a goat cheese salad, checking the time on my phone before signaling for the bill.

The walk to Louise's bookshop took ten minutes, and on the way I mentally rehearsed the script Jean-Luc and I had prepared the night before. "Get there exactly at two o'clock," he had instructed, and so I waited out the final four minutes on the sidewalk across the street from the building.

"*Bonjour?*" I called upon entering the shop, but the spot behind the cash register was empty.

I glanced around, taking stock of the layout. Located on the ground floor of a shabby *hôtel particulier*, Louise's shop was dim even at midday, the windows covered with an elaborate iron grillwork. The shelves spilled over with used books, and a couple of limp orchid plants offered the sole concessions to decor. Through a half-open door along the wall, I glimpsed Louise's private office: a large desk partially obscured by stacked boxes.

I shifted my bag from one shoulder to the other. "Hello?" I called again. At least five minutes ticked by, and then the sound of running water heralded Walker's appearance from a side door.

"*Bonjour*," he began, before catching sight of me. "Kate?"

"Walker, hey!" I smiled and moved forward to hug him.

"What are you doing here?"

"Surprise! I decided to come over for one final last-minute cram session before The Test." I hoped he hadn't heard the catch in my throat.

"Whoa, that is seriously hardcore." Walker lifted his dark brows. "Isn't The Test in like two weeks?"

"Nine days," I corrected him. "But who's counting?" I let out a girlish trill, inwardly wincing.

"Yeah . . . seriously hardcore," he said again, but this time he spoke more slowly. Did his eyes just narrow?

"How are you doing?" I said quickly. "It's good to see you! I—I've missed you."

"Really," he said with an undeniable chill in his voice.

"I've missed studying together," I amended. "I really learned a lot from you."

"What are you doing here, Kate?" He crossed his arms and eyed me shrewdly. "Why on earth are you taking such a long trip right before the most important day of your life?"

"I told you," I insisted. "I'm cramming for The Test—meeting with winemakers and sommeliers. As many as possible. I'm learning so much!"

"Like what?" he challenged.

"Like . . . I had the best wine and cheese pairing yesterday," I gabbled nervously. "Volnay and fromage de Cîteaux. Have you tried it? The wine really cuts across the earthiness of the cheese."

"Fromage de Cîteaux?"

"Um, yeah. Do you know it? It's this washed-rind cheese—"

"That's produced only at the Abbaye of Cîteaux," he finished my sentence. "So, I'm guessing you went to see him, too, huh? The old monk? Crazy as a loon, right?"

I pressed my lips together, furious with myself.

"You know"—Walker heaved a sigh—"we could've worked together. We could've helped you find the missing wine, and a buyer to boot. And obviously we would've kept everything completely discreet. Instead we've wasted all this time at cross-purposes. Why don't you trust me, Kate?" He tapped his chest. "I mean, we're both American. We both work in the restaurant biz. What about the fellowship of the somm?" Was he joking, or not? As so often was the case with Walker, I had no idea.

"Is, uh, Louise around?" I asked, after an awkward pause. "I'd like to ask her advice about a rare book that a friend wants to sell."

"Sorry," he said, though he did not seem very sorry. "She's at a meeting."

"Well, if she's coming back soon, I'll just wait. No problem."

"It could be a while," he said shortly.

"So are you saying that Louise would not be interested in a first-edition, hand-bound volume of *The Physiology of Taste?*"

He hesitated.

"In Danish," I added.

Walker glanced at the clock. It was nearing a quarter past two. I could see him calculating the amount of time Louise could possibly take for lunch. "Okay," he agreed finally, and I would have felt sorry for him if he hadn't heaved a gigantic, exasperated sigh.

I sat down on one of the skeletal garden chairs lining the wall and fiddled with my phone as if checking email. Instead, I set the timer, turned up the ringer, and waited. Three minutes later, my phone began buzzing and chiming, and I pretended to answer it. "Hello?"

I said to silence. "Oh, hi, Dr. Iqbal. Sorry, what? You have my test results back from the lab? Sure, I have a minute to talk. Hold on, let me go somewhere more private." I rose from the chair and caught Walker's eye. "Okay?" I mouthed, raising my eyebrows and pointing at the door to Louise's office. Without waiting for a response, I pushed my way inside.

While the shop's ambiance could best be described as barren neglect, Louise's inner sanctum was overflowing with boxes, cartons piled to the ceiling, except for a small island around her desk. "*Oh my God, are you serious?*" I said for Walker's benefit, while staring at the masses of brown cardboard. How on earth was I going to find anything in this mess?

I took a deep breath and pried open the closest box as quietly as I could. "*But how is it transmitted?*" I said loudly. "*I mean, we used protection.*" *Squirm, Walker, squirm,* I thought.

A quick rifle through the first box yielded a bunch of old cookbooks. I shoved them aside and pulled another from the stack. "*Sorry, sorry, no, no. I'm just completely in shock.*" I stared at a ragged pile of Georges Simenon novels. "*Can you repeat that?*" I tore open another carton. A flash of brick red beneath the flaps indicated a stack of Gault Millau wine guides.

"*What kind of scan?*" I said as I reached for another box. Outdated travel guides, dog-eared penny romances with creased covers, a wobbly stack of pocket dictionaries: English-French, Français-Italiano, Français-Español. My fingers brushed against thick, textured leather, and then closed upon a heavy volume. *Les Frères Corses.* My eyes traveled to the author's name: Alexandre Dumas.

My heart was suddenly pounding against my chest. Pulling the box closer, I scrabbled to the bottom, throwing the other books on the floor, heedless of the noise. Finally, I unearthed a book bound in tattered black cloth, its cover a portrait of an overweight man clad in an old-fashioned suit. The title read: *Le Comte de Monte-Cristo.* The spine slumped as I opened the cover and turned to the first page, which was marked with a name in careful, copperplate script: Edouard Charpin.

Angry voices boomed in the bookshop, causing me to leap to my feet. I clutched the book to my chest, lunging for my bag, but not before the office door flew open, revealing Louise in a slim grey dress, nude heels clicking as she stormed toward me.

"*Vous!*" she hissed. (Even in my shock, I noticed she was using the formal form of "you.") "*Qu'est-ce que vous faîtes!*" Her dark eyes darted to and fro, taking in the open boxes. "What is that?" she demanded of the book in my hands. "Where did you get it?" In two swift steps, she was in front of me, attempting to snatch it back.

I threw a glance toward my bag, but it was out of reach. "Louise! What a surprise to see you here! In your office!" I said feebly, trying to buy time.

"Don't bullshit me, Katreen. I know exactly what you're up to."

I wrapped my arms around the book. "I could say the same thing about you."

She took a step closer, so that I could smell the sickly musk of her perfume. "Give me the book. Give me the book and I will even"—her eyes narrowed—"yes, I will split the profits with you. That's what this is about, *n'est-ce pas?* Money. But you are forgetting that I am the one who has invested so much time collecting all this junk, hunting for the little needle in the stack of hay." She waved a hand at the boxes. "I know a French collector who is willing to pay top value—cash, under the table. He is dying to get his hands on those bottles of Gouttes d'Or, no questions asked. Just give me the book, and if it leads to anything I will give you a share. A two-way split, *d'accord?*"

Sheer outrage caused the blood to rush to my cheeks. "Those bottles belong to my family!"

"The wine belongs to France. This is part of our French heritage, Kate. How on earth could you sell it at auction to rich foreigners when its true place is here in our homeland?" Before I could respond, she grabbed for the book, her sharp-clawed fingers leaving a long red scratch on my arm. I stumbled away from her, the heel of my boot snagging on a corner of the carpet. I threw out an arm as I started to trip, and a steady hand shot out and grabbed my elbow, pulling me upright.

"*Qu'est-ce qui se passe là?*" Jean-Luc boomed. He released my arm, and I regained my balance by clutching at the wall.

"Oh, Jean-Luc!" Twin roses bloomed in Louise's cheeks. "What are you—Katreen and I were just—" She laughed. "I didn't expect to see you again so soon!"

"Obviously," he said.

Louise paused delicately. "Did you know Katreen was in town again?" The edge in her voice was barely perceptible.

Without answering her question, Jean-Luc reached over and plucked the book from my hand. "*Le Comte de Monte-Cristo.*" He smiled.

"Isn't it a wonderful book? What a treasure!" Louise held out her hand for the book but Jean-Luc neatly sidestepped her and turned toward me.

"*On y va?*"

Quickly, I snagged my bag off the floor and moved toward the door. Jean-Luc followed me out of Louise's office and neither of us paused to say goodbye.

"We were wrong." Jean-Luc slumped against the kitchen table. "There's nothing here." He reached for the book again, leafing through it for the hundredth time, fanning the pages, which were soft, slightly yellowed, but otherwise pristine. Once again he examined the spine, the cover and its endpapers. Nothing.

We had been sitting here all afternoon, puzzling over the book, trying to tease out its secrets. Outside, the shadows had lengthened and a chill was rapidly descending. Across the table, Jean-Luc's head was bowed over the pages, his expression perplexed. "Are you *sure* she left a message here?" he asked.

I searched my memory for details from the World War II books I'd read. A few of them had mentioned coded messages, which had played a large role in occupied France. "They used to put tiny pencil dots over letters, to spell out words," I said. "Do you see any markings?"

He shoved the book so that it slid across the table. "It's over a thousand pages," he said. "You want to inspect every one?"

His irritation left a wake of silence in the kitchen.

I could hear the tick of his watch, the soft crunch of a car passing on the dirt road behind the house. A bird chirping its high-pitched mating call.

"Do you have a magnifying glass?" I picked up the book, smoothing the flyleaf. "What?" I said in response to his look of incredulity. "No one said this was going to be glamorous."

Jean-Luc rooted around the top drawer of his father's old escritoire, shoving aside a handful of outdated francs and several desiccated fountain pens (did anyone in France ever throw anything away?), finally unearthing an ornate magnifying glass. Peering through the lens, I began the laborious task of inspecting every letter in the book. He pottered around the kitchen, emptying the dishwasher, wiping down counters, mixing vinaigrette in an old jam jar. "Salad and cheese okay for dinner?" he asked.

"You're cooking *again*?" I said. And then, "Sorry, sorry—I'll stop saying that. That sounds delicious, thank you."

I returned to squinting at the old-fashioned type. By page twenty-six, I was already regretting my insouciance. By page forty-three, I was beginning to feel cross-eyed. By the time Jean-Luc set a bowl of salad and a wooden board of softly oozing cheeses on the table, I was downright dizzy. We ate quickly, swiping baguette across our plates to catch the last drops of vinaigrette, and then I doggedly resumed my task.

Jean-Luc washed the dishes, and then came and stood behind me, so that his shadow fell across the page. "I need to answer some emails," he said. "I was going to bring my computer in here, if you don't mind."

"*Pas du tout,*" I assured him. And so he moved his laptop to the kitchen table and we sat in companionable silence, broken only by the click of the keyboard and swish of paper as I turned a page.

An hour passed. Then another. Jean-Luc closed his laptop and began reading the newspaper. Despite my best intentions, my eyelids began to droop, my grip loosening on the magnifying glass, my head falling forward. I jerked myself awake, turned the page, forced myself to concentrate. The letters swam before my eyes, black lines and speckles against the light-colored surface. *Speckles?* I gripped the magnifying glass more tightly and peered at the text. There, in the middle of the page, was a soft dash above a "C." Further along, I found another, above a "U." Now my eyes were speeding through the paragraphs, finding other marked letters. I reached for a pencil, scribbling the sequence on a piece of scrap paper. "It doesn't make any sense," I muttered.

"*Comment?*" Jean-Luc sounded disoriented, as if he'd been dozing behind the newspaper.

"Look." I scooted beside him. "These letters are marked in the book—but the message—it doesn't make sense. It must be in code." I showed him the piece of paper.

CUSOQUATREPLUSNADEUXCO3DEVIENTAU

"*Attends.*" Jean-Luc grabbed the pencil. "CUSO QUATRE PLUS NADEAUX CO TROIS?" he muttered, trying to force the letters into words. "DEVIENT?" He frowned. "Wait. What if it's a number?" He began scribbling.

$$CUSO4PLUSNA2CO3DEVIENTAU$$

"Nope." I groaned. "Still gibberish."

But he was staring at the page, the color draining from his face. "*Bouillie bourguignonne,*" he murmured.

"What?" I could barely hear him. I shook my head, faintly irritated.

"Burgundy mixture! Look! Copper sulfate plus sodium carbonate." He scrawled another line:

$$CuSO_4 + Na_2CO_3$$

He frowned in concentration. "DEVIENT—that means 'becomes.'"

"So, Burgundy mixture becomes . . . A.U.? What's that mean?" The letters tugged at my memory. Where had I seen those initials before?

A.U.

A.U.

A.U.

"Gold!" Jean-Luc shouted, and I started back in my chair. "Au. That's the abbreviation for gold on the periodic table. Except . . ." He paused and shook his head. "It doesn't make any sense. How does Burgundy mixture become gold?"

I stared at the formula scrawled before us. "What if . . . it's not gold?" I suggested. "Not exactly. But . . . drops of gold? Les Gouttes d'Or," I breathed, as the pieces began to click into place. "If Hélène was making Burgundy mixture during the war, the fruit from the vines she treated would have become Les Gouttes d'Or. It's genius."

"Except"—Jean-Luc's shoulders dropped—"it doesn't reveal anything about where she hid the wine."

Something was tugging at my memory, but I couldn't grasp it. "A.U." I closed my eyes and the vision of a dark room floated before me, needles of cold piercing a dry stone wall. I gasped. "*La cabotte!* My great-uncle Albert's initials on the wall. A.U. Albert Ulysse. But remember? *His initials were there twice.*"

Jean-Luc shoved his chair from the table, and stood. "Come on." He grabbed my hand and pulled me upright, then led me through the kitchen and out of the house, to his truck, opening the passenger door and guiding me inside.

"But she can't have hidden the wine at the *cabotte*," I pointed out once we were bouncing along a dirt road that led through the vineyards. "There's nowhere to put it."

"*Non*," he agreed. "I think it must be something else that she concealed there—a map, *peut-être?*"

We crested a gentle slope and the *cabotte* appeared. Jean-Luc pulled to the side of the road and we scrambled out of the truck. By this time, the sun had descended, leaving a mass of shredded clouds tinted with shades of pink, bronze, lavender. In the fading light, the vines were like a dark maze, but Jean-Luc was sure-footed, leading the way to the doorway of the small stone structure.

It was colder inside, and darker, smelling faintly of wood smoke. Jean-Luc swung a flashlight around the cramped interior, so that it bounced off the rough walls, onto the patch of wall embellished with letters— Nico's initials, Uncle Philippe's, Grandpère Benoît, Uncle Albert, Great-grandfather Edouard. And there it was: Au. Kneeling to the ground, I began digging with my hands, swearing softly. "Hold on," Jean-Luc said, before stalking off to the truck. A few seconds later, he returned with a shovel, handed it to me, and then held the flashlight while I plowed into the floor of the *cabotte*, turning over the earth, deeper, deeper. The clang of metal upon metal made my heart stop.

A few more shovelfuls and I had unearthed an old biscuit tin, striped in yellow and blue. I pried off the lid, and Jean-Luc trained the flashlight on my hands as I withdrew something flat from within, unwrapping a waterproof cloth to reveal a *cahier d'exercices*—a school notebook—with a thick brown binding that looked familiar.

"What is it?" Jean-Luc asked.

My heart hammered in my chest as I opened the cover. By the thin beam of the flashlight, I peered at the careful French copperplate covering the pages:

Cher journal,

. . . Well, I am not sure how to begin this journal, so I will start with the facts, like a proper scientist. My name is Hélène Charpin and today I am eighteen years old . . .

It wasn't a map. It was a diary.

6 JANVIER 1944

Cher journal,

Benoît's birthday today. Madame showered him with presents, a pair of shoes, used of course, but only lightly scuffed, a lumpy woolen hat and sweater knit with her own hands, and—*la pièce de la résistance* for a ten-year-old boy—a shiny, toy-size trap with teeth as sharp as needles, all the better to catch squirrels, wild hares, or other small creatures. She also baked him a cake, humming as she beat together butter, sugar, eggs, walnuts. The fact that no one in the village has tasted cake for months, if not years, did not distress her in the slightest.

After we had finished supper—potatoes fried in pork drippings for Madame and the boys, two bowls of watery cabbage soup for me—but before Madame had sliced the cake, we heard a motorcycle sputter in the driveway, then a quiet knock at the door. Madame went aflutter, as is her wont these days, opening the door to reveal the lieutenant. He kissed her on both cheeks before bowing to me, courteous as ever, and then turned to the boys and gave them each a bar of chocolate.

"Oh, Bruno, you're spoiling them!" Madame said in that horrible, breathless tone she uses with him, but the old Haricot Vert just grinned and plopped himself into a chair at the far end of the table. Papa's chair. I began clearing away the supper dishes so that I wouldn't have to look at his face.

While I was washing dishes, Madame cut the cake, serving first the Haricot Vert, and then the boys. "And you, Hélène? A small piece?" she called out.

"*Non, merci,*" I said automatically over one shoulder, remembering too late that my refusal could be construed as incendiary. "I'm—er, I'm not hungry."

"More for us, then!" said Madame in a laughing voice. The clink of metal on china indicated that they had begun eating.

"Why isn't Léna having any?" It was Albert, his small voice pitched like a clarion.

"Ask her yourself, *chéri,*" came Madame's reply.

I scrubbed hard at a bit of potato stuck to the sauté pan. "I've eaten well tonight, *ma puce,*" I said finally.

Silence again, broken eventually by the sound of the Haricot Vert clearing his throat. "Your sister is a young woman of great principle, Albert," he said.

"You should be proud of her resolve." His words hung on the room's warm fug before he continued: "Though, of course, it is silly and misguided. After all, we're hardly the horrible enemy she believes us to be. Isn't that right, young man?"

Blood rushed to my face, but I remained turned toward the sink and hoped no one would notice. A second later, I heard the sound of a plate sliding across the table. "If she's not having any, I'm not either," Albert declared.

"Albert!" Madame snapped. "Finish your cake!"

"*Non! J'en veux plus!*"

"Do I need to take you behind the woodshed?" she threatened.

He fell silent and out of the corner of my eye I saw him fold his arms across his chest. I counted eleven ticks of the clock and then: "I'll eat it," said Benoît. "If he doesn't want it." He pulled the plate toward him and stuffed a huge forkful in his mouth.

"Benoît," Madame protested. But she fell silent when the Haricot Vert began to laugh.

12 JANVIER 1944

A note was slipped among the messages I gathered at the *boulangerie*. Unfolding it, I found a Paul

Verlaine poem, copied in Stéphane's hand, and a message:

Learn this for the exam.

So strange. What exam? I can't think what he means, but just to be safe I have started memorizing the poem by heart. Here is the first stanza:

Les sanglots longs
Des violons
De l'automne
Blessent mon coeur
D'une langueur
Monotone.

17 JANVIER 1944

The Haricot Vert is here again. It's the third time this week. I saw him pushing his motorcycle across the gravel driveway, and then he tiptoed up the path and through the back door. A few minutes later, socked feet began creeping down the hall to Madame's room. I suppose she thinks they are being discreet with these late-night rendezvous, but I am not fooled—not when he appears at the breakfast table in the morning.

How can she stand to be around him? Yes, he

is polite, of course, in that stiff Germanic way, but his skin is obscenely ruddy with health, and his ice-grey eyes are as watchful as a hawk's, seeing everything, observing everything. I do my best to avoid him, and I think that pleases him. As for Madame, well—she is indebted to him, and I think that pleases him as well.

27 JANVIER 1944

Albert was sent home from school today with a bloody nose. Fighting at recess, his teacher said. When I asked him about it, he said a group of boys had ambushed him in the schoolyard, taunting him and calling him names. "What names?" I asked him. Tears spilled from his eyes, drawing tracks down his dirty cheeks, before he buried his face in my shoulder and sobbed. "What happened?" I pressed him.

"Maurice called me a *collabo*," he said, the words muffled against me. "Then Claude joined in, and I was so angry I just swung out and punched him. *J'suis pas collabo*, Léna. *Je suis pas.*"

I rubbed his back, even as my hands trembled with rage. He is eight years old; what does he know of collaborating? It is impossibly unfair.

Of course, I've received my own share of hard

stares in town, accidental jostles that were not accidental, globules of spittle narrowly dodged. My friends from the circuit think my situation could be useful if the Haricot Vert ever lets slip any information, though of course he never does. But why hadn't it occurred to me that the same aggression could trickle down to the schoolyard? I held my little brother close, wishing I knew how to protect him. What can I do? What can I say?

1 FÉVRIER 1944

Laundry day. I was in the scullery, so absorbed in scrubbing the bloodstains from Albert's shirt that I didn't see Madame until she spoke. "Is that blood? Is it Benoît's?"

My fingers were numb and swollen from the icy water, so perhaps I spoke more shortly than I intended. "It's Albert's."

"What happened?" she cried.

I wrung the shirt gently, trying to avoid tearing the threadbare fabric. "He got into a fight at school."

"Chuh!" she spat. "I *told* him to stop picking fights with the other boys. Well, it's obvious that he needs to be punished. First there was that dreadful outburst on Benoît's birthday, and now this. He's turned into a horrible little beast. You've spoiled him, Hélène. I'm sorry, but I really must blame you for this behavior."

"*Moi?*" I choked on my incredulity. "You are blaming *me*? Do you know why he was fighting, Virginie? The kids at school called him a *collabo*. A collaborator!"

"Who? Who said that?" She spun round to face me. "How dare they! Just wait 'til I tell Bruno—those little brats will regret ever opening their smug little mouths. And as for their self-righteous parents . . ." Her hands balled into fists.

An image flashed before me of the Haricot Vert and his underlings banging on the doors in the village, dragging our neighbors and their children from their homes. Oh, *cher journal,* how I wished I could snatch back my hasty words! Instead, I attempted to recant: "It was nothing—just a childish squabble. I have no idea who said it. Albert did not tell me. I think that probably he doesn't remember."

Her nostrils flared. "Forget it," she snapped. "I'll find out myself." She stalked from the room, and a minute later the door of her room slammed shut.

Recounting this now, my heart is breaking. Why

can't she see what she is doing? It's bad enough that she's destroying her own reputation—how can she also destroy the lives of her children?

4 FÉVRIER 1944

I was hurrying out of the house with my shopping basket over one arm when Madame stopped me. "Oh, good, Hélène, there you are. I need to speak with you. Come into the *salon.*"

I winced but followed her into the room that she has reclaimed as her own with furniture polish, plumped cushions, and a merry little fire that she feeds dry logs without the slightest twinge of conscience.

She sank into the sofa and nodded at me to sit in the armchair opposite. I perched on the edge of the seat, aware of her huge blue eyes searching my face. "Tell me." She picked at a loose thread on her dress. "Before your father . . . left"—she paused delicately—"did he mention anything to you about *les caves?*"

Despite the crackling fire, the fine hairs on the back of my neck stood on end. "*Les caves?*" I repeated, stalling for time. "Not that I recall. Were you thinking about something specific?"

She blinked, a cold reptilian flicker. "Before the

Germans arrived, didn't he say something about hiding the more valuable bottles?"

"Hmm, did he say that?" I frowned, hoping it would conceal my thoughts. Was it possible that Papa never told Madame about the secret *cave* and the treasure we hid there? When I think back to that winter before the Occupation—four long brutal years ago—and all the afternoons Papa and I spent in the cellar, toiling in clammy semi-obscurity . . . he had said he would tell her about it "eventually." In the end, had he decided not to? If that was the case, I certainly wasn't going to give away the secret. I took a deep breath, willing myself to keep my voice steady. "He never mentioned anything to me," I said.

Her lips thinned, but she maintained a pleasant expression. "Are you sure?" she pressed me. "Bruno says—" She caught herself with a cough. "I mean, we all know that every winemaker in the region tucked away his best bottles before the Occupation. That's simply common sense. The Führer remains eager to procure the best French wines. Did you know Goebbels simply adores Burgundy? It would be foolish not to take advantage of this interest."

I stared at her in disbelief. The Führer? Goebbels? Did she really just mention these animals like they are perfectly normal beings, and not the *espèces de connard* causing unspeakable misery?

Madame must have misinterpreted my silence, for she plunged ahead: "I was in the cellar yesterday and I couldn't find any of the 1929 Gouttes d'Or—not a single bottle!"

"Papa would sooner pour wine down the drain than let the Boches have it."

Her eyes narrowed. "Hélène, whether you like it or not, now that your father is gone, I am the head of this household. You can choose to cooperate with me or not. But you need to remember that I am making the decisions, and I don't care what your father would have done. Collaboration is shielding us from the worst horrors of the Occupation."

Was that how she justified her actions? I swallowed hard, and attempted to appeal to her more avaricious sensibility. "Papa says that wine is part of the domaine's legacy."

"Legacy?" she spat the word. "I'm more concerned with our current survival. And as for your high-minded father—well, you can stop talking about him as if he's coming back. It's time you faced facts." She lifted her chin. "He is dead."

The blood rushed to my face as if she'd slapped me. Dead? How did she know? Had the Haricot Vert told her?

"Be sensible," she continued. "All these months, and we haven't heard a thing? It's the only possible explanation."

Slowly, so that she couldn't see, I exhaled. She doesn't know for certain. This is just the excuse she has invented to justify her own actions.

"He's still alive," I insisted. "He's in a prison camp and they won't allow him to write to us."

"Believe what you want."

We stared at each other with naked displeasure. But we had reached a stalemate—there was nothing left to say—and so I awkwardly grabbed for my shopping basket and left the house.

Later, as I was bicycling to Beaune with a vicious wind biting at my face, I analyzed our conversation, hearing again Madame's cool, clear tones discussing the Führer, her plans for the hidden wine, her dispassionate pronouncement about Papa.

I have always disliked her. That has never been a secret. Much of my dislike was fueled by my own childish jealousy—I see that now—and our rivalry for Papa's affection and attentions. I have known her to be petty, manipulative, duplicitous, but I never believed she would actually harm any of us. Until now.

Ever since Benoît's birthday—no, it started before that. Ever since that night in December, when Benoît was so terribly ill and the Haricot Vert brought that Boche doctor to our house—she has carried herself with a new confidence. She is indebted to them, yes, especially the Haricot Vert—but she also basks in their power, taking genuine pleasure in flaunting the privilege bestowed upon her.

How could I have been so blind? I am embarrassed it has taken me so long to admit it. Madame isn't merely collaborating with the enemy. She has become the enemy.

8 FÉVRIER 1944

Our first meeting since the New Year this afternoon. 'Twas very, very subdued. We have strong reason to believe that the extensive "Prosper" circuit to the west has been broken up, and all of us are devastated. We talked obsessively of tapped telephones, Gestapo tails, paid informers, anonymous tip-offs. "I hesitate to say this," said Stéphane, "but I feel almost envious of them. Now that they've been taken, they no longer have to fear it." Everyone nodded in agreement.

In an effort to change our conversation to a more cheerful topic, I asked about the *messages personnels* we hear every night on the BBC. "Who is Yvette and why does she like big carrots?"

Yvette, Emilienne told me, might signify a successful parachute drop of weapons. "The tall blond man called Bill" could indicate the safe arrival of a plane in England.

Stéphane had been concentrating on an underground newssheet, but now he glanced up. "Did you all memorize the Verlaine poem I sent you?" he asked.

Everyone nodded. "Bit depressing, isn't it?" said Danielle. She's our radio operator, a round-faced girl with a thick fringe of dark hair. "The long sobs of the autumn violin . . . wound my heart . . . with the languor of monotony," she intoned dramatically.

He smiled faintly. "Just listen for it. Every day, keep listening."

"Why?" I pressed. "What does it mean?"

"D-Day," he said in English.

I frowned—Stéphane knows my English is poor. "What's that?"

"*Le Jour J,*" he explained. "It means we will be saved." But when I asked for details, he wouldn't say anything more.

10 MARS 1944

Cher journal,

It dawned dark this morning and looking at the sky I knew it would be one of those grey, grizzly spring days, the kind where the sun never reaches full strength. The air felt heavy, electric, and I briefly considered abandoning my plan to bicycle to the Côte de Nuits. But there were two messages hidden in the lining of my satchel, and so I donned Papa's waxed raincoat and trilby, hooked a basket over my handlebars, and set out just as a few drops began splashing from the sky.

I'd been cycling for about ten minutes when the downpour began in earnest, a gentle tapping that turned quickly to a roar, and then became hail, icy bullets pelting my head, face, and hands. I should have given up and headed home, but I continued for another kilometer, my visibility worsening as the hail returned to thick rain. I had just made the decision to turn around when I saw a police checkpoint looming straight ahead on the Route de Savigny—a new one, a surprise one that hadn't been there a day earlier. Every instinct screamed at me to turn tail and flee, but I forced myself to pedal straight toward it, the murmur of Stéphane's instructions an undercurrent beneath the thunder of my heart:

Always go directly toward a police barrier, never double back. Always walk against oncoming traffic so that a car cannot approach you unnoticed from behind. Always tear messages into tiny pieces and scatter them over very long distances.

Well, it was too late to tear the illicit messages into tiny pieces, never mind scattering them over a long distance. I struggled to appear calm as I approached the checkpoint. The blood was roaring so loudly in my ears, I thought I might faint.

"*Halt! Stopp!*" commanded one of the Germans as I drew near. He was tall and thick-limbed, his fleshy cheeks shadowed by the peak of a cap. I dismounted from my bike and walked toward him, gripping the handlebars to hide my shaking hands.

"*Guten tag,*" he said.

"*Guten tag,*" I responded dutifully.

"Papers," he ordered, switching to French. Silently, I handed him my identity documents. "What is the nature of your business?"

"I'm out gathering food for my rabbits." The lie slipped from my lips, before I remembered that the dismal weather would betray me. "I've been out for hours. I had no idea it was going to storm," I added.

His eyes darted across my face to my clothes, my bicycle, my bag, the basket hanging from my handlebars. "Why is it empty?" he said, nodding at the basket.

I flushed. Usually I remembered to stuff a few stray weeds inside but today the rain had distracted me. Before I could respond, he said: "Show me your bag."

I stared at the ground as he opened the flap and pawed through the contents, breathing very slowly to keep myself from being sick. My belongings came flying into the mud: A pair of worn gloves. A tube of India ink. Our ration books. Then there was a pause. I snuck a glance from under my eyelashes and icy dread dripped down my spine. In the German's hands was a copy of *La Voix*, our mimeographed Resistance newspaper, which I'd slipped into my bag last week and completely forgotten. How could I have been so stupid? Next he would rip open the bag's lining and discover the hidden messages sewn within. What information was in those letters? Whose names? How much of the circuit would be implicated? I gritted my teeth to keep from crying.

The Boche raised a hand at one of the military vehicles. "Herr Leutnant!" he shouted. I kept my face straight ahead, but out of the corner of my eye I saw a tall figure swing down from the truck and walk toward us. The two men conferred in Ger-

man, a long, ursine growl that seemed to go on forever, of which I understood only: "*La Voix.*"

The two Boches separated, and the lieutenant
moved closer. I lowered my eyes to the ground,
steadfast in my refusal to show the fear brimming
there. "Mademoiselle Charpin!" he sang. At this, I
raised my chin to look at him—and stifled a gasp. It
was the Haricot Vert.

"Mademoiselle." He nodded at me. "How de-
lightful it is to see you here—and how enlighten-
ing." His ice-grey eyes lingered shrewdly on the
empty basket perched upon the handlebars of my
bicycle.

"Is it?" I managed to croak.

"Very." He folded the newspaper into thirds and
slipped it into his pocket.

I could barely hear him above the blood rushing in my ears. He stared at me for a long moment,
appraising me with those glacial eyes. The rain fell
steadily in a continuous patter—Papa would call it
a "vigneron's rain"—running in rivulets down the
back of my neck. The Haricot Vert, too, was getting drenched, but he seemed hardly to notice. Finally, he took a step closer—too close—and spoke
quietly, so quietly only I could hear him above the

rain: "You and I both know that I should bring you in for questioning." He gazed down at me, so that his eyelashes fell upon his cheeks, a fringe of pale white against flushed skin. "But"—he leaned even closer—"as we have *friends* in common, I am going to let you go."

I felt myself go limp with relief, though I tried to hide it behind a shrug. "As you wish." I forced myself to lift my chin. "I have nothing to hide."

"Young girls with nothing to hide shouldn't be so careless as to get caught in a tempest, fräulein." He tapped a finger against his nose. "I suggest that you return home and leave the, ahem, *foraging* for more clement weather." He handed me my satchel and I clutched it to my chest before swinging a shaky leg over my bicycle seat. The Haricot Vert moved to let me pass, but as he stepped aside, he did something truly terrifying: He looked at me, and he smiled.

11 MARS 1944

I am restless, sleepless. Indeed, I haven't been able to sleep since the Haricot Vert stopped me yesterday at the surprise checkpoint. I still can't believe I was so stupid, so careless. How could I have forgotten to remove the copy of *La Voix* from my bag? That newspaper is full of Resistance information—coded, yes, but now it's in the enemy's hands. I keep analyzing my encounter with the Haricot Vert, examining it from every angle. What does he know? What does he suspect? What has he told Madame? Has she been more quiet of late—more pensive—or is that my imagination? Around and around I go, in an endless loop until I droop with exhaustion, and still my thoughts whirr, whirr, whirr.

The moon is like a beacon tonight, so bright it casts shadows. Gazing out at the rows of silvery grapevines, I am reminded of the night Papa and the Reinachs left—that terrible, luminous night. It has been eighteen months since I last saw them, but I feel like I've aged a thousand years.

I have been thinking a lot about something Rose said all those months ago, when we were making the copper sulfate at the *cabotte*. It was like alchemy, she said; we were turning metal into gold. She was being fanciful. Joking. But now, I think often about this word—"alchemy"—for what is it but a process of mysterious transformation? And I wonder if this war could actually be a form of alchemy—changing us, testing us, until each of us has revealed the truest part of our souls.

16 MARS 1944

Entering my room tonight, something feels strange. Off. I can't quite put my finger on it. My first fear was that someone had discovered this journal, but no, the rug was pulled smoothly over the uneven floorboard, the whole appearing entirely untouched. The rest of my room is as I remember leaving it this morning—the books stacked on my desk, my mustard-yellow sweater hanging on the back of the chair, the framed photo of Papa and Maman square on my dresser. But something is causing the back of my neck to prickle. It's ridiculous, but I feel as if the very molecules of the air have shifted.

Is it Madame? Has she been here? Do I smell her perfume? Like a mad dog, I just went around the corners of the room, hunting for her scent. Nothing.

Is this how paranoia begins? Yesterday I thought someone followed me to the mail drop in Beaune, but when I turned around, there was no one to be seen for meters. I've been sleeping poorly, eating poorly. It's no wonder my nerves are worn threadbare. These past few months have made me too brittle, too suspicious. Add to this the severe malnourishment we all face—it's enough to drive anyone to the brink of madness.

I must steel my nerves—there is too much at stake to falter now. *C'est rien, c'est rien, c'est rien.* If I repeat it enough times, perhaps I will start to believe it.

4 MAI 1944

Cher journal,

Sunlight woke me this morning, a shining ray of warmth caressing my cheek. For a moment I thought I was on holiday near the sea (which I've never seen). Albert was squatting nearby at the water's edge, digging in the wet sand with a shiny new shovel. "*Regarde*, Léna," he called, popping up and running toward a cresting wave. "I can swim!"

"Wait, Albert! Be careful!" I cried, grabbing for his hand. Pain shot through my arm so that I gasped, opening my eyes to find myself in the same grubby hospital bed that I've been in for the past two weeks. In the corner, two French policemen conferred with a nurse. A few seconds later, she approached my bed.

"Charpin, you're being discharged today." Her hair was pulled into a tight bun that emphasized her slightly bulbous eyes.

"Released?" I croaked. "Or transferred to prison?"

She pressed her lips together and ignored me, moving down the ward.

Was she telling the truth? Or was this another trick? My heart pounded, but I could do nothing but wait, my thoughts turning for the thousandth time to the events of the day that had brought me here.

It was a warm day, especially for mid-April. I had received word of a meeting in Beaune, two o'clock at the home of Docteur Beaumont on the rue Paradis. This was a new address, but that wasn't unusual; we had to change our meeting place often and Stéphane had recently mentioned the elderly dentist, describing him as "not one of us, but sympathetic to us."

I set out in late morning, hours in advance. The fine weather allowed me to take a circuitous route so that I could make sure no one was following me, and I zigzagged through the vines, enjoying the mild breeze on my face. At a quarter to two, I approached the doctor's street—a narrow, cobblestoned lane lined with attached town houses—very correct, very bourgeois—noting a shining brass doorplate that indicated he kept his consulting rooms on the ground floor of his home. I rang the bell, and a stout, grey-haired woman opened the door—the housekeeper, I assumed, from her apron—and directed me to an empty sitting room upstairs.

The room was dim and airless, the windows closed, shutters fastened tight. I sat on a stiff antique chair, and hoped fervently the others would soon arrive. The doorbell was ringing constantly— the waiting room downstairs filling with the doctor's post-lunch patients—and something about its sharp trill set my nerves on edge. At least, I reasoned, the crowd of patients would provide cover for our group. After what seemed like an eternity but was probably about ten minutes, I heard light footsteps on the stairs, and Emilienne appeared.

"Is this an odd place for a meeting?" she asked after we had exchanged cheek kisses.

I shrugged. "Stéphane's mentioned it before."

"The house has no back door," she observed. "It's an easy trap." She moved to the windows. "I suppose it's too high to jump?"

Before I could respond, Danielle arrived, her round face flushed and sweaty. Then Bernard, still limping from his escape from a Lyon prison, and close on his heels, our newest recruit—we call him The Kid—barely sixteen years old, his cheeks rough with acne. It was two o'clock. Then a quarter past. Two thirty.

"Where's Stéphane?" Emilienne asked. "Should we leave?"

We had abandoned a meeting in conditions far less dubious, disbanding and regrouping a day or two later. I glanced at Bernard, trying to gauge his opinion. He was leaning back in a chair, legs stretched before him, his face grey with exhaustion. Voices filtered up the stairs—the howl of a child and his mother's scolding—the murmur of the housekeeper dispensing pleasantries at the door. They were such normal sounds—sounds of domesticity, sounds of peace—that for a second I forgot where we were, and why we had gathered there. My eyes drifted to the mantelpiece clock, ornate gleaming gilt and anchored by a fat cherub, and that is how I know that it was three minutes to three o'clock when the pounding on the front door began. My eyes met Emilienne's—her face drained white—but we had no time to hide before boots stormed up the stairs and the sitting room door flew open.

"*Down on the floor! Get down! Get down!*" a massive ox of a Boche shouted in a guttural accent. Two other Germans loomed behind him, dressed in plain clothes, all of them brandishing pistols.

I threw myself to the ground. My face was pointed to the carpet, but I could see their feet moving around us, grinding heels into stray fingers. Fear rose to my throat, choking me, so that I had to bite my lip to keep from retching. *Where is Stéphane?* I thought desperately. *Did he escape? Please, God, please, God, please.* The great, stocky bull of a man—the leader, I presumed—kicked over a delicate side table, splintered off a leg, and began to beat Bernard.

"I recognize you, you little bastard!" he screamed. "You're not getting away this time."

With a merry jingle of chains, the other two Boches moved about the room, clapping on handcuffs, pausing to aim a few kicks at Bernard before wrestling the restraints onto his wrists, growling information at each other. One of them kneeled beside me and began to bind my wrists with a leather strap.

"They're saying there's no more handcuffs," mumbled Bernard, who after several months in prison had learned some German. "They're surprised we're so many."

"*Shut up!*" The Ox struck Bernard in the back with the table leg. "*Move.*"

They forced us to our feet, prodding us downstairs with their pistols. We shuffled past the downstairs waiting room—crowded, but eerily silent—and through the front door to the street, where cars stood waiting for us. Beside the first vehicle, a tall figure slumped, head bowed, shackled wrists preventing him from raising a shoulder to wipe his bloody face. My heart plummeted—it was Stéphane.

Our eyes met and flew apart. From now on, we would have to pretend we had never met—denial and feigned ignorance are our only hope of protecting our contacts. My other comrades, too, kept their gazes fixed on the ground as they were marched outside. Emilienne was in front, I came next—trailed by a Boche who held one end of the leather strap encircling my wrists—and Danielle was somewhere behind. The Ox and his minions began forcing everyone into the cars, Stéphane, Bernard and The Kid into the first vehicle, and then Emilienne was being led to the second. Before I could follow her, I sensed, rather than saw, Danielle bend over, and then I heard her gag, and a flood of sick hit the pavement.

"*Scheisse!*" roared the Boche behind me, leaping away from the vomit pooling at our feet.

I twisted to look behind me—and that's when I saw that he had dropped the end of the leather cord. Danielle lifted her head, our eyes met, and she gave me the faintest ghost of a wink. Quickly—

before I could reconsider—I shoved the Boche so that he went sprawling into the stinking puddle and I ran, wriggling my hands from the loosened leather strap as I fled.

The cobblestones were rough beneath my feet, but I managed not to stumble as I sprinted down the street. Glancing behind, I saw two Boches hard on my heels. If I could just make it to the park, I could find a place to hide. A shot exploded behind me, but I kept running, running . . . I was almost at the corner, if I could turn, I'd lose them . . . only half a block away . . . and then searing pain tore through my shoulder, forcing me to falter. In an instant, one of the Boches had tackled me. The last thing I remember is the weight of his meaty palm shoving my face into the cobblestones.

I woke in a hospital bed, my bandaged shoulder throbbing and hot. The left side of my face felt tender, and I couldn't take a deep breath without gasping. A nurse bustled past carrying a stack of folded sheets. "I can't breathe," I told her.

"Your ribs are broken," she said, and kept walking.

I closed my eyes against the pain, drifting into a twilight sleep. Minutes—or was it hours?—later, a hand touched my face, tenderly brushing the bruises. I opened my eyes to find a man looming above me, gazing at me with penetrating blue eyes set amid sharp features. "Such a pretty girl," he murmured, stroking a thumb across my chin. "It's a shame about the black eye."

I flinched and drew away, and his thin lips curved upward.

"Mademoiselle Hélène Charpin?" he said, straightening slightly. Behind his slight form stood the Ox, all fleshy features and thick limbs.

"Yes." I managed to look at him without cowering.

"We would like to ask you a few questions. It will not take very long."

Cher journal, what could I do but agree? He pulled up a chair and the interrogation began, questions about the house on the rue Paradis, demands that I identify my comrades, threats of physical harm: Who are they? How do you know each other? Why were you meeting? And, finally—asked with deceptive carelessness—who is Stéphane?

We are a wine appreciation society, I replied, reciting the details of the cover we had invented so long ago. In the beginning we hosted wine tastings, but now, given the current ration restrictions, we gather to simply *talk* about wine. I rattled off some nonsense about the Clos du Vougeot, and Maréchal Pétain's favorite vintages. Stéphane? I've never set eyes on him before yesterday, I lied, gazing at the picture held in front of me, an old school photo of a sullen and unsmiling *lycéen*.

My interrogator took notes with a knowing smile, as if he had no need to even ask any questions but was merely waiting for me to stumble over my own answers. On and on went the examination, one hour creeping into the next, until I grew limp with pain and exhaustion, even as my inquisitor's piercing blue eyes twinkled each time I shifted in discomfort.

I had just begun to describe the wine appreciation society for the fifth time when, as suddenly as he had arrived, my little Gestapo departed. Perhaps he was late for another appointment, perhaps someone had beckoned to him from across the ward—whatever the case, he sprang from his chair and vanished around the corner. I tensed, waiting for him to return, a flood of questions coursing through my brain: How had they found us? Who had ratted us out? Eventually fatigue overwhelmed me. I sank into my thin pillow, and slept.

The next day was the same—and the next day, and the next—on and on until one week bled into two. He always appeared without warning, always greeted me with a caress that made the bile rise to my throat, and always interrogated me for hours, the questions growing increasingly intimate—asking about my childhood and education, my parents, my friends—before he suddenly disappeared. I dreaded these meetings, even though they were the only human interaction of my day—even though they offered the only break from my silent, solitary purgatory of fear and worry. The effort to appear calm and composed before him taxed my energy more than the pain of my injuries.

And so, we arrive at this morning. As I gazed through the window at the leafing trees, I wondered if the nurse had been telling the truth. Was I truly to be discharged? And, if so, where was I going? A moldy prison cell? A grim Polish work camp? Would I be allowed to see Benoît and Albert before I was sent away? I wanted my brothers to understand that I had resisted because I believed it was the right thing to do.

Eventually a doctor came to check my injuries, pronouncing me fit and scribbling his name across the bottom of a discharge form. After more waiting, a nurse tossed a rough grey tunic on the bed and told me to get dressed. As I scrambled into the clothing, she reappeared to drop my old, battered shoes on the ground. "Let's go," she said, with a scowl.

I followed her meekly out of the ward, along the hall, down the staircase, all the while bracing myself for what surely lay ahead. A glance behind confirmed that a Vichy policewoman had trailed us to the ground floor of the hospital. The nurse opened a door and I stepped into a waiting room, steeling myself for the sight of the Gestapo's drab grey-green uniforms, the iron of their grip on my arms. Instead, a slender, tawny-haired woman came forward with a frown. "Oh, there you are, Hélène," she said. "Took your time, didn't you? I've been waiting for hours." It was Madame.

6 MAI 1944

It's two days since I returned to the domaine. At least Albert was happy to see me; he hurled himself at me, heedless of my injuries, giving me a squeeze that sent pain knifing through my body. Benoît was more reticent, offering a mumbled "*Ça va?*" and ducking out from my embrace. Madame watched us with a needle-sharp gaze.

At the first opportunity I came upstairs to my room. My belongings had been ransacked—which did not surprise me—the contents of my drawers upended on the floor, my books and clothes rifled and cast askew. I dropped to my knees on the threadbare carpet, groping beneath the uneven floorboard, closing my eyes in relief as I touched this journal, still safely tucked away.

"Happy to be home, Hélène?" Madame said from the doorway.

I kept my eyes screwed shut. "I was saying a prayer of thanks," I replied after a long minute, struggling to my feet.

"I do hope you included me. After all," she said, her voice dripping with vile sanctimony, "you'd be rotting in a Polish work camp if not for me." I'm afraid I could not hide my surprise, and she continued, "Don't look so shocked, Hélène. I'm not a monster. Yes, we've had our differences of opinion, but I still feel responsible for you, especially since I gave—" She broke off, her pale cheeks flooding with color. "I owe that much to your father, at least—to save you."

She was staring at me with an expression that looked strangely like guilt. "To save me?" I repeated. "*To save me?*" My brain churned, clawing through her words, trying to untangle their meaning. Suddenly, I put it all together. "You were spying on me!" Her eyes shifted from my face, and I knew

I was right. "You've been snooping through my things. And when you finally found something . . . you took it straight to the Boches!" I was shouting now, almost certainly frightening the boys, but I didn't care. "Do you have any idea what you've done? Do you know what happens to *résistants* who get caught? Their blood is on your hands, Virginie. Just like the Reinachs. Just like Papa's!"

Her eyes had turned to twin lumps of burning coal in her pale face, her arms crossed against her chest so tightly the tendons stood in high relief along her neck. For a fleeting moment I thought I had broken her defiance. Instead, she took a single swift step toward me, and hissed: "Whatever you think, you'll never be able to prove it!"

12 MAI 1944

Another sleepless night. When I close my eyes, I see them in the final moments before the Boches took them away. Danielle's flushed cheeks, a line of sweat beading her upper lip. The Kid, jiggling his left foot up and down, up and down, up and down. Emilienne, her lovely eyes dreamy and wistful. Bernard's exhausted pallor. Stéphane, lifting his shoulders with futile effort as he tried to wipe away the blood trickling down his face. Was that the last time I'll ever see them?

Every day I hope for news; every day my hopes are dashed. My injuries preclude a trip to Beaune and, anyway, my bicycle has disappeared. And so I remain here at the domaine, trapped in this fog of grief and guilt, my mind running over the details of that day, wondering what I could have done to prevent the outcome. I am afraid to sleep for when I do, I wake to the same ugly reality: The circuit has been destroyed, my friends are in trouble—and I am responsible.

5 JUIN 1944

For four days, the BBC has been impossible to receive, the signal jammed no matter how carefully I twist the radio dial. But tonight my patience was rewarded. *Cher journal*, I heard it. Forgive my shaking hand, the haste of these words. A few minutes ago, *I heard it.*

The program started out the usual way: *Içi Londres. Les français parlent aux français.* London here. The French are speaking to the French—followed by the usual announcement of a few personal messages—and then suddenly the announcer was reading words that I have whispered to myself a hundred times: two mournful stanzas of "Chanson d'Automne," the Paul Verlaine poem Stéphane instructed us to memorize all those months ago. He recited each line twice, with crystal clarity.

Could I hope—dare I hope—that the Allies are finally here?

6 JUIN 1944

All day I waited for news, so nervous and distracted that Madame grew quite impatient with me. After I accidentally fed the chickens some scraps she'd been saving for dinner, she snapped: "What's wrong with you?" Frankly, it amazed me that she could not sense the strange energy humming through the air, making the blood vibrate within my veins.

When, this evening, I was finally able to pick up the BBC's signal, it took me several seconds before I could concentrate on the announcer's words. But when I did, *cher journal*, I thought I might faint, for there was Général de Gaulle addressing us, the people of France, in clarion tones: "The supreme battle has begun!" Listening to his brief speech, the tears began streaming down my cheeks, so that I was wiping my face with a handkerchief as he concluded: "In the French nation, in our Empire, in our Armies there is one will, one hope. Behind the clouds laden with our blood and our tears, we see again the sunrise of our national greatness."

The Allies are coming.

The Allies are coming.

The Allies are coming.

Thank you, God. Thank you. Thank you. Thank you. Thank you.

21 JUIN 1944

Finally, I was able to go to Beaune today. In a rare (and strange) conciliatory gesture, Madame lent me her bicycle. I forced myself to ride there very slowly, to protect my shoulder, even though I was bursting to see Madame Maurieux at the café. I couldn't wait to finally discuss the recent events with someone who truly shared my joy.

Turning onto the rue des Tonneliers, I smelled an acrid stench. A few seconds later, I was staring in stunned silence at the burnt shell of the café. Flagging down a stooped woman creeping by on a cane, I gasped: "What happened?"

"You knew them?"

"I know them," I corrected her. "Where are they?"

"Missing. But . . ." She gave a regretful shake

of her head, and I struggled to contain a wave of panic. Her beady eyes peered at my face and finally she said: "The Boches are taking matters into their own hands—punishing anyone they suspect of sabotage. A word of advice, *ma puce*"—she took a shaky step forward and lowered her voice—"if you were a regular there, you'd better hurry home. Beaune is not safe for you."

Cher journal, I fled.

21 AOÛT 1944

I feel like I have spent the past several weeks in a fog, lost in a nightmare of terrible violence—disappearing neighbors, impromptu executions, looting, arson. At first Madame found excuses for these acts of German vengeance, but then something unexpected happened: the Haricot Vert vanished. Yes, the horrible old Boche String Bean up and left, without even a word of farewell. If I expected Madame to be upset—if I thought she had formed some sort of emotional attachment—I was mistaken. She acts as if he never existed.

7 SEPTEMBRE 1944

After weeks of heavy shelling, we woke this morning to silence. Madame was too afraid to venture forth, so it was I who crept up the cellar stairs to investigate. Given the explosions that have shaken the past days, I was braced for the worst—but far from scorched earth, I found our precious vines sprawling across the slopes in verdant innocence, cool and untouched.

I'm not sure how long I stood there mesmerized by the rippling leaves, but eventually a distant rumble made me stiffen. After four years of Occupation, I knew the sound well—it was a convoy traveling the main road. Were the Germans returning? The engines grew louder and louder and I grew more and more fearful. Finally, desperate to learn more, I began to climb the cherry tree, ignoring the pain throbbing in my side and shoulder. From high in the branches, I glimpsed a line of vehicles heading toward us, drawing nearer, nearer. I lifted a hand against the sun dazzling my eyes. Did I spy a flag? I squinted, trying to make out the colors: red, white, and blue. I opened my mouth, but found myself unable to utter a sound. They were Americans.

8 SEPTEMBRE 1944

Oh, what a scene today in Beaune! For as long as I live, I shall never forget the mad joy in the streets—the crowds of revelers, the flags streaming from every window, the bottles of wine passed from hand to hand, the cheers so loud they made my ears ring. My brothers and I danced until we gasped, paused briefly to catch our breaths, and danced some more. I embraced all our neighbors, including the old woman from the *boulangerie* who had handed me secret messages for a year, yet whose name I have never dared to ask. To my surprise, I even saw Monsieur Fresnes roll a barrel to the street and begin pouring wine for American soldiers as if he and his wife had never invited Germans to drink of the same vintage! When I greeted him (I couldn't resist), he handed me a cup of wine with a cold bow. "Where is your stepmother?" he asked.

"She's not feeling well," I told him. In fact, Benoît and Albert had begged her to join us, but she had irritably shaken off their pleas. "She has a migraine—oh!" Someone had shoved me from behind so that the wine in my cup sloshed across my dress. I placed a hand against my sore ribs.

"Whoops, sorry, didn't see you there." Madame Fresnes stepped into my line of vision. "*Bonjour.*" She offered me a hard little smile.

"*Bonjour,*" I faltered.

"*Chéri,*" she turned to her husband. "Didn't you

want to speak with Monsieur le Maire? I just saw him there with Jean Parent."

"*S'il vous plaît,*" I murmured, though they didn't acknowledge my politesse. *Go,* I thought as they moved away. *Go and attempt to fawn over the mayor while you still can.* The Fresnes are opportunistic old toadies—but judging from the hard looks being thrown their way, it seemed everyone else in town recognizes it, too. They revealed their true selves long ago. I feel certain fortune will not smile upon them for much longer.

19 SEPTEMBRE 1944

There are things four years of Occupation have taught me to fear. The flash of a grey-green uniform caught from the corner of my eye. Checkpoints. An unexpected knock on the door. It was the latter that roused us at dawn, a loud banging that echoed through the house. Benoît started crying, and Albert ran to me as I stumbled blearily into the hall. Madame appeared in her nightgown, whispering: "Who is it?" My first thought, foggyheaded, was of Papa, and the second it entered my mind, I flew down the stairs. "Wait!" hissed Madame. But it was too late—I was already opening the door.

"Madame Virginie Charpin?" said a voice. Suddenly three men were pushing past me and entering the house. I squinted at their faces: Monsieur Parent, the mayor, and *Monsieur Fresnes*? They wore hats and tweeds, with tricolor armbands wrapped around their sleeves—blue, white, red—the colors of France. The colors of the Resistance.

"Why are you here?" Madame cried. "What do you want?"

"Virginie Charpin," Monsieur Parent said again. "You are being arrested for crimes of collaboration." Monsieur Fresnes reached forward and grabbed Madame's arms.

"Please," pleaded my stepmother. "Why are you doing this?"

"Have you not, Madame, received all manner of material benefits in exchange for the—*ahem*—attentions of a German officer? Your children have been well fed. Your house has been warm. Even your hair has been coiffed!"

Madame's mouth fell open, as did my own. To hear these accusations issuing from the lips of Monsieur Fresnes, a man so close to the Vichy that he had gifted Maréchal Pétain with a parcel of Clos du Vougeot vines . . . well, I could have drowned myself in the irony.

"But you have no authority!" Madame protested. "The war is not even over!"

"The Comité de Libération was formed two days ago, Madame," said the mayor. "We are beginning tribunals immediately. You are accused of undermining national morale with your unpatriotic behavior."

Madame twisted violently in Monsieur Fresnes's hands. "*C'est pas possible!*" she protested. "*Ce n'est pas juste!*" Her words rang through the house. *It's not fair.*

"Come, come, Madame Charpin," said the mayor in soothing tones. "There's no need to get hysterical. I assure you all this will be easier if you just remain calm."

"Calm?" She struggled again to break free. "*Calm?*" Her eyes burned against her papery skin. "You barge into my home in the middle of the night, attack me with these ridiculous accusations, restrain me in front of my sons—and you expect me to remain *calm*?" She was screaming now, specks of spittle flying from her mouth, her features stretched like a madwoman's. "I have done *nothing worse* than any of *you!*"

At this, Monsieur Fresnes's face darkened, and he forced her hands behind her back, giving her arms an extra vicious twist. "The tribunal will be the judge, Madame."

Suddenly she wilted and began to cry, heedless of the tears and snot running down her face. "Please," she sobbed. "My boy, my Benoît, he is so frail—I couldn't bear to watch him waste away. I only did it to take care of my sons. With their father gone, I'm all they have in this world. Please let me stay with them—don't take me away. Find some mercy in your heart. Please. *Please.*"

The mayor and Monsieur Parent exchanged a look. "I am afraid, Madame, that you are being accused of more than mere, er, horizontal collaboration." The mayor coughed delicately. "More seriously there is the matter of your work as a Gestapo informant. The Comité has learned of a raid on a local Resistance network, which led to at least one execution—the leader, shot by a firing squad."

"*He was my nephew!*" boomed Monsieur Parent.

The air disappeared from my lungs. Stéphane was dead? I had suspected it—feared it—but hearing the confirmation, a wave of nausea caught in my throat. The image of the last time I'd seen him rose in my mind's eye—the slouch of his shoulders, the line of blood running down his face, his eyes blazing with pride. He was so alive, so vital—how could he be gone? I shot a look at my stepmother and hot fury coursed through my veins.

"Me?" Madame exclaimed. "An informant? I have no idea what you mean! I would never—I couldn't imagine—deep in my heart, I have always remained loyal to France."

Her audacity stunned me from my silence. "*Liar!*" I screeched. "You know exactly what they're talking about! You spied on me for weeks, and then gave the information straight to the Germans. You're a traitor, Virginie, and now everyone knows it, including your sons. *Fille de Boches!*" The words exploded from me, propelled by grief and rage.

"Let's go." Monsieur Parent moved forward to hustle Madame down the stairs.

"But why did Hélène go free?" Madame said quickly. "If I'm the informant—if I'm the traitor—why was she the only one of her group to be released? Why was she the only one who didn't get put in handcuffs? She tells a pretty story, but have you stopped to consider that maybe *she* is the one walking around in complete liberty—*because she set up her friends.*"

"What?" I reeled upon the stairs. "That is a complete fabrication! There are many who would vouch for me—just ask Madame Maurieux at the Café des Tonneliers." Too late I remembered she was missing, feared dead. "Or—or the old woman at the *boulangerie* on the place Carnot . . ." I faltered, recalling that I never even asked her name.

Monsieur Fresnes had loosened his grip on Madame, and now she crouched low, opening her arms to Benoît, burrowing her face into his hair, her shoulders wracked with sobs. It was a most touching portrait of motherly love. False as her words were, I had no doubt her maternal devotion—as well as her fear—was very, very real.

"You know," Monsieur Fresnes said to no one in particular, "I didn't say anything earlier, but my wife did mention some rumors about Hélène."

The mayor turned to me and an icy prickle ran down my spine. "She's lying!" I insisted. "She'll say anything to save her own skin."

"Shhh, shhh, don't cry," Madame soothed Benoît. "*Maman est là, maman est là.*"

"Hélène Charpin," the mayor said. "You will come with us for questioning."

"This is ridiculous!" I protested. "I've done absolutely nothing wrong—anyone in my circuit would tell you that."

"Everyone in your circuit is gone," said Madame.

In a flash, Monsieur Fresnes was beside me, encircling my wrists with an iron grip. "Tell them the truth, Virginie!" I cried. "Tell them I'm innocent!"

For a second, guilt flickered across her features, and I sensed her wavering. But before she could respond, the men began moving me down the stairs, bumping me painfully down each step. My last glimpse of Madame was of her head bowed over Benoît's slender form, her body limp with relief.

21 SEPTEMBRE 1944

The past two days have been the stuff of nightmares—worse, actually—a humiliation greater than any I could have imagined. All the way to Beaune, I held out hope for the humanity of my fellow townspeople. But when we arrived, there was no justice. There was no tribunal. There was no voice of mercy. There was only a crowd thirsting for revenge, straining to punish "*les putes*"—the whores, the women who had submitted in the most obvious, carnal way to our Occupiers—a group of six that somehow, impossibly, I had joined. The throng was so eager to disgrace us that no one paused to deliberate the truth. Hands tore at my clothes, stripping me naked. Sticks prodded me through the streets. Razor blades skimmed my scalp, shaving the hair from my head. Paint was smeared across my most private parts, daubed upon my skin in designs of swastikas. Jeers and taunts and globules of spit were hurled toward my face, along with chants of "whore" and "slut." Stones were plucked from the ground and flung toward me.

I write this account now, as plainly as possible, so that there is a record, so that no one forgets what happened to the group of us. I write this account now because I saw with my own eyes that today's most enthusiastic persecutors were the war's most spineless cowards—traitors, informers, racketeers—hoping to expunge their record by pouncing upon this most convenient scapegoat.

Later I heard them calling it the wild purge, and the wildness, yes, I understood it. Theirs was a savage fury, fueled by righteousness and fear. But the purge made less sense to me. They claimed to be cleansing the filth from our society. But what they really wanted was to scrub the guilt from their own souls.

Later

I left the domaine at dawn, and so I return to the domaine at dawn. It is the last place I want to be. But half-naked in my tattered clothes, shaved of my hair, with an open gash on my head seeping blood, I have nowhere else to go. At least the house is asleep so that I do not have to see Madame, hear her treacherous voice attempting to justify her actions. My head throbs and spins, bursts of light swim before my eyes as I stagger to my room and close the door.

Albert wakes me. He has a damp cloth in his hand, and is trying to clean the cut on my head. Sunlight shimmers from the window, a bright blaze that makes my stomach churn. I throw a hand over my eyes. "Ça va, Léna?" Albert says, looming over me, his voice so shrill it pierces my skull. Turning to my side, I retch, and retch, and retch.

What is that smell? Do you smell it? It fills my nostrils, choking me—blackening my lungs from the inside out—an acrid smell, burning, burning like the scorched rubble of the Café des Tonneliers. Albert raises a cup to my lips. "Drink some broth, Léna," he urges. I breathe the steam and recoil, the pungent odor stinging my nose. "Get it away!" I cry, knocking the cup from his hand. It falls to the ground and shatters.

I drift and dream of hands. Ripping my clothes. Tearing at my hair. Hurling stones at my face. Grasping my shoulders and shaking until my head bobbles like a rag doll's. I awake, screaming, to find a woman sitting on a chair at the end of my bed. She is frowning, her face creased into familiar lines of disappointment. "Hélène," she calls, "*comment vas-tu?*" I try to respond, but my words slip and slur, like a drunkard. Am I drugged? Perhaps that explains this heaviness of my limbs, this persistent drowsiness. I am so tired, so tired, so tired, and yet when I close my eyes, my mind refuses to quiet. I scribble within these pages, trying to still my spinning thoughts, hiding the book beneath my pillows whenever I hear footsteps on the landing.

Now there is a man in my room, his heavy features blurring as he draws closer. I do not know him—do I? He lifts the bandage from my head with gentle fingers. "Open your eyes," he urges me. With difficulty, I comply. His words float toward me. Pupils are dilated . . . she's disoriented . . . head injury . . . potentially fatal . . . do not let her sleep . . .

A woman hovers above me once more—I know this face—it's so very, very familiar. It's my mother. No, no, it's my *stepmother.* She grips my hands too tightly and I try to shove them away. "Hélène," she says sharply, "stay awake! Dammit, stay awake!" But I cannot.

Chapter 16

"That's it?" Jean-Luc gestured at the journal. "There's nothing more?"

I fanned the remaining pages of the notebook. "It's blank."

"But what happened to Hélène? She just . . . died?"

"I guess so." I took a deep breath and slowly exhaled. "Jesus, Jean-Luc, I can't believe what we just read." A slow, ugly churn turned in the pit of my stomach, propelled by a combination of sorrow and disgust. "*Now* I understand why they kept Hélène a secret for all these years." My voice broke. "It's even worse than I ever suspected."

Jean-Luc gave me a pat on the shoulder, but I barely registered it. When the clock in the hallway struck four, he moved to the kitchen and began making tea. We had been here for hours, I realized, reading Hélène's diary aloud. Now it was nearly dawn and I felt drained and emotionally hollow. How on earth would I tell Nico and Heather about what I'd discovered? At the thought of them, a dull twist of pain began radiating down the back of my neck. Over the past few months, I had imagined a thousand different horrific fates for Hélène, but nothing could have prepared me for this truth.

"Here." Jean-Luc handed me a steaming mug. "Tisane with honey." Then he reached across to the sideboard and produced a nondescript bottle, pouring a shot into each of our cups. "*C'est du marc*," he explained.

"*Merci*," I said. The brandy hit the back of my throat, the heat sliding down to my stomach, loosening the taut muscles in the back of my neck so that my head floated free. "How could they stand it?" I demanded. "Living with that huge lie for their entire lives? Uncle Philippe always says that our destiny connected us to this land—that we have a responsibility to care for these vines—that our family fought for generations to preserve this heritage. But now that I know that my great-grandmother was dishonorable, deceitful—" I sucked in a sharp breath. "She didn't care about protecting our heritage. She only cared about saving herself!" I shook my head, trying to process everything. "I always thought my mother was crazy to turn her back on this place. It seemed ridiculous—like a silly affectation—but now I see she was right. This place has way too much history for us to overcome. It's—it's insurmountable." A shiver ran down my spine, and I crossed my arms, clenching my jaw to keep my teeth from chattering.

"Here." Jean-Luc stood and removed his sweater, attempting to drape it over my shoulders.

"It's fine—I'm okay," I said, catching a cashmere sleeve between my fingers.

"Oh, Kat!" Jean-Luc burst out irritably. "Why won't you let me take care of you?"

I choked on a sip of tea. Take care of me? Glancing up, I saw Jean-Luc staring at the ground, a flush spreading slowly across his face. "Oh," I whispered.

"When I heard you were coming back, I thought I couldn't bear it," he said in a low voice. "Surely you must have guessed how I felt. It was torture for me, having you so close."

I shook my head. "But what about Louise?"

"Oh, Kat." He sighed. "There's only ever been you." In his face, I saw such vulnerable sadness that my heart began to melt, like butter on hot toast. I shut my eyes, expecting to feel his warm grasp, a tug pulling me toward him, the brush of his lips across my own.

I opened my eyes. Jean-Luc was motionless in his

chair, gazing at his tea with an unreadable expression. As quickly as he had revealed that flash of tenderness, he had tucked it away. If he had forgiven me, he hadn't forgotten the pain I had once caused him. I held my breath, my thoughts a jumble of impulse and consequence. What would it mean—for either of us? I stared at his hands on the table, his long fingers rough with callouses, strong hands, farmer's hands, heartbreakingly elegant, and suddenly I was overcome by a single emotion: All I truly wanted was for us to care for each other.

"Jean-Luc?" I whispered, stretching my fingers to brush them against his.

His smile sent a jolt through me even before we touched, our chairs tumbling sideways in our haste to reach each other. His hands were tangled in my hair, soft upon my neck, and we were kissing, our clothes falling to the floor, his tenderness at once familiar and unknown, like something I remembered from a dream of long ago, once upon a time when I was happy.

The sound of birds woke me, an insistent squabbling chirp. The room was dim, but the shaded windows were outlined in chinks of light. I stretched in bed, the sheets crisp against my bare skin. Slowly the events of the previous night returned. Jean-Luc and I in the kitchen. Streaking upstairs to his bedroom. Tumbling into bed. A blush spread across my cheeks.

On the bedside table, I found a cup of coffee and a note.

Chérie,

You were sleeping so deeply I didn't want to wake you. I have a meeting in Beaune that I can't miss. I'll be back at 2 P.M. to drive you to Paris.

Bisous,

J-L

The coffee was lukewarm, but it revived me. I found my thoughts turning again to Hélène and her diary, and all we had uncovered last night. In the bright light of morning, my initial, visceral shock was fading. But I still had absolutely no idea how to proceed.

I took a shower and began to repack my little bag, all the while wondering when I'd be back here again. What did the future hold for us? Last night had been like a dream, but now the mists were beginning to clear. Were Jean-Luc and I destined for a long-distance relationship? Was ours to be a romance of Skype conversations carefully orchestrated around time zones? Even considering the logistics exhausted me. I couldn't help but feel we were in the exact situation we'd been in ten years ago: older but no wiser, still wrestling with the same responsibilities and ambitions.

I shoved a sweater in my bag and struggled to close the zipper. Was it possible that our lives were incompatible? *Just focus on The Test,* I told myself. *If you love each other, things will fall into place.* But at the thought of The Test, my heart began racing. It was only a week away, yet here I was halfway around the world, tangled up in family tragedy when I should be reviewing rare grape varietals or the role of enzymes in winemaking. I pressed my hands to my head, which was suddenly splitting. Everything was bearing down upon me at once—my anguished turmoil over Hélène, my concern about a future with Jean-Luc, my anxiety about The Test—all of it assailing me so that panic was closing up my throat, choking me, stifling me.

I had to get out of here. I needed to go home and take The Test, and once that was done, maybe I'd be able to figure out what to do about everything else. At the thought of returning to San Francisco, the clamp on my chest began to loosen. I would leave Jean-Luc a note—I hoped he'd understand—and call a taxi to bring me to the train station in Dijon.

Fifteen minutes later I was in the back seat of a Renault, watching the familiar landscape tumble away.

"Can we make a stop before we get on the highway?" I asked the driver, and he nodded. "Turn into this driveway here. I'll only be a second."

I knocked at the back door, but when no one answered, I let myself in, just like I always had. The kitchen was barren, a yawning cement hole, with plastic tarps covering the carved woodwork. "Jesus, Kate, you scared the daylights out of me!" Heather shrieked when I found her upstairs folding laundry. "Wait a second. *Kate!* Shouldn't you be in San Francisco? Aren't you taking your test in like seventy-two hours?"

Conscious of the waiting taxi—and its ticking meter—I thrust Hélène's diary into her hands. "Jean-Luc and I found this last night. You and Nico have to read it."

She stared at me in complete bewilderment.

"It's Hélène's diary. I'll explain later. I've got a taxi downstairs—I can't miss my flight. Just read it!" I called as I ran down the hall. "And get in touch with me when you're done!" I dashed down the stairs and out the door, moving more swiftly than I had in days.

It took me over twenty-four hours to get home to San Francisco, more than a full day of travel. I stumbled up the stairs to my apartment, my legs stiff from being crammed into an economy seat, and my head aching. In my living room, I unearthed a stack of flash cards and began quizzing myself on Italian grape varietals, grimly focused once more on The Test that I would be taking in seven days' time.

"Kate! My dear girl!" Jennifer flung open her front door. "Big day tomorrow! How're you feeling?"

"Nervous," I admitted, kissing her on both cheeks.

"You're going to be fine!" she said with a wave, taking my coat and throwing it over the banister. "Anyway, we're not going to talk about the exam. Tonight is all about relaxing. Bax has been cooking up a storm, and we're just going to eat and talk and drink—one glass of wine each." She lifted an eyebrow. "After all, you've got to stay fresh for tomorrow."

I stepped into her house feeling, as I always did, embraced by its cheerful clutter. "Watch out for the shoes," Jennifer said, kicking several pairs aside. "*Kids!*" she shouted up the stairs. "*Say hello to Kate!*"

"*Hi, Kate!*" Two voices yelled back.

I followed Jennifer downstairs to the kitchen, breathing in the scents of sautéed garlic and chopped parsley. She immediately went to the fridge and poured us both a glass of sparkling water. "Poor man's Champers?" she joked, proffering a tumbler.

I smiled weakly.

"Oh, dear girl," she said. "You're looking a bit

peaky. I *do* wish you'd stop worrying. After all, at the end of the day, it's just a stupid exam." Her sharp gaze traveled over me, taking everything in. "Or . . . is something else the matter?"

I fell silent, a flush creeping to my cheeks. "Do you remember the secret *cave* I found at Domaine Charpin?" I said finally.

"Of course."

"Last week I went back to Burgundy. No, wait, let me finish," I said, when her eyes widened with surprise. "I thought I'd figured out a way to find the Gouttes d'Or. But instead, I found a diary from World War II, and it contained some pretty damning revelations about my family." I filled her in on Hélène's history, glancing away, too ashamed to look her in the eye. "The story, it's so horrible, sometimes it seems unreal. But then I catch myself, and force myself to recognize all over again that these things actually occurred. Honestly, I'm not sure how to live with the shame. Every day I find myself scouring my thoughts, terrified they'll reveal that deep down inside, I'm a bigot."

"Oh, Kate." Jennifer's head dropped.

I gulped at my glass of water. "Sorry. This was supposed to be a relaxing evening. I don't want to burden you with this stuff."

She stared at the floor for a long moment. "I think,

actually," she said slowly, "that I'm one of the few people who might truly understand. It wasn't pretty, you know, growing up in South Africa in the shadow of apartheid. If I rarely talk about it, it's because it still hurts. My father was Afrikaner and a racist in the purest sense of the word. My mother, too. I see that now, but it took me a long time to accept it. He terrorized my mother. Beat her. Me and my sisters, too. All of us—his girls." Her lips twisted into a bitter smile. "It's a little different for you because you never knew your great-grandmother. But I spent a lot of time trying to understand the choices my parents made. Sometimes I wonder if that was just another way for me to justify their actions." She sighed and fell silent.

"But how do you deal with it?" My voice rose. "How can you accept them as your family, and love them, and condemn them at the same time?"

"The same way," she replied simply. "By asking questions, and trying to understand their choices. Not in order to excuse them," she added, "but so I could take responsibility."

Before I could respond, a heavy figure trundled down the stairs. "Kate!" boomed Baxter, holding out a thick hand for me to shake. "How're you doing, darlin'? Big day tomorrow! I've made your favorite veal stew. If that doesn't bring you luck, I don't know what will!" He beamed at me, his smile faltering when he saw my strained expression. "Test be damned, Jennifer! Get this girl a glass of wine!"

For the rest of the evening, Baxter did his best to jolly us along, piling delicious food upon our plates and trotting out all the funniest stories from his South Carolina childhood. He even ignored his wife's protestations and poured me a second glass of wine. "It's medicinal," he insisted. By the time I kissed them all goodbye, I had managed once again to compartmentalize my feelings about Hélène.

Jennifer followed me outside to my car. "Call me tomorrow when you're finished," she said. "And remember: At this point it's more about luck than knowledge."

I smiled as brightly as possible. "Thanks."

I waited until she had closed the door behind her before starting the car and pulling onto the street. It was still early—barely eight o'clock—so I drove home through Pacific Heights, watching the lights of the Bay Bridge sparkle like sequins against the dark night sky. Usually I found this drive soothing, but as my car sped down the city's slopes, careening further and further from the center of Jennifer's calm confidence, a familiar anxiety began to set in. I wasn't ready for The Test. I still wasn't ready. Only last week, at my final practice exam, I had misidentified a French chardonnay as California. "Did you discern malolactic flavors?" Jennifer had asked pointedly. "Are you even analyzing what you taste?" I had mumbled an excuse and we had moved on. But her point was clear: If I was still making that kind of stupid mistake, I was going to fail.

With shaking hands, I pulled up outside my apartment building, parked, and headed to the door, so preoccupied that I didn't notice the figure sitting on the steps until I was right beside him.

"Kat."

I shrieked and tripped on the stairs, catching myself on the rail.

"Sorry, sorry—I didn't mean to scare you." In the urban glow of the streetlights Jean-Luc's face had half turned to shadow.

"What are you doing here?" My mind was so filled with The Test, I felt dazed, like I'd been shaken from a dream. Stepping forward to hug him, I felt his arms circle me, solid and strong. In the weak light, I could just make out the stubble covering his chin, his rumpled clothes belying hours of travel.

"Can I come in?" he asked.

I hesitated. More than anything in the world, I wanted to stay up all night with him. But The Test flashed in my face like an angry beacon.

"I know your exam is tomorrow morning," he said quickly. "But I have something you need to see, something important that I felt I needed to bring to you myself. It'll only take a minute."

Inside my apartment, he fumbled briefly in the inside pocket of his jacket, and handed me an envelope. "*Tiens.*"

"What is it?"

He took a deep breath. "It's a letter from Hélène."

With shaking fingers, I pulled the letter from the envelope, the sheets creased and brittle, covered with the careful loops of Hélène's handwriting.

1 novembre 1944

Chers Albert et Benoît,

By the time you read this, I'll be gone. Please don't try to find me. I'm leaving because I want to make a clean start and, anyway, I don't yet know where I am going. I wish things could be different. I wish I could watch you grow into the fine young men I know you will become. But I want you to have the chance to move forward from this war, the same as everyone, and I know it will be easier for you to do that without me.

You have, I know, witnessed some terrible things

these past few weeks. To be honest, I am not sure that I will ever be able to forgive your mother. But lest you judge her too harshly, there are two things I want you to know. First, I sincerely believe that her choices were made out of a deep love for you, her sons. For that I cannot blame her, because I, too, love you profoundly. Second, it is thanks in part to your mother that I am able to leave. Last night, she brought me her jewelry box, and together we sewed its contents into the lining of my coat. "I hope it will be enough, Hélène," she said in a low voice that belied her guilt. She feels ashamed—as she should—as she always will. This act is not enough to absolve her. Though I am unable to forgive, I do feel a shred of compassion for her. The war has brought out the best and worst in each of us.

Mes petits frères, I hope you will remember me and Papa, and the happy hours we spent together in the vineyards. Papa's truest legacy lives in this land, in the plants that flourish in our cherished rocky soil. But he also left us something tangible—a cellar of treasured bottles hidden in a secret place. No one else knows about it, not even your mother, but I have placed a clue in Papa's favorite book that will help you find it.

There is something else, too, that I have left for

you—my journal. I am giving it to you because I feel it's important to preserve a record of what happened. But I will understand if you wish to discard it with the past.

And here is where I must make my own confession: When I leave the domaine tonight, it will be with bottles of Les Gouttes d'Or tucked into my trunk. I am sorry to take away part of your heritage, but I see no other option. My plan is to go to Paris, sell the wine to the highest bidder, and use the money to leave France forever. Oh, how it frightens me to write those words—I, who can barely muster the simplest greeting in a foreign language—but I hope that the help I once offered others will be returned to me.

Alors, Albert, Benoît—I bid you au revoir. How I shall miss your little voices, your beloved faces. I hope that you will think of me sometimes—and if you do, remember this: What we fought for were the justice and compassion that define civilization.

Je vous embrasse,
Hélène

I raised my eyes from the letter and found Jean-Luc's gaze upon me. "Sh—she didn't die?" My voice emerged in a croak.

He shook his head.

"And Virginie—" I cleared my throat. "In the end, she helped her?"

"It's not enough to redeem her. But at least it's something."

I touched a corner of the stationery. "I wonder if Albert and Benoît ever found her letter."

He shrugged. "Who knows? Presumably, as soon as Hélène left, Virginie bundled all her stuff into boxes and moved everything down to the cellar. Out of sight, out of mind, right? I think the guilt and shame must have been unbearable. She couldn't forbid her sons from talking about their sister, so she told them Hélène had moved away and died. Eventually she had the bench and memorial plaque placed in the town cemetery."

"But where did you get the letter?"

"From Louise," he admitted, faintly embarrassed. "She brought it to me right after you left. She had discovered it months ago in a used book at the charity shop in Beaune. She tried to buy the box but you and Bruyère—"

"I remember. We outbid her." I snapped my fingers. "I knew she was up to something that afternoon."

"When Louise read the letter, she immediately started looking for the secret *cave*—and she enlisted

Walker to help. They suspected it might be somewhere at Domaine Charpin, but they were hoping Nico and Bruyère would give them a cut if they could lead them to it."

"Except I found it first. But why did she give the letter to you?"

"You and Nico have been so quiet about the *cave*, she didn't realize you had actually discovered it" he explained. "She came to me and asked if I would help her. It turns out, Louise is far more conservative than I thought—frighteningly extreme, actually. She's fanatical about keeping this wine in France. She knew we'd been to the abbey together, and she offered to split the profits of the French sale if I told her what you'd learned."

"Sounds like a pretty far-fetched plan."

He raised an eyebrow. "Isn't everything about the wine business far-fetched? Ninety-nine percent of my success relies on *the weather*."

I smiled faintly, and Jean-Luc pressed his advantage. "Listen, Kat, I came here because I knew how much Hélène's letter would mean to you. But that's not the only reason." He hesitated, running a hand through his hair. "I know a lot has changed since—since—well, since the last time we were together. We have become different people, perhaps. But my feelings for you have never changed. You're still the person I want to see every morning, and share a glass of wine with every night." He gave me a crooked smile that caused my internal organs to melt. "Kat," he said softly. "Would you—"

He broke off as I drew away from him. "Oh, Jean-Luc." I paused, trying to marshal my thoughts. "Ever since I left Burgundy, I've been thinking about this. Us. How we could make it work. I don't think either of us wants a long-distance relationship. I want to wake up with you every morning. Eat breakfast together. Cook dinner together. But my life is in California, and you have the winery in France, and, well . . ." I bowed my head. "I can't go back there."

"But wait, wait, wait!" Why was he beaming? "You didn't let me finish! What if I"—he gave a little flourish—"would like to leave France?"

My jaw dropped. "What about the domaine?"

"It's the Côte d'Or, *chérie*. I'd have no trouble finding a buyer."

"But how could you—why would you—your entire life—"

"Exactly!" His face flushed. "It has been my entire life. Even when I was a little boy, I knew I would become a vigneron and take over the family vineyard, just like my father, and his father, his father's father, and so on, and so on, until the beginning of time! But Kat, more than anything, there is you. Sure, yes, I could continue making wine in Burgundy forever. But I would rather do something else—if it means you are by my side."

I thought of the night, so many years ago, when Jean-Luc had kissed me for the first time. For many days afterward, I had been goofy with happiness, drifting through my classes with the sound of his voice in my ears. I remembered the day I had broken up with him—the tears, the doubts, and, ultimately, the self-righteousness that had stiffened my resolve. I had been so convinced that I was doing the right thing for both of us. How could I have known that sacrifice isn't always rewarded, that hard work doesn't always pay off, that luck plays a bigger role in success than any successful person would ever admit?

On the other side of the kitchen counter, Jean-Luc was watching me with those clear, tawny eyes. Jean-Luc, whose touch I still dreamed about. Jean-Luc, whose friendship I still longed for. Jean-Luc, whose absence I had felt so keenly, I had even rejected the type of wine he made. For ten years, I had denied it, most of all to myself. I took a deep breath and lifted my face to his.

"I missed you. A lot. No, no, more than that, Jean-

Luc—" My voice dropped, and I gulped, trying to swallow the tremble. "There hasn't been a day that I haven't thought of you." His face split into a smile. Before I could second-guess myself, I stepped around the counter, teetered up on my toes, cradled his face with my hands, and kissed him, softly at first and then, as he responded, with increasing passion, until the rest of the world fell away.

Twelve wineglasses sparkled on the table before me, arranged in a loose semicircle. With my fingertips, I adjusted the position of the furthest one, frowning at the watermarks clouding its foot. Why hadn't I polished them more carefully last night? Did water stains bring bad luck? I glanced at the guy to my right. His wineglasses were spotless. He caught me staring and gave a faint nod. "Nervous?" he asked, jiggling his leg up and down. I caught a glimpse of ladybugs on his ankles—lucky socks.

"My God, yes. You?"

"I could puke at any moment," he admitted cheerfully. "It took me forever to find a parking spot this morning. Thought I was going to miss the entire thing. I finally begged a garage to squeeze me in. They're charging me the equivalent of a month's rent."

A tall woman wearing a flowing crepe pantsuit and owlish glasses entered the room. "Good morning, everyone," she intoned. The room quieted and thirty pairs of eyes swiveled to her face. "Welcome to the first practical paper of the Master of Wine examination." She bent her head to the sheet of paper in her hand and began reading. "As you know, you'll have two hours and fifteen minutes to complete twelve blind tastings." A team of assistants circled among us, pouring wines into our glasses. "This morning we'll be covering still whites. You'll be asked to assess variety, origin, wine-making, quality, style."

I stared at the array of liquids in the glasses before me, ranging from palest lemon to buttery gold. Somewhere in their depths lurked the key to my future.

"You may begin."

A rustle filled the room as we broke the seal on our exam booklets. White wines were my weak link, and as I waded through the essays, struggling to make my responses as meticulously clear and analytical as possible, I felt my confidence slipping away. Was Wine 1 a sauvignon blanc or riesling? Was Wine 2 from South Africa or New Zealand? Germany or Austria? Jupiter or Mars? By the time I reached the fifth and final question I was shaking with self-doubt.

Wines 11–12 are from the same region.

For each wine:

» **Identify the specific origin as closely as possible.**

» **Compare the state of maturity, giving the vintage for each wine.**

» **Compare the quality of the two wines, within the context of large- and small-scale vinification. As a large corporation taking over a family wine business, should you keep the family values alive and, if so, how?**

Even without smelling or tasting them, I guessed the wines were from Burgundy. I took a tentative sip of Wine 11 and a sharp tartness hit my tongue, tapering to a smoky, flinty finish. It was as austere as a couture gown—draped with deceptive simplicity, sewn with meticulous stitches—meant to fill the taster with awe. I allowed the liquid to reach every corner of my mouth before I spat into my plastic cup.

Chablis, I thought. Premier cru? I reached for Wine 12.

The nose hit me first, lush notes of tropical fruits, peaches, and a wisp of lemon, as familiar and beloved as the scent of his hair. I closed my eyes and took a sip, rolling it on my tongue, that powerful wine, that muscular wine, with its supple, honeyed depths. Meursault Les Gouttes d'Or. It tasted of Jean-Luc. It tasted of home.

I began to compose my answers, my pen flying across the page, the words spilling from me. For the first time, I knew exactly what I wanted to say, and exactly how I needed to structure my essays in order to create the most impact and earn the most points. But when I got to the third part of the question, I paused, rereading it once, twice, three times, considering my response.

As a large corporation taking over a family wine business, should you keep the family values alive and, if so, how?

The words darted through me, and I was surprised to find tears springing to my eyes. *A large corporation taking over a family wine business . . .* Was that, then, to be the fate of Jean-Luc's domaine? Snatched up by a multinational conglomerate, run solely on profit margins and markups? I swirled the golden liquid in my glass so that the alcohol ran in spidery legs down the sides, and suddenly I understood that the greatest thing about this wine was not its supple beauty, nor the mark of its terroir—no, it was the love that its vigneron had infused into it at every step, a commitment that stretched, unbroken, to the beginning of wine itself.

If I had learned anything from Hélène's story it was that the stewardship of this land was a privilege, the responsibility a type of freedom. *Liberté.* The word could have so many different interpretations: Freedom from oppression. Freedom from the past. Freedom to stand up to injustice. To remain and fight for one's values was surely as important a legacy as the terroir itself.

As my pen moved steadily across the page, I knew with absolute certainty that it would be an enormous mistake for me to reject this land. I needed to be there, rooted, so I could confront the past and take responsibility. I needed to be there to ensure that nothing like that happened ever again. For better or worse, this land was in my soul.

"Time. That's time. Thank you, everyone. Pencils down."

I reread my final paragraphs and closed my exam book with a sigh.

"Not too bad, huh?" Ladybug Socks was grinning at me.

"What a relief, right?" I found myself grinning back.

He held up his hands. "God, not for me. I couldn't get a grip on that first question and it went downhill from there. I meant it seemed good for *you*—you were scribbling away like a maniac. You must've had a lot of great stuff to say."

"Oh, well." I blushed, and tried to hide it by twisting around and reaching for my tote bag. "We've still got two more papers. Plenty of time left for me to screw up."

He dabbed at his desk with a paper towel. "Nah." He glanced up and in his face I saw a flash of envy. "You got this."

Outside I found Jean-Luc, leaning against the car with his face tilted toward the sun.

"Hey!" I placed my box of glasses gently on the ground and flung myself at him just so I could feel his arms close around me.

"*Et, alors?*" he asked, after he had given me a hug that squeezed the air from me. "How'd it go?"

"Actually, it went great. Listen, I don't want to talk about The Test." I grabbed both his hands, and took a deep breath. "I realized something important right in the middle of the exam. Jean-Luc"—I leaned back to look him straight in the eye—"you can't leave Burgundy, I can't let you leave. We have a responsibility to this land, and now that I know Hélène's story, I understand it's our destiny to care for it. To turn our backs on it would be rejecting our obligation. We can't let it happen. Promise me that we won't let that happen." I held his gaze, unwilling to break eye contact until he agreed with me.

He laughed, confused. "But—but I thought this was what you wanted, to stay in the California? What about the job at Sotheby's?"

I shook my head. "I don't care. I mean, obviously, yes, I do care—but I'll figure something out. After all, it's Burgundy, not East Timor. There're tons of wine jobs there."

An expression of pure joy was suffusing his face, but still he paused to look at me, to make sure I was certain—this man who loved me so much he hoped I would never again regret a promise made to him.

I met his gaze and smiled. "As long as we're together, everything will be okay."

San Francisco
Three months later

"Kate!" Heather waved as I pulled up to the curb and double-parked beside the pale pink Edwardian behemoth that was her hotel.

"Hey!" I threw open my door and dashed around the front of the car to give her a hug. "I can't believe you're here! I know this is the worst time to be away— only a couple of weeks before *les vendanges*—you must have a million things to do."

"Seriously, Kate." Her shining eyes met mine. "We wouldn't have missed this for the world." A smile crept across her face, a reckless, joyful smile, and I found myself smiling back. "Anyway," she added, as we strapped ourselves into the car and adjusted our sunglasses, "a transatlantic trip without the kids is like traveling first class. Although Anna may never forgive me for not letting her come and do your hair and makeup."

"They're with Uncle Philippe and Aunt Jeanne?"

"Yeah, Papi is taking them camping at the *cabotte*. Can you imagine?"

"Anna likes camping?"

"There may have been a little bribery involved." She shot me a sly look and I laughed. "But Papi thought it would be a nice way to honor Hélène's memory. And I didn't want to throw cold water on the idea."

"You did exactly the right thing." I checked my blind spot and eased into the ebb and flow of traffic.

Heather swiped at the screen of her cell phone. "What time is Jennifer expecting Jean-Luc and Nico with the stuff?"

"She said she'd be home until five." I accelerated up a hill. "That should give them plenty of time to drop everything off for the reception tomorrow. Let's see, there's the wine, the flowers, the glassware . . ." I tapped my fingers against the steering wheel.

At first Jean-Luc and I had talked about eloping. But when Jennifer offered to host a reception at her house, she and Jean-Luc, the pair of them, had persuaded me into a small wedding ceremony. No gowns, tuxedos, or stiff hair—just family, friends, and a lot of really good wine. I bought a beautiful cream satin dress with a slender, cap-sleeved bodice and full skirt that brushed my knees; a pair of burnished gold pumps still left me several inches shorter than my fiancé. Jean-Luc's mom and sister were ecstatic to visit San Francisco, though my parents had, regretfully, declined. Luckily Jennifer would be there to walk me down the aisle.

"Are you nervous?" Heather asked.

"About marrying Jean-Luc? Nah." Without warning, my face melted into a goofy smile. "I'm . . . excited."

She smiled, pleased, and finished sending a text before letting the phone drop into her lap and falling quiet—so quiet I thought she might have drifted to sleep. At the Bay Bridge, she roused herself once again. "Aw," she said, as signs for UC Berkeley flashed overhead. "University Ave."

"We can make a pit stop at Top Dog if you want," I joked.

"Maybe on the way back." She gazed out the window, at the concrete and asphalt of the urban sprawl unspooling before us. "You aren't going to miss it?"

"What, this?" I gestured at the big box commercial center, a great, salmon-pink blight on the left side of the freeway.

"Well, yeah—the convenience. The weather. The . . . freedom."

Another half mile slipped by as I considered her question. "Sure," I said eventually. "I'll miss it. After all, this is the only place I've ever lived. But on the other hand . . . this is the only place I've ever lived. Know what I mean? How will I ever grow up if I don't leave?"

"I think I know exactly what you mean." She stared down at the backs of her hands, rough from dishwater, the nails clipped short, an heirloom diamond sparkling from her ring finger. When her mouth curled up in a wistful smile, I was reminded that Heather had made a similar leap a long time ago. Maybe, I thought, she sometimes regretted leaving her youth and freedom behind before she was really ready.

"Besides," I added. "I suspect we'll be back one day. Jean-Luc still hasn't given up his dream of owning a piece of California vineyards."

"Domaine Valéry Napa Valley?" she mused. "Actually, that has a nice ring to it."

By this time, the traffic had lightened, the landscape growing steadily more bucolic as we drove further north. Heather fell asleep again, but at the first sign for Davis she bolted upright in her seat, pulled her handbag to her lap, and began rooting through the contents. "You're sure it's okay that we came alone?"

I, too, found myself suddenly fending off a flutter of nerves. "You did all the legwork finding her," I pointed out. "I don't think anyone else would have guessed that Hélène had changed her name to Marie."

She peered into a tiny mirror and dabbed powder across her face. "Nico really wanted to be here, but I felt like this was something we needed to do on our own—as the women of the Charpin family—the female future." She clicked her compact shut. "And there'll be other chances. I'll make sure of it."

The campus of the University of California, Davis was an idyllic leafy sprawl intersected by a web of orderly paths. We followed a pack of polite bicyclists to the shimmery waters of Putah Creek, crossing over toward a glittering glass structure that had the words "Department of Viticulture and Enology" etched in large letters upon its side. Inside, the lobby was cool and shadowy, a respite from the midday heat.

"Mrs. Charpin?" A young woman came forward to greet us, pushing long dark hair behind her ears. "I'm Anita Gonzalez, a grad student here." She offered a shy smile.

"Anita, hi!" Heather's face lit up. "Thank you so much for your help arranging today." She nudged me forward. "And this is Kate Elliott."

Anita shook my hand enthusiastically. "I'm a huge admirer of your fiancé's winery. We studied it in my viticultural practices seminar, and everything Mr. Valéry has created is truly remarkable. It's—it's inspirational." Her cheeks grew red.

"Are you hoping to become a winemaker?" Heather asked as we moved across smooth, polished floors toward a bank of elevators.

"Oh, gosh no. My dad's a grape grower in Modesto, and I've spent way too much time out there." She pressed a button. "No, I'm thinking about wine sales. Or maybe the Master of Wine program."

"That's what Kate is doing!" Heather said.

"Seriously?" Anita turned to me, her brown eyes filled with awe. "That test—it seems almost impossible."

"It actually is impossible," I agreed with a laugh.

The elevator opened on the fifth floor and we followed Anita to a set of double glass doors.

"Mrs. Charpin! Ms. Elliott! I'm Professor Clarkson. Welcome to the Robert Mondavi Institute at UC Davis!" A large man moved through the open doors of the conference room, giving a nod of dismissal to Anita, who disappeared discreetly down the corridor. The professor seized first Heather's hand, then mine, giving them a vigorous shake. He ushered us into the room, introducing us to the faces around the table, all of them department faculty, their names and titles disappearing from my head the instant he uttered them. "May I offer you something to drink? Water? Wine? We have lunch all ready. Please, do help yourselves." He gestured at the buffet spread upon a side table—platters of roast beef, poached salmon, grilled vegetables, all beautifully arranged.

We selected some food and found seats at the table. "This is lovely—thank you so much," said Heather, once everyone had begun eating.

"It's the least we could do," said Professor Clarkson, with just a touch of unctuousness. "We are very grateful for your family's generosity. The Hélène Marie Charpin Scholarship will enormously benefit low-income students pursuing degrees in enology or viticulture. Seriously, this money will mean a lot to a lot of kids."

Heather smiled. "We hope to grow the endowment over time," she murmured quietly.

The Sotheby's auction of our family's secret cellar, entitled simply "A Private Collection," had attained a new record in wine sales. We had all traveled to London for the event, gathering afterward in the private dining room of a discreet restaurant to discuss our plans for the future. To my surprise, Uncle Philippe had suggested—to unanimous family approval—the creation of the Charpin Foundation, which would bestow donations on refugee aid organizations, as well as grants for wine research and scholarship. "Bruyère shall head it," he declared. "If, of course, she agrees." Heather had blushed and accepted with genuine emotion, and all of us had cheered.

As for the domaine, no amount of windfall could tear Nico and Uncle Philippe from their land. They remained passionately devoted to the vineyards and had high hopes for a *millésime* this year—an exceptional vintage to celebrate the opening of Heather's charming bed-and-breakfast, which had already garnered eight excellent reviews on TripAdvisor.

I cleared my throat across the silence that had suddenly descended. "I was wondering . . . did anyone here work with Marie? I know she passed away many years ago, but . . ."

"I did." A slender, silver-haired woman leaned forward in her chair. "I was her teaching assistant in the . . . oh, it must've been in the '80s. She was a tough cookie—all of us grad students were terrified of her. But there's no doubt that her work was influential. Her research on synthetic compounds really helped establish viticulture in Sonoma." Everyone around the table was nodding and murmuring in agreement. "The funny thing I remember about Professor Charpin," she continued with a frown, "is that even though she loved chardonnay, she absolutely refused to drink white Burgundy. In fact, I don't think I ever saw a drop of it touch her lips."

Without warning my eyes filled with tears, and I blinked them away. "And she didn't have a family?"

The woman looked uncertain. "No. No one. Only some nieces and nephews—in New Jersey, I think?"

"New York," Heather said softly.

"Somewhere back East," agreed the woman. "She used to speak fondly of them, but I got the impression they didn't see each other often."

"The Reinach family," I said. "They helped her come to America." This was the greatest discovery that Heather had unearthed. Rose Reinach and her parents had indeed been murdered at Auschwitz. But her brother Théodore had—somehow, miraculously—survived. Arriving in New York sometime around 1944, he had completed a degree at Columbia, launched a successful printing press, and—at some point in the late 1940s—sponsored the immigration of one Marie Charpin. He had died about ten years ago, and Heather had been trying unsuccessfully to find his descendants.

I think we could have lingered for the rest of the afternoon chatting with everyone, but Heather and I still had to drive back to San Francisco in time to change for the evening's rehearsal dinner. The professors left, bestowing handshakes and business cards, before disappearing down the corridor. Professor Clarkson walked us to the car and we each gave him a brief hug goodbye.

"You ready to head back?" Heather asked after he had trundled away on his bicycle.

I hesitated, fingering the edge of my cell phone. "The results of The Test are supposed to come out today," I admitted. "I told myself I wouldn't let it ruin the entire weekend if I didn't pass. But . . ." My heart had begun to skitter an uneven pattern in my chest.

She gazed at me earnestly. "Have you tried to visualize success?"

I rolled my eyes. "You can take the girl out of Berkeley, but . . ."

"I'm serious!" She shot me an injured look, but she was laughing. "Close your eyes. Imagine the email on your screen—"

"Heather!" I bleated her name, two syllables of pure exasperation.

"Would it kill you to humor me just this once?" she snapped.

And because she was my best friend, and cousin-in-law, and maid of honor—because she had spent hours listening to me fret about The Test—because she had housed and fed me for weeks—because I knew she truly loved me, just as I loved her—I obediently shut my eyes.

"Okay," Heather sounded greatly mollified. "Picture an email from . . ."

"The Institute of Masters of Wine."

"And it says . . ."

My eyes flew open. "This is ridiculous."

"C'mon, Kate," Heather pleaded.

"It says something like . . ." I closed my eyes again. "We are delighted to inform you that you have passed the practical element of the examination. Many congratulations on this wonderful achievement! Now go forth and get plastered on Champagne—only the good stuff! We're fairly confident you'll be able to recognize it. Winky emoji. All best from the old farts at the Institute of Masters of Wine!"

"Okay." I heard a smile in her voice. "Then what happens?"

"I jump up and down. You start crying. We call Jean-Luc and he starts crying."

"And then?"

"And then . . ." I swallowed hard. "I tell Jennifer tonight at dinner. Jean-Luc and I get married tomorrow and instead of a honeymoon we work *les vendanges*, but it honestly doesn't matter because we're together. In a month or two, I decide on a subject for my research paper, and start writing. Meanwhile Jean-Luc and I settle into domestic bliss at the domaine. And then, a year from today, praise be to Dionysus, I am officially declared a Master of Wine!"

"And then?"

"And then . . ." I hesitated. I'd never allowed myself to think this far ahead. "I start writing about wine for *Decanter*, *Wine Spectator*, and . . . oh, hell, sure, why not? The *Wall Street Journal,* the *New York Times, Bon Appétit.* I become an expert on rare Burgundies. The major auction houses beg me to head their office in Beaune, but I insist on being a consultant so I can balance life with Jean-Luc and our baby." I opened my eyes and took in her look of surprise and delight. "Just one baby."

She turned away, not quite hiding a grin. "See? That wasn't so hard, was it?"

"No," I admitted. "I guess not."

We stared at each other, and though my heart was no longer skittering in my chest, it thumped with a heavy, portentous beat.

The phone slipped in my sweaty hand. I tapped in my pass code and then pressed the envelope icon, waiting for the messages to load. "It's slow. I don't have much service," I said uselessly. *Checking for mail . . . Checking for mail . . .* A single message from The Institute of Masters of Wine slid into my box, followed by a buzz. Before I completely lost my courage, I gritted my teeth and tapped the screen with a trembling fingertip, scanning the lines until I reached the second paragraph.

"What happened? What does it say?"

Wordlessly, I handed her the phone. She read it in a glance, and then suddenly she was gripping my shoulders. "Oh, Kate!" she said, and her voice seemed to be coming from very far away. "You did it. You did it!" She threw her arms around me and squeezed the air from my chest, releasing me so quickly I staggered back against the side of the car, my entire body limp with disbelief.

The excitement would come later with the pop of a cork, and the fizz of Champagne. It would come with Jennifer's heartfelt emotion as she declared, "I'm proud of you, my girl." It would come with Jean-Luc's whoop of delight, with a hug that would lift me off my feet, with his whispered words telling me that his belief in me would never waver. It would come with a stream of congratulatory messages—of handshakes and hugs, emails and Facebook messages, bouquets of flowers and many, many bottles of wine. But now, as I waited for the news to sink in, I thought of the land, of the faint striated pattern of vineyard rows running to the village below, the crumble of cherished soil underfoot, the soft chartreuse of clustered grapes peeping through a screen of foliage. Burgundy, the place I had loved and resisted for so many years—it was calling for me, it was waiting for me, my once and future home.

Acknowledgments

In researching life in Occupied France, I relied on many histories, memoirs, and films. In particular, I found inspiration in the facts and insights of *Wine and War* by Don Kladstrup and Petie Kladstrup, which offers a fascinating account of all the French wine regions during World War II. *A Train in Winter* by Caroline Moorehead, *A Cool and Lonely Courage* by Susan Ottaway, and *Fashion Under the Occupation* by Dominique Veillon reveal the courageous—and often forgotten—role of French women during the war. *Outwitting the Gestapo* by Lucie Aubrac and *Resistance and Betrayal* by Patrick Marnham were invaluable in imagining Hélène's Resistance circuit and creating the details of her capture. For information about horizontal collaborators and the *épuration sauvage*, I referred to *Year Zero* by Ian Buruma, *Women and the Second World War in France, 1939–1948* by Hanna Diamond, and the Alain Resnais film *Hiroshima mon amour.*

I am indebted to the memoir *Resistance* by Agnès Humbert, whose story so profoundly moved me, I found it haunting my dreams. The character of Hélène is deeply influenced by Humbert, and Hélène's final words to her brothers are inspired by her book.

My heartfelt thanks and gratitude go to my agent, Deborah Schneider, Francophile, wine lover, and unwavering champion. My tireless and brilliant editor, Katherine Nintzel, shaped this book with her perceptive insights and the story is infinitely richer because of her. My thanks to the team at William Morrow—Kaitlyn Kennedy, Kaitlin Harri, Lynn Grady, Liate Stehlik, Stephanie Vallejo, and Vedika Khanna—for their enthusiasm and support. I am also grateful to the team at Gelfman Schneider/ICM Partners and Curtis Brown UK—Penelope Burns, Enrichetta Frezzato, Cathy Gleason, and Claire Nozieres.

For their sharp eyes and suggestions, I thank my early readers: Meg Bortin, Allie Larkin, Kathleen Lawrence, Laura Neilson, Susan Hans O'Connor, Amanda Patten, Hilary Reyl, Steve Rhinds, Lucia Watson, and my parents, Adeline Yen Mah and Robert Mah, who have read this book almost as many times as I have.

For information on the wine trade, high school chemistry, and/or French bureaucracy, I am grateful to Josh Adler, Jérôme Avenas, Gesha-Marie Bland, Claire Fong, and Adrian Thompson. Any inaccuracies in this novel are mine alone.

My experience volunteering at the Champagne harvest of 2015 first inspired this story, and I am grateful to Anne Malassagne and Antoine Malassagne of AR Lenoble for warmly welcoming me to their vineyards and *cuverie*, as well as Christian Conley Holthausen, who is a font of wine knowledge and good cheer.

To Shamroon Aziz I owe an immeasurable debt for giving me the space and time to write every day without worry.

My love and thanks to Christopher Klein, who read these chapters before they were a book and encouraged me to keep going—and who always knows the right moment to open a bottle of wine.

About the Author

ANN MAH is the author of *Mastering the Art of French Eating* and *Kitchen Chinese*. She is a regular contributor to the *New York Times* travel section, and her articles have appeared in *Condé Nast Traveler*, *The Best American Travel Writing 2017*, Vogue.com, BonAppetit.com, and *Washingtonian* magazine, among other publications. She lives in Paris and Washington, D.C.